PRAISE FOR *AND THE CROWS TOOK THEIR EYES*

"*And the Crows Took Their Eyes* is a devastatingly beautiful, complex portrait of a small community torn asunder by the Civil War. What Vicki Lane has rendered in this harrowing and profound portrait of life and death in one little corner of Western North Carolina is a world that would otherwise be lost to us or, at best, consigned to a dusty footnote of history. Lane, through the alchemy of her formidable imagination, has breathed life into unforgettable characters living through a time of upheaval and untold tragedy. I will never hear the words Shelton Laurel again without a host of Lane's powerful and heartrending images coming to mind. *And the Crows Took Their Eyes* accomplishes what only the very best historical fiction can ever hope to accomplish, connecting us, not only to our history, but to our humanity as well."

— Tommy Hays, author of *The Pleasure Was Mine*

AND THE CROWS TOOK THEIR EYES

Vicki Lane

Regal House Publishing

Published by
Regal House Publishing, LLC
Raleigh, NC 27612
All rights reserved

ISBN -13 (paperback): 9781646030118
ISBN -13 (epub): 9781646030385
Library of Congress Control Number: 2020930410

Interior and cover design by Lafayette & Greene
lafayetteandgreene.com
Cover images © by Nancy Darrell

Regal House Publishing, LLC
https://regalhousepublishing.com

The following is a work of fiction created by the author. All names, individuals, characters, places, items, brands, events, etc. were either the product of the author or were used fictitiously. Any name, place, event, person, brand, or item, current or past, is entirely coincidental.

Printed in the United States of America

For Pearl Massey's daughter who confronted me in the grocery store parking lot and told me to hurry up and write this book while she could still see to read...and for all the folks who helped.

NOTE

Inspired by *Braving the Fire*, Jessica Handler's excellent book on memoir, I have chosen five witnesses to tell the story of the divisions in one rural county during the Civil War in western North Carolina. Four of the witnesses are historical; one is fictional. I have attempted to stay true to the generally accepted narrative of a confusing time, imperfectly documented by incomplete and contradictory primary sources. But this is a novel, fiction not history, and I have let each character have his or her say, always remembering, as Handler says, that "in the space between the contradictions is where the most profound truth lies."

For the real story lies not in the historical events but in the myriad moments that divide imperfect humanity so that, though we may speak the same language, we sometimes find it impossible to understand one another.

"We know certain historical facts…. We try to imagine what went on in other people's minds and what they may have said or done, beyond the secure facts. Here and there it is just possible that I may have guessed right."

— Naomi Mitchison, *The Corn King and the Spring Queen*

PROLOGUE

~JUDITH SHELTON~

Shelton Laurel, North Carolina
1900

You want to know the way of it, what it was led to the hangings and the whippings, the massacre, and then the killings that went on after that? Folks still getting even nigh forty years on? I reckon most would tell you they know who was in the right and who was in the wrong. And I reckon was you to ask five different folks to witness, you'd get five different stories.

As for me, I ain't so sure. I've waited most of my life for God Almighty to speak unto to me and explain it all…maybe lean out from a dark thundercloud and roar down a mighty pronouncement or speak in tongues of fire from a bright red maple in the fall, or maybe just whisper in my ear on a still and starry night. I have listened and prayed and listened some more and here it is a new century but He ain't spoke to me, not once.

Just now, I remember thinking when they came upon us back in eighteen and sixty-three, and I felt the rough bite of the rope around my neck and harkened to the cruel sound of the whip, the weeping of the women, and the whimper of Mary Shelton's babe. *Just now*, I thought, *would be a good time for Him to commence.*

All that I know is that war casts a long shadow, both in the coming and the going of it and we ain't out of that shadow yet, not by a long shot. The hunger and the hangings and that terrible day…red blood on white snow…the black wings of them crows…it don't hardly bear thinking of…but it's every bit of it in my memory yet—and I ain't the only one what remembers.

Some say that all the meanness that came upon us here in Laurel begun back in '61 when Neely Tweed went after Sheriff Ransom

Pleasant Merrill with a double-barreled shotgun—went after him and killed him dead over there in the county seat.

I don't know—it could be. But I reckon it goes a ways farther back—likely Brother Norton would say all the long sorry way back to Cain and Abel.

1861

1.

~SIMEON RAMSEY~

East Tennessee
Sunday, April 21, 1861

And the Lord had respect unto Abel and his offering
But unto Cain and to his offering he had not respect.
And Cain was very wroth and his countenance fell.

I am puzzling out the words in my daddy's old Bible when a stranger sets down next to me. All the others here at the inn is busy drinking or gambling and Lathern, my particular friend, has gone off somewheres, most likely with that gap-toothed girl what was making eyes at him as she brought out the victuals. I nod to the stranger and skooch over to make room on the bench by the fireplace.

"You're right obliging, sir." The stranger holds out his hands to the red warmth of the glowing logs and remarks on the coolness of the evening. He is a dark-complected feller, something like an Injun, and with a strong nose like an Injun, but his hair is kindly curly and he has a big beard which Injuns never do and he don't talk like no Injun that I ever heard.

"Name's Aaron," he says, looking me up and down. "Jake Aaron, pack peddler working my way back to Greenville, South Carolina. Though had I a mite of sense, I'd head south to Mexico or north to Canada."

He takes a deep draft of his cider and stares into the fire. I close the Bible, keeping the place with my thumb.

"I hear Mexico's right hot and full of bandits," I say, "and I reckon Canada's right cold and full of savages. Up yonder you'd be carrying your pack through snow and ice nine months of the year if my geography schoolbook had the right of it. What's wrong with *this* country?"

He screws his head around and looks at me like I ain't got no sense.

"Son," he says, "haven't you heard about Fort Sumter? Oh, this is a fine country, none better, but it's about to be torn asunder. And we are setting right at one of the ripping places. War's coming, make no mistake."

Only last night, when our wagon train put up at Garrett's Inn near Warm Springs, we had heard something of Sumter and the cry of war. A feller there had a Tennessee newspaper and he was plumb full of talk about South Carolina taking the fort from the Union soldiers. There is always folks eager to tell the latest news whenever we stop at an inn so I already knew that sometime back of this, South Carolina, Georgia, Alabama, and maybe Texas, along with several others, had voted to leave the Union. Why, I even knew they had elected a feller name of Jeff Davis to be the head of them, but I hadn't paid it much mind, figuring that it wouldn't change my life none.

My life is set and arranged according to the seasons. In the spring and summer of the year I go with a wagon train on the Buncombe Turnpike, carrying goods between Greeneville in Tennessee and Greenville in South Carolina. Come fall I follow the droves of hogs along the same road when the packed dirt turns to a stinking slough of mud and hog shit. Hard, dirty work but a few more years and I'll have enough saved to buy me a place near Maryville in Tennessee where Cora's people are. And then I'll turn farmer and my life will still run according to the seasons.

"Mr. Aaron," says I, making light of the peddler's gloomy words. "I ain't got no slaves nor do I want none. I just want to tend a little piece of ground and raise up a family. What they do in South Carolina ain't none of my business."

He don't say nothing for a spell, just shakes his head and looks at me kind of pitiful like. Then he reaches out a hand and taps the Bible where I have it laying on my knee and he says, solemn-like, "And Cain talked with his brother Abel and it came to pass, when they were in the field, that Cain rose up against Abel his brother, and slew him."

It gives me something of a chill, hearing this stranger say the very words I was just reading, but as I am about to ask what he means, Lathern shambles back in with a grin on his face like a shit-eating dog. I can see he wants to tell me what he's been doing but quick as he worms in beside me, I speak up.

"Lathern, Mr. Aaron here says they's going to be a fight now that South Carolina's gone and turned the Union out of that fort."

Lathern just grins wider, looking every bit the fool he sometimes is. "Reckon *I* could make a soldier," he says, lifting up his chin and squaring his shoulders. "March behind a brass band carrying a rifle gun and wearing a fine uniform. Yeah, buddy, that'd be a sight better'n driving these blame wagons up and down the muddy ol' Turnpike."

He sniffs at his fingers and grins some more, then waves them under my nose. "Take a smell, Preacher. You know what that is? Gen-yoo-wine East Tennessee pussy."

I knock his hand away. "I know what it is, you fool," I tell him. He likes to call me Preacher on account of I read my Bible every night and because I don't go after girls like he does. Not that I ever did much, but now that me and Cora are promised, to my way of thinking ain't none of the others even worth looking at.

The peddler looks at his half-empty tankard. "It's coming, boys; will you, nil you, war's coming. Once they fired on Sumter—"

"I told you," I say, feeling some aggravated now, "I ain't no part of this. It don't matter none to me who the government is, long's I can have me a little piece of land and make a crop. Besides, I don't hold with fighting."

"Dang, Preacher," Lathern's grin is gone now and he is frowning at me. "You turned Quaker like that girl of yourn?" He stands, shaking his head. "That ain't no religion for a man. You'll be *thee*-ing and *thou*-ing, next thing I know."

He's funning me some, but I know that underneath he's serious. Then he slaps me on the back and heads off to where some fellers are hoo-rahing at their dice game. A cloud of baccer smoke is hanging low over the gamblers and through the blue haze I see the gap-toothed girl slip out the door with one of the other wagoners. He has his hand on her big old rump and is pushing to hurry her along.

"A Quaker?" The peddler raises his thick black eyebrows at me. "And are you an Abolitionist as well?"

Something in this feller's manner makes me want to explain myself. "Like I told you, I got no slaves nor do I want none. This whole slavery fuss ain't nothing to do with me. And I ain't no Quaker neither.

Lathern just said that on account of the girl I aim to marry. Her family are big Quakers over in Maryville, but she's living with her aunt in Greeneville, Tennessee, and she goes to the Presbyterian church there."

Cora has told me how her family helps runaway slaves on their journey north. When first I learned this, I had to study on it some, for it seemed to me that it was the same as stealing another man's property. But then she told me stories of how bad some folks treated their slaves and how nigger families got broke up and sold away to different states, and how all that the runaways wanted was to get to where they could make it on their own. Listening to her tell these awful tales in her sweet low voice, I had come to see that them runaway niggers weren't anyways different in their wants from me.

But still and all, I ain't no Abolitionist. I ain't a slave and I don't own no slaves so, as I see it, it ain't my fight.

The peddler is tapping on my Bible again. He has his eyes closed and is rocking back and forth a little. The words come out almost like a song.

"And the Lord said unto Cain, Where is Abel thy brother? And he said, I know not: Am I my brother's keeper? And he said, What hast thou done? The voice of thy brother's blood crieth unto me from the ground...." And he goes quiet but his eyes is still shut and he is still rocking back and forth.

I take a look in my Bible and he is saying the words exact. "You got a fine memory, Mr. Aaron," I say, "but I wish you could tell me what you mean."

"I mean," says he, opening his eyes and staring into the fire like he was seeing pictures in the flames, "I mean there's a storm coming, and a mighty flood that will sweep everyone—Union, Secesh, Quaker, Abolitionist—all of them caught up and swept along in the raging waters. Some will go under, some will survive, but none will be unchanged."

"Noah had an ark," I say, thinking of a hidden cove I know over in Tennessee. "He rode the flood high and dry, him and his family."

Mr. Aaron turns his great dark eyes on me. "So they say. And they say, too, that Noah planted vines and became a drunkard. And cursed his son Ham who had seen him naked. Cursed him and his seed forever, saying they would be servants all their lives."

He reaches out a finger and taps my Bible yet again. "Ask any church-going, Bible-believing slave owner and they'll tell you that their Negroes are the descendants of Ham and that God *meant* them for slaves. And now, here we are… and I tell you again, there's a storm coming."

He drains the last drops from his tankard and stands. Pointing a finger at me, he says, "My friend, you're young and think you can stay out of this. But I've seen it all, time and time again, and you'll not escape the storm. You can run from it but it'll be there waiting for you when you least expect it. And, sooner or later, after the storm has passed, there'll be a need for redemption."

His sad eyes bore into me and he says, low and most to himself, "And it will be a terrible redemption…."

For a moment he stands there, looking like someone trying to call up a word or a memory, then shakes his head and starts for the door. I call after him, "Ain't you sleeping here? It's black dark and cold outside."

He waves a hand in the smoky air like he is pushing my words aside. "I prefer the clean straw of the barn and the peaceful company of the brute beasts. Good night to you, Sim. Try to keep your head above the water."

In the middle of the night I wake and lay there in my blanket, listening to the sounds of the others in the big room. The coals in the great fireplace is banked but a red glow flickers on the humped shapes around me. We are all laying, feet to the fire, like the spokes on a wheel. Some are snoring and one feller calls out, "Gee up there, you sorry critter, gee!" and jerks about like he is having a bad dream. Over to the left, someone lets loose a fart and I think that maybe Mr. Aaron was in the right of it to sleep in the barn. Though critters is bad to fart, somehow it don't smell near so bad as with folks.

Mr. Aaron seemed a nice enough feller but that was some crazy talk he was doing. What I say is let the Unionists and the Secesh fight it out amongst theirselves. I'm not like Lathern, a fool for a brass band

and a fancy uniform. No, I'll keep on like I'm doing, putting by a little more coin every year. Two more years should see me married to my Cora and tending our first crop. I can see the rows of corn with bean vines twisting up some of the stalks and the broad green leaves of pumpkins and candy roasters spreading beneath. A big-bagged Jersey cow, a flock of red chickens scratching around, pigs in the woods, growing fat on acorns and chestnuts, Cora in a pink sunbonnet…

I think some more about the peddler, carrying that pack of gew-gaws and gimcracks to tempt the females who don't never get into town, and I think I'll ask him in the morning does he have some pretty I could buy to take to Cora. If nothing don't happen, we'll be in Greeneville tomorrow night and I'd admire to see her fine gray eyes sparkle at the pleasure of a gift.

When I fall asleep, I dream of her. Her and me riding in a boat down the French Broad River. It is running bolder than ever I've seen it and our boat skims along at a great pace, high above the hidden rocks.

When we get to Greeneville it takes an awful time to get the wagons unloaded and the beasts fed and stabled. At last I hurry to Cora's aunt's house, hoping to see a lamp or candle in the window, but all is dark and I know Cora and Miss Viney must be asleep. Honest folks aren't abroad at this time of night and, not wishing to be taken for a robber, I make my way back to the stable and bed down in the hay with my team.

At dawn I am back at Miss Viney's. Her house is a neat little brick cottage surrounded by a picket fence with a brick path winding from the gate to the front porch. Spring lilies of yellow and white are push-ing up through the dirt and the big lilac at the side of the house is heavy with purple blooms. The scent makes me think of Cora and as soon as I see the smoke begin to curl up from the kitchen chimney, I knock on the door, so eager to see my Cora again that I have to pull off my hat and hold it in front of me.

Miss Viney answers the door and while I am looking over her shoulder, hoping to see Cora come a-running, Miss Viney stands aside and motions me in.

"Come in, Sim, and get you a bite of breakfast. I hate to disappoint you but your sweetheart's gone back to Maryville. Her mother was taken bad and they needed Cora to help out."

All my happiness and eagerness disappears and I set my hat on a chair just inside the door. I find myself looking around to see if maybe this is a prank that Cora and her aunt are playing on me, but there is no gray-eyed girl with smooth chestnut hair coming smiling to meet me. Like always, the front room is full of bolts of cloth and baskets of lace and trimmings of one kind and another. There is a half-finished dress of some shiny blue stuff on the headless dummy and two more, one brown and one black, hanging from hooks on the wall.

Miss Viney makes dresses for all the high-toned ladies of Greeneville and Cora is learning the trade. I first saw her when I come to make a delivery of eight bolts of silk and velvet her aunt had sent off for. Miss Viney had asked me to bring them in the house and put them on her parlor table, and when I staggered into the room, weighted down by all them bolts, why, there was Cora. I won't never forget that first sight of her. She was setting in a little rocker, sewing wide cream-colored lace onto a light green dress and I like to fell over my feet for staring at her, she was such a pretty thing. When she looked up from her sewing and smiled at me, I knew that she was the girl I'd been waiting for.

And will have to wait some longer, I tell myself, trying not to be downcast. Miss Viney shoos me toward the kitchen, and I have to admit that the smell of coffee and biscuits and bacon is mighty welcome.

"Take some more bacon, Sim," she says, filling my cup again. "Cora left a letter for you. I'll just step into the parlor and get it."

My heart sinks for fear of what that letter may hold but I take another piece of bacon. Cora is fit to be the wife of some rich feller and I have always known that a better man than me could come along and claim her. The bacon don't seem to have no taste as I chew it and wash it down with the coffee that has suddenly turned bitter.

Miss Viney bustles back in with an envelope in her hand. "You set here and read your letter while I go tend to my chickens," she says and is out the door, skittering along like a plump little pullet herself.

I wipe my hands on my pants and open the letter.

April 18, 1861

Dear Sim,

I take pen in hand to say that I am needed at home and may not tarry even to see thee on thy return. Mother is taken ill and Father begs me to come at once to help with her care. His letter came by way of a Friend who was traveling to Greeneville on business and Father desired that I should return with this same Friend.

Nothing has changed in my feelings for thee and I hope that thine are the same. I do not know how long I shall be needed at home but trust that the Lord will bring us together in His good time.

Please, if thou are able, send a line to let me know that thou are well and unchanged in those sentiments professed by thee in February.

Through dark times and light, I am,

Yours as ever and in haste,
Cora

2.

~MARTHY WHITE~

Shelton Laurel, Madison County, North Carolina
Sunday, May 12, 1861

The sun is slicing through the stand of poplars above the path and there is bars of dark and light beneath our feet. I step slow and careful from light to dark and dark to light, taking care not to put my foot in both at once. Light to dark, dark to light, and back again. The pattern sings in my head, full of some kind of message—but what it is I cannot tell. I am filled with the same kind of feeling that comes just before I get a Seeing and I slow, then stop, waiting for what might come.

Mommy and Pap and the rest of them—Kate and Billy, Luvena, Josie, and Paul—is up ahead, hot-footing along so's to have extra time for visiting before the preaching begins. Just as they reach a bend in the trail, Mommy looks back to see am I coming. She makes an angry face at me and shifts Baby Sam to her other hip.

"I declare, Marthy," she puffs, hurrying back to grab my arm and give it a jerk that like to pull it loose, "when you don't get your way, you're as bad to bow up as any old mule. Now leave off that shuffling and step along smart-like or I'll cut me a switch."

Off a ways the church bell is beginning to ring. "Plague take it!" says Mommy, and she yanks my arm again and commences to pull me along at a trot, Sam's little head just a-bobbing above her hip.

I ain't much of a one for church going and such. Generally, I find a reason to lay out whenever I can. They's always too many folks turning to look my way and whisper behind their hands. And once, during a revival, they all of them mobbed around me and prayed that my tongue would be loosened and that I would be able to speak like any other young un.

That was three years ago when I weren't but nine years of age. It scared me right much and didn't do a lick of good—I still can't shape my mouth to make sounds a body can understand. And Mommy has about give up on trying to make a Christian of me. I won't go forward when they give the altar call and I ain't never going to let no one dip me under the water when they have the baptizing down at the Laurel Creek.

Most Sundays I slip away to the woods while Mommy is busy getting ready or I make myself take a coughing fit or some such, but this morning she latched on to me and said that like it or not I was going to the preaching with the rest of the family.

The bell has stopped ringing and the last folks is settling themselves on the benches when me and Mommy come up the log steps and into the church house. The room is full to overflowing, with some of the men standing at the back. Mommy cuts her eyes at me to let me know it's my fault if we can't find a place to set but then Sally Shelton and her girls scooch over to make room. Molly, who is the friendly one, smiles real sweet at me but I look away right quick and busy myself with lining up my toes along the crack between the puncheon logs of the floor.

First comes the praying—everyone offering up whatever is in their hearts. Some shouts out their prayers whilst others don't hardly raise above a whisper. It's a mighty racket, all them different voices together, but I make out one word being said over and over in the prayers and that word is *secession*.

I know what the word means, for Pap and Sol Chandley sat out on the porch late last night talking about the coming vote and what it would signify for us in the Laurels did it go this way or that. And I know that the vote in Marshall tomorrow is why the church house is packed full today—every man here wants to see which way his neighbors is likely to jump.

At last the praying stops and the preacher comes forward. Brother Ray is a tall skinny somebody with an old black frock coat that looks like it had belonged to a short fat man. When Brother Ray raises his arms, the sleeves pull back showing his great knobbly wrists, but you can see he don't pay that no mind. He holds his arms high while we all watch, hardly breathing, then he brings down the right one, finger a-pointing, and flails it back and forth like he is pointing at each and every one of us.

It is dead quiet except for the snuffling sound of a titty baby getting its dinner. Then the preacher's voice rings out so loud I see Emmeline Rice on the bench directly in front of me jump like she'd been stung by a wasper.

"*Brothers* and sisters," the preacher begins, commencing to walk back and forth. He talks that certain way preachers do, kindly jumping on some words and huffing them out special. "The book *says*, 'I was in the *spirit* on the Lord's *day* and heard behind me a great *voice*, as of a *trumpet*, saying, I am *alpha* and omega, the *first* and the last.'"

Some few give out an amen but Brother Ray keeps going, hollering something about seven golden candlesticks and the Son of Man with eyes like fire and a voice like the sound of many waters.

Folks is nodding and amen-ing like it makes sense to them but I just set there thinking on a voice like the sound of many waters. I decide that it might be like the roaring sound the creeks and branches make after a heavy rain, and I get to wondering what *my* voice would sound like, was I ever to gain the use of it once more. I have heard Mommy tell how I started off babbling and saying words like any young un but that by the time I was three, I had quit talking altogether. Mommy reckons it might have been on account of the bad fever I took that summer. She says the Angel of Death was hovering, and they had almost give up hope but then the fever broke.

Once that happened, Mommy says, I mended fast and was up and running about in no time. Only I didn't never utter another word. They even carried me to the doctor in Marshall but he couldn't do no good. Mommy says it don't matter, that I am as good a hand to work as any girl and not near so bothersome as some. She means my sister Little Kate who will jabber the live-long day unless Mommy or Pap makes her hush.

Even here in the Lord's House, Kate is jabbering—down the bench she is whispering to Nancy Shelton. Mommy reaches across me and pinches Kate on the arm without even looking at her. Mommy lets out a loud *amen* to cover Kate's squeak of pain and the preacher comes to the end of his message.

When church breaks up, folks gather outside like always. The women is talking, as is usual, of who's in the family way and who's sick and who's courting and who ain't here today. Judy Shelton is one who ain't here—she don't often come to meeting and besides, her babe is not yet a month old and kindly fractious. I look across the branch where I can make out the top of her tall rock chimney over the spring-green trees. There is a wisp of smoke curling against the blue of the sky and the sight of it makes me smile. Miz Judy is my special friend.

The menfolk is in a tight little bunch off to the side of the church-yard and over and over that word—*secession*—is being tossed from one to another. Ever one of the men looks angry and they are shaking their heads *no* and raising up their fists. Ol' Brother Ray comes hus-tling over, head sticking out like a skinny hen-turkey, and he tries to push in amongst them, perhaps a-feared that they is going to be a fight, but the men pay him no mind. So he falls back and looks around to see where else he can poke that long nose.

Under the big oak at the edge of the churchyard, Kate and a gang of her friends is sitting on the hard-packed clay and whispering secrets. Most of the boys is hanging round near the girls, shoving one another and laughing, aiming to make the girls take notice of them. But I see five fellers slipping off a ways and I reckon they are fixing to shoot marbles—though if Brother Ray catches sight of them, there'll be a mighty fuss and he'll most likely take the marbles away. According to Brother Ray, any kind of playing on Sunday is against the Book. And marbles, where you may win or lose some, is bad as gambling.

I can see that we are going to be here a while yet so I go over to a big flat rock where I can sit and watch all that is going on. The women is still chattering away and I hear Miz Unus Riddle holler, "Let me hold that little un." Mommy always says that woman is a pure fool for babies. Miz Unus has helped birth most of the ones born around here, and, though she's past eighty and crippled with the rheumatism, she will go out in the awfullest weather there is to help a woman at her time.

Off at the edge of the woods, I see the five boys are crouched in a circle over their marbles. One of them is Little Davy Shelton, with that fine black curly hair falling in his eyes. Kate always calls him my sweetheart because she seen him smile at me last time him and his pap come to trade for some garden seed.

Kate is all the time saying things like that just to be aggravating. Davy ain't even as old as me nor as tall. But he is the onliest one that has ever smiled at me like that. And he is a fine-looking boy with them black curls and blue eyes and he will make a fine man—if he lives, like the old folks say.

Just thinking them words gives me the cold shivers. Folks says that about little uns there's so many of them taken in the first year or two—but Davy is eleven years old. He ain't some puny babe, like to be carried off by the summer complaint. Over to the side I see Brother Ray. He has give up on trying to talk to the men and his eyes is darting all around. Preacher is the sort of somebody who always has to be finding fault—and knowing better than to try it with the grownups, he naturally goes after us young uns. There he is now, pussyfooting over amongst the girls, and I can hear him asking what lesson they had taken from his sermon. Whilst they are trying to answer him, I slip down from my rock and make my way to where the boys are playing. When they see me coming, some of them make faces at me, and I hear Lige Norton say, "What does the dummy think she's doing?" But Davy stands up and watches as I jerk my head and cut my eyes over to where Preacher is.

"*Hsst*, Preacher's on the prowl," Davy whispers, and the boys grab the marbles and stand up quick-like, making sure to scuffle out the circle they had marked in the dirt. I turn back to my setting place but first I hear Davy whisper, "Thankee, Marthy," and he smiles at me again.

His eyes are like pieces of the sky.

The Moores from the next holler are with us as we set off up the trail for home. Miz Moore and Mommy commence to talk about the sermon while Pap and Mr. Moore fall behind. I hear them talking solemn and, again and again, there's that word—*secession*. They are making plans to ride into Marshall early in the morning to be there for the vote. "All of them that's for the Union had best stay together," Pap says, "for they'll be a sight of them rich town folk *for* seceding and they'll do anything they can to stop us voting."

Pap sounds so stern that another shiver runs over me—somebody walking on my grave, Mommy would say. I run to catch up with her and hold out my arms for Little Sam. He is warm and sleepy and it feels good to hold him close, even though I can tell his hippins needs changing. I pay no mind to the soggy, smelly cloths wrapping his little bottom and bury my face in his yellow curls.

When we reach the place where the trail forks and the Moores go on their way, Pap falls in by Mommy. She just nods, like she knows what he's about to say.

"I reckon you'll be leaving out afore sunup," she says. "Sixteen long miles to Marshall. Tonight, I'll bake you a pone of cornbread to carry with you."

He puts his arm around her and whispers something in her ear. I think how it would be if Little Davy was whispering to me, how his curls would feel soft against my cheeks, and my face goes hot.

Later when all us young uns is in our beds and Kate and Luvena is already snoring next to me, before I go to sleep, I see Pap by the fireplace, cleaning his squirrel rifle and his pistol. Mommy is setting next to him and her face is sorrowful.

"I pray there won't be no trouble," she says, and for the third time that day, a cold shiver runs all over me. I wonder was I to go to the pool in the woods, would I get a Seeing that would tell me what was coming?

But I am afeared of what that Seeing might hold and I know that I won't.

3.

~POLLY ALLEN~

Marshall, Madison County, North Carolina
Sunday, May 12 - Monday, May 13, 1861

With Lawrence away, Juliann and I have taken the opportunity to do a most thorough spring cleaning. It has had me in its clutches for weeks now and I have put off answering Emmie's letter far too long but shall seize this moment while the little ones are in Juliann's care. Enticing aromas of gingerbread and the cheerful sounds of happy children emanate from the kitchen. In the parlor, all is tidy—the windows shine; the carpet is swept, the curtains and antimacassars are bleached and fresh starched. Carefully I lay out the paper on my writing desk, dip my new-sharpened nib, and begin, savoring the bliss of a moment's leisure and the beauty of the slanting letters, black against the creamy page.

Sunday, May 12, 1861

My Very Dear Emily,

Your most welcome letter arrived last week in a packet from the old home. How glad I am you thought to direct it thither. I have been reading and re-reading your dear words till I fear my eyes will wear away the ink, were such a thing possible. Certainly, the paper is growing soft and worn with folding and re-folding. And now at last I have a few free moments to pen a suitable reply and to answer, as best I may, your many questions.

It seems such a short time past that we were happy young girls, but a glance in the mirror and at my little ones reminds me that we are both *matrons* now and that with the joys of marriage and the blessing of children come their attendant responsibilities. So I will not chide you, dear Emmie, for this long lapse in our correspondence—has it indeed been eight years since you attended at my wedding and, soon after, eloped with Mr. Worth of Grand Rapids, Michigan?

I know I had a letter from you a few months after the event and I believe I wrote to tell you of my joy at learning Lawrence and I were to be blessed with a child—but that letter was returned and I had no way of discovering your new address. So I was unable to tell you how that first sweet hope had been soon dashed. How I wished for you in that sad time, my dear Emmie! But enough of old sorrows—on to present joys!

You gave me such a nice long budget of your family and your activities—I can almost see you, surrounded by your little ones, strolling the banks of the river and admiring the rushing waters that give your city its name, or tending the roses in the garden you describe so beautifully. Now I must try to paint a picture of our life here in the mountains.

Like any fond mother, I begin with the children—Annie is six, Romulus is rising four, and little Margaret (whom we call Maggie) is almost one. I will spare you, in *this* letter, a list of their perfections, only to say that Baby Maggie is trying to toddle and a charming sight she is, her face screwed up in concentration and the pink tip of her tongue protruding, while Romulus is a stout little fellow whose greatest desire is to "be as big as Papa and wear britches and shoot a gun." (His manly ways have, of course, made him the apple of his father's doting eye.) Annie plays the little mother to her siblings with such sweet solemnity that I have oft to turn away to hide a smile. Lawrence has purchased a pony for the children and, though Annie must be coaxed onto Dapple's broad gray back, Rommie bids fair to becoming an excellent little horseman.

We live in Marshall, the county seat where Lawrence was, until very recently, Clerk of the Superior Court. The town is small and lies on a narrow strip with the dashing waters of the French Broad River at its foot and a mountain of rocky cliffs and steep woods at its back. There is a rather unprepossessing brick courthouse and an ancient wooden jail, two hotels, and three stores—as well as a dressmaker and a blacksmith. Nine residences are crowded into this rural metropolis—ours is on the main street but a few steps away from the courthouse and looks especially fine now that my flowers are abloom. I brought 'piney' roots from the old home and they are making a bold show just below the gallery. They are the white ones, the ones with little splashes of red.

My dear brother John's family lives a few houses down from ours. John's wife Mary (you may remember her) has proven a true friend (though not such a Soul Mate as my Emmie!) and we are fortunate to have them near. John's Mary and I cling together, consoling one another in our loneliness, since, like my own Lawrence, John has 'gone for a soldier.' (John was always my favorite among my siblings and he and I have shared many a quiet hour together, talking over happy childhood days.) Lawrence's cousin (and the town's doctor) James Keith (yes, the same) and his young family live nearby and are another source of society—though I believe that Cousin James, too, will soon don the grey uniform and depart.

Truly, except for the distance between my Emmie and myself, I have heretofore been most content with my life here in Marshall, and I pray that this unpleasantness that grips our country will soon end and Lawrence will return to the peacefully humdrum existence that we enjoyed before the events at Fort Sumter. He vows that Honor requires he answer the call but assures me that there will be no war.

You may know that North Carolina has not left the Union—as recently as February our county voted against such an extreme measure. It is chiefly the big slaveholders who stand to lose should the Abolitionists have their way—and there are few slaveholders in these mountains, almost none with any large number of Negroes. (I doubt our few servants even think of themselves as slaves, such a part of the family they are.) Still, there is a strong sentiment that the South should be allowed to find her own way rather than submit to the dictates of the North. And I must admit that when, directly after Fort Sumter's surrender, a group of recruiters accompanied by a brass band marched into town to turn the young men out for the South, I stood on the upper front gallery of our home, hearing the martial airs and the cries of "Huzzah for the South," much to my surprise, my blood stirred.

Lawrence stood by me, watching the spectacle and saying little. But not a month passed before he resigned his office and joined the infantry, saying it was a matter of Honor and he could do no less. Even now he is in Raleigh at a Camp of Instruction.

Dear Emmie, can I hope that you will understand my feelings? As his Wife, I am proud of his fervor, his desire to defend our Homeland and our way of life but, O! how I pray that this unpleasantness will pass as quickly as might a misunderstanding between two hot-headed brothers.

Indeed, we are awaiting the public meeting tomorrow when the voters of the county will select delegates to another secession convention in the state capitol. Pray God that the vote will—

There is a thunder of boots on the front steps and the door swings wide to reveal my dear Lawrence—booted, spurred, and in the splendid glory of his new gray uniform. I throw down my pen and rush to greet him.

"But, how are you come here? What—"

I am all amazed, but his warm arms surround me; his beard tickles my cheek; I am enveloped in the masculine aromas of leather, tobacco, and horse. As we stand embracing, Annie and Rommie run in from the kitchen, crying out, "Papa! Papa!"

Releasing me, Lawrence bends down to sweep the little ones up in a vast hug. "It's only the briefest of visits, Poll; I could not miss the balloting tomorrow. And as soon as I've cast my vote and had a word with my deputy clerk, I must be in the saddle and back on the road to Raleigh. You have me for tonight, no more."

He has much to tell me of his training and of his duties with Company A of the Partisan Rangers, but Rommie quickly claims his father, desiring Lawrence to let him hold his sword and to show him how his pistol works. I hurry to the kitchen to direct Juliann to kill one of the pullets so that Lawrence may have his favorite chicken fricassee. She has anticipated me and is already beating up the batter for one of her delicious pound cakes. "And green peas, Juliann—I believe that there are sufficient on the vines for a mess."

Returning to the parlor, I find that Lawrence has rescued Baby Maggie from her cot and is dandling her on one knee, oblivious to the spreading dampness on his gray trousers. My desk chair has been commandeered by Rommie to serve as *his* horse and even sedate little Annie is astride the arm of another chair (alas for my starched antimacassar) as Lawrence urges them on to a mad gallop. I sink onto the loveseat and watch them all, aglow with the joy of reunion.

Indeed, Rommie and Annie engage Lawrence so fully and pelt him with so many questions, that it is not till they are all safely abed that there is time for my own anxious queries.

"And will it come to war?" I ask as we sit in the parlor, the uneven flicker of the oil lamp making the arabesques of the wallpaper seem to dance. In the kitchen I can hear the clink of china and the sweet low hum of Juliann singing to herself as she puts away the dishes and lays the table for breakfast. I clasp my husband's strong hand, hoping for reassurance. "Will North Carolina fight the Union?"

"I think it likely, my love." Lawrence yawns wide and looks toward our bedchamber. "Every man I've met is aflame with the desire to preserve the South's liberties. Some are even calling it the Second American Revolution."

He yawns again and stands, stretching his arms wide. "Inspiring times—and we must match them. I am proud to have answered the call. But mine has been a long day, Polly, most of it in the saddle. And I've been looking forward to the comfort of my own bed and…."

Taking my hand, he pulls me toward him. "Now, sweetheart, don't fret," he admonishes, seeing my brow furrowed and a few tears standing in my eyes. "When Lincoln and his cronies see how strong the South is—how united the Southern states are in their desire for independence, make no mistake, the North will back down before there's a real war. A few skirmishes perhaps, no more, and they'll be bound to admit that we have the superior men, as well as the superior cause."

His fingers are busy on the buttons of my dress and he stops my next question with his eager lips. "Polly, pretty Polly," he whispers, his words and the pressure of his body urgent, "come to bed."

෴

In the sweet joy of our reunion, I forbear to question him further but as he gives me a last drowsy caress and makes to turn on his side, I ask again if he truly believes a war can be averted.

He pats my hip absentmindedly. "My dear, do put away these fears. After all, the only thing the South asks is to be left alone, to manage our own lives..." A great yawn interrupts his sleepy words. "To manage...as seems best...to us..."

And with this, he begins to snore.

He is up early to cast his vote and then he is gone. His brief and unexpected visit might have been a fleeting dream, but for the lingering scent of his tobacco and Rommie's constant talk of "Papa's grand u-form." I wander to the parlor, thinking to finish my letter to Emmie but lay it aside, too distracted by sounds from the street and by my own misgivings to continue. The thought that even now, Emmie might be thinking of Lawrence as one of the Enemy is deeply disturbing. *Pray God that Lawrence is right and the North and the South will agree to co-exist as two great nations.*

But with the rising hubbub in the street, an unwelcome thought blossoms in my mind. *If it comes to war, might it not be that I will hear the clamor of enemy soldiers at our very doorstep?* A sudden chilling comprehension of what war—war waged here in our homeland—might mean floods over me. My heart races and, almost as frantic as if my imaginings were real, I feel a sudden need to see my children, just as a mother hen, alarmed by the shadow of a passing hawk, will spread her wings and call her chicks to her.

In our bedchamber, Little Maggie is sound asleep in her cot, pale wisps of hair tousled, thumb firmly thrust between those rosebud lips. I pull it gently out but a frown fleets across her sweet face and the comforting thumb pops back in. Sighing, I watch her slumber, glad that Mary is not there to see. Dear Sister Mary, so full of suggestions—mittens tied tight or something bitter on the thumb. *Soon,* I think, *I'll do something about it soon.*

I follow the sound of childish prattle to the kitchen when Juliann (a treasure, if ever there was one) is letting Annie and Rommie cut out biscuits. Annie, like a thrifty little housewife, is taking care to place the cutter just so in order to cut the most circles possible from her sheet of dough but Rommie's biscuit cutting is boyishly slap dash; indeed, as I withdraw unnoticed from the kitchen door, I hear him declare that now he will cut out a horse.

Back in the parlor, I uncork the ink and take up my pen to continue my letter to Emmie, but before I have so much as wet the nib, the shouting in the street becomes louder. *Perhaps the voting is over,* I think and go to peek out the window. Cries of "The Southland forever!" ring out, and as I watch from behind the curtain, I see throngs of men milling about, many of them sadly intoxicated.

I draw back a little, not wanting to be seen. With all my heart I wish that Lawrence had not gone back to Raleigh so soon, leaving me alone with the children at such an unsettled time. And then, catching sight of the unfinished letter on my writing desk, I wonder what Emmie would think if she could see the scene beyond my front door. Near our porch, a shouting group of townsmen cluster 'round Sheriff Ransom Merrill who, I am dismayed to see, looks as if he too has "a drop taken." I see Cousin James Keith with his nephew Mitchell and am a little comforted to think that I have at least one male relative still nearby.

James and the sheriff, both much excited, lead a cheer for Jeff Davis and the Confederacy and a great many of the crowd take up the cry. Across the street in front of the Mercantile, a little knot of rough-looking men raise a cry of "Washington and the Union!" These men wear homespun or buckskins and have that look of fierce arrogance that proclaims them the products of one of the more isolated communities of our county.

When he was Clerk of Court, Lawrence told me of his encounters with men of this type. He called them "the natural men"—uneducated, for the most part, and quick to take offense if they feel someone is attempting to bamboozle them. I have seen them on their infrequent forays into Marshall for provisions, sometimes riding, sometimes in a broken-down wagon pulled by a pair of slab-sided mules but standing aside for no one. "I'm as good as any other man," their scowling visages seem to say, "and maybe a good bit better." Their women rarely come to town but when they do, they are usually taciturn, relying on the men to do the bargaining. They buy little—only the barest of necessities—not even casting a longing glance at some of the fripperies on display. All the women are poorly dressed—homespun again—and all are work-worn. In spite of this, they appear to be as proud as their men. Mary warned me of this when I spoke of wanting to hire some country girl for help with the children—before Juliann came to us.

I remember a Saturday—it was the first summer of our residence in this house, and Lawrence and I were enjoying the air, sitting out on the upper gallery and watching "country come to town." Lawrence was exchanging bows and greetings with various acquaintances, then regaling me with whispered character sketches of each. This one was known as a pinchpenny, that one was a sharp trader—

Breaking off, Lawrence leaned close and directed my gaze to a woman striding down the street. Her confident gait and her bon-net-less head of flaming red hair set her apart from the other female pedestrians as did the unseasonal shawl she clutched about her in a token attempt to conceal her condition—heavy with child and inde-cently close to her time. She disappeared into the Mercantile, and I shook my head.

"Oh, heavens," I whispered, "to be seen in public in that state! These country women! Surely her husband—"

Lawrence had raised an eyebrow. "Perhaps she has none. The folk from the more remote parts of the county seemingly have little regard for the proprieties of God or man. Truly," he had declared, "some of them are little better than savages."

I remember those words as, from behind the parlor curtain, I watch the scene in the street. A rough-looking group of the Unionists—sav-ages, indeed, with unkempt hair and menacing demeanor—advance upon the sheriff and his supporters. Harsh shouts for the Union, answering huzzahs for Jeff Davis. As the rabble closes in, I see the sheriff pull his gun and cry out, "You damned black Republicans and Lincolnites."

There is a great scuffle between the two factions and, unbelieving, I press my hand to my mouth and watch in dismay as the two sides jostle for preeminence.

A shot and then another ring out and I hear the tinkle of glass as one of the sidelights of our front door shatters. I am frozen with fear—cannot move, cannot, indeed, even take a breath. In the dust of the street I see a fallen body—a young man, hardly more than a boy, clutching a bleeding arm, and Sheriff Merrill standing near, pistol in his hand. Cousin James is quick to come to the young man's aid and as he kneels there in the dust of the street by the wounded youth, an older man—perhaps the father of the fallen one—emerges from the group of Unionists. He carries a shotgun which he raises to his shoulder as he approaches. Without ceremony, Sheriff Merrill takes to his heels. I watch in horror as he clatters up our steps, bursts through the door, and, brushing against my skirts, makes for the stairs, heedless of my astonished presence.

Fearful for what might follow, I slam shut the front door. Above I hear the terrified children calling for me, and then the sheriff shouts, "Come up here, all you damned black Republicans, and take a shot about with me!"

I am turning from the door all amazed when I hear another gunshot—deeper, louder this time. Upstairs, the children begin to howl with fear. Half-demented, I rush to the staircase, knocking against the little writing desk in my haste. The open ink bottle overturns and the jetty liquid creeps across my unfinished letter to Emmie.

4.

~JAMES A. KEITH~

Marshall, Madison County, North Carolina.
Monday, May 13, 1861

A milling crowd of the Shelton Laurel men stand between me and the sheriff, preventing my seeing just what happened when the shot was fired. "Let me through," I shout, forcing my way through the useless mob. "I am a doctor. Let me see to him." The crowd parts, revealing young Elisha Tweed, bleeding profusely from his left arm. My nephew Mitchell has followed me, and he stanches the flow with my scarf while I make a hurried search for other wounds. The bullet appears to have passed through the flesh of the youth's upper arm and lodged itself against a rib. Elisha is conscious and moaning in pain but in no present danger. It is well for him that I was nearby.

I might have known what was afoot when I saw Neely Tweed, one of our county's justices, in close conference with the gang of Laurel Unionists. His wife is related to half of them and, no doubt emboldened by their presence, Neely has chosen this day, of all days, to address old grievances with our sheriff. My friend Merrill was already in a dangerous mood due to the unexpected number of Union supporters who have turned out to vote for their delegate. From the angry words I heard exchanged just before the shooting, I can only surmise that Merrill meant to shoot the father and, impaired by liquor, hit the son. I stand to look around and assess the situation.

Pandemonium reigns. The street is like an angry hornet's nest, abuzz with mindless malevolence. A tall bay, spooked by the gunfire, has pulled loose from the hitching post beside the courthouse and canters toward us, reins trailing. Men scatter and I wave my hat to turn the beast away from young Tweed and Mitchell who is kneeling at his side. A frantic young mulatto chases after the runaway, shouting, "Whoa up, whoa up there, you Prince." At last the brute tires; a bystander grabs the reins; and the mulatto leads the lathered bay back to its irate master.

By now the more timid citizens have sought the refuge of the nearby stores but most of the voters gathered here today are transfixed by the drama playing out before them. Sheriff Merrill is leaning out from the upper gallery of Cousin Lawrence's house, haranguing Tweed and the Lincolnites. I see that some of them have found Joe, the town constable, and are urging him to arrest the sheriff for shooting young Tweed. Poor Joe, undoubtedly desirous of avoiding a confrontation with Merrill, is being hustled unwillingly along by this rabble, when I hear another shot—the unmistakable boom of a double-barreled shotgun.

Merrill reels and slumps against the railing, while below Neely Tweed, father of the wounded Elisha, prepares to reload his shotgun. As best I can tell, he was using birdshot which, at this distance, means Merrill cannot be seriously injured. I abandon my patient to Mitchell's care and hurry to remonstrate with the elder Tweed who is fumbling with his powder flask.

"Neely," I call to him, keeping my distance as he shakes the powder into the muzzle and rams home a wad. "Neely, your boy is not much wounded. Don't make matters worse by shooting the sheriff in cold blood—see, the constable is coming to take him into custody. This is a matter for the law—"

Tweed turns an icy blue eye on me. "The high sheriff *is* the law and it was him shot my boy. Everyone knows the quarrel was betwixt me and Merrill—I called him out on his underhanded dealings and he shot my boy out of pure meanness."

The gang of Laurelites have moved closer to him and they nod agreement. "That's the way of it," a snowy-bearded patriarch avers and the others mutter like sentiments.

"For God's sake, man," I plead, "stand aside and let the court and justice deal with this matter."

"Justice?" Tweed all but spits the word at me and reaches for the leather shot pouch at his side. "What kind of justice is there for me and mine here in Marshall? We come here to cast our votes against secession and them fellers are trying to prevent us."

Tweed is pale with fury, but he has not yet reloaded, and I venture closer, believing that, surely, I can persuade him. "Neely, come see to your boy. We are going to carry him to that house over there so I can remove the ball."

He stands unmoving and I try again. "Come, man, help us to move your son out of the street."

From the corner of my eye I see the constable and some others entering Cousin Polly's house—whether to come to the aid of the wounded Merrill or to arrest him, I know not. Nor, at this point, do I care. If Merrill is in custody, I can treat his wounds and he'll be safe from further attacks by the Laurelites. And if he states that he was being menaced by the Tweeds, no jury in this county will convict him. After all, the boy is barely wounded.

I step aside and begin to direct two onlookers to carry young Tweed to the lower gallery of John Peek's house. When I turn back to engage Neely's assistance, he is gone. Then I see him, shotgun at the ready, bounding up the front steps of Cousin Lawrence's house and disappearing through the front door. My first thought is of Polly— with Lawrence already departed for camp, she is without a protector and will welcome my intervention.

I start for the steps. Then I see above me on the upper gallery, the wounded Merrill standing, bracing himself with hands outstretched to the railing, his back to the street. Before I can shout a warning, there is a second shotgun blast from the door opening onto the gallery and my friend is blown back by its force. He falls across the railing, his head shattered, and I realize that this time Neely must have loaded buckshot. Merrill is bleeding like a slaughtered hog and the blood flows down to spatter the white flowers and green leaves of the bushes below. I am momentarily frozen, watching the progress of my friend's life blood—dripping from petal to leaf to leaf to petal.

Above the exclamations of the crowd, I hear a woman shrieking.

It is Polly and I bound up the steps, heedless of danger. Polly needs me.

"My cousin was understandably distraught at having been witness to such a scene but she and the children are unharmed. They will all be the better for a little rest," I assure the neighbor women who have gathered to support Polly and, I suspect, to observe the denouement of this drama. "I have administered a soporific and they are all sleeping quietly in the bedchamber."

The good wives nod and cluck like a parcel of hens and I hear a knowing whisper. "He'll have given laudanum to Polly and then a drop of Godfrey's Cordial for the little ones."

Mary Peek has taken charge and is directing a manservant to clean all traces of blood from the upper gallery and from the stairs where my poor friend's body was carried down. A competent woman, she has matters well in hand so, leaving instructions to send for me when Polly awakens, I proceed to the jail where young Elisha has insisted on being taken to join his father. Mitchell has returned home to secure my medical bag and will be there to assist.

My patient is awake and alert, though in obvious pain. They have put him in a room with a tall window so that I can have the advantage of what light remains in the day. Mitchell helps young Tweed onto the rough table and, at my direction, undoes the make-shift bandage and cuts away the torn and bloodied shirt. I send him for a bucket of water and begin to examine the wounds.

The arm is the bloodier, though the less serious, I judge. But it will be easier to probe for the ball in my patient's side with the arm bandaged and out of the way. Elisha is trembling slightly, his pale flesh all goose-bumped, as my fingers explore the entry and the exit of the pistol ball in his biceps.

"You were lucky here, Elisha," I tell him. "So far as I can tell, the humerus is untouched. The ball passed cleanly through the distal end of the biceps but with no damage to the tendon."

He gazes at me blankly, his pupils dilated with shock, and I rephrase my words. "It went through the flesh only—the bone wasn't touched. The arm should heal fully as long as there is no sepsis—no infection."

He nods wordlessly. My bucket of water has arrived and I direct Mitchell in sponging the arm clean, at the same time explaining to him my findings. He is touchingly eager to follow in my footsteps as a doctor and shows real promise in both his manner and his understanding. Taking some carbolic and lint from my bag of supplies,

I wipe the entry and exit wounds, demonstrating to my nephew the best way of extracting the bits of fabric carried into the wound by the force of the ball. I consider whether a poultice is necessary and decide it is not.

After wrapping the wound with lint, it is time to see what further damage the ball has done. My patient is still trembling slightly but he uttered not a sound as I dealt with his arm which bodes well for what is to follow.

"Now, Elisha," I say, calm and low as if gentling a skittish colt, "I must probe for the ball in your side."

A sharp intake of breath is his only reply. I direct him to lie back and gently position the bound arm away from his side so I can work unimpeded. I call for a lamp to be brought and have Mitchell hold it so that the light falls on the pale torn flesh and the bloody hole that gapes just nipple high.

Elisha catches sight of the probe as I lower it to the wound and shuts his eyes tight. An involuntary whimper escapes his lips.

"I'll be as quick as I can," I assure him. "But we must find and extract the ball."

He utters a stifled sound and I insert the probe. As I thought, the ball is lodged against a rib; I lay down the probe and, using the straight forceps, extract the ball in a matter of seconds.

"You see, Mitchell," I say, placing the bloody piece of lead on a square of lint, "the ball is still round, not flattened. Thus we can be confident that it lacked the force to splinter the rib."

A splash of carbolic and I mop the wound clean, once more extracting any errant fibers.

"It's over," I tell my patient, assisting him to sit up so I can wrap a bandage about his chest. "I expect you'll heal quickly. You'll have three scars to show for the one ball."

He opens his eyes and essays a weak smile. "Thankee, Doc, much obliged." He seems to feel some confusion. "I…ah…what do I owe you?"

Assuring him that he owes me nothing, I offer the bloody ball as a keepsake. He takes it and studies it, turning it this way and that. At last he pockets it and asks if he can be taken to his father.

The thought of seeing the man who, not an hour ago, killed my poor friend Merrill is—daunting. As a physician, I have done my best for the boy but I can hardly trust myself to be in the presence of his father. Still, I swallow my anger and lead the boy back to the cells, reminding myself that at least the murderer is in custody and will face trial.

The first cell is occupied by two of the town's habitual drunks—one sprawled comatose on the plank bunk; the other on his hands and knees, vomiting copiously into a bucket. The sour stench assaults our senses, and I see Mitchell pull out a handkerchief and put it to his nose. Neely Tweed is in the next cell, standing rigid as an image.

"Pap, the doc has fixed me up fine." Neely's stony visage softens and he puts a hand through the bars to grasp Elisha's good shoulder. The lad has regained his color and his father is visibly relieved to see him in such good case.

"That scoundrel Merrill had no cause to shoot my boy," he says, looking over his son's head into my eyes. "I know he was your friend but he was a goddamned thief. He used his office to line his pockets and today he was turning away from the ballot box anyone who was fixing to cast a vote for the Union."

I bite back my retort, knowing that some of what he says is true but taking comfort in the knowledge that my friend's murderer will soon face a jury—and, in all likelihood, the gallows. Young Elisha declares that he will stay with his father and I, not trusting myself to remain impassive a moment longer, return to Cousin Allen's house to enquire after Polly, Mitchell following behind like a faithful hound.

"We heard gunshots earlier," my wife says, looking up from her interminable knitting as I enter the parlor. "Little Laura was alarmed and cried but Baby Douglas clapped his hands at the sound. The usual election day rowdiness, I presume?"

"That," I tell her, dropping into my particular chair with a grunt of relief, "that and cold-blooded murder."

When I have recounted the events of the day and answered her many questions—women never apprehend these matters fully—she is little moved. Margaret never liked Merrill, calling him vulgar and uncouth. She knits on, unconcerned.

I study her placid, matronly countenance. A good woman, an excellent mother and wife but somehow… Of course, one should not expect youthful beauty in a woman who has borne two children and is entering her third decade. But, I muse, Cousin Lawrence's wife is the same age and *she* has borne three children. Yet Polly retains the bloom of youth.

The room seems suddenly stuffy—too much dark red velvet, too many uncomfortable little chairs. Even the wax flowers under their dome of glass—Margaret's especial pride—make me melancholy and I excuse myself to take a turn on the veranda.

My thoughts are with Polly—the delicate violet of her closed eyelids, the feathery lashes, her fine complexion, her sweet lips—and it rankles yet that Cousin Lawrence should have bested me in wooing. Still, I am the wealthier man and, if war comes, as I am sure it will, it is there I will look for further advancement, winning honor "even in the cannon's mouth."

From down the street I hear a roar of voices and cries of "Jeff Davis forever." A milling throng has formed into an impromptu parade and, as they march toward my end of town, behind them I see a cloud of dust as a gang of horsemen make a hurried departure in the opposite direction. I surmise that the votes have been counted. Undoubtedly, McDowell, a staunch secessionist, has been elected to the state conventions and the damned Laurelites have gone back to their sorry little valley and its meager homesteads, frustrated in their desires to advance the Union cause.

As the shouting victors come my way, I light a cheroot and walk down the steps to join in the cheering.

The following night, I am awakened by the constable and his deputies pounding on my door and the unwelcome news that the God Damned Laurelites have broken into the jail and helped Neely Tweed to escape justice.

5.

~JUDITH SHELTON~

Shelton Laurel, Madison County, North Carolina
Wednesday, May 15, 1861

Me and Ellender and Dan'l are near done with hoeing the taters and I am stretching the kink out of my back when I see three men on horses coming up the lane. I shade my eyes from the morning sun to see who it is. Something about the one in front seems like I ought to know him, but his slouch hat is pulled down and I can't make out his face. The other two are a man and a boy, and the boy is having all he can do to stay upright.

Another few paces brings them closer and I see that it is Abner Tweed. I can't help but think how I must look with my faded sun-bonnet, my raggedy old linsey skirt, and my shirtwaist showing two wet patches in front. Little Armp has been fretting there on his quilt at the end of the row and my milk has let down like one thing. It's been a long time since Abner and me was sweethearts, but the sight of him still makes my breath catch—though he's been wed these ten years—and me as good as.

"Judy," he calls, pulling his horse to a stop at the edge of the field, "we need a helping hand."

The young uns are standing all amazed, but I tell them to keep on with their work. I make my way down the green rows of tater plants toward him, stopping to pick up the babe and wondering what Abner Tweed can want of me. Since we parted, I've seen little enough of him and, from all I hear, his wife is a jealous somebody who'd not look kindly on him straying. Though the Lord knows, between Mama and the children and Sol, it's not me he'd be straying with.

I come up to him and stand at his stirrup. "Abner," I say, looking up into that handsome face of his. "What is it that you need? You know I'll help youns anyway I can."

"I reckon you heard," he says, "how they stole the vote from us on Monday. And how that no-good rascal of a sheriff shot my brother's boy."

"I did," says I. "And I heard that Neely was in the jail house for killing the sheriff."

The fellow on the second horse coughs and I look over to see that it is Neely and that the sick-looking young un must be his boy.

"Some of us rode into Marshall last night," says Abner, looking up at the sky and pulling on his beard. It puts me in mind of how he used to scratch his chin when he wasn't sure what to say—back before he even had a beard.

"And you busted Neely out and now here he is." I step back and look beyond Abner to the abiding mountains, hoping to take strength somehow from them. I knowed this was going to be bad for us folks in the Laurels, directly Sol told me about the shooting. And now here sets the three of them, looking at me like there was something I could do about it.

"It's like this, Judy." Abner knees his horse toward me and leans down till he is almost whispering in my ear. "Neely and Elisha are set on riding to Tennessee and joining up with the Union army just as quick as they can. But Elisha's wounds need tending to and I need time to gather up some supplies. All I'm asking is for you to let them rest here till dark and for you to see to the boy's wound. I'll be back once it's full dark, and then they'll be on their way."

He reaches out his hand and tips the brim of my sunbonnet back so as to look me in the eye. "Judy, if they catch up to Neely, there won't be no trial. They'll shoot him like a dog. And had we left him to stand trial, do you think those Secesh would have let him go free? They'd have hung him for sure."

I know it ain't no use but I ask anyways. "Ain't there no other—"

He shakes his head. "They'll start by looking amongst the Tweeds and their near kin. I figured here for being the last place they'd look—there not being a man here."

He ain't comfortable with saying that but I let it pass and tell them to put their horses in the barn and come on to the house.

Mama is there on the porch doing a churning, and the least uns,

Little Sol and Linnie, are playing with some old cobs. "Where's Frank?" I ask Mama.

"I sent him to pull me some branch mint for tea," she says, peering over my shoulder toward the barn. "My bowels is in an uproar. Who are those men over yon?"

Her eyes is clouded up and not so good anymore. And she ain't always real sensible. She has gone down bad ever since Pap died in '58 but she can still get around some and she purely loves tending to the little uns.

"It's some of them Tweeds, Mama," I tell her as they come up on the porch. "You remember Abner and Neely. And this here is Neely's boy—his arm is hurt and they want me to take a look."

Mama smiles at Neely and says, "It's been a right smart since we seen you, Abner. Come in and get you a chair. Judy'll be back soon."

I pull off my sunbonnet and motion them to come into the house. In two minutes she'll forget she ever saw them. That's how she is these days.

The boy is leaning on Neely and looks like to pass out.

"Let him lay down over there on the bed near the window and help him off with his shirt so's I can look at that arm," I tell them. While Neely is tending to his boy, I see Abner looking about the room.

It ain't all that much changed from back when he used to come around. Fireplace with the cooking things, table, benches, Pap's chair, and the beds—Mama's near the fire and the other two farther off.

Abner's frowning and counting on his fingers. "How many young uns do you and Sol have now, Judy? Them two hoeing taters—"

"The big girl's Ellender," I tell him. "She's eleven and the oldest. T'other's Dan'l and he's nine."

Abner nods. "And the two little uns outside make four. And five with this un." He nods down at Armp who has got a hold of my shirtwaist and is trying to suck the cloth.

"There's six, you didn't see Frank." I kneel down to stir up the fire and put a kettle to boil, reckoning to clean the boy's wound when I change the bandage. Abner is still gazing about and finally his eyes come back to me and Armp. He hunkers down aside of me and whistles.

"Six young uns—law, Judy, you are the *breedingest* woman." He looks at the babe rooting at my milk-wet shirtwaist and chuckles. "Give that baby some titty, Judy. Not like I ain't never—"

I tell him to hush but I move to the bench beside the hearth and put Little Armp to the breast. Abner stands over us, watching. "Six young uns. Why ain't you never married Sol?"

"Same reason I didn't marry you, Abner Tweed. I heired this house and this land from my pap and ain't no way I'll marry and let some man have the say over it. This is Shelton land and my young uns is all Sheltons—no matter what name their pa carries."

We keep our voices low. I reckon everyone in the Laurels knows all this old story but somehow it don't seem fitting to talk of it before Neely and the boy.

Abner was a fool for me back when I wasn't but fourteen or fifteen. He was up in his twenties and aiming to marry but when I told him I weren't looking to wed, he sulled up like a young un who's lost his play pretty and went to courting a cousin of his. Said he didn't want to sire no young uns iffen they weren't to have his name. But he took his time with courting that cousin and every now and again he'd come by to see had I changed my mind. The last time he came was some months after I'd took up with Sol Chandley and I was already in the family way with Ellender. After that, Abner stayed away. I was carrying my second when he married that cousin of his.

My thoughts is wandering in the past when Neely calls out, "Miz Judy, you want me to unwrap these bandages? They're near soaked through."

Little Armp has dropped off to sleep and I lean over to lay him in his cradle. Abner is on his feet and he holds out his hand to help me up and then, for a moment, he don't let go. We stand there, holding hands and looking at each other.

"You don't change, Judy," he whispers. And he squeezes my hand, then lets loose of it. My heart is pounding and I can feel the heat rising on my face. I move away from him, quick like he is the fire that is burning me, and go to the bed where the boy is laying.

"If you don't care, Abner, just set that kettle on the hearth," I say, bending down to sniff at the boy's arm and at his side. The flesh around the wounds is proud and angry red but there ain't no smell of mortification. Still, just to be sure, I go outside to pick some feverfew for a tea. Abner follows me.

"I'd best be getting on," he says. "There'll be someone keeping watch on the road should the folks from Marshall come this way. But I don't expect no trouble."

I nod and make for the clump of feverfew that grows up next to the chimney. He lingers a bit, watching me cut the stems. Finally he says again, "I best be getting on."

I look at him and then, not quite knowing why, I hand him one of the strong-smelling, ferny green stems with its pretty little yellow and white flowers. "I'll be seeing you later, Abner Tweed," I say and turn and hurry back into the house.

The day drags on with Neely and the boy napping and then Neely pacing the floor, saying that maybe they had ought to make a run for it now, and me telling him he had best wait till dark when Abner and the others will go with him. I cook some side meat and cornbread for our dinner and feed Mama and the young uns. Neely and the boy say they ain't hungry, but I make them drink some buttermilk and take a little cornbread. When they both drop off to sleep again, I hustle the young uns outside and send Ellender to kill one of the old hens, thinking to cook a chicken stew to tempt them Tweeds to eat before making another long ride tonight. I set the boys to picking the new peas, even Little Sol. He won't do much good but he likes to be counted in with his brothers.

Armp is happy in his cradle, sucking on a sugar tit, while Linnie is napping on a pallet by Mama. Mama is half-asleep in her chair, but when I carry the plucked chicken into the house, she rouses up. "Who are those fellers in the bed?" Mama asks again. It don't matter what I tell her, she'll not remember.

"Does Sol know those fellers?" Mama is all the time worrying about Sol and where he is. I have told her time and again that Sol is married now and can't be here as much as he used to but, like I said, she don't remember much.

Sol was a good bit more patient than Abner. He kept thinking that once the babies started coming along, I would change my mind and marry him. It wasn't till the fourth that Sol bowed up. "Here you've named this un after me," he said, "but he's Sol Shelton, not Sol Chandley. You're a fine woman, Judy," he said, "and you make some fine babies, but I'm of a mind to get me some Chandleys."

So he went to courting Polly Riddle and now he has him some Chandleys—two so far and another on its way. But he still comes around now and again. I reckon Polly knows he's the daddy of Linnie and of Armp too. They say she don't care, long as he provides for her and hers.

Sol is an awful good man and he has give me some fine young uns—but he ain't never made my heart leap in my bosom the way that it does when I see Abner.

It is black dark when I hear horses coming up the lane. Neely and the boy had went out to the barn at nightfall, saying did the law come after them, they would hide or make a break for it ,and I could claim I didn't know they was there.

Mama and the young uns is all abed and the only light in the house is the flickering of the dying fire. I open the door a crack to see who it is. A quarter moon is on the rise and in its pale light I can see four horses standing in the lane between the house and the barn. In the still of the night, I hear the jingle of a bridle as one of the beasts shakes its head and the creak of leather as a rider swings down from his mount. I can just make out the shape of him and the set of his shoulders as he comes my way. He stops a little ways from the steps and whistles.

It is the same call that him and me used for a signal so long ago. My mouth has gone dry but I work my lips till I can manage to whistle back. *Kee o WEE, kee o WEE.*

Abner bounds up the steps and I open the door and slip out to the porch. "They're waiting in the barn," I tell him. "The boy seems a good bit better now and had ought to be able to endure another long ride. They've et and I put up some corn pone and bacon for them to travel on."

Abner calls to the other men and in a moment the Tweeds come out of the barn, leading their horses.

"I thank you kindly, Judy," Abner says, coming right up close to me and talking low. "We'll be on our way to Tennessee now. Come morning you might want to run your cows down that lane to hide our tracks from the main road. Not that I think it likely the Marshall people will get this far, but I want to make sure you don't have no trouble on our account."

I had already been naming to do that very thing but I thank him for thinking of it. "Let me get you some rags to silence all that jingling harness," I say and turn back into the house.

I grab up my ragbag and pull out a handful, wishing there was something more I could do, wishing he could stay a while longer, wishing all kinds of foolish things.

"Will youns ride with Neely and the boy all the way to the Tennessee line?" I ask as I hand over the rags.

Out in the lane, the horses are stomping, restless to be going. Abner looks their way then turns his back on them, to where can't none of the others see as he puts a hand to my cheek.

"Judy, we're going, every one of us, to join up with the Union Army. There are folks in Marshall who saw us at the jail and it ain't safe for none of us to stay. Best we can do is light out for Tennessee."

There are so many things I want to say to him but all that comes out is, "Abner…"

He lays a finger against my lips. "You take care of yourself, Judy. I'll be looking for you when I come back."

And before I can say ary word, he is up on his horse and gone with a parting wave of his hat. I stand on the porch, shivering a little in the night chill as I watch the gang of them trotting off to war, laughing and joking like it was some play-party they was going to.

6.

~SIMEON RAMSEY~

Greeneville, Tennessee
Thursday, May 16, 1861

I tromp through the woods above the Chucky River till I come to what is left of my daddy's farm. I don't know if my stepmam and that fellow she married after my daddy died still own it, or if the county has took it for taxes. Everwhat, the fields has growed up bad and the cabin roof, which was in bad shape when we lived there, has a great hole in it where the shingles has blowed off. I reckon didn't none of them think it was worth mending—the ground here is poor and it always was hard to make a crop. Daddy weren't much of a farmer; my stepmam used to say that he spent so much time reading his Bible he had come to think that he was one of the lilies of the field and that the Lord would provide for him and hisn.

Daddy would look up with his sweet smile and wave an arm at the woods and the river. "Can't you see, Sairy, all around us? The Lord *does* provide. Fish in the river, game in the woods, chestnut mast for the hogs, berries and apples and peaches in season…"

I don't know what she thought she was getting when she married a wandering preacher, a widow man with a boy that had run near wild all fourteen years of his life. But she done her best to make a garden, and she brought a cow and some chickens with her when they married. For a few years, we lived pretty good, between the Lord's providing and Sairy's hard work.

And I didn't fault her none when Daddy died of a fever and she took her cow and her chickens and went back to her own folks over in Blue Springs. She would have took me too, but I was sixteen and was ready to see some of the world. That's when I went to work for Big Quinn in the wagoning trade—and then, not so long after that, I met Cora.

Thinking of Cora, I feel beneath my shirt for the little silver locket I bought off the peddler. I could have left it with Miss Viney, but I took a notion to wear it till I saw Cora again and could put it around her neck myself. I like the feel of it warm next to my skin and thinking that soon it will be hanging betwixt Cora's breasts.

When Miss Viney told me that Cora was gone to her folks, my first thought had been to light out for Maryville, so strong was my wanting to see her. But Big Quinn had one job after another waiting for me at his place, and I had already promised to drive a team on the trip to South Carolina this month. And all this meant another sum to add to my savings. Beside which Miss Viney kept saying she was certain sure Cora would be back soon as there was a particular dress she was working on that had to get done. The old lady kindly giggled when she said this, as if her and Cora had a secret betwixt them. So I asked Miss Viney would she write to Cora for me—I ain't much of a hand to write—and tell her to be making us some quilts and bed ticks and such for I aim to marry her sooner rather than later.

Now almost a month has gone. I must be back on the Turnpike leaving for South Carolina in the morning and still no word from Cora. If I could have only had another letter to carry with me, it would have made the going more easy.

I look at the little house where I was raised up and at its falling-in roof and sagging porch. When I was a little un, I never knowed how sorry a place it was. There was always food on the table, and if Sairy spoke sharp some of the time, my daddy could always make her smile by bringing her a woods pretty—a bright feather, a spring flower, a hatful of berries—or by reading from his Bible.

Sairy could be all bowed up, put out by something Daddy had left undone—a gate not closed and the cow out wandering or the roof not mended and the rain dripping—and he would set in to reading to her from the Song of Solomon. "Behold, thou art fair, my love; behold thou art fair; thou hast doves' eyes…"

He'd read it real elegant, waving his arms like a master elocutioner, and pretty soon she couldn't help herself. Her mouth would start to quiver and a smile would break out. "You old honeyfuggler," she would say, and he'd pull her down on his lap and afore long he'd send me off on some errand that would keep me gone a spell. They was quite a pair, them two.

I climb through the woods up to the little knoll where Daddy and my mama are buried, and I think about how Daddy's Bible opens right to them love songs. I picture me reading those words to Cora one day—them and some others farther on that you wouldn't hardly think to find in a Bible—all about breasts and bellies and such.

At the top of the knoll, the trees, which is mostly young locust and poplar, have growed up thick, and I have to prospect around before I can come upon the graves. Daddy had hauled a white rock up to mark my mama's place and when we buried him next to her, Sairy fussed till I found one like it for him. Both rocks is sunk in the dirt now, half covered with dead leaves and growed about with weeds. On the other side of my mama is a pair of little rocks for the two babes Sairy bore and lost. She said she liked to think of my mama caring for them in heaven.

I use the heavy stick I have brought with me to prize up my daddy's marker, and I scrape away the dirt beneath it to get to the flat stone that is atop of my bank. Under the flat stone is the little crock, its heavy lid all crusted over with dirt. I grabble around it till I can get a purchase and then I pull my bank up outen the ground.

Daddy never had money enough to put in a real bank. But he would talk of bank failures and the Panic of '37 and say that the lesson was not to lay up treasure on earth nor to put faith in banks. Now here I am, doing my best to lay up some treasure so that me and Cora can marry, but all that Daddy said about banks failing has stuck with me. So, when after several years of wagoning steady, I had me some gold pieces to put by, I thought it seemed fitten to let Daddy watch over them for me whilst I was traveling up and down the Turnpike.

The flash of the gold when I pull the lid off the rough brown crock is a sight on earth. There's mostly quarter and half eagles, but there is one big old double eagle and I take it out just to feel the warmth and the weight of it in my hand. Pretty Lady Liberty with her crown and thirteen stars looks off to the side, just as calm as can be and putting me something in mind of Cora. I study her a while then turn the coin over and there's the Eagle, with the Stars and Stripes of the Union on his breast, the arrows of war in one claw, and the olive branch of peace in the other.

I purely love the look of the thing and the feel of it in my hand. Big Quinn tried to pay me in greenbacks this last time, but I told him I didn't see how a piece of paper that could get tore to bits or burnt to ashes could ever be the same as gold. He took on some but at last he come across with the coin.

I am admiring Lady Liberty and thinking how I will use these coins to buy a place for me and Cora when I hear something moving down the other side of the ridge. At first, I can't make out what it is—there is nothing but woods and thick undergrowth betwixt this knoll and the river and the road, and the crossing is a good ways upstream. Then I realize that it is horses I hear, and I quick put my earning back into my bank and my bank back in its hole. It don't take hardly a minute before the white rock is in its place and when I have half hid it with dead leaves, I slip quiet as an Injun to the far side of the knoll top and get behind a big buckeye to see are the horses coming this way.

There are six horses with riders moving along the narrow riverbank under the bluff. I figure they must be making for the trail a little ways on that joins up with the road into Greeneville. It don't make much sense to me why they are here—the horses are wet hock high like they must have crossed the river at the shallow part a ways downstream. But there is only woods beyond the river, woods and then the North Carolina line. If they are from over yon, I wonder they didn't come the usual way.

As they get closer, I see that they have rags wrapped about the metal of the horses' bridles to stop them jingling. Then the man in the lead, a big, strong-looking somebody with a slouch hat, holds up his hand, and the whole lot of them stop and look back the way they have just come, like they are watching for someone.

They stay right still for a little time, some of them cupping a hand to an ear and not none of them speaking. At last the big man motions them to get going and they move on. I creep to the top of the bluff just in time to see the last horse clambering up the steep trail that leads into the woods and on to the Greeneville road.

They pass out of my sight with nary a sound and when the woods swallow them up, I am left wondering if they was living men or if maybe I have seen a band of haints.

That night at the inn where me and Lathern and some others of Big Quinn's men is getting our supper, I see the same six fellers—Slouch Hat and the rest. They ain't no haints but there is something not quite right with them, the way they are bunched up at a table in a dark corner. They are all of them watching the door and looking skittish as wild turkeys, clenching up and running their hands under the table ever time the door opens.

Me and Lathern get us a dish of burgoo and squeeze in at one of the tables. The place is fuller than usual—all sorts of folks, a sight of them strangers, and the room is loud with talk of which states is leaving the Union and which is not.

One heavy set feller in a dark frock coat is talking bold. He throws back a shot of whiskey and slams the empty glass down on the table. "By God, I say that if the state legislature votes for secession from the Union, why then East Tennessee had ought to secede from the rest of the state. It's happening in Virginia—over in Wheeling the western counties are meeting right now to free themselves from the rest of the state. Mark my words, before long there'll be a new state—West bygod Virginia—a state that's loyal to the Union!"

Someone brings him another dram and he raises it high. "I say huzzay for the Union and huzzay for East Tennessee!"

There is considerable muttering in the room but finally one and then another takes up the cry. I see the big man in the slouch hat looking all around. When it is clear that this bunch is mostly all strong for the Union, he gets up and makes his way over to where Frock Coat and some others are talking loud about *regiments* and *cavalry* and *infantry* and such. I hear Frock Coat bray out that his brother in Flat Lick, Kentucky, has wrote him that more and more Union men from Tennessee was coming there since Kentucky had decided to stay out of the Confederacy.

"Brother Charles says that there is great demand to form a Tennessee Regiment there in Flat Lick and he urges all patriotic Tennesseans to rally round the Union Stars and Stripes."

Lathern is listening hard as he spoons down the last of the beans and gristle and gravy that the old woman here calls burgoo. Big Quinn has some kind of an agreement with her—he lets her have meat, mostly from old wore-out critters that he has took in trade—and she feeds his wagoners when we are here in Greeneville. I ain't choosy about my food but I'll sure be happy when me and Cora are married and have our own place. I have eaten Cora's cooking at her aunt's house, and her chicken and dumplings is fit for the President of the United States.

Lathern is jobbing his elbow into my side. "Hey, Preacher, let's me and you do that—quit the wagoning and go to Flat Lick and join up."

"We can't do that," I tell him, moving away a little. "Big Quinn needs—"

"I ain't funning, Sim," he says, and for once he ain't sporting a foolish grin. "I've made up my mind to go for a soldier—like that feller there said, to rally round the Stars and Stripes. I had an old grandmam who used to tell how some of my kin was with General Washington, way back when we threw out the king of England. Don't you see, I got to stand by the Union those fellers fought for?"

I look at him close. His eyes is kindly glittering and he is breathing fast and shallow. This ain't like his usual self. He is caught up in some kind of fever—like those that take a notion in church to confess their sins and give their lives to the Lord. And I can see there ain't no way I could persuade him different.

The next morning Lathern is gone. He gathered up his few belongings and lit out before sunup, shaking me awake to say that he had found some other fellers who knowed the way to Kentucky. I wished him well with a great lump in my throat. Fool though he might be, Lathern has always been a good friend and all at once it come over me just what this war is like to mean.

7.

~POLLY ALLEN~

Marshall, Madison County, North Carolina
July 1861

Though we cannot bear arms, yet our hearts are with you, and our hands are at your service to make clothing, flags, or anything that a patriotic woman can do for the Southern men and independence.

There is a low hum of assent in the roomful of women as Cousin Margaret reads these words from the newspaper clipping she has pasted into her commonplace book. I see Miss Gibbs, the desiccated little dressmaker, lift a handkerchief to her eyes before bending with renewed vigor to stitch at another pearly star on the silken folds of blue draping her lap.

I think back to the morning after the sheriff was murdered in my house and I awoke to find my world a shoreless sea and myself adrift. And so I still am but Cousin Margaret has taken the helm and insists that I row, that we *all* row, though the shore remains out of sight.

The patriot fervor in the county has grown to such a pitch that a new company of one hundred and twenty-five Madison County men, including my beloved husband and my dear brother John, has been organized and my own Lawrence unanimously elected captain. I know not whether to be thankful that the two men closest to my heart will be together to support one another or rather to fear the old adage about the dangers of keeping all one's eggs in one basket. It matters little—when Honor is concerned, a foolish woman's fears are of little account to her men.

Orders came at once from the War Department and the new formed Company set off for Richmond where, if Lawrence's suppositions prove true, they have joined with General Wharton Green's battalion. Cousin James is Lawrence's second in command and James's wife Margaret immediately insisted that she and I would stitch a flag—the recently adopted Stars and Bars—for the Company and send it after them as quickly as it was finished.

Though I am no great seamstress, I agreed that it would be fitting—like the ladies of olden times bedecking their gallant knights with silken favors. "But where," I asked, "are we to find the silk? I was at Miss Gibbs's yesterday to plan a dress and she had no silk other than somber blacks and purples, suitable for widows and old women."

"We shall manage," Margaret said, infuriatingly calm as usual, and she produced several lengths of crimson silk, draping it over her horsehair sofa to show off the glowing folds. "I'd put this by some time ago, having decided it was too bold for my taste. We shan't need nearly so much of the blue—I believe there's enough in the lining of my winter cape if I cut carefully."

"Oh, Margaret," I cried in horror, "your beautiful cape—"

"I shall replace it with Canton flannel," she said, her face smug with virtue, "much warmer and much more practical. I think it an honor to make so small a sacrifice for our brave men. Now, as for the white..." Her eyes bored into mine. "Were you not married in a white silk gown? I don't recall to have seen you wearing it since those first weeks of your wedding tour. You've not had it dyed, have you?"

The memory rankles and I bite my lip as I look down at the seam I am stitching—a bar of crimson joined to a bar of white—alas for my wedding dress, put away so carefully in hopes that someday it might adorn one of my daughters. As Margaret said, I could do no less.

After several trials, Margaret and I found that neither of us could produce a passably close-stitched embroidered star capable of withstanding the wear the banner would undoubtedly suffer. Accordingly, we enlisted the aid of Miss Gibbs to embroider the circle of eleven stars on the field of blue. Her work is perfection—each star symmetrical and sharp-pointed, almost as if they had been woven into the fabric itself.

Feeling my gaze upon her, Miss Gibbs looks up from her needle and ventures a smile. "See, Mrs. Allen, I'm closing the circle." She holds up the square of blue with its nine completed stars, a tenth, centered in a hoop and well underway, and the chalked outline of an eleventh. The silver thimble on her finger flashes as she tells them off for all of us, in order of secession. "I've done South Carolina, Mississippi, Florida, Alabama, Georgia, Louisiana, Texas, Virginia, Arkansas…" She takes a breath. "And *this* that I'm working now is our own dear North Carolina star, stitched with special care. That leaves just Tennessee to do."

There is a soft patter of applause as we less skilled seamstresses acknowledge her workmanship. The six of us have been meeting once a week in my parlor to knit socks and comforters for the men and to talk over such news as has reached us. In June we had thrilled to word of a battle at Big Bethel in Virginia—a battle in which our troops suffered only eight casualties with one killed while the Union forces lost eighteen men and had fifty-eight wounded. Such a one-sided tally seemed to foretell a speedy and favorable end to the war and we all rejoiced—little Mrs. Morris waving her half-finished sock in the air with such vigor that it fell unravelling from her needles.

That was nigh a month ago. We continue to pray for a rapid conclusion to this unnatural state of hostilities between North and South (and my conscience pricks me as I think of my letter to Emmie, lying, black with spilled ink and still unfinished, in my desk drawer). What little we hear from our men is of camp life—boredom, drilling, dull food, and the humorous shifts they must employ to secure basic comforts.

Mrs. Morris, always the most cheerful of our group, launches into a story of her husband's paying an outlandish price to a local farmer's wife for a laying hen so that he might have a fresh egg every day. After achieving a sort of coop for the biddy behind his tent and feeding her on biscuit and cornmeal, Captain Morris crowed with pride when after several days the hen produced an egg. He set it carefully aside till there should be three for a sumptuous omelet and fell asleep in blissful anticipation of the feast to come.

"Alas, 'twas not to be," Mrs. Morris tells us, her merry eyes at odds with the solemn set of her mouth. "In the night, a skunk or some other vermin, tore into the coop and all that was left of the hen were a few sad feathers. Captain Morris said that he cooked and ate the single egg with a gloomy relish, thinking that it *should* be delicious as it was the most expensive egg he had ever consumed."

A general chattering breaks out, but Margaret clears her throat and lays aside her sewing. "Ladies," she begins, and the room falls silent. As always, I am a little annoyed that she has this trick of summoning attention—we meet at *my* house and it is *my* husband who is the first officer while hers is next in command, but during these meetings, it is *she* who is in command and I am but a shadowy second.

I see little Annie peeping round the kitchen door and crook my finger at her. She slips in silently and leans against me as Margaret speaks.

"Now that we have completed a goodly store of knitted items, I wonder if we might turn our efforts to rolling bandages and making lint. My husband Dr. Keith has written of the potential need..." Opening her commonplace book to a page marked with a blue ribbon, she looks round the room to be sure that we are all attentive, then continues. "He has sent me this clipping from the January 7th issue of *The Charleston Mercury*. I think that we will all find it inspiring." Clearing her throat again, she reads: "Lint. An interesting circumstance connected with the lint, which the teachers and pupils of the Columbia Female College (during this their present recess) are preparing for the use, if need be, by our Southern army, is, that it is from linen sheets, spun and wove by a woman of the Revolution of 1776 (the great-grandmother of one of the teachers of the institution). The women of one revolution, thus, as it were, coming up to the help of the women of another, even as the memory of the patriotism of the women of the past causes to glow with increased ardor that of the women of the present. Signed, Carolinian."

I see a few uncomfortable glances exchanged and can imagine the thoughts behind my neighbors' eyes. If our army continues as victorious as it has begun, will not this conflict soon be ended—with no need of ripping up our precious linens? But Margaret ignores the anxious looks, settling firmly into her subject, and I have no doubt that my beautiful linen sheets and tablecloths will soon go the way of my wedding dress.

"We all know the efficacy of lint in dressing wounds," she continues, in that pedagogical tone that she is all too apt to fall into on these occasions, "and already there is concern that lint will soon be in short supply. As long as this conflict endures, it is our duty—and our privilege—to supply this commodity. Who knows, as she cuts to bits the tablecloth her grandmother wove, if those very pieces of precious fabric may not save the life of a beloved husband or son? Who among us—"

"But how does one *make* lint?" It is one of the unmarried girls who has dared interrupt, but Margaret is prepared.

"My dear, it's the simplest thing in the world. Every wife and mother should know how to prepare bandages." Suddenly she is aware of Annie at my side and holds out an imploring hand. "Annie, will you help me?"

Annie, ever obedient and pleased at being included, goes to her cousin who takes from her sewing basket a small square of linen and a little knife. Stretching the fabric on the table before her and holding it taut, Margaret shows Annie how to scrape the surface to produce a fine lint. Annie's brow furrows in concentration as she works, and she beams with pleasure when Margaret pats her on the shoulder, commending her labors.

"You see, even a little child can assist in the defense of her homeland by making lint," Margaret proclaims, "and so *much* may be needed." She takes a folded paper from her sewing basket and opens it. "In his last letter, Dr. Keith writes he is much concerned that, should real fighting break out, the supplies of lint will be quickly exhausted. Already, he says, much has been expended in dealing with the incidental wounds attendant to training…"

Margaret squints at the close-written page, shakes her head, and continues. "He says that army regulations suggest eight pounds of lint as a three-month supply for a regiment—four pounds per battalion and two per company. He adds that hospitals, too, will be in need of quantities of lint."

My eyes blur and all at once my crowded parlor feels airless. I look down at the red silk in my lap and can see only the oceans of blood that we may be called on to staunch with our tablecloths and sheets. Red roiling waves soaking into the white of our homely dressings as the precious life blood of our men drains away… I am stitching a flag of blood and bandages… My very fingers are stained…

I stagger to my feet and, murmuring an excuse, hurry from the room, through the stifling kitchen and to the shaded back steps where Juliann is snapping cow peas. I stand there swaying and reach to steady myself against the door. *I will not faint...*

"Are you taken poorly, Miz Allen? Set yourself down and let me get you some cool water." Juliann is already on the move to the spring-house and I sink gratefully onto the straight-backed chair, taking deep breaths and attempting to compose myself.

Little Maggie lies sleeping on a pallet nearby while Rommie ramps about the packed dirt of the back yard, singing and running a stick along the pickets of the fence. In his thoughtless play he has broken or bent my beautiful hollyhocks which had stood soldier-straight and proud. Now the ground is littered with fallen flowers of red and pink. I want to cry out that he must stop at once but no sound comes.

Perhaps my stays are too tight, I think. *Or the heat of the crowded parlor and so much talk—the clatter of women's voices.* I can hear them still, like a swarm of bees with Cousin Margaret's voice the loudest and, as I close my eyes, once again I see the rising tide of blood threatening to wash over all that I hold most dear.

Vapours, Cousin Margaret called the spell I took last week, after she had questioned me closely to determine if I were with child. When I assured her that I was not, she nodded wisely in just the manner Cousin Keith does. Of course she has had occasion to observe more of medical practice than most but I, for one, am not yet ready to rely upon her diagnoses. The idea!

Now, a week later, our Ladies Aid Society is wholly dedicated to producing lint, as well as rolling bandages and the tedious manufacture of something Doctor Cousin Margaret calls *charpies*. We are to meet Tuesdays and Thursdays, and today my parlor and front gallery are full, every chair taken by women pulling alternate threads from linen squares to make the absorbent *charpie*—the advantage of which, Margaret tells us, is that it can be lifted in one piece from a healing wound, bringing away pus and dead matter with it.

We hear and speak of these things with equanimity—*assumed* equanimity for my part. But amidst these preparations, Margaret has found her voice, and with her admittedly overbearing husband safely (if that is the right word) away at war, she is free to practice medicine herself and be every bit as overbearing as Cousin James.

Even the children have been called into action today. I count five dutiful little girls sitting on low benches, scraping at bits of family linens stretched over shingles. Margaret had hoped to conscript the brothers of these girls as well but the experiment was not a success. Little boys and sharp scraping knives, amid talk of war, are not a happy combination and the boys (my Rommie among them, alas) have quickly deserted their sisters to enact the battle of Big Bethel in the back yard. "See me!" my Rommie shouts as he brandishes his wooden sword. "Mama, see me!"

The outcome of this is to dismiss the boys from future attendance at Ladies Aid meetings and to provide Margaret with one slight but bloody wound on which she happily demonstrates the efficacy of our lint and bandages.

"There," she says, pressing the new-scraped lint against the cut on Rommie's arm and wrapping a long strip of muslin about it, "the first to receive the benefit of our labors. You see, ladies—"

She is interrupted by a sound of huzzahing from the street. Every woman there crowds onto the porch to hear the cause of the celebration. I suspect that, like I, all of them are hoping to hear that the Union has decided to recognize the Confederacy. Margaret, perhaps, looks a little disappointed. I believe she is enjoying her newfound importance and would regret relinquishing it.

I see our friend Donal Blevins in a group of men clustered around one tall man waving aloft a newspaper and when I catch his eye, he lopes over to the front steps and sweeps a bow.

"And is it over, Mr. Blevins?" I ask, my heart pounding with joy. "Have they given in?"

"They have, indeed, ma'am," he whoops, "given in and run like frightened rabbits. We whupped 'em good at Bull Run."

8.

~MARTHY WHITE~

Shelton Laurel, Madison County, North Carolina
November 1861

"And I say if the damned Secesh hadn't whupped the Union boys at Bull Run back in July, this war would likely be over by now. But I reckon the Union will outlast them in the end."

There are three of them strung up from the trees by the creek, all pink and white and glistening in the morning sun. The three heads are already off and set lined up on a log, solemn and quiet like they are watching us. A bloom of hoar frost turns the dry grass and few remaining leaves to a silvery white and Davy's father's breath makes little clouds all around him as he works his shiny knife under the skin and makes a long cut between the two rows of tits lined up like little buttons on the belly of the hog. The guts come bulging out and Davy's father has to skip backwards out of their way as they tumble into the wooden tub on the frozen ground.

We are over at Davy's family's place, helping with the hog killing, and in a few weeks, they will come and help us with ours. There is several men I ain't seen before, hard-looking somebodies but good hands at scraping the bristles off the hog. One of them cuts a real shine, singing out, "Barber, barber, shave a pig, how many hairs to make a wig?" and trying to put a handful of the bristles in Davy's hair.

The women hurry to haul the tub over to the creek—there's the purply-red loops of gut to wash out and scrape clean ready for sausage meat. The men go on talking of the war while they pull out heart and liver, kidneys and leaf lard, laying them in different tubs.

"Sounds like East Tennessee is still holding strong for the Union," one of the stranger men says as he watches Davy's pap cut out and tie off the bung hole of the second pig. "Union fellers over there are burning railroad bridges ever chance they get—on the direct orders of old Abe hisself."

Davy's pap don't look away from what he's doing but I see his mouth kindly quirk up on one side and he says, "Reckon how you'd know about that, Jacob? What else are they saying?"

The stranger laughs and wraps his arms around himself, putting his hands in his armpits to warm them. It is blamed cold today, as it must be for a pig-killing, and we all of us take it in turns to go and warm ourselves by the fire. Davy comes over to stand by me and whispers that his ma has made gingerbread and he has some in his jacket pocket.

"It's still warm," he says. "Reach and get you some; my hands is dirty."

If it was any other boy, I wouldn't do no such thing, being sure that what I'd find in their pocket would be a dead mouse or some such nasty surprise, but this is Davy, and me and him are sweethearts. We decided it last month when we had an apple butter cooking at our place. There was several families and a sight of young uns there. After supper we went to playing Blindfold and when Davy caught me, he said he couldn't guess who it was but kept feeling of my face and putting his hands in my hair and such till the others hollered that if he went much farther, we'd ought to be sweethearts.

Later on, outside in the dark, he said he had knowed it was me all along.

The gingerbread is sweet with honey and I smile my thanks at Davy. He winks at me and goes back to fetching more wood to keep the fire going.

The men come up to the fire to warm their hands. "They burned nine bridges in Tennessee?" says Pap, letting out a low whistle. "Shit-*fire*! Old Abe's got him a long arm, looks like." The stranger they call Jacob pulls a flat little bottle out of his coat pocket and hands it to Pap who takes it whilst he pats me on the head without paying me anymore mind than if I was a pet hound.

"Well, they was nine on the list, but only five of them got de-stroyed," Jacob says, cutting his eyes at me.

Pap sees what he is thinking and pats my head again. "You can speak free around Marthy," he says. "I guarantee she'll not repeat a word of what you say." He laughs and catches me up for a quick hug. I wrinkle my nose at the whiskey smell on his breath and he sets me back down. "They's considerable to be said for a woman-child who don't talk," he says, winking as he passes the bottle to Davy's pap.

"Ain't that the truth!" says Jacob. "And even more for a silent woman. But what's wrong with this one? She looks peart enough."

Once Pap and Davy's pa have told Jacob more about me, Jacob eyes me funny. "A mute, is she?" he says and takes a long pull from his bottle. "Well then, I'll tell you the way of things in East Tennessee. There was this preacher feller had put out word he was looking for loyal Union men to help in burning nine railroad bridges. He had twenty-five thousand in cash money—sent straight from Old Abe to pay the men bold enough to try it. And before long that preacher had it all planned out, with different teams set to burn different bridges—Loudon, Union, Watauga, Strawberry Plains—Lick Crick was ourn—"

He claps his mouth shut like he hadn't meant to say that last but Davy's father just laughs. "Go on, Jacob," he says, "we're all Union men here in Shelton Laurel. You can speak as plain as if you was butchering hogs with Old Abe hisself."

"With General Winfield Scott and Andy Johnson toting the water," Pap puts in, and they all of them laugh like one thing as they turn back to the hogs. They lower the first one and lay it on the sled where they cut it into pieces—hams and shoulders first, then the long business of getting the backbone cut free and carving out the tenderloin to feast on fresh for supper. The rest of the meat will be left in the barn to half freeze overnight so it will be easier to cut up. We will come back tomorrow and the men will salt down the big pieces while the women grind up the trimmings for sausage and cook down the white fat for lard.

Davy's mam comes over, drying her hands on her apron and holding them out to the fire. They are bright red with the cold. "Oooh-ee," she sings out, "that icy water like to froze my fingers off. But there's a nasty job done." She nods her head at a tub full of clean pig guts, glimmering shiny white and waiting to be filled with sausage meat. "We'll have us a world of sausage this year."

My mouth waters to think of it—full of sage and hot pepper and tasting of the hickory-smoke, I like it better than most anything.

"Are you going to take care of them hog heads now, James?" she calls out to Davy's pa. "We'd best get them brains out and into cold water before they go blinky on us. I've been saving up eggs so we can have us a good mess of eggs and brains later on."

Mr. Shelton has been using his ax to cut the long backbones into smaller pieces, but he stops what he is doing.

"My woman is right hicky about them hog heads. But she makes the best souse meat you ever tasted," he tells the other men.

He brings the ax down between the eyes of the first head, splitting the clean shaved face in two. It is an awful sound and sight but I can't help watching.

When it gets too dark to see good, they all of them come into the house where the women have cooked a fine supper—eggs and brains, scrambled together soft and moist with the edges fried brown and crispy, fried tenderloin slices, shucky beans, kraut, hominy, fried pies with dried apples and peaches, biscuits and crackling bread. When the men have et their fill, they gather round the fireplace, smoking and talking some more of how the war is going. There is the question of whether the Union will come to the aid of East Tennessee and there are whispers of *outliers* and *bushwhackers*.

This is the first I've heard those words and I listen hard to hear what manner of beast an outlier or a bushwhacker might be. As the talk goes on, I realize that it ain't no beast but a feller who is laying out of the army but likely fighting his own war. One of the men is talking low of a cave up in the laurel thickets where some of them have a store of guns and powder and balls.

"Just let them Secesh come riding into old Laurel, there'll be a gun behind every bush and in every tree—"

Davy's pap shushes the man right quick. "Enough of that—let's us step outside a minute."

The women and children are at second table now. I have never seen so much food—there is a plenty, even after the hungry men have had their fill. The sweet pork tenderloin is my favorite—fresh pig meat don't come but once a year. After all the pig killing is done, it'll be salt pork and fatback from the middlings, smoked sausage and hog jowls, and the rest pickled in big crocks. Some of the backbones will get cooked and stored in crocks covered with lard and these will keep, long as the weather stays cold. The hams will hang in the meat house, curing in the dry cold air, drawing in the salt that drives out the water and keeps them from going bad. Most folks sell off the hams, for cash money or they give them in trade at the store.

It's a marvel how much eating there is on a hog. Liver mush, souse meat, lard, pickled pig feet—there ain't much goes to waste. I once heard Pap say, "Long as I've got a pig in the pen and salt to cure his meat, I'll tell any man, be it the President hisself, to kiss my ass."

Just then I hear Davy's mam tell Mommy, "They say salt is going to be high this next year, along of this plagued war. I told James we best lay us in some more next time he goes to Marshall."

Davy comes and sets between me and my brothers. They have about wore themselves out with teasing him about me, but right now they are too busy eating to say one thing. I push the dish of tenderloin in front of Davy and reach him some of the pickles too. He nods a thank you and goes on talking to my brother Billy but under the table we are holding hands.

It is late when Mommy and Pap and the rest of us walk home, and a little snow is drifting down, sparkling in the light of the waning moon.

"Good hog-killing weather," Pap says. He has had several swigs from Mr. Shelton's jug and is in as fine a temper as ever I've seen him. "Yessir, cold enough without being plumb bitter."

Mommy pulls her shawl tighter around her. "Just right, thank the Lord," she says. "Come morning that pig meat'll be half froze and all the easier to cut up. I purely despise fooling with meat that ain't cold enough."

Mommy is in a good mood too. She loves visiting with neighbors, even with all the work of pig killing. We'll be up early tomorrow to do our chores and tromp back over to Shelton's. There's meat to cut up and grind for sausage, the big kettle over the fire outside to tend while we boil the cleaned and split pig heads for souse meat, lard to render—the leaf lard from the insides makes the best pie crust you ever tasted—liver mush to cook—oh, it'll be a long, long day but there'll be plenty of funning and fine things to eat. And at the end of it all, Davy has told me that they have settled with old man Norton to bring his fiddle and there will be dancing.

Davy has asked me will I be his partner in the dancing and I have nodded my head *yes*.

Up ahead on the path, I can see that Pap is thinking ahead to the dancing too, for he is whistling "Turkey in the Straw" and has his arms around Mommy. He is swinging her in a circle there on the path, and she is laughing and trying to shush him so he don't wake little Sam who is swaddled close under her shawl. But Pap, he busts out singing:

As I was going down the road
Tired team and a heavy load…

And Mommy can't help but laugh, he is cutting such a shine, capering about like he was at a play party. She shakes her head but joins in on the chorus:

Turkey in the straw, turkey in the hay

And the pair of them are laughing hard and all us young uns join hands and dance around them.

Pap starts in on the last verse:

Oh, I jumped on the seat and I give a little yell,
Horses ran away, broke the wagon all to—

"Sam!" says Mommy, in that warning voice she has, and he leans down and kisses her hard then finishes out the verse:

Sugar in the gourd and honey in the horn,
I never was so happy since the day that I was born.

And I feel just the same. I am so filled up with happiness I could bust. I think what a fine thing it is to be here safe in Shelton Laurel, while not so far off bridges is burning and soldiers is fighting. If I could hold this moment for ever—the moon turning the old familiar trail to silver, the snow falling slow and lazy, and Mommy and Pap and all of us dancing amongst the moon-touched trees that seem to sway and dance with us—and the smooth feel of the carved bone ring that Davy gave me—if I could, I would put it all in a little box, seal it tight, and set it away on a shelf in my heart forever.

1862

9.

~JUDITH SHELTON~

Shelton Laurel, North Carolina
April 1862

These is queer and troubled times but fields has still got to be plowed, corn and taters planted, and cabbages and such set out. Now that the Confederates has passed a conscription law, most of the men here in the Laurels has slipped away to join the Union army, and them that ain't is laying low up in the mountains. We have already had a gang of Secesh march into our valley, looking to conscript any able-bodied men but on meeting with gunfire from most every tree and bush, the damned rebels galloped away empty-handed, not even bothering with the bodies of two of their men what was kilt. Likely the feller in charge'll tell his boss they killed a plenty of us Laurel folk but the truth of it is that, except for one of them Nortons falling out of a tree and busting his collarbone when he was hoo-rahing after the Secesh had rode off, weren't none of our men hurt.

Still and all, it's a terrible thing to be called a traitor for staying true to the flag your people fought under back in 1776 and it's even worse to be hunted in your home place, on the land where your kin have lived since 1790, the only home you've ever knowed or wanted to know. Why should our men fight for slavery when don't none of them own slaves? And the rich men that do, they stay safe in their homes by paying to send someone in their place. It don't seem right.

Mama ain't doing no good these days—mostly she lays in her bed under a pile of quilts and sleeps. When she wakes, she'll call out Pap's name real pitiful like. I have give up on telling her that he's dead these four years and more and just say, "Hush now, he's gone hunting and he'll be back soon." Mostly that calms her and I can get her to set up and take a little buttermilk and cornbread or get her onto the chamber pot. Between her and Little Armp and all there is to do here at planting time, I am most wore out and am thankful for any help I can get.

I say this to Marthy White, who showed up at my door this morning like she sometimes does when there's something bothering her. She was carrying a note from her mother saying that Marthy had come to tend the young uns or help me everhow she could.

Kate White is a good woman and a good mother, but sometimes I think Marthy feels easier coming to me in search of answers to whatever it is that's troubling her. Probably because, along of her not speaking, it takes a world of patience and guessing to get at what the trouble is. And Kate ain't the most patient woman.

So I send Ellender and Frank and Little Sol off to hill up the taters that are thrusting their strong green leaves out of the dirt, and me and Marthy and Linnie head up the mountain in search of ramps and spring greens to make a tonic. Little Armp is riding on my hip but Marthy holds out her arms and I am happy to let her tote him awhile. Seems like I ain't hardly ever without a young un on my hip or at my breast or in my belly, and as we move out of the sun into the coolness of the tall trees, I feel most as free as a wild thing. Here I am, a woman almost thirty, and I am fairly skipping along the path. It puts me in mind of the happy times back when me and Abner was courting, back before my pride and hisn commenced to butt heads and we parted.

Then Linnie toddles after me, holding up her little arms and calling out *Mama, Mama* and I am pulled back to who I am—Judy Shelton, mother of six and wife of none.

We pick some dandelion and burdock greens and climb till we find a nice patch of ramps just nigh a level spot above the trail where we set Linnie and Armp down on a quilt I have brought. Marthy finds them some little twigs and rocks to play with and then we go to digging. Not far off, one of them great old woodpeckers is hammering on a dead tree and somewhere down in the valley I hear the sound of a gunshot and then another.

"Groundhogs is awful bold just now," I tell Marthy. "Reckon that's someone protecting her new peas. Them varmits purely love those tender vines."

The ramps are like hundreds of little green flags, waving under the big trees. They are easy to loosen from the soft woods dirt and my basket is already half full.

I set back on my heels and study one, brushing the dirt from it. "My grandmam called these *ramsens*," I tell Marthy, breathing in the strong oniony smell of the slender white bulbs and their broad green leaves. "She said that was what *her* grandmam had called them and that was what they were called in the Old Country over the water."

At these words, Marthy's blue eyes open wide and she makes a beckoning sign with one hand. This is her way of asking for more—a story or an explanation or some such.

"What is it you want to know, honey?" I ask her. "About the ramps?"

She shakes her head.

"My grandmam?"

She frowns and starts to shake her head again and then I know what it is she's after.

"The Old Country? You want to know how it was we come from there?"

A smile lights up her face, making her right handsome for a moment. Marthy is always so shy and downcast that folks has got in the way of hardly seeing her, but in this moment, I see the pretty girl that she really is. And I see that there is a good bit more to her than any of us has ever reckoned.

"Ain't your mama told you that story?" I say and want to bite my tongue, remembering that because Marthy don't talk, folks mostly don't talk to her, other than to say *Come here* or *Do that*.

So I hurry right to the story, the way my folks always tell it, and we go on with our digging while I talk.

"Well, our people, yourn and mine alike, come from over the water—Ireland and before that Scotland, and in both of them places we was treated bad by the rich men who owned the land, treated not much better than the black slaves all this fuss is about. But we didn't have to stay put like the slaves do, so we come to America in search of a place that would be our own, where couldn't nobody take the crops we grew. My grandsire was Roderick Shelton, who is reckoned to be the first white man to settle these parts, and he come here all the way from Virginia with my grandmam Sarah. It was him built the house I live in now, and my pap heired it from him, and I heired it from my pap."

She nods at me, all big-eyed and I know she wants me to go on.

"They say Grandpap Roderick was a big red-headed man, six-foot-tall and two hundred pounds. He had fought in the battle at King's Mountain to set the States free of the king of England, and it was with a land grant on account of what he'd done in that war that he took up this place right here. Now it needs a strong man to make a farm in the wilderness—clearing trees and breaking ground, hunting for meat and building house and barn with not much more than an axe. And it takes a strong woman to help her man—to bear him children to help to work the land, to lay by food to make it through the winter—you know, there weren't no stores in Marshall back in them times for they weren't no Marshall. Why, they say that Grandpap Roderick once walked all the way to South Carolina just to buy salt. What do you think of that for hard times?"

She shakes her head and rolls her eyes, glad that things is easier now. We have already filled two baskets with ramps and I tell her that's a plenty.

"You don't never want to take too many, or they may not be here when you go to look for them next year. Take care of the land and its gifts, my pap always said, and it'll take care of you."

Marthy nods and looks over to the quilt where Little Armp and Linnie are both fast asleep, curled around each other like kittens. I'm in no hurry to wake them but set down and stretch out and go on talking. It's a pleasure to tell my stories to someone who ain't always breaking in with questions like my young uns do.

And it's a pleasure to enjoy a peaceable moment, setting in the spring green woods with the sunlight dodging in and out of the leafy branches. I used to be a fool for roaming the woods—greeting all the flowers and such at their different times of blooming. Once, about this time of year, me and Abner found the prettiest patch of yellow moccasin flowers a little ways farther up—and I think when the young uns awaken, maybe we'll go see if them pretty flowers are blooming yet.

But Marthy is watching me, eager-like to see what else I can tell her, so I go on with my tale.

"You see how it is. Coming from a place where we didn't have no land, this is holy ground to most of us. Over the years, the old folks has handed down a love for the land that almost passes the love of God, though I'd not say that to anyone else. Ever one of my young uns, one of the first things I do, soon as I'm outten childbed, is to put their little bare feet to the dirt, same as my mama done me, and tell them that the land is their birthright, theirs to have and to hold."

Her face tells me that she ain't sure what to think—is Miz Judy speaking heresy? Miz Judy who don't bother with marriage but bears one woods colt atter another?

Marthy's face stays solemn but she picks up a handful of dirt and presses it to her lips, and I know then that she understands me. So I go on, filled with a church solemn feeling that I must testify to how precious the land is. I am made bold in my talk by the knowledge that she'll not pass on whatever I might say.

"This place has been good to us Sheltons and to all the other folks that have settled here. Easy laying fields, water a-plenty, fish in the creeks and game in the woods—and far enough off from town not to feel crowded—leastways not till this secession business come along."

I see Marthy ain't attending no more but is turned, looking down the way we came. There is the sound of someone running fast up the path and two of the Cutshall men come into view, followed close on by Pete McCoy. They are all of them carrying knapsacks and squirrel guns and I know where they are headed. They hurry on up the trail without seeing us but Pete stops right below us to catch his breath.

"Hey, Pete," I say, soft-like, and he jumps like one thing. "Thought you'd gone with the Rebs."

"Shitfire, Miz Judy, you like to scared the—" He wipes his face with the back of his hand and don't finish what he was saying. "I *was* with the 64th but I reckon you could say I seen the error of my ways. Slipped away a few weeks ago and come home. But now the goddamned Secesh have sent a whole troop of soldiers clear from Asheville and they have rounded up near fifty men already. They aim to conscript them or shoot them. If they know I'm a deserter, it'll be a quick bullet for old Pete."

Marthy makes like she's about to leap up and run off but I grab aholt of her arm.

"Set down, Marthy. You go running down that way, all distracted, if any of the Secesh are following these boys, they'll suspicion that you'd seen them. Pete, you go on along. I reckon you best get off the trail and hit the woods now. Me and Marthy'll walk on down and tromp out any footprints youns left."

Pete winks one blue eye and grins at me that crooked way he has and heists his knapsack higher on his shoulders. "Much obliged, Miz Judy. They ain't like to get over here for a good while. We gave 'em the slip down at the Norton holler and cut through the woods to just above your place. I'd of stayed and fit them Rebs some more but I'm near out of powder. You can't do no good, hunting without powder."

The sound of them words lifts the hair on my arms and I feel like I am taking a chill. But Pete, he takes off up the mountain, lighthearted as a boy playing hide and seek. I wonder what it is about some men, maybe most men, makes them act that way—like war is just a game and the killing ain't real.

Marthy is about to jump out of her skin and I try to make out what is troubling the child. She is trembling and, were it not for the tight hold I have on her, I believe she would be off down the mountain like a runaway horse. But what is it has her in such a state?

"Are you worried about your daddy, Marthy?" I ask, hoping to set her mind at ease. "They'll not conscript *him*—or if they do, they'll soon discover that he ain't able—the poor man's been ruptured these past four or five years. He can't go for a soldier."

She shakes her head impatient-like. No, it ain't her daddy she's worried about. She looks to be struggling with whether or not she wants to tell me, and at last she pulls on a string that is around her neck and shows me a finger-ring, smooth carved from a bone of some sort. There is a crooked little heart and on one side of it, a letter *D* and on the other, an *M*.

"Marthy, honey," I say, putting a hand to her cheek, "so you have a sweetheart," and she colors up and nods. Now it's all clear—the young un has a sweetheart and she's afeared he'll be conscripted.

Just as today is the first time that I have noticed that Marthy is a pretty girl, it is also the first time that I take note of the swell of her bosom. I reckon because she don't talk, all of us has been in the habit of counting her as a child. But now I think on it, she was born the same year as my Ellender.

"I disremember, honey, just how old are you—eleven?" She holds up all ten fingers and closes her hand and shows two more. Twelve. Old enough to bleed; old enough to breed. I wonder has one of the older fellers tried to have his way with her, thinking that she'd be easy pickings.

"So you're worried about your feller. And his name begins with a *D*?"

She is eager for me to guess but I string it out, wanting to keep her up here a while. Whatever is going on down there with the conscription troops, it ain't in our power to stop them. And I would wager that ever how many they take into the Rebel army, the most of them will find an opportunity to slip away and enlist in the Union army or come back to hide out here in old Laurel.

She has settled back down and I commence to name off all the fellers around here with D names. I just pray it ain't one that is like to hurt her.

"Well, let's see. There's several Daniels and Davids and a Donal and a Douglas…"

She shakes her head and makes the *more* sign. I am relieved it's not none of these for to my certain knowledge, two of them is the trifling sort.

I smile, pretty sure I have hit on the right one. And a good un too. "Wouldn't be that curly-headed Davy Shelton, would it?" and she is nodding for all she's worth.

"Honey, them Rebs won't bother Davy, he's not even as old as you are. Your sweetheart is safe—and this foolishness is all like to pass afore he's of an age to fight."

She flings her arms about my neck and hugs me hard. I hug her back, hoping that my words was true.

Linnie and Little Armp are stirring and I judge that we'd best head back to the house and tromp out any marks Pete and them left on the trail. As we make our way down, Linnie is on my hip and Marthy is toting Little Armp. We each have a basket of ramps and are scuffling along like a bunch of hogs to hide the traces of Pete and them. It ain't my place but I think to say a needful word or two. No telling what Kate has or hasn't told this young un. So I ask her if she's had her monthlies yet and she holds up three fingers. *Three times.*

Then I ask does she know how babies get made and she blushes and nods and looks away. I stop and wait for her to look me in the face.

"Marthy, honey, now that you have a sweetheart, sooner or later he, or could be the both of you, may be wanting to fool around that way. It's only natural but I want you to be careful. You and him ain't old enough to be making babies."

She looks kind of surprised at this thought and I know there's some would say I am putting ideas into her head. But them ideas will come of their own soon enough. I want her to think what she's about, rather than get swept up into something without thinking. I tell her things I know her mother never would and warn her about some other things. It is the same talk I had with Ellender when she turned twelve, though she's not gotten her monthlies yet. I aim to make sure my girls know how to take care of themselves.

As we near the edge of the wood, Marthy grabs my hand and squeezes it hard. Then she brushes my cheek with a kiss. I give her a hug and wonder how I could have ever thought she was plain-looking.

When we get down to the tater patch, Ellender and Frank are still hoeing while Little Sol is setting off to the side just a-bawling.

"Whatever is the matter?" I holler to Ellender. "Youns should have finished long since."

"It was them blame soldiers, Ma." Frank is hurrying toward us, hip-hopping over the rows and I can see now where horses has been in the patch and the end of one row is all tore open. "We was near done, all hilled up pretty and here come six men on horses. They started asking was there any men in the household and while Ellender was telling them there weren't none, a couple of them ran their horses right in here and one of them said he was gonna dig him some taters. I told him there hadn't been time for no taters to make but he went to grabbling and pulling up the plants. Then one of the others hollered at him to leave off. Said they'd come back when the taters was big."

Frank is fighting hard not to cry. Ellender's face is hid behind her sunbonnet and she brings her hoe down hard, again and again, moving down the row, rebuilding the hills that the Rebs trampled.

10.

~JAMES A. KEITH~

Marshall, North Carolina
July 1862

July 22, 1862, at Home in Marshall, North Carolina

My Dear Cousin Sallie,

You will be surprised to see that I am at Home. Let me hasten to assure you that I am not wounded nor in any way indisposed but am, rather, on leave—and finding it most grateful after the Perils of War I have thus far endured. I charged Margaret with the task of keeping you informed of my situation but, having at last a brief cessation of my onerous (and like to grow more so) duties, I take pen in hand to relate to you my "adventures" since last I wrote.

I know you have been given the bitter news of nephew Mitchell's untimely passing. You will excuse me if I do not elaborate on what a pen more skilled than mine has already conveyed to his friends and family. A brave lad, basely slain in the service of his country. Slain by cowards and brute ruffians—but I say no more.

I pull the tintype—the likeness Mitchell had taken soon after he enlisted in the 64th—from my breast pocket and open the velvet case. He stares out at me in all the glory of his new uniform—cradling an ancient musket and attempting to look as fierce as his smooth fourteen-year-old face will allow. The old feeling wells up in me once more and I understand how men have been driven mad by sorrow. Margaret upbraids me that I cannot find consolation in our own children but they are little more than prattling babes whereas Mitchell…

I snap the little case shut and force myself back to equanimity and back to my letter.

After some little time in Richmond, from whence I last had the pleasure of writing you almost a year ago, on December last the 2nd N.C. Battalion (to which our company was attached) was ordered to Wilmington in anticipation of an attack somewhere along the coast by General Burnside's Federal fleet. We encamped at Mitchell's Sound (an unfortunate reminder of my lost nephew) and drilled regularly in preparation for meeting with the Foe.

I have here to relate an humorous event occasioned by our unschooled mountain men. When we reached the waters of the Sound and they found that body of water (larger than any they had ever seen or imagined) salt and unfit to drink, the rumor went round that the Yankees had purposely dumped salt into the water 'to pizen it.' As the price of salt has steadily been on the rise and it already grows scarce in our mountain counties, this rumor led to some dispirited talk of the superior financial resources of the Federals.

Thankfully I was able, by means of a few well-chosen words with some of the more intelligent of the enlisted men, to dispel this notion. Indeed, I believe—

"James, do you have everything you need? I'm on my way to a knitting party at Mary Peek's."

Margaret is drawing on her gloves. Her hat is on her head and an oak split basket brimming with fat rolls of gray wool yarn hangs from one arm. I assure her that I want for nothing and send my compliments to her working party on their tireless efforts to keep our men in socks, comforters, and mittens. She withdraws and I turn back to my letter.

Indeed, I believe that the men begin to hold me in higher esteem than they do Cousin Lawrence, our *duly elected* commander, and were that same election to be held today—but this is idle surmise, my dear cousin, (as always, I can open my heart to *you* as to none other) and I beg you not to repeat my speculations).

After some weeks at Mitchell's Sound, on the 30th of January, we were ordered to proceed *in haste* to Roanoke Island. This we did by way of Norfolk, Virginia, from whence we were tugged in barges over the Chesapeake Bay to Roanoke. There we found an engagement in process and we disembarked amidst whistling shells and the booming shots of enemy artillery. Forming up as soon as we were once again on terra firma, the battalion double-quicked the three miles to headquarters where orders were received. Though all our forces did credit to themselves in the engagement, the defenses were inadequate. General Wise, whose command it was, had invalided to Nag's Head and it fell to Col. Shaw to protect the Island. Despite his noble efforts, the enemy was too strong for the small force we could muster and on 8th February, the Island was surrendered to General Burnside and the Federal forces.

Imagine your poor cousin's chagrin at finding himself a Prisoner of War! I was seized with the fear that, for me, the war might end almost before it had truly begun and wretched, indeed, were my sentiments. On the third day after the surrender, all the Confederate officers were marched *under guard* to the steamer *Spaulding*, and placed in the hull of the vessel, still well-guarded. (Having seen what we could do in an unequal fight, the Yankees were not disposed to handle us like *gentle lambs*.) But I cannot complain of our treatment—we were fed well and soon were moved to Elizabeth City where, to my inexpressible relief, we received our paroles. Here though we quickly felt the pangs of hunger as Elizabeth City had been evacuated and there was little food to be found—lending added urgency to our return to Norfolk, which was accomplished on tugboats.

Our company took the Petersburg route to Lynchburg, then gratefully boarded the cars of the East Tennessee and Virginia Railroad to Greeneville in East Tennessee—the nearest point by rail to our own Madison County. It was eleven o'clock at night when we tumbled off the train in Greeneville, sleepy, hungry, and irritable. Cousin Lawrence went to make arrangements for the men, some ninety-one in number, to be fed and bedded at a hotel while I made my way to a livery stable to wake someone and arrange horses for Lawrence and myself for the return to Madison County.

My pen sputters and I realize that I am pressing too hard on the paper. Writing the words *livery stable* has awakened an unpleasant memory and I see the insolent grinning face of that young oaf as clearly as if he stood before me.

It had taken persistent knocking and hallooing to raise anyone at the livery stable but finally a bleary-eyed youth had appeared, rudely demanding to know what the hell we wanted at this time of night.

"Boy," I remonstrated, "don't you see this uniform? I am an officer in the Army of the Confederacy and I am here to requisition two horses—two *good* horses, mind you, none of your spavined, sway-backed nags."

The ill-mannered youth was unwilling to comply with my demand, saying that the boss—one "Big Quinn"—was not on the premises and I would have to come back in the morning. Weary with travel and impatient for food and bed, I brushed aside the stable boy's objections and pushed past him to take a look at such horseflesh as the livery stable possessed. The young yokel followed me, protesting, till I turned on him and put my hand to my sidearm. Disgruntled, he fell back, muttering that Big Quinn would have something to say to me in the morning.

Still grumbling, he lighted a lantern to show me the horses. Noting that the youth appeared strong and well made, I asked why he had not enlisted.

"Ain't my fight," said he. "Do I look like someone with a passel of slaves? Old Abe can free them ever one, far as I'm concerned."

I opened my mouth to speak of defending our beloved Southland and of the honor of answering the call to arms but recollected myself and followed his bobbing lantern to view the stock.

The best animals in the place were the half dozen big workhorses—none of which, the youth warned me, were broke to saddle. But amidst the usual complement of sorry-looking, wall-eyed, worn-out old hacks, were two decent appearing mounts—a chestnut and a bright bay.

"I'll have these," I told him. "I want them saddled and brought to our hotel—the Lane House—by eight in the morning. Your employer can put in a request for compensation."

The youth nodded a surly acquiescence and, thinking no more of it, I retired for the night, happy to think that I would be a-horse once more for the return home.

As I was, but not on the chestnut nor on the bright bay. Waiting for us outside the hotel the next morning were two sad *Rocinantes*, both well past mark of mouth, ill-groomed and dull-spirited. I sprang into the saddle of the nearest, caught the reins of the other, and turned toward the livery stable, determined to exchange these sorry nags for the horses of my choosing.

Big Quinn himself was there to greet me but of the stable boy there was no sign. When I apprised Quinn of my dealings with his employee on the night previous, he scratched his head and looked blank.

"Sim didn't say nothing about none of that to me, Captain, sir. He told me a feller over near Blue Springs had sent for them horses particular and he left out of here an hour agone."

I find that while lost in these unpleasant recollections, I have been mindlessly driving my pen back and forth till I have ruined the page. Stifling an oath, I crumple the paper—then smooth it out, fold it, and tear off the undamaged part. Margaret has already been complaining about the price of paper—rising to four and five dollars a quire—if, indeed, it can be obtained at all. This war forces privations on us all.

Still I see the sullen face of the stable boy. If he had been under my command, I should have taught him respect. But now, now that the Draft Law has been enacted, the next time I find myself in Greeneville, I shall make a point of seeing if the stable boy is still at Big Quinn's. Big Quinn called him Sim. I'll not forget that name.

In an attempt to shake off the foul humor I find myself in, I stand and take a turn about the room to dispel the vexing memory, then reseat myself and resume my pen to complete my letter.

I am pleased to say, Cousin Sallie, that since first we were organized in May, Company A of the Partisan Rangers has increased in strength till it is on the verge of becoming a full Regiment. I expect that this will take place very soon and that we will be designated the 64th N.C.—as we are the sixty-fourth to be organized.

It is a further source of pride that we have enough men from Madison alone to make up six full companies of 100 men each. The remaining four—for a regiment requires ten companies—will be as follows: one from Henderson County, one from Polk County, and two more from East Tennessee. I cannot help feeling a bit aggrieved that we could not fill *all* the companies with loyal Madison men—the traitorous behavior of a certain area of our county is a constant vexation. But of this, more later.

It occurs to me that you and the ladies who look to you for news of our men may not fully apprehend some of our military terms. Just as when we were children together and I tutored you in your ABCs, I shall write out here, for your instruction, a little primer on military organization.

The *Regiment*, 1,000 men strong, is made up of ten *companies*, Company A thru K. (I hear you reciting your alphabet and thinking that you have caught me out in a mistake, but I hasten to assure you that what I have written is correct—the letter *J* is not used because of the similarity in sound to A.) Each company has ninety-seven men and three officers—a *Colonel*, a *Lieutenant Colonel*, and a *Major*.

Beyond the Regiment, is the *Brigade*—which may encompass anywhere from two to six regiments and is commanded by a Major General. (Many brigades bear the name of their commanding officer or some nickname.)

The pen sputters and I pause to clean it with the pen wiper. Dipping the nib into the inkwell, I pull a scrap of wastepaper to me to test the pen. Idly I scribble my name. *James A. Keith...Keith's Brigade...*

It will come to pass. Lawrence's little game of conscripting men and accepting payments—ostensibly to purchase replacements but in reality, I suspect, to line his own pockets—has not gone unnoticed, thanks to a well-placed word or two in the right places. His suspension without pay over yet another irregularity in bookkeeping has put me in nominal charge (though he carries on as if nothing were changed). But when the extent of his defalcations is known—I make it at almost twenty-thousand dollars—when *this* comes to the attention of his superiors, they will be forced to take stronger measures, to remove Cousin Lawrence altogether, and then I shall come into my own.

Keith's Legion. Almost without my volition, the pen continues to form the names. *Keith's Marauders...Keith's ~~Mountain Lions~~ Catamounts....*

"More company business, Jim? We're supposed to be on leave."

At the sound of my cousin's voice in the door, I hurriedly crumple the scrap of paper and shove it up my sleeve for later disposal. The floor creaks as Lawrence comes across the room to take the only chair not plump with horsehair and red plush.

"I am well forward with company business, Lawrence. It is family correspondence that occupies me. I thought to apprise Cousin Sallie of our past movements and of the increasing burden of leadership that is like to fall upon me with our conversion to regimental status. Shall I send her your regards?"

Lawrence appears, at first, not to hear me—indeed, appears to be struggling with some weighty conundrum. At last he replies, somewhat perfunctorily, "My regards? Oh, by all means." Then he seems to recollect himself and says, "I came to tell you that we have received our marching orders." He pauses, looks at his boots, then up at me. "Allen's Legion, so designated, is to proceed to Greeneville, Tennessee. I am promoted Colonel and have no doubt that you and Polly's brother John will soon receive your own promotions."

I hardly hear the rest of what he says as he stands—the fury at being once again passed over in favor of Lawrence is like a roaring in my head. I force myself to my feet and extend a hand in congratulation, mumble some words—I know not what—and move quickly to place my foot over the crumpled scrap of paper that has fallen from my sleeve. At last he leaves and I fall upon my unfinished letter and, in my frenzy, reduce it to inky shreds.

11.

~SIMEON RAMSEY~

Greeneville, Tennessee
August 1862

Miss Viney's house has a different look to it now. Shades pulled down like someone died though it ain't nigh dark yet. And her pretty flower beds is all growing up in weeds. She is afraid to spend much time outside, what with all the soldiers about—says that a woman alone must be careful. I would laugh at her fears—she is most fifty if she's a day—but there has been some ugly tales about drunken soldiers and what they get up to.

I peck at the front door with the certain knock she told me to use—one-two-three, one-two, one-two-three-four—and wait. I have been seeing about her as best I can—making sure she has a store of wood and mending the shingles that blew loose in that big thunderstorm last month. Now I have come to take my leave before we make another haul to South Carolina—and in hopes that there may be a letter from Cora, who is still in Maryville.

When the drives was all ended last year, I went to Maryville and stayed with Cora's family for several months, making myself useful around the place and trying to win her daddy's good opinion. Cora's mama died last fall and her daddy ain't yet remarried, and him with all them young uns to do for. Cora is the oldest of eight and the youngest is not but four or five. "They need me, Sim," she said, when I asked if she wouldn't come back to Greeneville with me. And now I have not seen her since March—all those long months. One more season, I told her, of driving the wagons and I'll come back for good. We'll be married and set up housekeeping in that hidden cove I know of, away from all this war foolishness.

I hear soft footsteps in the house and call out, "It's Sim, Miss Viney."

It takes her a time to lift the bolt I fixed for her but at last she pulls the door back. The house inside is dim and stuffy and I wonder how she can see to do any sewing. The parlor has been empty of the bolts of cloth and half-finished dresses for some time now—there is very little dress goods to be had and Miss Viney's work now is mostly helping those ladies what can afford it to make the best of old dresses—turning them or making some little change so they seem different. Women is still women, even in the midst of war.

Miss Viney is not as plump as what she was but she still steps along like a chicken in a hurry. She shoos me back to the kitchen where the windows is open and the curtains is all drawed back. I see she has got her rocker by the window and a piece of sewing in the basket beside it. She fusses around, opening a cupboard that I can see is near empty, and pulls out a plate with some cornbread on it and a little dish of jam.

"I wish I could offer you better fare, Sim," she says, tucking her hands under her apron and looking down at the plate. "Wheat flour is such a price these days, if you can get it at all, that I hardly remember the last time I made biscuits."

"Miss Viney, I thank you but I just come from the inn and I am full up to here with stew."

She tries to get me to eat the cornbread and jam anyway but I keep shaking my head. At last she puts it back in the cupboard, saying all the while how she wished she'd knowed I was coming for she had an old hen she was fixing to butcher. She closes the cupboard door careful-like, and I realize that sorry little scrap is probably her supper.

She looks a mite more cheerful as she goes to her sewing basket and pulls out a letter. "At least I can give you this—I had one too. Our dear Cora is in good health and doing such fine work—but no doubt you'd rather read it for yourself." Still she goes on chattering about the Abolitionists and the Underground Railroad in Maryville.

I am eager to get away and read my letter in peace so when she pauses to take a breath, I tell her why I am come.

"We leave first light tomorrow," I say, "but I wanted to see was there aught I could do for you afore I leave—or anything you're wishful for that I might be able to find in South Carolina."

The wrinkles on her face sag downwards. "Oh, Sim, there are so many things. But, you know, I hardly dare part with my little savings, not knowing how long this dreadful conflict will go on."

She perks up some when I ask can I bring her needles and thread and she pats me on the arm. "Such a thoughtful boy you are. But I don't want for needles and thread, nor pins either. Jacob, the pack peddler who makes the rounds, was here not long ago and I laid in a goodly store in exchange for doing some mending for him. Such an interesting fellow and quite well read…" and she is off again while I stand there, nodding and fingering Cora's letter in my pocket.

Finally she recollects herself and tells me to set down and read my letter while she gets on with a piece of knitting she is doing. I go out to the back steps to catch the best light and pull the letter from my pocket.

July 5, 1862

My Dearest Love,

How long it seems since we were together and how many long days must wear away till thou return to Maryville and thine own Cora. As thou well knows, I am kept quite busy with the cares of a busy household and with overseeing the schooling of the younger ones. Thou wouldst laugh to see how solemn and stern I can be when little Hezzy and Isiah would try to cajole me into doing our lessons outside or, indeed, putting aside those lesson in favor of a ramble.

The special work thou saw some small portion of while thou was abiding with us engages much of my time as well. Thirteen more precious souls saved, eight of them children. Despite the dangers of war, the work goes on.

I look up from the letter, remembering what Cora had showed me of the 'work' her folks was doing. While I was staying there, it hadn't been long before I saw that there was something out of the way going on—more food being cooked than seemed to get eaten and Cora slipping off of an evening with a heavy basket and returning with it empty. I had my suspicions and one evening I stopped her and told her that she had ought to trust me and I would carry that basket for her everwhere it was she was going.

She colored up and said that she trusted me with her life but some of the other Friends…and she looked away, confused-like. I took the basket from her, warm and heavy and smelling of the beans and streaky meat we had had for supper. "Cora," I told her, "*I* am your truest friend."

At last she gave in and led the way along a path to an outbuilding behind the main barn—a shackledy old place that she said had been the cabin her great grandpap had built when first he settled there. In the dusk it appeared to be empty—but then I heard a baby's gurgling laugh. The sound stopped short and Cora shook her head.

"Poor little thing. Before long I hope she'll be safe where she can laugh out loud all day long if she wants." And I followed Cora around to the back, along a narrow path through great tall bushes and to a little door, low to the ground.

It was a kind of half cellar under that old cabin and she said that her great grandpap had dug and hacked it out of the limestone to be used in case of an Indian raid and later for a root cellar. "But these troubled days," she said, pulling open the door, "it's a place of rest for poor souls on their way to freedom."

When she opened that door, at first it seemed only a dark hole lay beyond, but then I saw there was a candle burning down there and, in the dimness, there was shapes huddled together on the floor. Cora went down the little ladder and I followed, not right sure what to make of this.

As Cora lit a tallow dip that she had taken from her basket, I begun to see some better. There was pallets of straw and old quilts along one wall and a rough low table with a bench on either side taking up the most of the little room. A big man, the blackest of any man I had ever seen, was setting on the pallets with one leg stretched out so's his bandaged foot could rest on a folded-up blanket. Another man, some younger and not so black, was at the table next to an old woman wrapped in a shawl. Across from them was what I took to be a white woman holding a white baby and two young uns beside her, one kindly coffee-and-milk colored—what folks call a 'mule'—and the other real dark. I couldn't make no sense of what the white woman was doing there with a bunch of runaway slaves. They had all of them perked up at the sight of Cora and the basket but when they saw me, they looked scared. The big man started to stand but Cora stopped him.

"Stay down, George," she says. "Sim is a friend. Let me share out the food and then I'll tend to thy foot."

"Bless you, Miss Cora," the woman says and the men and the young uns says it too, "Bless you. Bless you."

Cora shared out the food in bowls and you never saw people so happy to eat beans and bacon and cornbread. She had a jug of new milk too, which they passed around, and the young uns licked their lips over its sweetness.

Then she called me to hold the tallow dip close while she undid the big man's bandages. When I saw the nature of his wound, it took all I had to keep my supper from coming back up. Ever one of his toes had been cut off. It looked like old healed-up wounds that had reopened, likely from the hard traveling he'd been doing. Cora was as gentle as could be, unwrapping the cloths and daubing some sweet-smelling stuff from a bottle onto what was left of his foot, talking soft and low all the time and telling him how brave he was.

The white woman got up from the table and came and handed the baby to the big man then set herself on the pallet beside him, leaning up against him in a loving sort of a way. Just then my world turned itself upside down for I had never thought to see such a thing.

I said as much to Cora as we walked the narrow path back to the house. She laid a slender hand on my arm. "Sim, Tabby is George's wife. She, all of them, were slaves on the same plantation in Alabama. How they managed to make it this far with his foot so mutilated—"

"His *wife*?" I said. "But she's white and he's a ni—"

She put a finger to my lips then for she can't abide that word. And I have tried, for her sake, not to use it. She began to explain, slowly as if I was a young un, that Tabby was the daughter of a white man and a light-skinned slave. And that it was likely the same white man who was the father of her least un. That the old woman and young man were George's auntie and brother and the other children were George's. That they had tried to run away before and because of this, George's toes had been chopped off.

I am remembering all of this and how just thinking of what all them poor folks had gone through made me so mad that I could see why a body might join in on the Union side to fight against people who would do such things. Back then I had told Cora this but she had begged me to stay out of the fight. "When thou return and we are married, then thou can help in the work. We have so many poor fugitives seeking refuge all the time and we are always in need of brave men to guide them to the Free States."

I turn back to Cora's letter but the light is fading now and Miss Viney is calling from the door that I should pick some early apples to take with me. I look quick at the next few lines.

> Now and again I am able to do a little sewing for our future home. My dear mother had laid aside some lengths of linen of her own weaving for me and I am making pillowcases, though I fear some of this precious stuff must be reserved for bandages. As thou knows, we Friends are pledged to aid the needy and suffering, whether they wear the Blue or the Gray—or whether their skins are Black or—

At the door Miss Viney is fussing about them apples so I take a hasty peek at the last page then fold the letter back into its cover and put it in my pocket. There is a lantern at the stable and I can read it all again.

The crooked old apple tree that stands near the house has dropped some of its early fruit. I expect Miss Viney has been quick to collect the windfalls but a few broken apples are laying there, covered with the crawling bugs that are feasting on the fermenting flesh. There is a rich cidery smell in the air and as I reach me down some of the apples, I wonder if bees and waspers ever go to war or if that's a thing only people does.

I take the back ways to Big Quinn's. Ever since the Confederates passed that dratted Conscription Act in April, I have had to be careful where I go. Conscription agents is roaming about and I would have been taken up before this if Big Quinn hadn't stepped in. Long as he needs me to drive one of his wagons, I reckon I'm safe. But with so many men in the army, leaving only women and children to tend the farms, there ain't that much in the way of goods to haul. And there is always the chance that some gang of soldiers, be they Reb or Union, will take a mind to requisition those goods. Big Quinn's wagons are loaded for what he says is likely our last run to South Carolina tomorrow. He ain't even sure will there be aught at the other end to haul back to Tennessee, though goods of all kinds is needed here.

I light the lantern and walk through the dim sweet horse-smelling stables, looking over the wagon teams. I have spent the last few days tending to them and to the harnesses. The horses is all new-shod and the harnesses are clean and mended. I have brushed and curry-combed the beasts till they fairly shine. If this is our last trip down the Buncombe Turnpike, we'll do ourselves proud. Old Heck and Old Brutus—my particular pair, look up from their oats and whicker at me as I stop at their stalls.

They are fine looking horses—bright sorrels with pale manes and tails. Brute turns his long face to me and tosses his head. I reckon he can smell the apples in my pocket. I am reaching for one when I hear the sound of marching boots. Not so very strange anymore now that a gang of Secesh are stationed in Greeneville but it ain't usual for them to be marching about after first dark.

The tromp of boots stops and I hear the heavy tread of one man coming into the stable. We ain't got nare horse for hire just now so I will have to disappoint him, I reckon. As he gets closer, his spurs jingling and his breath coming heavy, I see that it is the same ill-tempered officer that I disobliged some little time ago and I make ready for a fuss.

"It's Sim, is it not?" he says when he is so close I can smell the cigar on his breath. He speaks gentlemanly enough but in the lantern light I can see that the glittering eyes above that black beard are crazed-looking and that he has drawn his sidearm.

"Sim…" he says again, rolling the sound around in his mouth. "Oh, Sim, I want you to come with me."

12.

~POLLY ALLEN~

Marshall, North Carolina
December 1862

My Dear Emmie,

I take up my pen once more to add to my never-sent letter, begun when the world was still a sweet and rational place. Never sent and never shall be for it is only here that I can unburden myself. Before Lawrence and the children, indeed, before all my acquaintances, I must maintain a façade of strong determination. It is the role the Colonel's lady must play, even to the bitter end. But to you, nay, not you but rather to this papery semblance of you, I will speak truth.

Our glorious second American Revolution is going badly. The too sanguine hopes for a rapid conclusion of hostilities have been dashed and the naïve dream of two great nations existing amicably side by side seems like to prove a nightmare. Lawrence does not speak of it, neither during his brief visits home nor in his letters, but I hear from all sides that East Tennessee is showing itself a rebel to the rebellion. And in our own county, adjacent to East Tennessee, the whole of remote unruly Shelton Laurel is reckoned a hotbed of Unionists. Brother John's last letter confirms this.

My pen stops, and I remember the day back in the spring when Cousin Margaret came to my door, waving a newspaper and so filled with indignation that she could barely form her words.

"S-savages!" she sputtered. "Savage, degenerate brutes, all of them! Just see how they used my father's friend, poor Mr. Kennedy," and she thrust the paper at me. "Read that."

I took it, noting that it was a recent number of the *Greeneville Banner* and I surmised that one of Margaret's family must have sent it to her. Margaret was a Jones from Tennessee and, as she is quick to remind all her acquaintance, her family were people of consequence in the Greeneville area, her father owning much land as well as a part of an iron foundry.

"Oh, Margaret, my dear," I cried, opening the door wide, "please, come in and rest yourself while I look at the article." She bustled in and sank onto my parlor sofa, still simmering with anger and letting off little puffs of outrage in just the same manner a boiling kettle lets off steam. After calling to Juliann to bring a glass of water for my guest, I sat at my desk and began to read.

THE MARAUDERS AGAIN

The band of marauders who infest the mountains on the head of Laurel Creek in North Carolina are still slipping over in this county, committing their depredations of pillage and plunder, robbing smokehouses, money drawers, and cutting up in general. On last Friday night a band came to James F. Kennedy's, six miles from Greeneville, broke open his meat house, and carried off a thousand pounds of bacon. They represented themselves to be a hundred and fifty in number. They threw rocks against the door where the family were sleeping, threatening to kill Mr. K. and to burn his house. They however left without doing further mischief. A few nights previous to that, they took from another man in that neighborhood some five hundred pounds of bacon, and beat and abused a good Southern man, leaving him almost lifeless.

These marauders are a portion of renegades from Tennessee and North Carolina, who have fled, some of them from Justice, some for fear of being drafted into the Southern army, and others no doubt for the purpose of plunder. These renegades have taken up their abode in the fastnesses of the mountains for a shelter. This den of thieves and robbers should be looked after by the authorities of Tennessee and North Carolina and broken up at once. Property and life is unsafe while this gang of land pirates are suffered to remain in their dens. This was the headquarters of the notorious Fry who has caused so much trouble in this country.

This gang has been suffered to remain there unmolested for the last five or six months, at least since the bridges were burned last fall. All honest men ought to feel and take an interest in the arrest of such iniquitous conduct and see that the perpetrators are punished as their conduct merits.

When at last I finished my perusal of the article and ascertained that Margaret's family friend had suffered no more injury or loss than was reported, Margaret broke in on my questioning. "But don't you see? These are the same lawless ruffians who shot Sheriff Merrill right here—in this very house. The same cowardly, illiterate, godless…"

She had paused, seemingly at a loss for suitable invective, and as I waited for her to continue, a chill ran over my body, perhaps a foreboding. *Land pirates,* the article had called them and they were within an easy ride of Marshall.

At the memory of those ominous words, again that involuntary chill takes me and my pen slips from my fingers, leaving an evil-appearing splotch on my letter. I hasten to blot it. Almost a year has passed since the incident in the article, and we in Marshall have so far been safe from the depredations of the aptly named land pirates. They dare not invade a town, much less the county seat with its Home Guard. Surely, they will confine their cowardly thieving to isolated farms in lonely places.

I wipe off the pen nib, dip it in the ink, and resume my letter to Emmie.

It falls to Lawrence and his men to ride into this hostile Laurel Valley and root out those men who have not complied with the mandated conscription. And to what end? Those captives, once sworn to the Southern Cause and provided with clothing and arms, shamelessly desert at the first opportunity. It is said that many make their way back to Shelton Laurel where they join with other outliers in attacking our forces from hidden places. Bushwhackers, Lawrence calls them and grinds his teeth for these forsworn villains take a heavy toll on any troops sent into their miserable little valley. Savages and villains without honor they may be but they are also excellent marksmen. One of the saddest losses inflicted on our gallant 64th was that of young Mitchell Keith—the nephew and protégée of Lawrence's cousin James…

My pen stops. I feel almost that I am writing sedition. No matter that this missive will never be sent, I must take care that none but I ever see it. But these scribbled pages—now crossed and re-crossed—are my refuge. Here I can speak truth as I see it.

Cousin James took Mitchell's death exceeding hard—his fondness and preference for the boy was always clear, indeed, I believe that it was an ongoing point of contention between James and his wife Margaret, who disliked to see her children overlooked in favor of another.

Some things, I realize, are better not recorded—even in this phantom form. And Margaret's bitter words on hearing of Mitchell's death were not meant for my ears. *And this is his reward for his misplaced affection—his own children little regarded while Mitchell had all his attention.*

No, no more of this. I rise, stretch, and go to the front gallery. Far down the street I see Juliann with Annie and Rommie, their little faces shining and rosy, picking their way homeward through the remains of yesterday's snow. They begged to accompany Juliann on her errands, being impatient with the close confinement occasioned by the weather. So, as the sun was out and the air a bit warmer, I allowed them a taste of liberty. Little Maggie cried most piteously after them but was soon distracted by a rag dolly I had put by for just such a moment.

I peek into her crib where she is sleeping happily by the fireplace. Her right arm circles her dolly, holding it close, and once again her thumb is in her mouth. I reach down to pull it free but hesitate, fearing to wake her. *No,* I tell myself. *Let her sleep. There will be time to wean her of this habit, time and a-plenty.* I tuck the soft blanket around her and return to my writing.

Back in October a great wind of hope swept through our Ladies Aid Society, indeed, through the South as a whole. Dame Rumor insisted that France and Great Britain both were on the verge of throwing their support to the South—and with such allies, could victory be far behind?

"Mama! See my pistol!" The door creaks open and Rommie is upon me, snowy boots leaving a trail across the floorboards. Juliann calls after him to no effect as she helps Annie pull off her boots.

I hurry to blot and fold the pages so that I may return them to their hiding place, knowing all the while that I should simply burn them and be done with it. Why do I keep this sham of a letter, this too truthful record?

But Rommie is demanding that I admire the crooked stick that he proclaims is a pistol and I play my part, lavish with my appreciation of his war-like demeanor, all the while wishing to snatch the "pistol" from him and throw it on the fire. Why must men and boys be so warlike? Thank God, Rommie is still young! The thought of this precious boy with his confiding smile and tousled curls caught up in the horrors of war... I kneel down and hug his squirming little body to my breast, breathing in the smell of boy. He is so dear to me—so infinitely dear. How do mothers bear the loss of sons at any age?

And now Annie is at my side, telling me about the new kittens they saw when they went to visit Dapple at the livery stable.

"The mama cat is gray and one of the babies is gray all over, just like her. But then there's a gray striped one, and one is patches of black and white and orange, and one is white with a stripedy orange tail. I think she must be a very special cat to have babies of all different colors."

Annie confides this with such wide-eyed wonder that I have to suppress a smile and when she goes on to ask if she may have one of the kittens when they are old enough to leave their mama, I find myself saying yes. A kitten will, perhaps, make up for the lack of the usual Christmas candies for there are none to be had and Christmas only a week away.

"Up, Mama. *Up!*"

Baby Maggie is wide awake, roused by the commotion, and she is standing at the bars of her crib, feet planted firmly apart, her little arms outstretched. She is growing so fast—by this time next year, the crib will have to be relegated to the attic.

Next year...what will next year bring? Surely this terrible war will be over—one way or another. God...Fate...or whatever Power I might name has spared Lawrence and my brother thus far. I thanked God when I heard of a friend's husband mustered out with nothing more than a disabled hand but Lawrence shook his head. "Poor fellow," said he. "Poor fellow to miss out on the war."

Lawrence chafes at the fact that no glorious battles have fallen to his part. Have my prayers kept him safe and away from the great battles? He would not thank me. And Cousin James, when last he was here, even as he mourned his nephew, was outspoken to the edge of frenzy in his wish for battle and for revenge. His eyes glittered with something like to madness as he spoke of the "cowardly bushwhackers" who had taken his nephew's life.

Evidently, having the good sense to hide behind a tree to shoot at your enemy is a thing no honorable man would do. I am sick of Cousin James and his talk of honor. I see neither honor nor glory in war—only death and destruction and desolation.

"*Mama!*" Maggie's sweet face is growing red and her mouth is shaping that ominous square that precedes a mighty roar. I lift her from the crib and set her down on the rug where Annie makes a lap and begins to tell her about the kittens. Rommie rampages up the stairs in search of his wooden sword and I follow Juliann to the kitchen to see what she has managed to find in the stores. We are all but out of wheat flour—biscuits no longer make a daily appearance on our table, having given way to cornbread. I had hoped to be able to have a cake for the children's Christmas and have put by enough sugar and raisins to achieve a modest one—if only I can have some flour. Alas for the towering lemon-filled coconut cakes of happier years—coconuts and lemons are but dim memories.

Juliann's usually placid face is stormy and her lower lip is set in just that way that warns me to tread softly. She is removing a few small parcels from her basket and muttering under her breath. I assume a cheerful face so that she will not think I am blaming her for whatever shortages she has encountered.

"What have you been able to find?" I ask, hoping that the larger parcel may hold my wished-for wheat flour. "Did they—"

"They don't have much. Mr. Gudger say that the Yankee blockade is keeping out most all the supply ships. What little supplies do get through, he says, are bought up by rich folks at the coast or taken by the army. No tea. No sugar." She snorts and opens the smallest parcel revealing a handful of green coffee beans. "These was the last he had—he knowed you'd want to have some by, for when the colonel comes home."

I want to laugh, the amount is so pitiful. One good pot, perhaps two if I eke it out with parched acorns. "And wheat flour?" I ask, trying not to sound too eager.

Juliann shakes her head. "Mr. Gudger say maybe later but he couldn't promise nothing. He let me have a jar of 'lasses—weren't no other sweetening to be had. And I got some mustard for mustard plasters—we'll need it if the children take the croup again." She swings around, her hands on her hips. "Do you know he wouldn't even sell me salt? Said it's at a special salt store and likely you'd have to go with me if we wanted some."

Juliann is close to tears as she slams about the kitchen, throwing open cupboard doors to reveal our scant supplies. "What am I gonna do with our share of that hog Miz Peek is fixing to butcher next week if I don't have a plenty of salt to cure it? And kraut—I was aiming to put up more kraut from some of them cabbages—can't do that without salt. What about—"

I hold up a hand to silence her. "We will have salt, I promise you. I should have remembered—Cousin Margaret told me only yesterday that since salt is in short supply, the authorities have appointed a salt commissioner to make sure that it stays in Confederate hands."

Juliann gives me one of her sullen looks, brows lowered and lower lip stuck out. I can see there will be no peace in the kitchen until I've secured our ration of salt.

"I'll step over there right away," I tell her. "I was just wishing for a breath of fresh air." She looks somewhat mollified and I cast about for something to bring her to her usual sweet temper.

"Perhaps you could make some of your delicious cornbread for supper—with those molasses on it, the children will gobble it up."

"Reckon I could," she agrees and her expression softens. "And I might fry up some apples from the barrel. They're starting to swivel up right much."

As I put on my walking boots, gloves, bonnet, and cloak for the visit to the salt commissary, I can hear a hum of contentment from the kitchen where the children are "helping" sift the meal in preparation for making the cornbread. Thank heavens for the supplies we *do* have—cornmeal and cabbage, dried beans, potatoes and apples in plenty, with the promise of fresh pork in time for Christmas. Our little flock of chickens still provides a few eggs and, though our cow is dry and will not freshen till spring, we can buy milk from a neighbor. I should not let the absence of the usual holiday victuals make me downcast. But oh! for a few oranges or lemons, and the fat oysters that came in barrels from the coast…

My brief walk to the salt commissary is accompanied by memories of Christmas feasts past but my greedy thoughts cease as I catch sight of a jostling knot of people in front of the little building that, in happier times, housed a cobbler. A hastily painted sign by the door proclaims it to be the Office of Salt Commissions. The crowd seems to be mainly women—countrified creatures in rough homespun—and they are haranguing a harried-looking man who is at the door, blocking their entrance.

"Ladies, please—I have my instructions. I am not to sell salt to any Unionists. And all of you…" He is looking each of them in the face. His own face wears a dismissive smirk. "All of you are Laurelites, are you not? How many of you have men in our glorious Army of the South?"

There is a grumbling and muttering and one of the women, a hard-faced, flinty-eyed piece pushes forward. "We got the money to pay for salt. We have lived in the Laurels since our kin settled there atter fighting to free us from the king of England. This war of yourn ain't nothing to do with us—and we got to have salt."

"That's right," say several of the other women and one of the men—a ramrod straight white-haired patriarch chimes in, "You tell him, Judy."

The agent at the door ignores the clamor and looks over the heads of the Laurelites to see me, standing indecisive a little way off.

"Mrs. Allen, please, step into the office. It will be an honor to serve the colonel's lady."

He beckons me in and one of the Home Guard who had been inside the door emerges and disperses the muttering group. I avoid their eyes as I walk past them toward the open door. I can see the bags of precious salt are piled ceiling high, but the woman called Judy steps in front of me. I see a lock of red hair escaping from her bonnet and wonder if she is the same one Lawrence pointed out to me on that long-ago summer day.

"They call us traitors and homegrown Yankees," she says, piercing me with her gaze. "But I reckon my granpap, him that fought agin the king, would say it was you and your husband the *colonel* and all these other Rebs what is the traitors. And all so you rich folks can hold on to your slaves."

I hesitate, searching for a reply. She stares at me for a long angry moment then, as the agent motions me in, spits at my feet and turns away. Before the door swings shut, I see the patriarch raise a lean arm and point toward my house. But the Home Guard has summoned two of his fellows and they are escorting the Laurelites away toward the other end of town. I sigh with relief and turn to the business of ordering enough salt to see us through.

While the clerk is entering my order in his books, I glance down and see a shining bit of spittle slide off the polished leather of my right boot to mingle with the muddy tracks on the floor.

1863

13.

~MARTHY WHITE~

Shelton Laurel, North Carolina
January 5, 1863

The snow is just beginning to fall as I set out to feed the hog. Now that Pap is laying up with a broke leg and Mommy plumb distracted with trying to care for him as well as Little Sam whose coughing keeps us all awake at night, a lot more of the work falls to me. I am glad of it for now people will see that I can do all that any woman could do, even if I can't talk. Just last week I heard Miz Riddle tell Mommy, "Law, that Marthy'll make some man a fine wife one day," and I smiled to myself, knowing that Miz Riddle would repeat them words all over, for she does love to visit around and tell all that she's learned. I hope she goes to Davy's house.

I get two ears of corn from the crib and see that some critter has been gnawing at the door trying to get in. There is hardly enough corn to do us—and the cows and the mule and the chickens and the hog—without the rats or squirrels getting at it. I will have to try to cover the gnawed spot, always supposing I can find a nail to hammer something over the place. And if I can't find a nail, well, I'll figure a way—as this war drags on, we are learning more and more to make do or do without.

And I will set a trap of some kind. If it's a squirrel, just a little squirrel gravy on our cornbread would make us all happy. But if it's a rat—well, we have never eaten rat but when I think on it, but for the tails, they ain't much difference in looks betwixt the two.

The bucket of food scraps and buttermilk for the hog is hardly worth toting. He snorts and pushes at the logs of his pen as I empty the bucket down the chute. The sorry little bit of leavings trickles in and he gobbles it up and squeals, wanting more. I give him the corn then go to the branch to fill the bucket with water. At least there's a plenty of that. He drinks most of it and looks up hopeful-like, then goes and lays in the corner of the pen where he has dug out a bed. He is losing weight now, not putting it on like he should be. The pigs was both fat from mast when we brought them in last month. We butchered his sister back at the first snow and she was considerable heavier than he is now.

We would have killed him before this if there'd been enough salt. Davy's family and the Moores have said they would come and help everwhen we wanted. But the only salt we have is less than two hand-fuls in the gourd by the fireplace. Enough to give some taste to the cornbread but nowhere near the half-bushel or so that's needed to salt down the meat from a hog, even one as sorry as this.

Miz Judy was in a great taking on account of the way our folks was treated when they went to buy salt in Marshall. She said words I ain't never heard from a woman before and carried on something fierce when first her and the others came back and had to tell us that the goddam Rebs in Marshall weren't going to sell us none of the salt they had piled up there in great bags.

I make my way along the snowy path to the meat house, meaning to cut off a little piece of the side meat hanging there to cook with our shucky beans. Where would we be without the pig meat to see us through? And we ain't the only ones in need of salt, here in the Laurels.

Back in the house Mommy is spooning mullein tea into Little Sam's mouth as best she can between his coughs. Pap is in the bed and I can see he is hurting for he grinds his teeth and pulls at the quilts covering him. I get a dipper of water from the pail by the door and take it to him. He smiles at me and calls me a good girl, then shuts his eyes.

Mommy looks up from Little Sam and motions me to her. "Marthy," she whispers, "I wrote a note to Miz Judy, asking could she spare a little corn liquor. It would help your pap to sleep and a little mixed in with honey might soothe this young un's pesky cough. Will you go over there for me?"

I take the path through the woods and as I come out into the open just above Judy's house, I can see something out of the ordinary is going on for they is a lookout set down at the foot of the lane. I figger maybe the outliers must be here—them fellers what are hiding out and taking shots at the Rebs any time they come into our valley. They sometimes come down to Judy's to get the news and for supplies to take back to their hidey hole up on the mountain. They dasn't go to their own homes for fear the Rebs might be laying in wait.

I can hear the buzz and wrangle of what sounds to be a whole gang of men as I come up to the house and while I'm knocking at the door one of the fellers inside hollers out, "By God, Judy, I've half a mind to take my men and get salt for you and for all that needs it. We'll not abide them damned Secesh treating our people like—"

He breaks off, and all the other talking hushes too, as I push open the door and stand there looking for Judy. There is a dozen or more of them—all Laurel men what has gone for the Union—and ever one has pulled out a pistol and every pistol is aiming at me. We all stand there like the pillars of salt in that Bible story. They don't make no other move nor do I. I reckon I look like a haint for I can feel my face go pale and my mouth is hanging open and there we all stand. Up in the loft, Judy's young uns is laying on their stomachs close to the edge, watching the room below. Their heads is all lined up, peering down, like baby birds peeking out of a nest, and they every one of them have the same round-eyed, open-mouthed look on their faces.

"Put away them pistols," hollers Miz Judy from over by the fire where she is setting on a bench next to a big man. "Don't you fools know who that is? It's little Marthy White from down the road—Sam and Kate White's young un. The child can't speak a word and ain't hardly like to tell on youns."

And all them men standing there so still and serious let out their breaths and holster their pistols and begin to talk and laugh amongst themselves like I ain't even there. I make my way through them to Judy and hand her the note from my mommy.

Judy opens it and frowns. "How long has Little Sam had that cough?" she asks and I hold up three fingers for three days.

"Does he kindly whoop at the end of the cough?" she asks and when I look puzzled, she draws in a deep breath making an *ooh* sound. "Like that—is he doing that?"

I nod *yes* for that is the very sound that is keeping us all awake of a night.

Miz Judy frowns again. "The whooping cough—law, I hate it for that young un. But she's using mullein tea That should help." She sets studying on something for a minute, then calls to one of the men. "That jug I let youns have. Can you spare a sup for medicine?"

One of the men says he'll go get some and is out the door in two steps.

Miz Judy watches him go. "Thank the Lord I still have a little put by—there ain't nothing like it for medicine. I'm proud to be able to send some to ease your daddy's suffering. And you mix a little with honey and give that young un a spoonful. See if it don't soothe his cough."

She furrows up her face and goes to thinking. "I *have* heard," she says, "that one way to cure the whooping cough is to have a woman who married a man with the same last name as hers to bake some bread. But it don't do no good iffen *she* gives the bread to the one that's sick—no, it works best when someone steals that bread."

Judy cuts her eyes at me. "Now you know I can't help you none with it, but they's a world of Sheltons married to Shelton cousins around here. If Little Sam ain't better in a day, you go heist some bread from one of them."

The big man comes back, grinning at me and Judy, and hands me a scratched-up wooden canteen that sloshes as I take it in my hand. I duck my head *thank you*, then I tap my finger on the canteen and look a question at him.

"You keep that canteen, honey," he says. "There's plenty more where that come from."

A chill runs over me as I understand what he is telling me—that this canteen was taken from a dead Reb—and my fingers tingle as I brush them over its flat side. I look close at it and see that amidst the scratches is some letters. Turning the canteen to the fire, I can just make out the words DIXY and E.B. Ray. I wonder who E.B. Ray was—was he old or young? Did he own slaves and was that why he had joined up? Or was he just one of them fools who loves a fight? Maybe he didn't have no say in the matter. Once they started conscripting, less a feller had the money to buy a substitute, he had to go for a soldier whether he wanted to or not.

I flat my hand over E.B. Ray's name and picture him—maybe a young man, not much past being a boy, shot down and all his belongings stolen. And for what? Even though he was the enemy, at least as far as us here in the Laurels would see it, I am sorry for him. And I think if it was Davy… I take hold of the carved bone ring that hangs from a cord around my neck, the ring Davy made for me, and the tears begin to fill my eyes.

I turn my back to the room so don't no one see me all swimmie-eyed but ain't none of them studying on me. A big feller who I heard one call *Kirk* is saying how they had ought to ride right into Marshall to bring back salt and the room is loud with the voices of the men—all of them eager be a part of this.

I feel a tug on my skirt and it is Miz Judy. "Set here by me and warm yourself before you go back out," she says. "These fellers ain't going nowhere tonight but when they do, I'll make sure youns get some salt too—I know youns got a hog yet."

She scooches over on the bench and I set down beside her. One tear is sliding down my cheek and she reaches out and wipes it away with the tail of her apron.

"Did you know today is Old Christmas Eve? Remember how we used to celebrate with bonfires and serenades and fellers shooting guns into the air just to make a racket?"

I had forgotten all about it. In these hard times we don't have any extra for such carryings-on. Christmas got by with no more notice than Mommy telling us the Christmas story and making a kind of sweet cornmeal cake. The most we ever done at Christmas was to go visiting around—but they ain't much of that now. Ain't no one got food to spare and having company means putting out as big a feed as you are able. I wonder how Judy is providing for this gang but I see some big pokes over in the corner and suspicion that these fellers has brought along their own army rations.

"…something laid by I want you to have," Miz Judy is saying and she goes to a chest at the foot of the big bed. Two fellers is setting on the chest top and she shoos them off like they was chickens, then opens the big lid and takes out something folded up.

She comes back to me and shakes out a white night shift. It is the prettiest thing, with little white flowers worked all around the neck and the hem.

"I made this for myself, a long time back," says she, "but it wouldn't hardly fit me now, and besides, I want you to have it. Call it a Christmas gift but put it by till you marry. Times like this, it helps to have something to hope on."

My eyes fill up again, but it is happy tears this time, and I take the night shift from her and hold it to my breast. Then I grab her hand and kiss it, before I head back out for home.

As I near home, I pass the path to the little pool where I have sometimes got a Seeing and I almost go up it, thinking maybe a Seeing would give me a notion of when me and Davy might wed and when I might put on my pretty night shift for him to take off. But the air is icy and I think to myself that the pool is likely froze over anyway so I keep straight on.

When I reach home, I can hear Little Sam's terrible cough and I trace a quick charm on the door post that he'll get better soon. I know women that have lost children—it's a common enough thing—but some of them mothers don't never get over it—they turn sour and bitter, sometimes to their man, sometimes even to their children that didn't die. Night is coming on fast and I hurry into the house, the canteen slung around my neck and the beautiful night shift in my basket.

I give Mommy the canteen and bring her a cup with a spoon and some wild honey in it.

"You are my smart girl, Marthy," she says, and she quick mixes a little of the corn liquor in and feeds Little Sam a spoonful. He sneezes and makes a face at the taste, but then he grabs the spoon away and goes to licking it for the honey. And he don't cough.

Mommy pours Pap a tot of the whiskey, and he pulls himself up in the bed to take it. He is looking some better than he did. Luvena is tending a hoecake on the hearth, and Paul goes out to the spring house for buttermilk. For a little time, as we fill our bellies by the warmth of the fire, Pap not groaning with pain and Little Sam not coughing but every once in a while, I think again how happy we are.

Pap is still sipping on his corn liquor and when he finishes his hoecake, he begins to tell the young uns all about how on Old Christmas Eve, if we was to go out to the barn at midnight, we'd find all of the critters kneeling to give honor to Baby Jesus. And, of course, everyone says they want to stay awake till midnight to see is this true.

The sound of a log shifting in the fireplace below wakes me and I wonder is it midnight. The two low beds up here in the loft—one for the boys and one for the girls—look like squirrel nests with young uns snuggled up to one another to stay warm. I untangle myself from Luvena, tiptoe to the ladder, and, quiet as I can, climb down into the big room. All the house is still but for the sound of breathing and Pap snoring. Mommy and Pap are two rounded shapes under the quilts. Baby Sam is quiet on the trundle beside the bed but he has thrown his covers off, and I tip over to him and pull them up. His sweet little face is squinched up and his thumb is in his mouth. This is the first time in days that the coughing has stopped.

I take my shawl from the peg by the door and slip out into the moonlit night. The logs and the shakes of the barn are frosted silver in the light of the setting moon, and, at first, I think there are lightning bugs in the bare branches of the trees. But it is a thousand stars twinkling and I throw back my head to look at the blue-black sky. It seems like I can hear the stars singing, high and clear, to one another.

Inside the barn it is warmer and the sounds are of quiet breathing—the milk cow and the mules. And in the dimness, I can see that they are kneeling.

I think that this must be a special holy time and I fall to my knees to pray for Little Sam, for my mommy and my pap, for all my family. I pray that Davy won't have to go to war and I pray for all of us here in the Laurels. And tomorrow at sunrise I will make another charm to keep us safe.

14.

~JAMES A. KEITH~

In winter camp, Knoxville, Tennessee
Early January 1863

The feather bed cradles us as we embrace one another. Our limbs in-
tertwine; our breathing quickens. Fragrant linen, plump pillows, a dim
half-light creeping through the curtained windows—and her silken
flesh quivering against mine. Her lovely face with its parted lips smiles
up at me. She whispers and I feel my manhood harden—

"Sir, Colonel Keith, sir!"

I start awake to the unlovely face of Private Simeon Ramsey bending over my cot. The insolent smirk he is trying to conceal puzzles
me till I realize that my aroused condition is evident beneath the thin
Army-issue blanket. I mumble something and roll on my side but the
young fool persists.

"Sir, last night you said did I fail to call you at sun-up, you'd have
me walking guard duty till my feet was wore to—"

"Dismissed, Private!" I roar, and he backs out of the tent with a
hasty *yessir* that sounds like a barely suppressed laugh.

I close my eyes again and attempt to resume my dream but alas! the
soft feather bed and the lubricious bed partner have vanished, leaving
only my throbbing member. I deal with that at once and then force
myself to my feet to make ready for the day.

Outside, the morning is dawning fair and clear but the air is sharp
and my breath clouds around my head. I am pleased to see Ramsey
shivering as he stands there with my new-polished boots and the
message that I am to wait upon Colonel Allen at my earliest conve-
nience. Do I catch a glimmer of mirth in Ramsey's eye as he holds the
boots out to me? After conscripting this insolent stable boy, I made
it my business to keep an eye on him by appointing him my personal
servant. I know his type—an unwilling soldier, a bumpkin with no

concept of honor who will desert at the first opportunity. It is my intention to ensure that he does not. But this enforced intimacy of master and servant is proving to be something of a trial and I wonder which of us is suffering more.

No matter. I send Ramsey off to see to my mount and, after pulling on my boots, make my way along the neat rows of tents to Lawrence's headquarters. The men are, for the most part, engaged in the small morning duties of camp life but there is far less military discipline in evidence than I should like to see. The troops are drilled regularly, to be sure, but it is difficult to find occupation beyond make-work and these weeks of enforced tedium are eating away at the enthusiasm for the Southern cause that swelled our ranks only last year.

And now dysentery is beginning to take its toll. If something is not done, we stand fair to lose far more men to disease than to battle. I call a sergeant over and instruct him to detail a party to dig new latrines—the old sink pits are near to overflowing and, I make no doubt, have already contaminated our water supply. We have been tarrying here at Knoxville far too long.

I am turning away, leaving the disgruntled sergeant to collect his victims when a pleasant thought occurs to me.

"Oh, Sergeant, my servant is idle this morning," I tell him. "Make sure you include Private Ramsey in your party."

My cousin, whose tent like mine enjoys the comfort of a chimney, is seated by his fire, perusing what looks to be an official dispatch. Cousin Lawrence has aged much in the past months. More and more white besprinkles his dark hair and beard, and his face bears the lines of a much older man. Perhaps it is the effect of the disbanding of Allen's Legion, that Legion in which he took so much pride, as well as the assignment of his cavalry battalion to another commander. I find I cannot suppress a smile and the words *I almost fucked your wife last night* tremble on my lips.

Lawrence looks up. "You appear to be in a cheerful mood, Cousin," he says and offers me a cup of the vile brew of parched wheat that passes for coffee these days. He sips his own and his eyes return to the page.

I take a seat on an upturned box by the fire and wait for what he has to say. The 64th has passed many wearisome days in petty scouting parties and the rounding up of suspected Union recruiters as well as our own deserters. Even our part in the battle at Perryville, though successful, culminated in the less than glorious capture of several hundred government mules, the which we were then obliged to drive here to Knoxville to turn over to the Chief Quartermaster. When I made some small disparaging remark to Lawrence about officers and gentlemen turning muleteers, he only laughed and said the mules would be of far more use to the Cause than any number of prisoners.

Indeed, he remained completely oblivious to the hoots and jeers of the civilian population as we drove the cantankerous, long-eared brutes before us. He even essayed a literary jest, asserting that if for the want of a horse, a kingdom was lost, perhaps two hundred mules could ensure the Confederacy's victory.

The memory still rankles. I long for some glorious action and think back to the Mexican War…magnificent fighting…actions to stir one's soul—but that was a different time, a different place. I toss the dregs of my cup into the fire and clear my throat.

"You sent for me. Is there something—"

His head snaps up and there is a startled look on his face. It almost seems that he had forgotten my presence. He shakes his head, as if to clear his thoughts, then holds up the missive.

"Forgive me, Jim. This dispatch arrived a little after midnight but I saw no need to disturb your dreams. The 64th is ordered to Bristol, to report to General Marshall. The Yankees are sending forces from Kentucky in an attempt to destroy our salt works at Saltsville and we are to push them back."

Again I am struck by the weariness on his face and in his voice, which is faraway and without the enthusiasm I already feel welling up within me. The past months of suspension and the still-pending charges of falsifying his muster rolls have weighed heavy on his mind. Should those charges be proven…

No, that is an unworthy thought. I must content myself with the certainty that my time is at hand. Perhaps this coming encounter will prove decisive. At long last, a real military action—my mind is a-brim with possibility. But for Lawrence, I should…

"…six more deserters," he is saying as he leans to add a billet of wood to the fire. "I find it hard to blame the men—letters arrive from their families, sad tales of deprivations and hardships, and the men take French leave. We none of us expected this conflict to last so long and I have chosen to turn a blind eye to brief unauthorized absences. But more and more fail to return and now—"

I interrupt, impatient with his softness. "And now, since the Conscription Act last April, all those one-year volunteers have had their terms extended by three years and they don't like it. Hell's bells, Lawrence, this is war! That same Conscription Act mandates punishments for draft avoiders and deserters, punishments including death. We can't fight a war without soldiers."

He cocks his head to one side and gives me a wry smile. "It seems to me, Jim, that it makes small odds then, whether we lose a man to desertion or to execution. With desertion, we are less one unwilling soldier, less another useless body to feed, arm, and keep watch over. But with execution, not only have we lost a soldier; a family has lost its provider."

I can scarce believe my ears. My cousin, my so-called *superior*, is treading dangerously close to treason. I could wish there was another officer of my mind here in the tent with us at this moment.

"Certainly I would not suggest *wholescale* execution," I say, choosing my words with care. "But sometimes setting an example can prove efficacious. Recall last August, just before Manassas? General Stonewall Jackson had three habitual deserters marched to the side of their new dug graves and shot in a public show witnessed by thousands. I believe that little piece of theater slowed desertion rates considerably."

"Perhaps…" Lawrence says, prodding gloomily at the sullen fire and rousing the coals to a fiery glow before adding another chunk of wood.

The bitterness in his tone and on his usually placid countenance surprises me. There is something more at work here than January melancholy and the lassitude of winter camp.

He pours us each another cup of the muddy brew, this time adding a tot of whisky, and offers me my cup with an apologetic smile.

"I don't wish to argue the point, Jim. It's just that I'm feeling low these days. Polly writes of illness with the children and dwindling supplies to be had at home, while we spend our days scouring the woods for stragglers and outliers, men who simply want to be left alone to pursue their lives—much the South's avowed reason for secession. I cannot help but see the irony."

I nod wisely and attempt to sound sympathetic. "There's something in what you say, Cousin. But how many of those deserters take up arms against us in their own communities? You know that the Laurels are a hornets' nest of outliers and bushwhackers, many of whom once served with the 64th. You know and *I* know, none better, the damages they have inflicted on us. My own nephew…"

Lawrence shakes his head. There is real pain in his eyes and his voice brims with sympathy. "That was a sad pity. A fine young man—I understand your feelings." He seems to want to say more but merely shakes his head again and sighs. Then, remembering that it was he who had sent for me, he manages a graceful dismissal, saying that I probably have things to do to prepare for our march to Bristol.

The warmth of the fire and the whisky in the coffee have produced a buzzing effect in my head, and I step out into the brisk morning air to survey my domain. The itinerant photographer who, with Cousin Lawrence's permission, has set up temporary shop on the edge of the camp, has attracted a mob—a jostling mass of men, attired in the best uniforms they can muster and carrying an assortment of weapons—pistols, rifles, muskets, knives. I stroll in that direction to assure myself that nothing is amiss. As I draw closer, I see that the photographer, having made countless images of the camp and of the officers, in groups and singly, is now offering his services to such of the enlisted men as can pay to have their likeness taken, to immortalize themselves as warriors. Many a tintype, I make no doubt, will be dispatched home to anxious parents or find its way to the soft bosom of a waiting sweetheart.

Soft bosom… Images from this morning's interrupted dream drift through my mind and I stand transfixed as the haunting notes of a German harmonica rise above the genial chatter of the waiting men. A very young, very lanky private—one I've remarked previously for his resemblance to my lost nephew—is playing "Lorena." One hears that melancholy love song whenever the men gather, as well as at such social functions as are still held. Indeed, some generals have tried to ban the singing of it, believing that it exacerbates the already prevalent homesickness among the troops and encourages desertion.

There may be something in that, I think, as I feel a lump swelling in my throat. Soon all the waiting men have fallen silent to listen and then, voice after voice is lifted in the refrain.

> *Oh, the years creep slowly by, Lorena,*
> *The snow is on the ground again.*
> *The sun's low down the sky, Lorena,*
> *The frost gleams where the flow'rs have been.*

I find I am mouthing the words, substituting, as I always do 'my Polly' for 'Lorena.'

> *But the heart beats on as warmly now,*
> *As when the summer days were nigh.*
> *Oh, the sun can never dip so low*
> *A-down affection's cloudless sky.*

And it *was* a summer day so long ago, a never-to-be-forgotten day when I thought she would be mine. Could I have misread her blushes, her gentle words?

> *A hundred months have passed, my Polly,*
> *Since last I held that hand in mine,*
> *And felt the pulse beat fast, my Polly,*
> *Though mine beat faster far than thine.*

The chorus of voices swells and I am forced to turn away before the moisture in my eyes betrays me.

> *And what we might have been, my Polly,*
> *Had but our loving prospered well?*
> *But then, 'tis past, the years are gone,*
> *I'll not call up their shadowy forms…*

Alas, my dreaming mind betrays me and I *do* call up those shadowy forms. I think it no wrong, when *he* has the reality, to allow myself the dream.

> *A duty, stern and pressing, broke*
> *The tie which linked my soul with thee.*

Of late I have wondered if this might have been the case. Some parental obligation—some obscure notion of a prior claim. I cannot otherwise account for her choosing Lawrence instead of me.

The song has come to an end and I catch sight of a solemn-faced Private Simeon Ramsey standing before the canvas-draped side of the photographer's cart, one hand resting on a small rug-covered table, the other clutching a Bowie knife which, to my startled eyes, appears to be the very knife I saw last lying atop some papers on my writing table.

I am quick-tempered, I'll not deny it. The gently melancholy spell of "Lorena" dissipates as a red rage descends upon me. I stride into the midst of the throng and catch Private Ramsey's arm, wrenching him from the photographer's metal brace and pulling him away. I must contain the impulse to batter his wretched face to a pulp, to fling him to the frozen ground and trample him into insensibility. But I am an officer and a gentleman and the men are watching.

"Private Ramsey," I hiss through clenched teeth. "Why are you not with the party digging new latrines?"

His eyes are wide and he struggles to speak. "Sir, no sir, I took care of your horse like you said and then I come over here. No one said nothing to me about latrines."

I am not appeased. He is still clutching my Bowie knife. I flick it with my glove.

"And as for *this*—do you know the punishment for theft? You've seen the wooden mule—a long enough time astride that thin rail and you'll be of little use to that young woman whose letters you await so eagerly."

15.

~JUDITH SHELTON~

Shelton Laurel, North Carolina
January 8, 1863

Me and Marthy are making our way through the blowing snow up the Butt Mountain. The sun is only now topping the ridge and it sets the world a-sparkle, turning the woods and the fields below into a sight on earth. We stand a minute, just marveling at it, and all at once I feel closer to God than ever I have in the church house. The stillness and the sun shining through the snow and the clean cold air on my face is so like a blessing, I could almost think to hear God speak. I look over at Marthy and I can tell she is touched by this special moment too. She has ahold of that bone ring she wears on a cord around her neck and is staring off into the yonder, as if she is looking at a happy time to come.

Then a rooster crows from down in the valley and some dogs set in to barking and the moment is gone. Me and Marthy look at one another and go back to climbing. We have set out early to bring news and some supplies to Pete McCoy and the other outliers who are hiding up here from the Rebs. This cold time is hard on them fellers and though we can't tote much, we have a couple of jugs of corn liquor to help the boys keep off the bitter chill.

We come up careful, brushing out our tracks behind us for the first half mile. Now that we've left the trail, I tell Marthy she can leave off and she tosses her fir branch aside. She points up the mountain and looks a question, then taps her fingers to her lips. She is wanting me to tell her something, most likely more about where we are going.

The girl is just hungry for talk. Too many folks think that because she can't talk, she can't hear or just ain't worth talking to. So I set in to telling her all about Pete McCoy.

"Now, I told you who we was carrying this to. Pete McCoy is

brother to Patsy Shelton, your Davy's mama. You can see how the family looks come out in Davy—Black Irish, some call it. You remember, you saw Pete back in April when we was at my place hunting ramps for a spring tonic. You mind how he had run off from the Reb army that had conscripted him and was hiding out in a rock house up yonder—"

Marthy taps my arm, raises her eyebrows, and uses her stick to trace the outline of a house in the snow. Then she raises her eyebrows again.

"No, honey, not a real house. Hit's a place where some big rocks are leaned against one another and another big rock has made a kind of roof. Hunters used to shelter there, and Injuns too, back of this. And it *has* been used to hide a still." I smile, thinking of happier times. And of one particular time—me and Abner, laughing and just a little fuddled on white liquor from that still. God willing, those happy times will come again. But Marthy is impatient for me to go on and I continue my tale.

"Well, you remember how not so long after that time we seen Pete, the Secesh was like to overrun Laurel, taking up our men and stealing our provisions. So Pete made his way over to near Flag Pond in Tennessee where Mr. Lawing and his boys build them some fine squirrel rifles. 'I'll be hunting men, not squirrels,' Pete tells them, 'and I want me a .44 caliber rifle.'

"Now the Lawings is strong for the Union, so they told Pete to come back in thirty days and they'd have him a dandy. And they set in and built him that rifle with a fine curly maple stock, all polished smooth, and sights in the notch and a shining silver fifty cent piece cut down and fitted for the front sight.

"Thirty days passed and here come Pete to claim his rifle. It was ready for him and he walked all the way back to Shelton Laurel that very night and run him a batch of bullets for his new rifle which he had named Betsy."

Marthy's face is a study. Partly happy, for she likes hearing stories and learning about folks, and partly troubled-like. She is still worried that something may happen to her sweetheart—so many men have either gone off to fight for the Union or have been conscripted by the

Secesh. But Davy ain't of an age yet and I pray that he—and my boys too—will stay safe at home and that this fool war will get over with so's we can get on with the business of living.

Marthy taps her lips again and nods impatient-like so I go on with my story.

"Well, the next morning, Pete sets off with a horn full of powder and a pouch full of bullets and goes up in the woods just this side of my house, for I had told him how the Rebs had been stealing my provisions and would likely be back for more. And sure enough, the sun was just rising over Tater Gap Mountain when here come a sorry Reb up the lane with a bucket on his arm, making straight for the place where I'd put my taters. Pete just lay still and when the Reb had his bucket full and was heading back to his camp, Pete took careful aim with Ol' Betsy. The bucket with the taters flew up in the air and the man dropped down in the dirt of the lane, dead as a hammer."

Marthy bites her lip, for she is such a soft-hearted thing that talk of killing hurts her bad, but then she nods, solemn-like. She has to know, hard as times are, that if the Rebs get all our food, ain't no way we can make it through the winter. I shift the poke I'm toting to my other shoulder and we keep climbing.

"Ever since he got that Lawing rifle, Old Slick Pete McCoy, for that is what they call him, has been a one-man army. Any time the Rebs go to travel up or down the valley, Slick Pete is there, firing on them from behind trees or rocks. Why, he is reckoned to have accounted for near thirty Rebs. They send out parties to look for him and post soldiers at homes where they think he might stop for a night, for the Laurels is plumb full of Pete's friends, but he always outsmarts those thieving Secesh."

We are close to the spot where I usually meet up with Pete—he hasn't showed me just where they camp now and I don't want to know. Was the Rebs to suspicion that I knew how to find Slick Pete, I mistrust what they might do to make me tell them. I believe I could hold out against most anything—unless they was to threaten my young uns.

That's one reason I brung Marthy along today—was something to happen to me, at least she'd know the way. And she can't talk.

We stop at the big chestnut with a great broad rock at its base and I make the high long whistle Pete showed me. There is still a good bit of snow up here and a nearby balsam's feathery branches are weighted down with it. Once, then three times, then once again I whistle. Marthy has her lips pulled up and is frowning hard.

"Well, go ahead," I tell her. "See can you do that."

Her first try is a sorry little fizzle that puts me in mind of a young cockerel just learning to crow, but she tries again and manages a fair whistle. I clap her on the back and tell her she done good. "You know, Marthy, might be you could use whistling to talk." I am full of ideas about how this could work, but just then the heavy-laden balsam gives a little tremble and snow begins to sift down from its branches. Pete slides into view, Old Betsy in his hand. I swear, I never heard a sound, not a footfall. That feller comes and goes like a ghost.

"Thankee, Miz Judy," says Pete McCoy as I hand over the poke and the jug. Marthy does the same and I tell him that Kirk and a world of other men are home on leave from the Union army, scattered all through Laurel at their different houses.

"They say they'll be heading back to the Union lines afore long," I tell him.

His blue eyes light up. "If I'd a knowed that, I could have saved you a trip. This laying out up on the mountain is hard on a feller—I've about made up my mind to go for a soldier again—but this time I'll enlist with the Union."

He shoulders the pokes and gives a whistle. Another fellow slips out from behind the balsam and takes up the two jugs in one hand.

"We'll take this on to the others and I'll gather up my necessaries," Pete says, giving me a wink and a grin, "but you can look to see me later. Tell ol' Kirk not to fight no more of this war without me."

Early afternoon and I am on my knees in the meat house, using a knife and a wooden spoon to scrape the dirt from under where the hams and salt meat used to hang, when John Kirk walks in. He looks round at the empty hooks and bare shelves and clears his throat.

"Your girl said you was out here and I wanted a chance to talk to you alone, Judy."

"Well," I answer, jabbing my knife into the hard dirt, "here I am. Go on and say your say."

I tip another spoonful of the half-froze dirt into the vessel I have brought with me and go on scraping. He leans down to look at the vessel. "Not to be too quizzy—but what in hell's name are you doing there?" he asks.

I set back on my heels and stare at him. "We are in bad need of salt," I say. "Folks and critters alike. If I boil this dirt and strain it, then boil it some more, sooner or later I'll have me some salt."

He stands there another minute, then reaches inside his coat and holds out a letter. It is creased and dirty, like it has been carried for months and passed from hand to hand to get here, but I make out the writing and my heart jumps.

"Is he all right?" I ask, afraid to open it. It has been so long since I had any news of Abner—never a letter from him—but I know that he has written his wife for the news went around that Neely had died of the fever someplace in Kentucky not long after they all joined up.

"I couldn't say." Kirk gives me a strange look. "I'm the third or fourth to carry this letter. The man who gave it to me said that the Tweed boys was with Sherman's army now."

I put the letter in my bosom and get to my feet. "I thank you kindly for bringing it to me," I say and pick up my vessel and reach for the door. He stops my hand.

"Judy…"

The lust heat is burning behind his eyes. Like many another before him, he thinks because I am raising a gang of young uns without never a husband that I am fruit for the taking, ready to spread my legs for any man who asks. With Sol not around the way he used to be, I have got used to these looks from fellers. I can't fault them for wanting a little comfort of that kind before they go back to soldiering, but I ain't aiming to bring another child into this hungry world of ours—not now, not if I can help it.

"I got to get to the house," I say, pushing past him out into the chill night air. He stands there watching me go. In the lane I see more of the Union men gathering, and I hope that this means they will be moving on soon. While they are here, they keep the Rebs off—but there ain't no one to protect us from them. And Reb or Union, they all got to eat.

Back in the house I dip water from the bucket into the dirt-filled pan and set it on the fire to boil. Ellender is at the loom and Dan'l is outside bringing more firewood to the porch. The rest of the young uns is all under the bed covers to keep warm, and Frank is telling them a story about Jack the Giant Killer. It's the same story my granny told me, but in Frank's telling, the giant is a big old Reb soldier with a black beard. I can't wait no longer and turning my back to the room, I pull out my letter and unfold the single page to read by the light of the fire.

My Dear Friend,

I hope this finds you well as it leaves me. Me and John are with the 1st Tenn Cavalry, Neely having taken a fever and died soon after mustering in at Flat Lick. He spoke several times of how good you was to us that day and wanted to send you his thanks. Which I now do along with my own.

I think about coming back to Laurel if I am spared and I think about things I might have done different when you and me was young. My feelings for you are the same as they ever was and what I said to you that last night before we lit out for Tenn is true as gold. ~~You know my situation with my family.~~ I can only hope this war is soon over and that I can return to old Laurel and my one true love.

Your true friend,
A. G. Tweed

The crackle of the fire, the giggling of the young uns, and the steady *clack-clack thump* of the loom fade away, and I remember a summer's day so long ago, when I was slender as a willow wand and Abner in the glory of his young manhood. I remember all the foolish and loving promises we made and it puts me in mind of that song a gang of them in the Rebel camp was singing the other night. I reckon there's many a one in these dark times thinking back to summer days and lost loves. What was that line that near brought the tears?—*the frost gleams where the flowers have been—*

"Momma!" Dan'l busts through the door and, like that, my summer day with its flowers is gone. "Momma, that man's come back and they's a world of men on horses down the lane."

Ellender drops her shuttle and runs to the door, while the least uns set up a wailing, hollering that it's the Rebs coming back and that they are going to be eat up, like in the story. Little Sol and Linnie duck under the covers and wiggle like a pair of moles to the bed foot while Armp tries to follow them.

"It ain't the Rebs, young uns," I say, going over and giving each little poking-up bottom a pat. "It's John Kirk and them others, same ones as have been around here all week."

But they are taking pleasure in being scared and won't come out. I tell Frank to stay with them and I go out to the porch to see what all the commotion is about. Here comes Kirk on his big bay gelding and he reins up right at my steps.

"Judy, you can throw out that damned pan of dirt. I'm taking these men into Marshall and getting you some salt!"

He is red-faced and puffed up, all full of himself. I say something about the Rebs coming after them but he cuts me off quick. "There ain't no force of Rebs within a day's march," he says. "The Home Guard there in Marshall ain't nothing but a bunch of old men and cripples. We'll ride into town, get the salt they should of let youns have, bring it back here, and be on our way to the Union lines. Let them try to follow us *there*!"

He wheels the big bay around and waves his hat over his head. The men nearby let out a whoop and it is answered by more hoo-rahing down the lane and out on the road that leads to Marshall. There is a great thudding of horse hooves and I reckon to myself that there must be over fifty men and, from the sound of them, a good deal of liquor has been going around.

I pull my shawl around me and cross over to the barn. Down in the creek I see a broken grey jug, and I hurry into the barn and back to the stall where my liquor is hidden at the bottom of a manger.

Was hidden. The stall door is open and the hay that was in the manger is all throwed out. Jugs is laying on the dirt floor and the smell of spirits is strong in the air. I see a big wet patch in the dirt where

I reckon they must of stood and filled canteens. When I look in the manger, all that is left is one sorry little demijohn.

I pick up the empty jugs and set them back in the manger, wondering how they found my store. And I shake my head at the thought of fifty some drunken fellers riding into Marshall to get hold of salt. Lord knows we need it bad. But then those fellers will be gone, back to Tennessee and beyond. And what will we do when the Rebs come after their salt?

For come they will.

16.

~POLLY ALLEN~

Marshall, North Carolina
January 8, 1863

For a blessed moment the children are asleep, curled up under their warm blankets. The sore throats that have plagued all three since Christmas have turned to chills and fever, accompanied by a rash that consumes their little bodies with itching. Annie suffers the least—or bears it the best—but my Rommie tosses day and night in his bed, begging me to '*do* somepin.' And Little Maggie wails piteously till she exhausts herself. They have no appetite, though I tempt them with whatever dainties our meager larder can provide—a spoonful from our last pot of strawberry preserves, dried apples, stewed into applesauce, rich broth from the old hen Juliann was able to snatch back from a marauding possum. And even if I can wheedle them into taking a bit, it almost all comes back up again.

Pray God it is not the scarlet fever. When I sent Juliann for Cousin Margaret—in her husband's absence, she is my only resource—Margaret stood halfway up the stairs, excusing herself from closer approach by the fear of carrying contagion back to her own house, and called out questions. Where was the rash? Were there little bumps? Was there streaking? Were their tongues rough and red? What did their throats look like? And with every answer I gave, she retreated down another step. Finally she advised me to continue spooning liquids into them, to keep them warm and quiet and, with God's help, the malady would run its course. She left a small pot of some soothing balm on the steps, saying that it might be efficacious in calming the itching. She also advised that, when the children were recovered, I should burn their bedclothes and what clothing they had worn as well.

"It's quite contagious," she warned as she hurried away, "if it *is* scarlet fever."

Pray God it is not. I can ill spare any bedclothes, so many of my linens already gone—sacrificed to provide bandages and lint for the Glorious Cause.

Oh, God, that I had never heard those words! Were it not for the thrice damned Glorious Cause, my noble husband would be at my side; our cousin, our doctor would be here to attend to my children, and I—

I am growing fevered myself and I go to the window to cool my forehead against the glass. At least, I think, my brother John is at home on leave and safe for the moment. Perhaps later he will stop in and brighten my gloom. If the sun broke through once on this dreary day, I was not aware of it. I watch as evening twilight creeps over the desolate town below. Gray upon grey, black mud and, in some sheltered spots, dirt-spattered snow. The few stores are closed—those few that bother to open anymore. A solitary figure stumps along the side of the half-frozen road, hunched against the cold. A rider going the other way passes by and out of my sight.

The cold glass is grateful to my brow, and I stand a moment longer, wishing…wishing I know not what.

A thudding of hooves and the rider returns at a gallop, shouting something as he goes. I cannot make out the words but his alarm is evident. And then I hear the sound of many horses and stand there all amazed as a great band of horsemen thunders into the street. My first thought is one of heart-stopping terror—that the Yankees are come upon us, but as I look closer, I see no uniforms and nothing that bespeaks military discipline. Indeed, they seem little more than a drunken mob, milling about as if unsure of their purpose. But then a number of them dismount, tossing their reins to mounted companions whose heads swivel back and forth, as if on the lookout for interference.

As I watch, the intent of this gang of ruffians becomes clear—they are breaking into the salt commissary and hauling out bags of salt which they sling over their horses' backs. I see nothing of our Home Guard—whether they are not aware of this invasion or, as seems more likely, they are too far outnumbered to challenge this increasingly bold force. I watch helplessly as the men, like a stream of ants to a sugar bowl, carry bag after bag of our precious salt to the waiting horses.

And now some are breaking in to the Mercantile and the other stores, emerging with a seemingly random assortment of plunder. One grinning, ugly brute has tucked several bolts of cloth under one arm and a pair of child-sized boots dangle from his elbow.

"Mama?" I whirl around to find Rommie wakened and plaintively scratching at his arms.

"*Shh, shh,* my good boy," I whisper. "Hush now so you don't wake your sisters and I'll put some more of the nice ointment on."

But as I take one last glance at the street below, I am horrified to see five of the looters at my front gate. Without pausing to answer Rommie's cries, I dash down the stairs, calling for Juliann to bolt the back door. Her startled face appears then, as I cry, "*Now!*" ducks back into the kitchen.

I lock and bolt the front door and lean against it, almost unable to breathe. It is my old nightmare—war at my gate. And now boots are on the porch and the door latch rattles against my hand.

"Shitfire, looks like ain't nobody to home," growls a drunken voice almost at my ear.

"Well, maybe you got to knock louder, Joe," another says. "Could be ol' Allen's wife's already abed."

The ensuing laughter and crude talk chill me to the marrow. These *animals*, these *savages*—

I dart to the fireplace and take up the poker, just as the parlor window shatters into a thousand pieces. The glass lies all around me, sparkling in the firelight, and I feel a tiny trickle of blood run down my cheek where a flying splinter has lodged. Half-dazed, I stand there, poker raised, as a huge man with a matted beard and long unruly locks beneath his hat steps through the window frame. He regards me with amusement as I brandish the little poker before me and squeak out a warning. A quick step forward and he has seized it and twisted it from my hands. With a contemptuous laugh, he takes hold of each end and, as though it was nothing more than a willow switch, bends it into an arch and tosses it into a corner.

"Come on in, boys," he calls. "The colonel's woman is to home after all."

❧

I have been somewhere else, somewhere a long, long way from here, and, but for Lawrence and my babies, I would not have come back. Juliann is leaning over me, dabbing at my face with a damp cloth and crooning to me as if I were one of the children.

The children! I force myself up from the sofa and stare about me at the ruin of my parlor.

"Juliann, the children! They were screaming—I must go to them!"

She presses me down. "Lay back now. They ain't come to no harm, no thanks to that thievin' gang from Laurel. The babies are in their beds and gone back to sleep at last. Miz Doctor Keith come with more blankets and some soothing syrup for them. She set here with you and took the piece of glass from out your face and dressed the cut while I was upstairs with the babies. She's gone now to see to Cap'n Peek."

I hear her words without comprehending them. My brother John—Captain Peek—is home on leave. Why would Margaret be going to see him? I close my eyes. It seems I have wakened to madness. I try to make sense of the jumble of scenes in my head: the window exploding…the boots coming through… I open my eyes and in the light of the oil lamp see that same window is blocked with a thin mattress, held in place by my grandmother's tall bureau. I see the splintered wood of the drawers and begin to remember.

They demanded money and the keys to the bureau and the chests. The big man held me to him, his hands running over my body, while from upstairs Rommie called for me and Little Maggie screamed.

"Where do you keep the keys?" the big man asked, over and over, his hands never still, plucking at my dress, but I did not speak, only struggled to free myself. I saw three of the men run up the stairs, heard the children shriek, and would have gladly given over the keys. But before I could speak, another emerged from the kitchen with an ax and proceeded to hack his way into the bureau and then the chests. They plundered them of all they could—clothing, my few remaining linens, and money—shoving it all into the bags they carried.

I remember seeing the three who had been upstairs come thundering down, trailing the very bedclothes from my children's cots, and

I remember seeing the head of Annie's beloved china doll peeking from a jacket pocket. And then my captor released me with a final brutal squeeze and flung me to this sofa. As the brutes gathered up their spoils and made for the door, I could hear the children shrieking and started for the stairs—and there, my memory fails me.

"You must have swooned when you stood up, Miz Allen." Juliann kneels beside me and offers me some mint tea. It is heavily sweetened with molasses and the taste is unpleasant but I force myself to swallow it.

"Are the children truly unharmed?" I want so badly to run up the stairs and see for myself, to hold them, but my limbs seem to have turned to water. "You said that Margaret—Mrs. Keith was here?"

Juliann sits back on her heels, delighted to tell her part of the story. "Now you rest easy about them babies. They are sound asleep, all three. And, yes'm, Miz Doctor Keith was here. As quick as those villains rode out of town, I ran down to her house to get help. Hadn't no one bothered the Keith's place and when I told her you had swooned and the babies was a-howling, she grabbed up some things and called for a servant to follow her. She come right here and between us we got you back onto the sofa. Then we went upstairs.

"The babies got real quiet when they heard us coming, likely thinking it was the bad men again. Then when they saw us, they set up a howl. Them sorry thieves had taken all the bedclothes. Annie was holding the baby, trying to keep her warm, and Rommie was standing by the bed with his little wooden sword in his hand, like he was protecting his sisters. All three was shivering so hard their teeth was chattering.

"Well, Miz Doctor Keith, she took one look and told Rommie to get on the bed with the girls. She pulled off her shawl and wrapped it round the three of them, and she hollered down to her man to run back home and get some blankets. Then she set down with the babies and told them the bad men wasn't coming back, and she gave them some of that soothing syrup. She took and rocked Little Maggie in her arms, and she told Rommie that his papa would be proud of what a brave boy he was. Annie was crying because one of them villains had took her doll, and Miz Doctor Keith told her not to take on, that she had a pretty doll put away that she would bring over in the morning. By the time the man got back, their little eyes was heavy, and they was sound asleep when she covered them up and tucked them in."

Juliann pauses to catch her breath and I feel ashamed of the uncharitable thoughts I have had about Margaret in the past. Then I remember Juliann's earlier words and clutch at her arm.

"Juliann, what of my brother John? Did you say that Mrs. Keith had gone to see to him?"

"Yes'm." Juliann swallows and looks away.

I do not believe I can bear one more sorrow, not my dear brother too, but I close my eyes and ask anyway, "Has something happened to John?"

17.

~MARTHY WHITE~

Shelton Laurel, North Carolina
January 9, 1863

By heaven's mercy, we have salt at last! Or maybe it weren't heaven but that little charm I worked with a pinch of salt from the gourd. Mama don't know nothing about me and my charms, but I slip off now and again to do what I can. Lots of folks round here does charms, whether they know it or not—like knocking on wood or putting a horseshoe over the door. I just have more of them. Of course, charms don't always go the way you want—but then praying don't either. In hard times like these, I don't see no harm in doing both.

Miz Judy sent word for us to be looking for someone to bring us our share of the salt after dark and we was all round the fire waiting, though it was dreadful late. At last come the sound of boots on the steps and a heavy rap at the door. Pa was setting up in bed with his squirrel gun across his knees, and he motioned for Mommy to open the door.

Lo and behold, it was one of them Union soldiers with a great large bag of salt. He said Miz Judy was sending some folks to butcher the pig for us, being as Pap wasn't able, and that we should get our wood and water ready at first light.

"For," said he, "best youns get that meat salted down right quick and hid good for it's likely the Rebs will come looking for the salt."

A cold chill ran over me at those last words, but Mommy wasn't paying no mind for all she could think of was that big bag of salt. "Oh, what a blessing!" she sang out, as the soldier set the salt down just inside the door. She put her hands together like she was praying, and it looked for all the world like she might jump up and plant a kiss on that rough-looking feller. "You are a true angel of mercy. I thank you kindly and I thank Miz Judy for sending you. We are so near the end of our corn that rather than feed the hog the corn we need for bread, I was near to turning him loose to root for himself. And that would like as not end with the Secesh getting him. Oh, thank heavens for this salt!"

The big feller looked round the room, at all us young uns staring at him and at Pap in bed, his broken leg bound to a hickory splint. The man kindly shuffled his feet, then he cleared his throat. "Ma'am, it weren't right the way they done you folks here in Laurel over the salt. We just aimed to set matters square. I hate it we can't stay and help youns but we got to get back to the Union lines first thing in the morning."

Just then little Josie slipped up behind Mommy and hung on to her skirt, peeking around at the big man. Her eyes got real wide and she whispered, "Mommy, that man has a dolly in his pocket."

We all looked and, sure enough, there was a little china head with shiny black hair painted on it and a sweet white face with red lips just peeking out of the rough blanket jacket. Judy's girls have a doll like that but most folks don't have the money for such. Mommy has made rag dolls for each of us but they ain't a patch on a china doll.

The big man looked surprised and reached down and pulled out the doll. *How did that get there?* his face seemed to say.

Oh, she was such a pretty thing in her sweet ruffled dress of shiny blue cloth with lace all round the bottom and tiny little china feet painted with black boots. I could see that Josie wanted that doll in the worst way—she reached out for it but Mommy gave her hand a gentle slap.

The big man looked at Josie and looked at the doll in his hand. Then he squatted down till he was eye to eye with Josie. "Come here, young un," he said, in a real soft voice. "You want this play pretty?"

Mommy tried to say something, but he put the doll in Josie's hands and patted her on the head. "You take good care of her, you hear?"

He stood back up and said to Mommy, "I'd thought to take that to my little girl, but the Lord knows when I'll see home again and the doll'd likely get busted all to pieces along the way. I'm proud for this un to have her."

He looked all around the room again and opened his mouth like he wanted to say something else but then he closed it again and went out the door.

Pap's leg is still paining him but he got hisself out of bed before first light and set in to sharpening the ax and all the knives. Then he hopped around with a crutch stick, telling each one of us what needed to be done. We toted a world of water and wood, and now the big pot is on the boil and me and Mommy and Kate is hard at work making a dinner to feed the men what have come to butcher our pig. We will even have biscuits because there was a little poke of wheat flour in with the salt. I don't know when we last had wheat flour.

I am full of happiness. Partly because of not having to watch the poor hog grow thinner every day; partly because of knowing that we will have meat to eat again; but mostly because Davy and his father are with the men who came to butcher our pig.

The big Dutch oven is before the fire, full of browning biscuits. There is tenderloin stewing with apples and onions, there is cabbage frying and potatoes roasting and kraut and cornbread, and there is wild honey that Mommy has been saving. The good smells fill the house, and Mommy is humming as she flies about setting plates on the long table. It will be a fine feast.

Just as I am taking the biscuits out and readying another batch, I hear the sound of men talking and Pap's crutch on the porch. "Come in the house," he says and I can tell that he is happy too.

Pap's leg is still paining him but he got hisself out of bed before

The long day is over at last and all of the meat salted down and hid away. The men is setting before the fire, talking of the everlasting war and what the Rebs are likely to do next. Me and Mommy and Kate has done up the dishes and the little uns is in the loft, tucked under their quilts. Davy and me are back in the shadows, setting side by side at the end of the table, and Mommy is by the fire, leaning up against Pap. Her eyes are drooping shut but there is a little smile on her face. Having a good store of meat laid by has eased her mind considerable.

Davy's father is talking on about Pete McCoy and how many of the Secesh Pete and his gang of outliers has killed. "There's like to be more notches on Pete's Ol' Betsy afore long," he says, winking one eye kindly sly-like. "He was dead set on going with Kirk to join the Union Army, but Judy begged him to stay in Laurel and be on the lookout, for the Rebs are sure to come this way right soon. Hellfire—'scuse me, Miz White—you *know* the folks in Marshall is bound to set up a holler about what them fellers did to the salt commissary. And it appears…" Davy's father's voice drops low and solemn, "it appears that some of them fellers broke into Colonel Allen's house and did a little looting."

I think of the doll that is upstairs with Josie, and I wonder if Colonel Allen has a little girl and if this was her doll. I wonder, but Davy is talking low in my ear. He is so close that his dark hair brushes my cheek and sets me to shivering.

"You know, Marthy, I bet I could go with Pete and the bushwhackers. I'm a good enough shot. But Mama takes on so, and she has made me give my solemn word to stay home. She says that though I ain't yet fourteen, I'm as good a hand at the farm work as the others and she is counting on me if the others was to get conscripted. And it's true, she can't run the farm by herself."

He sets up a little straighter on the bench beside me and gives my hand a squeeze. "It's aggravating to have to stay out of a fight but it makes me kindly prideful too, to know I can do the work of a man. Besides, to speak the truth, all that I have ever wanted is to live here in the Laurels and make a crop every year, like Sheltons have done, time out of mind."

I squeeze his hand hard, and he scooches closer to me. The men are too full of talk to notice us and Mommy's eyes are shut.

"Back in the fall, me and Pa got to talking about when I'm growed." Davy is whispering in my ear again, and I can feel his breath stirring my hair just the least bit. It is a pleasing sort of tickle and I nod for him to go on.

"Pa has give my big brothers pieces of land, and he says that when I'm sixteen, he will give me the little rise on the west side of the farm."

His eyes catch the firelight and shine as he talks on. "Oh, Marthy, it's the prettiest place you ever saw, with a spring not far off, a good-laying field just below, and apple trees growing all around. I know Pa'll help me build a cabin, like he has the others—"

There is a big laugh over by the fireplace. Davy hushes and looks to see are they laughing at us but they ain't paying us no mind. Mommy is sound asleep, still leaning against Pap, and the men are passing around that wooden canteen I brought from Miz Judy's. Davy breathes a little sigh and slow and careful-like puts an arm around my waist.

"Well, I been going up to that little rise right much," he whispers. "I just set up there and think about what it will be like to have a house of my own. I have paced off the ground and marked how I want the cabin to lay, with the door facing east so's the rising sun will wake us."

At that word *us*, I catch my breath and stay still as can be, waiting for what comes next. Davy don't seem to notice what it was he said and goes on talking, his eyes all dreaming and happy.

"Every time I go up there, Marthy, I carry a rock with me for the foundation. And pretty soon, if nothing don't happen, I'll go to cutting trees and hauling logs."

He keeps his arm tight around me and turns to look in my face. The firelight dances in his blue eyes and almost takes my breath away.

"It's going to be a fine cabin and a fine life—there's just one thing I need…"

If I could talk, I would have to fight to keep from hollering out *Me, you need me!* But as it is, I just widen my eyes and look a question at him.

He gets a little flusterated and turns his head away for a moment. Then he turns back and takes a deep breath. "Marthy, would you… would you want to live in that cabin with me? I can't think of any girl I'd rather spend my life with. You are just so blame peaceful to be around."

I wish I could shout out a great *Yes* but before I go to nodding, I wonder, is he asking me to wed? Or just to live with him? I'd be happy either way but Mommy would take a fit was I to go off with Davy without first standing up in front of the preacher. I am looking at the little bone ring and twisting it on my finger when he all of a sudden tightens his arm around my waist.

"I'm saying I want you for my wife, Marthy. When I'm sixteen we can stand up before the preacher or the magistrate, ever how you want. It ain't that long to wait—two years and a piece. And by then I'll have that cabin fixed and ready to bring you home. Will you—"

And I nod like one thing and then, not caring whether the others see me or not, kiss him right on the lips. Under the table, I lay my hand on his lap and feel the stirring there.

When they have all gone, I climb up to my pallet in the loft and crawl under the quilts. The others are asleep so I wrap my arms around my feather pillow and pretend that it is Davy. I kiss it over and over and then I lie awake, making plans. Davy has a heifer—he would have had two if the Rebs hadn't took and butchered one—and her a fine critter what would have brought many calves. Seems like Rebs just don't think the way we do. But in two years' time, there will be more calves and I know Mommy will give me a hen or two and maybe a setting of eggs—and I have already made a quilt and will make more. I would like to make a fine fancy one with boughten cloth—if just this dreadful war would be done with to where there is cloth to buy again.

As I drift into sleep, I get a kind of Seeing—the little cabin with the sun shining in the door and the apple trees all abloom. I can see myself setting in the doorway in a blue dress, piecing a quilt and watching——watching for my husband to come home.

18.

~SIMEON RAMSEY~

Knoxville, Tennessee
January 14, 1863

I have never knowed a feller as hateful as Colonel Keith. He has had it in for me ever since first he saw me at Big Quinn's. I make no doubt that he conscripted me for his servant so as to pay me back for keeping them horses from him. And pay me back he has. Extra duty, extra drill, the worstest jobs he can find. Take, for instance, his damned old chamber pot. The colonel is too high and mighty to go along to the latrines like everyone else. Oh, no, he won't even piss outside but takes a delight in filling that pot to the brim and then calling me to go haul it off on the double. One time he made shift to trip me as I was carrying that stinking thing out the tent, and some of that piss and shit got on my britches—and then when I got back with the chamber all scoured clean, he lit into me about the "disgusting condition of my uniform."

Also, he is the quickest to anger of any man I ever seen. Back last week, when he saw me with my Bowie knife, which I had bought it from Harce Plemmons, the colonel right off thought that it was hisn and that I was fool enough to steal it from him. He wouldn't listen to a word I said but snatched the knife from out of my hand. He got all puffed up like a turkey gobbler and was threatening to ride me on that narrow rail they call the wooden mule and see me flogged too. I kept trying to *tell* him that his own Bowie knife was back in the tent, but he wouldn't pay no mind. He was working up to a screaming rage, all red in the face and spit in his beard, when Harce, who by the mercy of God was there to get his picture took too, stepped up to him and saluted real polite and soldierly-like.

"Colonel Keith, sir," said he, and ol' Keith swung around, looking for all the world like a mad bull about to charge.

"What do *you* want?" he bellowed. "Can't you see I'm disciplining this sorry excuse for a soldier?" And afore Harce could say ary a word, Colonel Keith rared back like he was making a speech. All the fellers what was waiting to have their likenesses took was watching close, and he swole up and set in, pleased as a preacher with a full church house.

"Thievery," says he, wagging a finger in my face, "cannot be tolerated in the army. It is detrimental to discipline and to the trust which ought to abide betwixt brothers-in-arms."

"Sir, excuse me, sir." Talking low, Harce tried again to save the colonel from making a fool of himself before all the men. "Sir, I need to explain something about that there Bowie knife."

But the colonel paid him no mind and settled in to his subject, pointing the Bowie knife at me and calling me all manner of names. He was speechifying like one thing and taking a deal of pleasure in it too.

"And *this*," says he, waggling the broad shiny blade under my chin, "…this loathsome object, this Private Ramsey has dared to steal from his superior officer, thus rendering the offense still more grave. Scurrilous behavior such as this cannot, nay, *will* not be overlooked and, by God, will not go unpunished. I intend to make an example of Private Ramsey so that others will think long and hard before succumbing to the lure of another's property."

Harce's face was all twisted up with wishing he weren't there, but he spoke up like the brave and honest man that he is. "Sir, Colonel Keith, sir, that there knife belongs to Sim rightful. I sold it to him this morning and you can see my mark on it." And Harce laid a finger real gentle on the brass guard. "Them three little *X*'s just there, sir."

Colonel Keith brought the knife up to his eyes, and when he saw that what Harce said was true, he looked most like he had been shot. His mouth was open but not a sound came out, and I took the moment to put in my word. "Yessir, Colonel Keith, sir, *your* Bowie knife is back at your tent. It was laying on the table under some papers last time I seen it."

Colonel Keith looked at Harce and then at the brass guard and scowled. Them three *X*'s was plain to see. Harce stepped back and a great silence fell as all the watching men waited to see what the colonel would say.

At first, he didn't say nothing but just stared hard into my eyes with a kind of crazy look that sent the cold shivers all over me. "If I find," says he, bringing the knife up to my throat again, "if I find that you *arranged* this little charade…"

And then he seemed to recollect himself. His mouth snapped shut and he dropped the knife at my feet, made a quick about face, and marched hisself off. For a wonder he didn't even remember about the latrine digging and I got to get my picture took after all.

The colonel weren't at the tent when I reported back after mail call so, after putting things to rights and emptying the damned old chamber yet again, I set in to polishing his spare boots. He is mighty hicky about all his belongings, and I sat there on an upturned keg and worked on those things till they was like a looking glass. But all the time I was wondering would I ever get a letter from Cora. I had made the mistake of letting some of the fellers know about her, and it got back to the colonel who has taken a delight in aggravating me about her. "Perhaps your sweetheart has found a likelier swain," is his favorite thing to say when he sees me come back empty-handed from mail call. I don't pay it no mind for I know that Cora will be true to the grave and beyond. But the other thing he does is far worse. He asked me one time where my sweetheart lived and, thinking he was trying to be friendly for once, I told him.

"Maryville?" he quizzed me. "Maryville in Tennessee?"

When I told him that was where, he pulled a long face. "I hope, Private Ramsey, that your sweetheart is not one of those home-grown Yankees, those traitors that infest so much of East Tennessee."

"No, sir," I told him. "She's a Quaker and they don't take sides."

He shook his head kind of sorrowful-like. "Oh, Private Ramsey," says he and lays a hand on the big old Bible he keeps on his writing table. "He that is not with me is against me," he says in a preaching voice. "It's here in God's Word. It appears that you have been consorting with the enemy." He smiled then, a smile like a dog's snarl, and I knew that he was no friend to me.

He went on to describe how enemy women was treated in Bible times, made into slaves and their babes torn from their bosoms and dashed against a rock.

"Of course, that was long ago. None today would attempt to enslave a *white* woman…" He pulled at his moustache and gazed off into the distance, then closed one eye like he sometimes does when talking. "Still, in times of war, the appetites and passions of the men cannot always be contained. During the recent Mexican war, for example…"

And he went on, describing the hateful things some of the Americans done to one Mexican woman who they had suspected of being a spy, all the while darting glances at me to see was I discomfited by his words.

Which I was, though I didn't let him see it. Finally he came to the end of his tale. "When the men were done with her, the wretched woman was more dead than alive. The kindest thing, I believe, would have been to put her out of her misery."

I had terrible dreams that night and have had them ever since, dreams of Cora tied up and Colonel Keith doing her like those others done that poor Mexican woman. In the dream Cora is crying out to me and I am standing by, helpless to do aught but look on.

Now the camp is all abuzz at the news that the 64th is ordered to Bristol to guard the salt works there. "Anything for variety," said one feller, and it is true that camp life is right tedious. But the best of us making a move, I think, is that on the march I might have some chance of slipping away like so many have done.

Colonel Keith is tickled at the news. He has me polishing his sword and cleaning his pistol and getting everything just so. I heard him talking with Colonel Allen. "God grant we may see some action at last!" said ol' Keith, and Colonel Allen, who is a sensible man, said something about being careful what you wish for.

We made the march to Bristol in such haste and was so close-watched the whole way that a man couldn't even step behind a bush to relieve himself without there was a corporal or a sergeant keeping him company. I was sore disappointed not to have gotten away but will keep my eyes open for the first chance that offers.

If ol' Keith had hoped for action once we got to Bristol, like me

he was a disappointed man. After one little skirmish when we helped
to drive back the Yankees who were advancing on Saltsville, the 64th
was ordered back to Knoxville, where it is camp life and scouting and
more of the same. Short rations—there being no green stuff growing for long forage at this time of year—the eternal weevily hardtack
which we call crackers or biscuit, though it don't eat like no biscuit my
step-mam or Miss Viney ever made, salt pork, and, if we are lucky,
cornmeal. Sleeping on the hard ground in one half of a little dog tent
with only a ground cloth and a blanket, if you have them. Many a
feller got shed of his ground cloth on the march, thinking to lighten
his load and now, with the weather cold and wet, has come to regret it.
We are as sickly a bunch of soldiers as you're likely to find—coughing
and sneezing and bowels griping with the Tennessee quickstep. Was
a force of Yankees to come upon us now, we would be whupped for
sure.

I am writing to Cora but I don't tell her none of this—just that
camp life is boring and that I miss her and hope for a letter soon. I am
sending her the picture I had took. I don't tell her that since that picture, I have growed a beard and it is coming in like one thing—thick
and black. And I am glad for it. When I saw what a boy I looked in
that picture, I imagined some Yankee soldier just laughing at me for
a raw recruit, still wet behind the ears. Anyways, shaving ain't all that
convenient, especially when we're on the march. And in this raw cold
weather, a beard helps to keep my face warm.

Something is afoot. Ol' Keith found me jaw-boning with some other
fellers after my rightful work was done and, just to be hateful, he
has set me to roaming round the camp, picking up every least bit of
rubbish there might be—cigar ends, scraps of paper, and such. I am
working over the ground near Colonel Allen's tent, when I see a rider
come galloping into camp. He reins up and heads my way, making for
the colonel's tent. There is an oilskin packet in his hand and I move
around to the back of the tent, hoping to hear something. The ground
back here ain't been tended to in some while and there is plenty to
keep me busy and out of sight. I am still picking up trash—someone
has lost a fine brass button, and I slip it into my pocket.

Through the walls of the tent, I hear a rustle of paper and then the colonel draws in his breath right sharp. "What else can you tell me?" says he to the messenger and there is a kind of fearful sound in his voice. "A raid on the salt depot in Marshall, you say? Were there any casualties, any looting? My house stands near the depot—"

The fellow what brought the message says that he weren't on the spot when it happened, but he understood that there had been a right smart of plundering of stores. "And Captain Peek, he was shot but is expected to recover. Now, I ain't for certain sure about all of this but I believe some private homes was broke into—"

There is a crash like someone's fist has hit the table, and the colonel god damns and the next I know he is hollering out the door for his orderly to go after Colonel Keith. I want to hear what they have to say in the worst way but not wanting to fall afoul of ol' Keith, I move away at double time. It don't matter; Allen's orderly will likely pass on whatever he hears and it will be the talk of the camp afore nightfall.

19.

~JAMES A. KEITH~

Knoxville, Greeneville, and Shelton Laurel
Mid-January 1863

"By God, Lawrence, it makes me furious! Long ago we should have come down on those accursed Laurelites like the wolf on the fold. And now this outrage! They ride into Marshall, bold as brass, and raid the government salt stores." A useful classic tag comes to mind—Seneca? Cato? No matter. I bring it out with all the force it deserves. "To paraphrase the old Roman: 'Laurel *delenda est*'—Laurel *must* be destroyed!"

Lawrence says nothing but nods distractedly as he drives his pen over the paper before him. His face is weary, and his eyes are those of a much older man. The ambiguity of his situation—suspension with the charges of muster roll irregularities still unresolved—has taken its toll, rendering him hesitant and tentative in all things. I step closer to the fire and try to curb my impatience. Heretofore, Lawrence has been slow to act against the Laurelites, but now he claims that his period of suspension is over and he is petitioning General Heth to allow us to lead our forces once more into that accursed valley. The necessity of an act of retribution against those blackguards, who plundered the salt depot and carried out who knows what other heinous acts, is self-evident. I am eager to be on the move but Lawrence is cautious and will not act without Heth's orders. Oh, that *I* held the command—there is a time for hesitation, but surely there is also a time for bold initiative—and I am the man for that time.

The scratch of Lawrence's pen and, even worse, the long pauses while he considers what to say next infuriate me. Words tremble on my lips but when I dare to venture a suggestion, he shakes his head, muttering, "Not now, Jim," and turns back to his tedious composition.

Again and again, have I expressed myself to Lawrence on the

subject of the Laurels—that traitorous nest of Unionists. After their raids into East Tennessee, their thievery, their brutal assaults on Confederates and slave owners, the bridge burnings, we should have put the entire place to the torch—wiped that vile breeding ground of savages clean from one end of the valley to the other. The manifold sins of the Laurelites plead our cause. They are all utterly savage—men and boys, women and children. But those in command choose otherwise, choose to send us on limited sorties. What, I say, is war if not absolute? We are at war—they are the enemy. It is as clear as can be.

Scratch, scratch. Lawrence pauses to reread what he has written. He dips his pen in the ink and begins again. How can he remain so composed? Is it that the transgressions of the Laurelites have not touched him so nearly as they have me? By God, when I think of my friend Merrill, gunned down in cold blood, and the escape of his murderer—both the work of Laurel men. And an even deeper wound, my nephew Mitchell's untimely death at the hands of a bushwhacker—God send that I may have my revenge.

On the move at last! I lead two hundred troops to Greeneville where we will rendezvous with Lawrence's three hundred, as well as with Nelson's Independent Company of Partisan Rangers—some ninety strong of the Georgia Cavalry. It is my understanding that the Rangers will be under my command and I exult to think that at last I will be able to hit these Laurelites and hit them hard. General Heth made himself clear: halfway measures are not sufficient, and he will require no tedious reports nor does he wish us to encumber ourselves with prisoners. Our only task is to break the back of the insurrection in the Laurels.

Heth is an officer after my own heart—a West Point graduate and close friend of General Lee—he understands these cowardly bushwhackers from his experience with others of that ilk in Mexico as well as in the Mormon Wars in Utah. *He* understands, as Lawrence does not, that in cases of this nature and with combatants like these, the long-established rules of so-called *honorable* warfare can have no jurisdiction. Lawrence prides himself on his honor but, in times like these, honor is nothing but a stumbling block.

The hard-frozen ground of the road to Greeneville makes our going the quicker and the icy air is an added spur. The men step out with a liveliness that is a pleasure to see. They are as eager as a pack of hounds on a scent for I have let it be known that *this* time they will not be restrained, and we shall have our revenge on the dastardly bushwhackers who have impeded our every sortie into that valley.

As we approach Greeneville, I feel as lighthearted as a boy. What might I not achieve with ninety of cavalry added to my troops?

"…and Nelson and his cavalry will accompany my column when we march into Laurel. My men will enter the valley *here*…" Lawrence traces a finger along the map laid out on the table before him, and I try to follow his route but the red tide of anger is rising behind my eyes and there is a roaring in my head that makes his words seem garbled and far away.

We had rendezvoused as planned with Lawrence's column and Nelson's Partisan Rangers in Greeneville and are now encamped. It was only when I reached Lawrence's tent that I discovered the change in what I had understood to be our orders. Once again, he has taken what should have been mine. I am thunderstruck and must summon all my will to keep my emotions under control.

"Did not General Heth's orders—" I begin, but Lawrence brushes my words aside.

"I take those orders to have been provisional," he says, without looking up from the map. "Now that my suspension is ended, I must resume my command." His finger moves along the inked lines of the map. "While Nelson and I begin our sweep at this point, you and your troops will enter the valley *here* at the other end, bottling up the Unionists, while we move from house to house in search of those who perpetrated the raid on Marshall. This time they'll not escape us."

I instruct my officers and especially my sergeants to be watchful on the coming march into North Carolina. The mountainous terrain and thick forests will tempt would-be deserters to slip away unseen. And the divided loyalties of East Tennessee—almost as bad as the Unionist nest for which we are bound—make it easy for those deserters to find a hiding place. I am pointed in telling my sergeants that Private Ramsey, who has no reason to love me and who is on familiar ground here, should be watched closely as I judge him most likely to run.

The 64th continues to suffer much from desertion. The men call it 'French leave' and say they *intend* to return after they have seen to their families' needs. Some few do return but there are many more that we will never see again—except perhaps, facing us on a battlefield.

Lawrence is to blame for much of this. He finds excuses for the men who run—they were conscripted; their enlistment term was extended; and when their wives send piteous letters bemoaning their state—food and firewood low, fields in need of plowing, little Billy sick—why then the men melt away into the woods, head for the ridgelines, and strike out for the miserable little hollows that spawned them. If *I* were in command, we would hunt them down and execute them as an example, but Lawrence merely marks present those whom he hopes will return and sends in a false report. Indeed, it was the revelation of this practice of his that brought about his recent suspension, that suspension of which I had hoped so much. If there were justice in this army, he would have been broke and I would be in command now.

The driving snow has hampered our advance, as has the knowledge that sniper fire can come from behind any rock or tree. The men have taken some slight injuries, and I myself had my hat knocked off by a ball from an unseen musket. But we have accounted for a round dozen of the traitors and our blood is up. Though frostbite has taken a severe toll, the men are eager for revenge, eager to—as I heard one corporal assert—"wipe every last one of these homegrown Yankees off the face of the earth."

The meager little farmsteads are set far apart, and it is a slow business to enter and search each one and to question the women—for men there are none, save for a doddering graybeard or two. And, to a woman, they vow they know nothing of any salt and that their men are away—in the army or hunting. We upend their paltry households but find no more than scant leavings of salt. Yet bushels and bushels were taken in the Marshall raid—and those bushels must be somewhere.

I am in the midst of interrogating a snaggle-toothed harridan, whom I would have taken to be sixty or more but for the child she held, snuffling and rooting, at her opulent breast. Hard-eyed and silent, she watched as my men tore apart her corn shuck tick then climbed into the cabin loft where they rummaged noisily for a time only to emerge, shaking their heads and munching on withered apples from the barrel they overturned in seeking the plundered salt. From upstairs come cries of children, wailing that the Secesh have stole their apples, and for a moment I see the hag's lips tremble.

I am about to press on with my questions when I hear the beat of hooves on the ground outside and the thump of boots at the door. I am surprised to see Lawrence, looking ravaged and as near to frantic as ever I have seen him. He jerks his head, motioning me outside.

"It was good luck that I saw your men as we came along. I'd sent word to your encampment but I may as well apprise you of the situation now. Word has come that my children are desperately ill. The message went first to Knoxville and has been some days in getting to me. I am on my way now to Marshall with a party of riders. Pray God I am not too late."

I say all the appropriate things about his children and assure him that I shall carry on here to the best of my abilities.

"Do that, Jim," he says, clasping my shoulder. "Root out those beasts. I will be back as soon as I can."

I walk with him to his horse and watch as he and his party clatter away across the hard-frozen ground. My heart lifts and before I turn back to the cabin, I call to one of the men standing guard to find a likely tree and to cut some rods, such as one uses on recalcitrant children. Now that I am in charge, I believe we can take sterner measures.

20.

~JUDITH SHELTON~

Shelton Laurel, North Carolina
January 1863

They bust into my cabin just after midday, and when I don't tell them nothing they want to hear, they put a rope around my neck and lead me outside like a dog, not even letting me get my shawl.

We have got used to seeing the Secesh soldiers from the 64th for they have been up and down the valley all along, thieving our food and trying to conscript our men, but they have never before offered to do violence to the women. Oh, there has been some ugly words whispered amongst some of them, but until now the ones in charge have scorned to let the common soldiers go on a rampage. Why, last year, the first time they come up the lane in search of Pete McCoy, Colonel Allen even lifted his hat to me, and I spoke to him sweet as sugar and said I had heared that Pete had lit out for West Virginia.

Back then, ol' Allen studied me for a time and then he said, "Sad times, Miz Shelton, when those who ought to be neighbors are enemies. I remember registering your deeds when your father passed. And I hope that someday I can serve you again. But just as I was bound to follow the law then, so am I now. Honor requires it. Good day to you, ma'am," he said and lifted his hat once more. But he sent his men to search my house and barn all the same.

That was last year. Today they are like a pack of wild animals. Instead of Colonel Allen there is another one in charge. It is Dr. Keith from Marshall—the same as saved the Norton boy's leg when he smashed it all to pieces falling out of a tree. Keith was reckoned a good man and a clever doctor but today it is as if a mad dog is looking from out his eyes.

He is sitting atop a tall bay that stomps and huffs a cloud then shakes its head to cast off the snow. Dr. Keith's hat and shoulders is covered with snow, but he sets like a rock and watches as they drag me across the icy yard to him.

"Another un that don't know nothing, Colonel Keith, sir," says the feller who has hold of the rope. He gives it a jerk and the rough hemp scratches at my bare neck.

"Very well," says Keith. "Bring her along."

I had thought to beg for mercy, to plead that I can't leave my young uns, but when I see the look in ol' Keith's eyes, I think it best not to mention them and give him ideas. I am suddenly afraid as I have never been before and can do naught but stumble after the feller that has the rope and pray that the young uns has the sense to stay where they are in the house and keep the fire going.

The ruts in the road has froze hard and make the going unsteady, especially as the feller holding the other end of the rope is stepping out like he is in a big hurry. When I trip and fall, he don't offer to help me up, just yanks on the rope till it cuts into my neck, and I scramble to my feet the best I can.

We look to be headed for Mary Shelton's cabin. Her man is off with the others and she not long out of childbed. Miz Unus is staying with her to help with the babe, and several of us has been taking it in turns to look in on them and do what we can. Mary has never been strong and this birth was a hard one, a long labor and a wrong way round britches baby at the end of it.

My hands are so cold I can't hardly feel them and my feet the same. I would wrap my hands in my skirt to warm them, but I dasn't let go of the rope lest it choke me. My eyes are watering and snot is running down my face. One of the soldiers who has kept close behind me, poking at my bottom with his rifle barrel to hurry me up, comes along side of me and lets out a hoot.

"Lord God, this un's a sight on earth. Crying like a baby and in sore need of a snot rag."

"I ain't crying," I say, and try to spit in his face but it only lands on his coat sleeve.

His face darkens. "I'll learn you manners, Union bitch," he growls. Then he hauls off and hits me a good lick across my face, and I fall again.

By the time we reach the familiar turning at the two big oaks, I am plumb give out. My neck and hands are chafed raw from the rope and my feet are blocks of ice. As I toil up the path to Mary Shelton's place, my heart is beating loud in my ears and the ragged sound of my own breathing is all I know. The flying snow is stinging my face, and it seems I have been walking forever.

I think of my children. If something happened to me, would Sol see to them? Would that wife of hisn take them in? Folks is mostly kind-hearted but ain't no one got the wherewithal to take on so many these days. Come what may though, I ain't going to tell these Rebs aught of where our men are or where the salt is. Better the children mourn a dead mother than live with the shame of one who betrayed her neighbors and her kin.

Through the drumming in my ears there comes the wail of a baby and the sound of a woman weeping, and for one crazy moment I think it is *my* baby and that it is me crying for having left hit mother-less. Then the soldier gives a sharp yank on the rope and I recollect myself.

"Step along, Miz Judy," says he. "Sounds like they're starting the play party without us."

There is a crowd of soldiers outside of Mary's cabin, milling about and making all kinds of ruckus. And then I see a big soldier toss a rope over the branch of a maple, and another soldier comes out of the cabin pulling along poor old Miz Unus who is eight-five if she's a day. She is trembling and can't hardly go.

"Boys," she calls out in her quavery, old woman's voice, "boys, what would your mothers say to see you treat an old woman so?"

One of the fellers looking on hollers out, "My mam is strong for the South and she'd say, 'Beat the truth outten that old hag and make her tell what went with the Confederate salt.'"

And there is hooting and hollering from some of them as Miz Unus is drug to the big maple and a noose put round her neck. I can see the tears running down her wrinkled old face and her lips all a-tremble as Keith rides up to where she stands.

He reaches out his riding whip and touches her cheek. "I'll wager that you're a church-going woman," he says, and Miz Unus looks up at him like she ain't sure what he is saying.

He has one eye shut and he prods at her again. "Well, am I correct?" he asks and Miz Unus nods her head and says something I can't make out. "And will you lie, forswear your immortal soul, to protect lawless thieves, men who not only stole from the government but who looted stores and homes?"

Miz Unus, she pinches her lips together and don't answer. Ol' Keith leans down. "Where are those men hiding?" he asks, real low and calm like he was passing the time of day. "And where is the salt?"

Miz Unus just shakes her head. Keith sets there on his horse, studying her for a minute. Her eyes is squinched shut now and her lips is moving but there ain't no sound. I reckon that she is praying.

At last Keith gives a wave of his hand and reins his horse around. "Carry on, Sergeant Jay," he says to the man holding the end of the rope that is over the limb. And as the horse trots away, the sergeant hauls on the rope till Miss Unus is pulled up to where her toes just barely touch the ground. Another man comes around the house with several long hickory rods in his hand and as he commences to thrash that poor old woman hanging there, her face turning blue and her feet skittering on the frozen ground, I think to myself that this is hell and these are its devils.

When they get done with Miz Unus, who is in sore straits but yet alive, thank God, they start on me. Having seen that little granny woman stand up to them and bear the pain and the fear and still not say nothing, I am so heartened that I almost laugh when the rope tightens on my neck. If she can bear it, I think, surely I can.

The whipping ain't so bad, though it tears through the cloth of my shirtwaist and leaves welts in my flesh. The hanging is the worst—having to stand on tippy toes to keep from choking and the muscles in my legs keep cramping up. I try standing on one foot to rest the other, but the rope tightens till I can't hardly breathe.

When they decide I ain't going to tell them nothing, the soldiers go into the house to warm themselves. They leave me hanging and Miz

Unus propped against the tree trunk. She had swooned when they took her down but I can see her bosom rise and fall, and I ain't much surprised when she opens one eye and whispers, "We done good, Judy girl. We'll hold out agin them sonsabitches, yes, we will."

And my heart lifts and I whisper back, "We'll go it, Miz Unus!"

But then there is a commotion in the cabin and one of the soldiers comes running out the door with a bundle in his hands. After him comes Mary Shelton, hair all tumbled down and howling, "Give me back my baby!"

The big sergeant is right behind her and he grabs her and holds her there just beyond the door. "Unwrap the brat and lay it in the snow," he hollers, and the soldier pulls the blanket offen the babe and lays it in a snow drift beside the woodpile.

"Now," says the sergeant to Mary, "the brat can lay there till it freezes, iffen you bitches don't tell where them damned outliers is."

It breaks my heart to see the babe's pale little legs kicking while it howls and flings its head from side to side looking for its mommy. Mary is babbling all sort of things but she don't know nothing to tell. Miz Unus probably knows but her lips are tight though tears is running down her face.

Mary is straining to get loose from the sergeant, and I can see that the babe's crying has made her milk let down for there are two big wet patches on her shirt front. The sergeant takes notice of this and an ugly smile spreads across his face. His filthy hands reach around Mary and he rips open her bodice. "Men, I got a notion to treat this piece like the dumb brute she is. I believe I'll milk her like a cow and ride her like a mule."

And with that the sergeant yanks her back inside the house. Most of the men are in the doorway but their eyes are turned on what is happening inside. I hear Mary scream and there is the sound of a slap and then the thump of the bedstead hitting against the wall. Some of the men in the doorway laugh, others turn away. The thumping goes on and then the sergeant hollers out, "Goddamn, she's so loose, a man might as well open the door and fuck down the road. Reckon I'll try the back door—" and there is a terrible, bubbling shriek, the sound of a fist hitting flesh, more thumping, and a cry like some kind of dying critter.

❧

I can't make out how long it is I been hanging here. Miz Unus is bunched up at the foot of the tree, either swooned or asleep. The baby's cries are getting weaker, like it, too, has give up thinking someone's coming to save it.

They are most of them in the cabin still except for a few that are searching the barn and outbuildings. Not a one of them even looks my way, but I can see that they all have that shame-faced look that a dog gets after he's been caught chasing cows.

I find myself wondering about them—most of them no more than boys. Is this their nature, to torment women and children? Or are they like dogs—mostly good on their own but bad to do slaughter in a pack? I have noticed a few looking troubled by all this—one young feller with a big black beard lit out for the barn when first they drug Miz Unus out and he ain't come back yet. Of course, there is some dogs and some men—like that sergeant—that is just eat up with meanness and the onliest cure for that is to knock them on the head or put a bullet in them.

"Judy, honey?" Miz Unus is whispering to me. "How're you holding out?" She is no more than a little heap of clothes there on the snowy ground but her sweet old face peers up at me and she tries to smile.

"I'm holding out, Miz Unus," I try to say, but I croak like a strangled toad frog and I doubt she can understand me. So I force my mouth into a grin and try to nod my head.

"Good girl," she says and scrabbles around trying to rise up. "Iffen I could get myself to my feet…"

Just then I see that black-bearded feller who's been hiding in the barn coming our way. He is looking left and right but there is no one but us to see. He slips up to the tree and starts in to untie the rope. As it slackens, I gulp in great deep breaths and feel the strain go off my legs.

"I best not let you loose," he says real low. "But I can give you some relief and likely they'll take it that the rope stretched."

He ties the rope back to where it is pulled taut—but now my heels are on the ground and I feel the salt tears snaking their way down my face.

He is gone before I can make a sign of thanks.

And just in time, for the rest of the soldiers come out of the cabin, all looking like men that have been on a spree and are feeling the worse for it. The big sergeant looks at me and narrows his eyes. I can tell he has a notion to do me like he done poor Mary, but then it seems the thought passes—likely he realizes he couldn't get hard again so soon. He shakes his head and hollers out for someone to let me down and tells the men they will make for their encampment.

When the rope is took from my neck, I set down on the ground with a bump. My legs won't hardly go but I got to see to the others.

Somehow or another, I get Miz Unus up and give her the baby to hold. She wraps it in her apron and holds it close to her bosom as I help her to hobble back to the house. I ain't right sure if the babe is dead or alive for it is awful quiet, but just holding the little thing seems to give Miz Unus the strength to move. The snow is setting in harder now and stepping into the cabin out of the wind heartens me right much. Then I see Mary Shelton.

She is face down on the bed tick, her skirts flung up and her arms stretched out like she is crucified. There is blood and shit smeared on her legs and all under her. I help Miz Unus to set down by the fireplace where one little log is flickering and tell her to tend the baby whilst I see to Mary.

"They hung me and Miz Unus and beat us too but they used Mary the worst."

I tell Marthy and her mother something of what happened, leaving out the ugliest parts. "Still, I left them all in tolerable shape," I tell them. "Miz Unus was limping round making catnip tea for Mary and setting things to rights. And the babe was reasonable peart once it got to suck a while—it fell asleep in Mary's arms."

Kate White tells me of the trials others has borne. They had got word of Polly Norton, tied in the snow while her babe cried in the cabin and the soldiers hung up little Enoch with a pair of his pa's overalls. Then the soldiers had come this morning while Kate and Marthy was over to the Moores. They had whipped Sally Moore till her back bled and they had hung Marthy like they done me and Miz

Unus. Marthy looks at me and makes a little half of a smile. She passes her fingers across her lips as to say she didn't tell them nothing. I am glad the child can make a joke after such treatment and I reach over and hug her.

Kate goes on. "Sally Moore told them over and over that Marthy couldn't talk, that she hadn't never talked in her life, and that they was wasting their time—even if she had knowed anything which none of us did anyway. Then ol' Keith come riding up, and Sally ran to his horse and grabbed his stirrup and begged him to spare the girl. When he finally understood that she couldn't talk a lick, he scowled and called out to his men, 'Cut her down; the girl's an idiot.'"

Kate grabs Marthy's hand and squeezes it. "Which you ain't no idiot but I reckon Sally weren't inclined to set the colonel straight."

"We have come through a hard time," I say. "Pray God things don't get worser."

"Amen," says Kate, and she asks me to take a look at little Josie who has been feeling out of sorts.

"She's here in the trundle with her dolly." Kate lays back the blankets to show me the little girl, one arm around her china doll and the other hand at her face so she can suck her thumb. Her cheeks are bright pink against the doll's blue dress, and when I lift her little shirt, I see the rash.

21.

~POLLY ALLEN~

Marshall, North Carolina
January 1863

I think I went a little mad when Rommie died. Had had it not been for brave little Annie and my stalwart Juliann, I should have flung myself in the icy, racing river and found a kind of peace in ceasing to be. As I tended my sweet Maggie, who was, minute by minute, loosing her hold on life, my rage swelled and I lifted my voice to heaven, calling down retribution on the Laurelites whose theft of my sick children's bedclothes must surely have worsened their state. When Juliann and I washed Rommie and dressed him for that last long sleep, I knelt by the bed in the cold chamber where my darling boy lay and prayed aloud that the stolen bedclothes would carry contagion to the children in the Laurels. And then I was seized by a fit of crazed laughing that would not stop.

Juliann brought catnip tea which I dashed from her hand and, all afraid for my safety, she ran in search of help. But it was when Annie, who had, as Margaret said, "turned the corner," rose from her bed and tottered into the cold chamber to fling her arms around me, crying, "Mama, please, don't!" that I returned to my senses and to my duty. Poor little girl, she has so much to bear.

By the time Juliann returned with Margaret at her side, I was calmer and myself again. No, not myself, only a diminished portion of who I was. There was a vacancy in my heart that will never be filled, no matter how many more children I may bear.

Margaret clucked over me and pulled a brown bottle from her basket. "Come, Polly, and lie down. A messenger is on his way to Colonel Allen and nothing need be done till he arrives. I have just been to change the dressings on your brother John's arm—he does very well and wanted to come to you but I forbade him. Juliann and I will see to Annie and little Maggie; you must rest," and so saying, she poured out a dose of laudanum.

I made some feeble protest but exhaustion overcame me and with a last kiss on Rommie's cold brow, I allowed Margaret to dose me and lead me from the chamber to my bed. I scarcely remember more than that the bed seemed to rise up to meet me—and then there were dreams filled with wanderings through dark meadows in search of lost things—a pincushion, a blanket, a child's blue dress, a china doll.

Juliann shook me awake with the welcome news that Lawrence had come at last. "He's in with little Maggie," she said, her voice breaking, and I could see through my sleep-bleared eyes that her face was streaked with tears. "He says you best come quick."

Maggie breathed her last in my arms, her father holding one little hand. I could hardly fathom how I might bear such double loss but there was no time, no time for anything but to make her ready. Make her ready so that she and Rommie could be buried at once and Lawrence might return to his accursed war.

Margaret drew Lawrence aside and I heard busy whispering and the word *remembrance*. Lawrence shook his head but Margaret persevered and finally he nodded and she hurried out. I still held my baby—she was warm yet and her angel face was peaceful at last.

"Sweetheart," said Lawrence, touching my cheek. "Margaret has made a suggestion…"

We have no portraits of the children. It had been our intention to have their likenesses taken, all three together, but the tumult of war intervened. Now it seems that a traveling photographer is in town, waiting out the worst of the winter weather, and Margaret has prevailed upon him to bring his apparatus to our parlor. I am too numb with grief to make any objection to what seems a grisly business and perhaps in time I shall be glad of the picture. I find my Maggie's pretty blue dress, one that escaped the clutches of the Laurelites as it was in my sewing basket waiting to have its hem let down.

My hands tremble and the tears fall. *No need now to let it down; she will never grow taller.* I hear the sound of voices in the parlor and Lawrence comes into the room. Laying a gentle hand on my shoulder, he says softly, "Polly, sweetheart, the photographer is here. I will carry Rommie to the parlor; will you bring Maggie?"

I nod and take up my babe. Her little body, cool and stiffening now, seems heavier than in life. I clasp her to my bosom as if to warm her and follow Lawrence. Rommie's dangling stockinged feet break my heart again. The Laurelites stole his new boots and he will have his likeness taken without them.

A wooden box on three legs stands in the parlor with a shabby, red-nosed, unctuous man at its side. "Colonel, Madam, my deepest condolences on your loss." He bows and comes forward, wringing his hands as though he were washing them. "May I commend your fortitude as well as your forward thinking in choosing to immortalize your beloved children in this manner. It was Providence, no doubt, that stranded me here in the hotel just across the road. Now, sir, if you will position the little boy here in this armchair—just so, prop him in the corner, and then the little one next to him—yes, very nice, very natural."

He catches sight of Annie, watching from her perch halfway down the stairs. "Would you not wish to have all your children together in this portrait? The little girl could stand just beside the chair."

And gentle Annie allows herself to be positioned with her hand on the back of the chair—she shrank from holding Rommie's hand as the photographer had suggested.

He steps back and appraises the scene. "Perhaps a special toy for each child—to enhance the illusion of life?"

The illusion of life. Those words catch in my mind and repeat, over and over, while Lawrence sends Juliann in search of Rommie's wooden sword and something for Annie and Maggie. What has my life been but an illusion? The illusion of a safe and happy home in a peaceful land—the illusion of a husband always by my side—the illusion that I am a Christian woman, bound to forgive those who sin against me. I gaze at my children, dead and living, and through the blur of rising tears, they seem all the same—all phantoms of illusion.

At last the sword is found and Lawrence wraps Rommie's stiff fingers around it and places it across his knees. Juliann, tears streaming, tucks a much-loved, worn cloth rabbit under Maggie's little arm, hands Annie her doll, then darts into the kitchen, trying to stifle her sobs.

"But where is Annie's china doll—the one I gave her? The blue creature?" Lawrence is glaring at the red-clad doll Annie is holding.

"The bad men took her, Papa," says Annie, her voice quavering. "Aunt Margaret gave me this one. Her name is Lorena Lee and—"

The photographer interrupts. "The little boy's shoes?" When Lawrence explains the theft of the boots, the photographer nods wisely. "Perhaps we might drape a shawl—"

It is I who interrupt, surprised at my own ferocity. "No! No shawl! Let his stockinged feet be a reminder of what those devils did!"

And the crazed laughter begins again, broken by sobs, till Juliann leads me away to recover myself.

The photographer is wrestling his apparatus out of the door as Mr. Gudger, who serves as Marshall's undertaker, arrives. He is come to tell us that all is ready for the burial. His men have managed to hack out a grave by dint of keeping a fire burning half a day to thaw the frozen ground and the preacher is waiting.

"No, not yet," I cry, tugging at my husband's arm. "Let me keep them here another day, only a day."

But Lawrence is impatient to be gone, to continue the work in the Laurels of capturing the men responsible for the raid, the men responsible for the death of our children. We both have no doubt that the terror of the incident: the men rampaging through the sick room, tearing the blankets from the children's suffering bodies, stealing their clothes and even their toys was surely the cause of their death, weakened as they were by the fever.

"The Laurelites shall pay for this," Lawrence declares. "We will hunt them down like the animals they are. Honor will be satisfied and justice will be done." His face is set in a pale mask of anger and I draw back, a little afraid of this husband of mine who seems utterly transformed with rage. He does not notice my shrinking away but bids the undertaker bring in the coffin and make all ready.

Because of the haste, my darlings are laid to rest in one coffin. Rommie's arm is circled protectively around Little Maggie and his wooden sword is at his side. For all time.

Life is the illusion. Only death is certain.

22.

~MARTHY WHITE~

Shelton Laurel, North Carolina
January 1863

I reach Miz Judy's house as the sun is dipping behind the mountains. The snow has laid and the last low rays of light touch the white-topped mountains, turning them to pink and gold against the clearing sky where the clouds is piled up like purple and gold pillows. I stand on the porch watching, all amazed that there is still such beauty in a world of meanness. My neck is sore yet from the rope and the welts on my back still pain me, but I rejoice to see there is something the damned Rebs couldn't harm.

Judy must have heard me knocking the snow from my boots for the door opens and she bids me come in and warm myself. I have come after some more balm to sooth little Josie's rash. She is much better, which is a mercy, for two of the Norton children who took the fever have died. Judy is telling me what is in the balm and how she makes it when we hear the sound of hooves outside. Peeking through the window, I see the Secesh soldiers again and that big Sergeant Jay, the one who used Mary Shelton so bad. My heart sinks and I start in to trembling, wondering will they begin on us again. Miz Judy motions me to get under the bed but I shake my head *no*—I will try to be as brave as her and all the rest, no matter what.

There is a stomping of boots outside and the door busts open. The big sergeant is standing there, and he tells Judy that they are going to use her house to hold some prisoners overnight.

"What prisoners are you talking about?" says she.

"Why, some of the black scoundrels who did the mischief in Marshall," he says and jerks his head at the open door.

Outside six Secesh soldiers, rifle guns at the ready, are guarding a bunch of our men who are standing there with their hands tied behind their backs, looking cold and tired. I recognize them all: a bunch of Sheltons—William and Azariah and Roderick and Old David—along with Halen and Henry Moore. I see Jim Metcalf and Ellison King crowded up next to Joe Woods and the Chandler boy—I think his name is Jasper. In the back of the gang stands Johnny Norton, shivering and looking scairt to death, and behind him I am surprised to see Pete McCoy who is grinning like this is all a joke. And then I see Davy's father and his big brother and I can't hardly catch my breath.

Judy goes to the door and looks out. "What are youns doing with these fellers and most of them little more than boys or men not able to fight? Ain't none of 'em had ary thing to do with taking the salt. It was all Union soldiers what rode into Marshall that night."

The big sergeant rounds on her, snarling like an angry dog. "I can tell you this, you home-grown Yankee bitch; some of these men is deserters: King and Wood there and them two Mooreses all run from the 64th—run like the cowards that they are. They'll pay for it, whether they was part of the thieving or no."

Judy starts to say something sharp and the sergeant lifts his arm, like he is meaning to backhand her, but just then an officer rides up and the sergeant thinks the better of it. He tells her and me to get out of the cabin but Judy bows up and refuses.

"I got sick young uns here, up in the loft. Me and Marthy'll stay here and fix some vittles for the prisoners."

The officer is Colonel Allen. Though he's been up and down this valley for several years now, I almost don't recognize him; he is so worn and old. He looks over at the group of prisoners then calls out, "Sergeant Jay, provide those women with meal and salt pork for the prisoners. They'll need their strength to walk to Tennessee tomorrow. Post your men all around the cabin and be ready to march in the morning with Colonel Keith."

The prisoners file into the cabin followed by two of the soldiers with their rifles. Some of our men are shame-faced at having been took up; others is making a bold show of it. Most of them move toward the fire but old David speaks up, saying he needs to piss and wondering which one of the Secesh wants to hold his pecker for him. "For unless you untie our hands, youns are going to be as busy as a pack of nursemaids, spoon-feeding us and tending to our needs."

Sergeant Jay looks black and opens his mouth to say something but Colonel Allen, who has left his horse and is standing in the doorway looking round the room, cuts him off. "Untie the prisoners. Let them be escorted out by a guard, one by one as necessity dictates. With armed guards inside and out, there's no need to keep them bound, Sergeant."

And he is gone, closing the door behind him. The sergeant stands there scowling for a minute then orders one of the soldiers to untie the prisoners. "And you, Carter," he says, nodding to another, "take this one out to piss. Shoot his pecker off if he offers to run."

When they return, behind them is another soldier, herding two more prisoners into the house. Their hats are pulled down low and knitted comforters are wrapped around their faces till I can't tell who they are.

"We picked up these two coming down out of the woods. Desperate men, the both of them," the new soldier says and gives the smaller one a kick that sends him sprawling to the floor.

His hat falls off and the comforter drops away from his face. He looks up and his beautiful blue eyes meet mine.

I start for him but Judy's hand clamps like iron on my arm. "Marthy, let's you and me go to the spring for water. With all this bunch to make mush and corn pone for, we're going to need us a-plenty." And before I can even look at Davy again, she has picked up the buckets and pulled me out the door. As the buckets are filling under the little stream of water, Judy talks fierce and low to me so the sentries near the house can't hear.

"Marthy, don't let on nothing of your feelings for Davy or them guards will watch you extra close. You do like I say and maybe we can help him and some of them to get away."

And she tells me her plan.

By the time the prisoners are all fed and laying down to sleep, the inside guards is yawning too. That was a part of Judy's plan. She made a great show of hiding a jug under her apron and slipping over to slide it way back beneath the bed.

"Oh, ho," called out one of the guards, "what do you reckon Miz

Judy is trying to hide?" and he stepped to the bedstead, knelt down, and used his rifle to scoot the half-full jug to where he could reach it. He pulled out the corn cob stopper and took a sniff, then a big smile spread across his ugly face.

"I believe we'll have to requisition this," said he to the other guard, "that is, oncet I take a sup and make certain sure of what it is we got here." And they went to passing the jug back and forth and guzzling, and all the while Miz Judy giving them down the road for stealing her likker.

Now they have drunk enough to put them into a friendlier frame of mind, and Judy asks is it all right if we pass among the prisoners and tend to their wounds, for several of them had been knocked about right much. The guard with the jug motions to her to go ahead and sets hisself next to the fireplace. He lays his rifle across his knees and upends the jug and swallows. I have never seen no one hide that much likker in one go and I'm not surprised when his head begins to nod.

I recognize the other guard, the one at the door, by his big black beard; Miz Judy says he is the feller who made hisself scarce when all the whipping and hatefulness was going on but then sneaked back later and loosened the rope that tied her.

Me and Judy take the balm and go from prisoner to prisoner, dabbing the good-smelling grease on cuts and bruises but mainly trying to hearten them some. Azariah Shelton whispers he believes they will be taken to Tennessee for a trial and another says he thought it would be to Marshall. Several of them, who was caught whilst out hunting, ask Judy to get word to their wives or mothers and say what had happened and that they would be all right.

When we get to Davy and his daddy, who are laying next to the bedstead, my eyes start to leak and I grab his hand, right there in front of everyone. Judy looks around at the two guards but the one has nodded off and Black Beard at the door is looking at something shiny dangling from his hand.

"Marthy," Judy whispers, "just you stand here aside of me. Make your skirts wide so's them two can't see, and Davy, you slide right under the bedstead. Get all the way to the wall. It might could be a chance."

I nod and beg him with my eyes to do this, but Davy says he ain't going to hide; he is going to stay with his father. "I reckon they won't go hard on us oncet they realize we wasn't a part of that raid. And if they do put us in prison for a spell, why, I can bear it. But I'll be back, Marthy, to see to the building of our cabin; don't you forget that."

Johnny Norton, who is laying nigh the bed whispers that if Davy don't want to take the hiding place, he will, and under he slides, quick as a blacksnake pouring down a mouse hole.

Judy grabs my arm and pulls me toward the ladder to the loft. "We can't do nothing more, Marthy, honey," she says in my ear, and we climb up. Judy lays down on a pallet with her least uns and is asleep almost at once, but I stretch out on the floor near the edge. There is a little railing there, but I can look down into the room and in the flickering light of the fire, I see them all—prisoners sprawled across the floor and guards in their places, all quiet, some sleeping. Davy is on his side looking up at me, and he seems so near I can most feel his breath on my face and hear his heart beating in time with mine. We might almost be alone, laying together and gazing into each other's eyes.

This is our wedding night. The thought comes out of nowhere and I shake my head *no.* I look again and Davy's eyes is closed. There is a little smile on his half-open mouth and I wonder is he dreaming of me. I close my eyes, hoping to have that same dream and am drifting off when a metal *chink* pulls me out of sleep. Looking down I see the black-bearded guard leaning to pick something off the floor. The firelight glints on a silver chain with what looks like a little locket hanging from it. The guard puts the chain around his neck and then he lifts the little locket to his lips before tucking it inside of his shirt.

My eyes are closing and I am sinking back into my dream of Davy and me and our cabin that is to come. But in the strange way of dreams, Davy has grown a big black beard and instead of a ring, I am wearing a silver locket.

23.

~SIMEON RAMSEY~

Shelton Laurel, North Carolina
January 19, 1863

"Up and out! Up and out!"

I startle awake and look outside to see that Colonel Keith and most of Captain Nelson's cavalry is back. It ain't even daybreak, and ol' Keith is hollering that we must get the prisoners up and be on the move at once. Shelt Ray, who was guarding the house with me and had put down most of that demi-john, is snoring hard but I am able to rouse him afore the sergeant comes inside. The prisoners is getting to their feet and milling around, and the woman named Judy is giving each of them a little pone of cornbread. She gives me and Shelt each one too. The girl, the one they called an idiot, is staying close to that young boy and his daddy. She is crying and trying not to let the boy see.

We hustle the prisoners outside and the colonel is in such a hellfire hurry that he don't even take a count. Which is a good thing for no one misses that boy I saw hide under the bed nor that grinning feller Shelt took out to piss when everyone else was asleep. The feller had sidled up to Shelt, who was drunk as an owl by that time, and the two of them had whispered back and forth a considerable while. I let on to be dozing but my eyes was only half shut. And what I saw was the two of them going out and Shelt coming back by hisself a quarter of an hour later. Now I don't know what went on out there. Maybe him and Shelt struck a deal. Or maybe that feller run off and Shelt didn't raise an alarm for fear of the sergeant seeing how drunk he was and that he had forgot his rifle.

Everwhat it was, it didn't matter none to me. I seen that the colonel was out for blood and that he didn't care a lick iffen we got the ones who stole the salt or not, long as we had a gang of the Laurelites to

160

take to trial. Old and young, lame and halt, he had us take up any that we saw. So iffen two get away, that is two less I need feel guilty for.

The Lord knows, I feel bad enough already after seeing the way them women and that idiot girl was treated. I had to slip away and vomit up my breakfast whilst they was tormenting that poor old woman. Even worser was what the sergeant and the others did in that cabin. It don't bear thinking on. And some of these was men I'd messed with or shared a blanket with. It was like seeing a pet dog run mad.

I have made up my mind that during the march to Tennessee, I will find my chance to slip away. I know these parts right well and I can make my way to Maryville and Cora. Maybe her family will hide me like they do the runaway slaves. Seems to me, I'm in as bad case as any slave ever was. Though we ain't fought in no big battles or such, in the past few days I have seen how war makes devils of some men. I want no more part of it.

It is coming on to snow right hard as we set off down the lane and take the turn that will lead us to the gap and the road to Knoxville. A few women run after us, wanting to catch sight of their menfolk, maybe speak a word, but the colonel gives orders that they must not follow us and when Sergeant Jay fires a shot that kicks up the snow and dirt at the feet of one of them, they fall back. As we march on, I think I make out a shape slipping along amongst the trees and laurels above the road but the snow makes it hard to tell for sure.

The prisoners is at the front, cavalry men on either side, and they are stepping along at a right smart pace. Not far off the road I see a barn, smoldering and black against the snow, and what is left of three cows laying stiff in the nearby field in the midst of bloody snow. The feller marching next to me whispers that there was some burning and slaughter done yesterday when the women wouldn't tell where the men was.

We have gone the better part of two miles when Sergeant Jay calls out an order and our column turns off the main road to a little trail. I am puzzled, for this ain't the road to Knoxville. We march a little farther and the sergeant calls a halt near a dry branch, a kind of shallow ravine. I am holding back a grin for I figure Jay or ol' Keith has got hisself turned about somehow and now we will have to backtrack.

Everwhat it is, we are all happy for the rest and, standing easy, I reach for the pone of cornbread the woman pressed into my hand afore we left the cabin. I take a little bite and it tastes like home. I am trying to decide whether to eat the whole thing now or save some for later, when I see the prisoners being marched to stand beside the little ravine. Then Sergeant Jay passes down the column, calling out one after another of us and I am the sixth to be called.

He forms us into a squad and marches us over and lines us up at attention, not ten paces from the prisoners. Colonel Keith is setting on his horse a little ways off, watching all this with a stony cold face. He raises his hand and Sergeant Jay motions five of the prisoners apart and tells them to kneel there at the edge of the ravine. They are beginning to look from side to side, all wide-eyed, and I see the same look dawning on their faces that comes to a beast being led to the slaughter.

Our squad is put at *Port Arms* and then at *Ready,* our rifles aimed at the prisoners. I tell myself this ain't nothing but more of the colonel's meanness, like he pretended to hang them women. He is having him a mock execution, wanting to scare the Laurelites till they shit their britches.

One of the kneeling prisoners, a white-haired old man, holds out his hands all a-tremble and hollers, "For God's sake, men, you ain't going to shoot us?"

He looks over to the colonel who makes no sign. The poor old man clasps his hands together and calls out in a piteous voice, "If you're going to murder us, give us at least time to pray!"

"There is no time," says Keith, in a voice I hardly recognize. If the devil hisself was to speak, I reckon it would sound the same. "Sergeant Jay," Keith says, "you may proceed."

The sergeant is enjoying this. He stiffens, raises one arm, and calls out the *Ready.* We have our rifles to our shoulders and I cut my eyes to the feller beside me. His face is sickly white and his lips are pressed tight together.

"Aim," cries the sergeant, and our whole line of rifles wavers then steadies. Most of the prisoners have their hands over their faces and I wonder are they praying or are they trying to hide from the rifle fire. I can see the colonel from out the corner of my eye and I am waiting for him to call this off and let us get back on the way to Tennessee.

But he don't utter a word, just sets there watching.

"Fire!" shouts the sergeant, slicing his hand down through the icy air.

And the whole line of us stands there frozen. It's one thing to kill a man when he's shooting at you. It's right awkward when he is kneeling on the ground before you, praying or begging for mercy. A many of these prisoners were neighbors of some of the men of the 64th and some was members of Company A before they ran.

One of the deserters calls out, "Shelt Ray, Sol Carter, can youns shoot your old comrades in cold blood?"

At this, Colonel Keith pulls his side arm and points it our way, sweeping it back and forth. "By God," he shouts, "fire or be fired on, damn you all. Fire or join the prisoners."

And there is a ragged burst of shots. I pull my trigger but aim high, not able to do this terrible thing. Four of the prisoners fall dead, clean shots to their heads or hearts. They are the lucky ones for the feller who called out to his friends in the firing squad is gut shot, thrashing and howling on the ground with blood and foulness pouring from his belly. He lays there screaming till Sergeant Jay finishes him off with a bullet to the head.

Shelt Ray is bent over vomiting, but the sergeant makes him stand back in the line and five more prisoners is brought over. They have a faraway look in their eyes and are as quiet as if they was already dead when they line up before us. The blue-eyed boy is there, supporting a limping man. He looks at the dead men laying at the edge of the ravine and lets out a sob. "Youns have killed my father and my brother," he says, trying to deepen his voice and speak steady, and it seems his blue eyes is boring into mine alone. "You shot my father in the face. Please, boys, don't shoot me in the face," he begs as the sergeant pushes him onto his knees.

Once again comes the order to fire and once again I aim high. And once again four men fall dead. But not the blue-eyed boy. He is shot in both arms and he looks down all amazed from one to the other. One hangs limp with a splinter of bone showing where his jacket sleeve is torn and bloody. The boy raises up the other arm, calling out for mercy.

"Youns have killed my father and brother," he cries again, taking ragged, gasping breaths. "And shot me in both arms." He is fighting for his breath and tries to wipe away the tears and snot running down his face. "But I will forgive youns all this. I can get well." He turns that blue stare on each of us in the firing squad, then looks over to where the colonel sets atop his horse. The boy's voice cracks as he calls out, "Please, let me go home to my mother and sisters."

The words are hardly out before the sergeant shouts, "Fire!" and the boy's body jerks and collapses. He is hit in the arms again and in the legs and both shoulders. He lays on his side, shuddering and screaming. There is bloody spittle coming from his mouth. I see Keith looking at me particular and realize that I am the only one that ain't fired yet. And I take careful aim and squeeze the trigger.

After that, the last three men die quick and clean and the firing squad is dismissed, Shelt is vomiting again and I feel like I'm about to do the same. Six privates what weren't a part of the firing squad are set to heaving the dead into the shallow ravine. They grab the bodies hand and foot and swing them over the edge where they land all of a heap, like so many broken dolls. My eyes light on a bright spray of blood that has made a fan shape in one bit of clean snow that ain't yet been tromped on.

Colonel Keith gives the order for us to cover the bodies and we set in to scraping up snow and brush and what little dirt we can. He tells the sergeant to carry on, then reins his horse around to move down the trail back to the main road.

The ground is hard froze and we can't make no headway covering the awful pile of corpses. Then Sergeant Jay jumps right atop the heap and begins to jig about, slapping his hands agin his cheeks, his chest, and his legs. We stand all amazed as he sings out, "Pat Juba for me, boys, while I dance the damned scoundrels down to and through hell!"

And the crazy look on his face and the slapping of his hands and the dull sound of his boots thumping on the helpless bodies tell me that I am already in hell, watching one of the demons a-capering.

24.

~JUDITH SHELTON~

Shelton Laurel, North Carolina
January 1863

As soon as all the soldiers has marched away down the lane with our men, my first care is to get Johnny Norton out from under the bedstead and bid him to slip home to his mam. Having just buried two young uns who took the scarlet fever, she is in bitter need of some good news. The Lord knows, there's little enough of that for us these days. I tell Marthy to come in and get the ointment for her sister, then hurry home to let her mama know she is all right.

She don't say nothing, just stands there staring down the road. Watching her sweetheart Davy being marched off to prison has hit her awful hard, and I start to say something but then I hear one of the young uns set in to wailing and hurry back inside.

Back in the cabin, my gang is peeking wide-eyed over the edge of the loft, and Linnie, all teary, wails that Frank told her ol' Keith would get her if she wasn't careful. I reckon I scared them all right much when I told them to stay put till I give the word, for the soldiers might come back.

"The Secesh is all gone," I say, trying to sound easy in my mind. "You rascals come down and get youns some breakfast." And they scamper down the ladder, Ellender helping little Armp and all the rest as nimble and frisky as a passel of squirrels.

I go over to the bedstead and whistle. "You, too, Johnny. They never missed you. But sooner or later someone's like to make a count and you'd best not be here was they to come looking."

Johnny mumbles something and I lean down to hear what it is he's saying. The poor young un has pissed his britches and don't want my girls to see. Telling him to stay put, I send Ellender and Linnie to the spring for water. Then I go find an old tattered quilt he can wrap around himself. I give him a pone of cornbread and tell him to be careful and go through the woods, not by the road. It is not till he has gone and I have had a minute to see what's what that I wonder why Marthy ain't come back in and got the ointment. I look on the porch but she is gone. Her footprints is in the snow, heading for the woods that run along the road. I puzzle over why she has taken that way instead of the quicker path she usually follows, but then a commotion breaks out amongst the young uns in the house and I go back in.

When things is quiet once more, I get the little tin of ointment and tell Dan'l to take it over to Marthy's folks and make them acquainted with what all has passed. They will have seen that Marthy is in a state, but the poor thing won't be able to tell them what was the way of things here last night. I warn Dan'l to be careful and hide if he hears the soldiers coming back. He is only eleven but big for his age. I can't help but worry—Davy Shelton is only thirteen and they took him.

Frank and Little Sol go out to bring in more firewood and I set in to sweeping out the cabin of all the mess that got tracked in last night. I think about the men who were taken and wonder how their families will make it without them. Like I do, I reckon.

The snow has begun again and the fierce wind is driving it sideways. I hope that Dan'l is either staying safe at the Whites or that he is almost home. This is the kind of blinding snow that can get a body turned around iffen he ain't careful. *He'll be all right*, I tell myself, *the boy has good sense.*

I have stepped out for the third time to look up the path through the woods when here he comes, gasping for breath and fair covered with snow. He hits the porch and shakes like a dog, then stomps his boots to loose the snow before coming inside.

Getting right up nigh the fireplace, he takes a minute to catch his breath and warm his hands which are bright red with the cold. Then he starts in with his tale. He is the most long-winded of any of my young uns and I set myself down to listen.

"Mommy, when I got there Marthy weren't come home and Miz White was just setting out to look for her. I told her how come Marthy to stay the night with us, and I told 'bout the soldiers and the prisoners and Davy marching off, for everyone knows them two are sweet on one another, and I told her we thought Marthy had gone home, and I give Miz White the ointment like you said, and she said praise the Lord, Josie is doing good and—"

"Whoa up, Dan'l," I interrupt before he gets into more about Josie, "You say Marthy weren't there?" My heart sinks, fearful for the girl. "Did Miz White—"

"I'm a-trying to tell you, Mommy, Miz White was just going to look for her and she said that whenever Marthy was troubled, she would sometimes go up to the barn loft and hide herself in the hay. 'I reckon I ought to take a look there first,' said she, and I said I would go look for her and she said—"

"Son, don't tell me what all ever one said. Did you find Marthy?"

"I did, Mommy, just like Miz White said, she was all burrowed down in the hay, curled up like a baby rabbit. But she was shaking like one thing and wouldn't pay no attention when I called her name. Then Miz White clumb up the ladder and made her sit up, and the two of us got her back down the ladder and into the house. Miz White put her on the bed and pulled off her boots. Her feet was white as snow, and Miz White took two taters from where they was roasting in the ashes and she wrapped them in a cloth and put them by Marthy's feet to warm them. Then she made Marthy drink some catnip tea with honey and she covered her with quilts and told her to close her eyes and sleep. After a while, Marthy wasn't shaking so bad, and Miz White just sat by her side, a-stroking her hair till Marthy dropped off to sleep—"

I wonder what made the young un to lay out in the bitter cold barn like that. Wanted to grieve in private for her sweetheart that was taken away, I reckon. I thank Dan'l for making the trip and for helping Kate White. Tomorrow, if nothing don't happen, I will go over to the Whites myself and see how Marthy is doing and have a look at little Josie.

❧

I have just set out the next morning when Marthy appears on the trail. She looks plumb crazy, her mouth open and her eyes wild and red-rimmed. I start to say some words of comfort but she grabs at my hand and motions at me to come with her. "Now, Marthy," I say, "just you come in the house and get warm." But she will have none of it and keeps tugging at my hand. She is past listening to me so I holler at Ellender to mind the others and I follow as Marthy pulls me along the lane to the main road. We are following the way the soldiers took, with me wondering where we are going and why.

"Honey," I say to her, "I don't see what good we can do. Davy and them are long gone, likely in Tennessee by now."

At that her mouth opens, as if she would say something but of course she don't; she just shakes her head *no* and *no* and *no* then points down the road and keeps dragging me on.

We have gone the better part of two miles when I see the crows rising, like black ashes flying up from a fire. They wheel about, stark against the gray sky, and drop back down behind the trees. *They have been at something,* I think, *some carrion, a deer or such, and something else has scared them off.*

Marthy don't have to pull on me no more. I am fearful of what lays ahead but know that I must keep going. She leads me up a little side trail, in the direction of where the crows landed.

I hear the squealing and grunting of the hogs before ever I see them. Quite a few folks has let their hogs run loose, not having aught to feed them, and they have gone most wild. I find stout sticks for me and Marthy in case of need and we follow along the little trail. Marthy is running now, making *uh, uh* sounds as she breathes. She is even more crazed-looking, her hair flying wild around her face and her mouth still open like she was screaming.

Up ahead there is a cleared field and a gang of hogs, black and red ones mostly, rooting at something in the shallow ravine at the edge of the field. Some are squealing and fighting, trying to run the others off, while others is busy snorting and gulping and eating fast as they can. The bare branches of the trees on all sides is full of crows, like bitter black fruit, and they are scolding the hogs. I take a closer look at the snowy ravine and the frozen shapes the hogs is tearing at.

An ugly, old black boar with mean long tushes looks up at me, then puts his head back down and takes ahold of something. He goes to worrying and slavering over it, and all at once I see that it is an arm with the fingers gone from the hand.

I let out a banshee shriek and go to feeling with my boots in the snow, hoping to find a rock to fling at the hogs. I find a big un and hit the black boar a good lick on the flank. He squeals and skips away. Marthy is waving her stick at the hogs but they pay her no mind. Then I see a jumble of rocks at the side of the ravine, rocks someone has cleared from the field and piled there. Me and Marthy take hold and rock them hogs till every last one runs back into the woods. And now we see it all.

It is our men, shot and flung in this shallow place like they was of no more account than varmints. I can see that some dirt was throwed on them, but it didn't take the hogs long to root through it and go at them.

Joe Woods, Jasper Chandler, the Mooreses, and all the Sheltons— eight, nine, ten, eleven, twelve, and thirteen. They are all there. Frozen stiff and gnawed bloody in places. All that talk of a trial in Knoxville was a lie, and the goddamned Secesh have kilt our men in cold blood. I feel swimmie-headed for a minute and want to sit down but we ain't got time for that now. We have got to get our men out of here and to a proper burial.

Before I can stop her, Marthy is clambering down the side of the ditch, making for what is left of Davy. He is laying there, half-under Halen Moore, but his snow-covered face is clear and I can see that the crows have taken his eyes. Marthy kneels in the snow beside him and strokes his hair and his cheeks. I am in fear for her reason—if only she could cry out.

"Marthy," I call to her. "We have to go get help to move these bodies off to where we can bury them." She don't look up, just goes on running her hands over the cold ruined face.

"Marthy." I clamber down to where she is, tripping over my dead neighbors to reach her. "Marthy, you have to come with me. Them hogs will be back afore long, and one person ain't enough to scare them away. You know how dangerous a hog can be—you come with me now, Marthy."

She lets me lead her away but it is almost as if she is a corpse herself, stumbling along silent and stiff and cold beside me. The sorrow and the woe of it all is most too much for both of us but we keep on.

As we start round a bend, I hear a cawing and look back to see the crows swooping down.

☙

The Franklins still have their ox, thank God, and it is with old Patch and the Norton's sled that Rock Franklin, me and Frank and Marthy, and the few other able ones I could find haul the bodies from the ditch and straighten them out best we can. I wish that we could spare quilts or blankets to wrap them decent, but the living need every covering there is in this cold winter. We load the corpses like so much cordwood on the sled and scrape through the snow back to the ridge near my place. It takes three trips, and when we come back for the last load, the hogs have been at the bodies again and one of the men's head has been most chewed off.

For a mercy, the snow has stopped and the rays of the setting sun are peeking through the clouds as we bring the last sled load up the lane to my place. Some of the other women have been digging two big graves atop the hogback ridge near to my cabin. The ground there ain't so rocky and the soil is loose, after they get past the first couple of inches. They is all of them weeping as they attack the ground with mattocks and shovels, the tears making white streaks through the dirt on their faces. Wives and mothers and sweethearts, they are doing the last thing they can do for their men.

We have to whip old Patch to make the hard climb up there again. He has had enough of this and snorts and tosses his head as he pulls the sled over to the open holes. We lift them gentle, one by one, and drop them into the graves. It ain't as any of us would wish to do, but it is the best we can manage with night coming on and our strength failing. At least they will be covered proper.

Once they are all in and the dirt thrown back over them, we stand there breathing hard, heartsick at the ugliness of this final rest our men has gone to. Then someone says that we had ought to offer up a prayer.

"*I'll* offer up a prayer," says another, wiping the dirt from her face with the back of her hand. "I pray that ol' Keith and them burn in hell for this and that their consciences don't give them no rest for all the days of their miserable lives."

And everyone, barring Marthy, says amen.

25.

~JAMES A. KEITH~

Big Creek Gap, East Tennessee
February 1863

My conscience is clear.

"Every last one of them ought to be killed," General Heth said, when news came to him in Knoxville of the further depredations of the Laurelites. "Every last one. I want no prisoners and I want no reports from you about your course at Laurel."

This is my answer to Lawrence when once again he questions the wisdom of the late action in the Laurel valley and deplores the lack of honor therein. Honor—he is besotted with the notion of honor and unable to grasp the realities of modern warfare. He belongs in one of Scott's ridiculous novels, astride a white horse and rescuing maidens. *Honor*, forsooth!

"I stand by my decision," I repeat, reminding him that I was faithfully carrying out the orders Heth had given. "Recollect, Lawrence, what manner of officer General Heth is: a graduate of West Point and friend to General Lee himself. Think of his vast service experience—in the Mexican War, on the Western plains against the bloody Indians, in Utah during the Mormon wars—must not Heth understand, better than any, the sort of irregular warfare, *guerilla* warfare, we are faced with? *Heth* understands that a fighting army, beset on every side, cannot overburden itself with prisoners."

Lawrence breathes a heavy sigh, pulls his camp chair to the paper-littered desk, and begins to page through the muster rolls. His unspoken disapprobation rankles and I feel compelled to bring him to a clearer understanding of the affair.

"Do you forget that many of those Laurelites were deserters—had run from our own company? An example *had* to be made." He makes

171

no acknowledgement as he slides his finger down a list of names. Surely the state of that diminished roster pleads my case.

I point to the telltale page. "Between diseases and desertion, the 64th is shrunk from three hundred to one hundred, and our numbers will continue to shrink if we don't instill a proper fear and sense of consequences in the men. It *had* to be done."

My cousin forebears to answer but reads and rereads the muster rolls as if this would swell our numbers again. The air in his tent is smoky and close, adding to my irritation.

"By God, Lawrence," I say, forcing myself to contain my anger. "Even General Lee recognizes the importance of making an example. He has ordered deserters shot on numerous occasions, executed by and before their former comrades. What I ordered was no more than this."

He shakes his head and lays aside the muster rolls to reach to the side of his desk for a letter held down by a chunk of white quartz.

"This came with the mail yesterday, Jim," he says, unfolding it and holding it before him. "From a friend with strong connections in the state government." He pauses and looks up to catch my eye. There is something in his expression, some guarded message—he seems to be steeling himself to an unpleasant task as he continues.

"For some little time I've been hearing rumors that the attorney general is out for blood. And, according to my friend," he nods to the letter in his hand, "Lawyer Merrimon of Asheville, who is hungry for political power, sees this as his opportunity. Merrimon has been speaking out against the action in Laurel to anyone who will listen, crying it up as a grievous crime."

"A *crime*?" I expostulate, impatient with this nonsense. "How can anyone—"

Lawrence holds up a hand. "And now Merrimon has made a report to Governor Vance, full of the most piteous and gruesome detail—reported, so he says, by 'a reliable source.' My friend, who has seen the report, commends this passage especially to our attention."

He clears his throat and reads. "'I learned that all this was done by order of Lieutenant Colonel James A. Keith. I know not what you intend doing with the guilty parties but I suggest they are all guilty of murder.'"

"*Murder?*" Resisting the urge to snatch the offensive pages from his hand and throw them into the fire, I take a deep breath and attempt to remain composed. "How can Merrimon speak of murder? We are at war, are we not? These contemptible wretches—deserters, outliers, bushwhackers—made war against the Confederacy, killing our soldiers, plundering our stores."

I can contain myself no longer. Lawrence's bland equanimity enrages me and I stand, placing both hands on the desk and leaning close to force him to some reaction. "Those Laurelites we executed—*legally* executed—were all of them heedless, lawless, desperate men."

His eyebrows lift and he opens his mouth to speak but I forestall his objection. "Yes, I say *men*. Even the youngest of them was fully capable of hiding behind a tree and firing on our troops. Those savages are little better than animals. Lawrence, you *saw* how they behaved in Marshall, in your own house, to your wife, your children—"

"Jim, please, no more!" He shakes his head and turns from me to the picture of his three children that stands atop his trunk by the side of Polly's lovely likeness. His face contorts and he covers his eyes with his hand.

I hold my tongue though there is much I would say. I could almost feel sorry for this weary, beaten man across the table from me. The death of two of his children has hit Lawrence exceeding hard. And though he has never spoken of it, Polly's fragile mental state, as recounted to me in my wife's recent letter, must weigh heavily on his mind. Margaret hints at outrages carried out by the Laurelites and the images that arise in my mind—a drunken Unionist pawing at a swooning Polly, her pale limbs sprawling, her gentle—

But now Lawrence is standing and coming around his desk to put a hand on my shoulder. "Forgive me, Cousin, the wound is still too fresh. I cannot bear to speak of it."

He moves to put a chunk of wood on his fire and stands staring at the sullen flames till at last the new green wood begins to sizzle and hiss.

"We have been encamped here too long; there is no more dry wood to be had," he pronounces with a gloomy satisfaction before returning to his chair. Reaching behind him he produces a case bottle and a pair of tin mugs. He fills each mug halfway, sloshing the whisky onto the papers scattered over his desk, then downs his in a gulp.

"It's early but, by God, I need it," he says, refilling his mug. He scowls and shoves the other mug toward me. "And so will you."

Anger spent, I resume my seat and let the fiery liquid trickle down my throat.

Again he picks up the letter from the well-informed friend and turns the page over. "My friend tells me that Vance has been pushing Secretary of War Seddon to begin an investigation into the affair at Laurel—naming you as the officer responsible."

I am in mid-swallow when Lawrence utters those last words and almost choke on the whisky. "An investigation? What would—" I begin but he holds up one finger and continues, looking at the pages rather than meeting my eye.

"Furthermore, my friend reminds me that under the 1806 Articles of War, which the Confederacy adopted, murder is a matter for the civil courts, not the military and—"

"It was not *murder*!" I try to keep my voice low, aware of the thin walls of canvas and the invariable listening ears. "The customs of war—"

He shakes his head. "I'm sorry, James. I'm afraid the newspapers and journals are out for blood. Lurid accounts have been published of women subjected to whippings and mock hangings. Stirred up by these reports, much of the public is appalled and the men who are the face of the Confederacy—men like Vance—have been forced to defend what they are calling 'the honor of our rebellion' by seeking a scapegoat."

He falls silent, his eyes on his boots. I can find no words and my hand is shaking as I pick up the tin mug. Can this be happening? Is that a note of pity in Lawrence's voice? I down the remaining whisky in one swallow and am beset by a coughing fit. When I am recovered, Lawrence is regarding me with a quizzical expression.

"My friend, who is most sympathetic to your position as well as anxious for the Army of the Confederacy to escape the ignominy of an officer tried and hanged for murder—"

The coughing breaks out anew and Lawrence hands me a canteen of water. At first it chokes me but I gain control of myself and, eyes streaming, signal Lawrence to continue.

"My friend suggests a simple solution: that you accept a *pro forma* court martial and resign," again he holds up a hand against my protestations, "but he promises that this resignation will be left undated and held in confidence against future need."

Resign. The word is a funeral bell, tolling the death of all my glorious hopes and dreams. I shake my head in negation and begin to speak but Lawrence continues, a dogged determination in his voice as the words fall like hammer blows.

"My friend reminds me also that should you be accused of a capital crime, and he assures me that this is a certainty, it would be my unhappy duty to use my utmost endeavors to deliver you to the civil authorities or risk being cashiered myself."

He puts the damned letter aside and looks me in the eye at last. "Jim, I have considered the possibilities and I fear this is the only way. The investigation is already in motion and we are helpless against the forces roused by Merrimon and the press. But a *pro forma* court martial, much as I dislike the necessity, will allow you to resign and leave the state long before Seddon's investigation can reach you. And if I do not know where you have gone…"

I say nothing while wild schemes race through my mind. I could walk from this tent, take a horse, and make for the territories—or even Mexico. I could shoot Lawrence and turn the gun on myself. I could fight the charges—and briefly I see myself standing before a jury and swaying them with impassioned oratory. I see my speech, my vindication, printed in the same newspapers that have excoriated me. I envision promotion, a political career.

"Pray, Jim, consider this carefully." Lawrence's quiet words break in on my whirling thoughts. "Think of Margaret and your children— give thought to how this may be accomplished with the least clamor. We still have some time and we can be deliberate—Secretary Seddon is beset with so many problems that he can hardly move swiftly."

He pours another tot into each of our cups. Raising his, he pauses and fixes me with a steady gaze. "But such is the gravity of the situation that my friend has enjoined me to say to you—" He looks back at the letter and reads, "Tell Lieutenant Colonel Keith, and tell him in these words, that the likely result of too much delay will be that he will—" Lawrence clears his throat and continues without looking up, "that he will hang by the neck until he is dead."

He has trouble getting out these last words and I see the tears standing in his eyes. His pity is perhaps the worst of it all.

26.

~SIMEON RAMSEY~

East Tennessee, Western North Carolina
March 1863

The dream of the boy—if it is a dream—begun a good while back, the very night after all them prisoners was shot and throwed in the ravine and Sergeant Jay done his devil dance on their bloody corpses. We had left them there, half-covered, and marched on for Tennessee, the snow spitting right in our faces, then coming harder and harder, like it wanted to hide us from sight. At last, when it had got so thick it near blinded us, we took shelter in a half-burned barn and paired off to sleep back to back for the warmth.

I woke to see him standing there at my feet—the same mournful big blue eyes, the same shattered arms, and his chest with the dark blood like a flower over his heart. I sat up slow, waiting for the dream to fade, waiting to hear Ned at my back cuss and tell me to lay still. But Ned went on snoring and the boy went on staring.

And how's my mama goin' to make it now, with all her men folk dead? he asked me.

I shut my eyes and shook my head and when I looked again, weren't no one there. I lay back down, keeping still but not wanting to sleep for fear of falling back into the same dream. Ned snorted and mumbled something and I wondered was he dreaming too—I wondered was he having the same dream or if one of the other dead Laurelites was visiting *his* sleep, but then I heard him say a woman's name and felt him beginning to jerk to and fro like he's fucking something.

Cold as it was, I pulled away from him and, with my blanket around my shoulders, stepped outside the barn to piss.

The boy was back the next night and this time both his hands was gone. I sat up and looked right into those mournful eyes. Only they was naught but black holes now. "What do you want with me," I asked him, "and what went with your hands and your eyes?"

He lifted his arms and turned those empty eye sockets to the stumps. I could see the white bone shining inside the dark wounds. *Hogs,* he said. *And crows. Youns had ought to have buried us deeper—maybe throwed some rocks on the grave. A great gang of hogs got at us. It was a big black one with the longest tushes you ever seen took my hands. And then the crows came.*

Bile rose up in my throat and I felt like I was about to be sick. I turned my head to spit and when I looked back, he was gone.

The 64th is encamped at Big Creek Gap now and the boy is still with me. Every night I have the same dream—if it is a dream. But whether it is or isn't, don't alter the case. I lay awake most of the night for fear of seeing that boy again. And every night when I can't hold off sleep no longer, he comes back, asking the same question, wanting to know who will take care of his mama, now that the 64th has shot all her menfolk.

The weather continues miserable cold but the officers keep sending out scouting expeditions to capture deserters or any Union recruiters. After what happened in Laurel, the word has spread throughout East Tennessee of how the 64th deals with prisoners, and now the people round here are set against us harder than ever. I seen more than one woman spit as we go by, and there is nothing but hard looks and low muttering from any folks that we meet.

We are most of us mighty low and every morning someone else has slipped away. Near as we are to some fellers' homes and farms, many a one has taken French leave, meaning to come back sooner or later. And some did return, in the beginning, once the plowing or the harvest was done. But anymore, they don't. Others has crossed the lines and joined up with the Union. They say there are guides all around who will show the way to the Union troops.

I would have run before this but ol' Keith keeps me close, finding task after task for me to do. One time I asked if I mightn't go on a scouting party and he just laughed. "You'd be off like a shot," says he, "running to see that sweetheart of yours. And what would I do without you to empty my chamber?"

It seemed I would be stuck with him and his piss pot for the rest of this sorry war, but then there came a time when he was busy writing letter after letter and mostly forgot I was there. A story was going 'round that Keith was in deep trouble for shooting them prisoners in Laurel. Some allowed as how he was going to have to stand a court martial, but others said that was so much hogwash. Everwhat the truth of it was, ol' Keith got plumb distracted and after he was done with all them letters, early one morning he lit out for Marshall with three of our best scouts, saying he'd be back in two days.

"What the hell does he mean by taking my three best men?" Sergeant Jay was stomping round the camp, *god-ing* and *damn-ing* with every step. "Colonel Allen wants me to send a scouting party to Warm Springs. Word is that Union recruiters is operating over that way."

Then the sergeant's eye lit on me where I was setting in front of ol' Keith's tent, putting a shine on his second-best boots. "You there, Ramsey, ain't no need for you to laze around while the colonel's gone. Time for you to do a little soldiering for a change. Get your haversack and be ready to move out with the scouting party in twenty minutes."

So here I am. Free of ol' Keith. I tell myself that this will be my best chance and I must not falter,

Tonight we are stopping just outside Warm Springs. We pitch our tents near a little farm and the sergeant sends me and Ned to go foraging for vittles as rations has been dreadful short.

We tromp across the frozen furrows of a last year's corn field and send up a black cloud of crows with a dreadful clatter of wings. There ain't but a sorry little cabin and a barn with a shed on it, all of them in poor repair. The shingles of the cabin roof are curling up under the snow, and I can see from here that there's a gap where some has blowed off. A spindly looking ladder is leaning against the house like someone was of a mind to do some patching.

Ned hellos the house and after a spell, the door cracks open and a woman pokes her head out.

"They ain't no men here for youns to con-script," she hollers, "and there ain't a thing worth thieving neither."

Ned takes a step closer. "We ain't aiming to thieve nothing, ma'am,

179

just hoping maybe for a bite of meat or whatever youns might spare."

The woman looks hard at both of us, then steps out onto the porch. Even wrapped in the shawl as she is, I can see that she is big-bellied and near her time.

"Ma'am," I say, easing a little closer, "did you want, I could maybe patch that roof for you. Cold as it is, it must be worrisome. And I don't reckon you had ought to be climbing no ladders just now."

Her face twists in what might pass for a smile. "No, I reckon I oughtn't." Her eyes search across the cornfield to the little knot of our tents and the men dragging in firewood and the campfires starting to burn. She hugs her shawl tighter. "We ain't got much but I might could find youns some kind of vittles." She points to a rough basket setting on the end of the porch by the ladder. "The hammer and nails and shingles is in there. I'd be evermore grateful could you mend the roof."

It don't take no time at all to set the shingles right, and by the time I am back on the ground, the woman has come out to the porch, carrying a poke that looks to be full of apples. I puzzle at the greasy stain on the bottom, then I see from the shape that it must be a cut of middlins and my mouth is all a-water at the thought of home cured bacon.

"We thank you kindly, ma'am," I say and she draws up her mouth.

"I don't reckon as I had no choice, did I?" says she, looking at me hard. "I heard how your gang treated them poor women over to Laurel. Still, it was good of you to patch my roof, and I thank you for it."

With that, she is gone, back into the house, the door shut behind her and the latchstring pulled in. Me and Ned look at one another then set off for the camp.

"What took you so long?" the sergeant grumbles and snatches the poke from Ned's hand. He hefts it, then reaches in and pulls out the greasy middlins. "A hell of a lot of sorry apples and a hell of a little piece of bacon. Had I gone, I'd of brought back a ham."

"There weren't no ham, Sergeant Jay," Ned says. "This was the last piece of meat she had."

"Was it?" says the sergeant and lifts his head to look toward the house. "What did the woman look like?" he says, and his nostrils flare like he is scenting something.

"Just about the sorriest old hag you ever saw," says Ned, cutting his eyes at me.

I am glad to hear Ned say this for I'd not like to see that poor woman abused. Sergeant Jay don't answer, just looks sour and cuts him a thick slice of the bacon, leaving the rest for us to divide amongst ourselves. The apples ain't much wanted by those fellers what has the quick step and me and Ned come away with three each.

We get our fire going and set some cornmeal to parch for coffee. Our ration of crackers is weevily, but we break them into pieces and put them to soak in hot water while I cut up the little piece of bacon and let it sizzle in the pan. When it has made some grease, we slice up two of the withered apples and let them stew, then stir in the soaked biscuit.

We take it into our tent to eat as the wind has come on to howl something fierce and we don't have enough dry wood to keep our little fire going. The apple bacon mush ain't bad, as eating goes, but it ain't what you would call good neither.

I am on sentry duty till midnight, just me and one other. It is blowing bitter cold and dark till I can't see across the tents to where the other feller is. I am stationed near the edge of the woods that runs alongside the cornfield and as I march back and forth, trying to keep warm, I start hearing the boy again.

You said you was goin' to run. Looks to me like this is as good a time as any. Just you wait till your relief comes, then back to your tent, get your haversack, and high tail it into the trees. It ain't that far to Tennessee and there's a many would take you in and help you get to the Union lines.

The boy is still whispering when I am relieved, and I think I glimpse his sad face and empty eyes in the blowing snow as I hurry to the tent and pull out my haversack from beside Ned's sleeping body. When the boy tells me again to head for the woods, I do it, every minute expecting to hear someone call out and then the crack of a rifle. I imagine the thump of the ball in my back, the slow toppling into the snow, and the feel of my warm life's blood gushing out.

But it don't happen. Scarce daring to breathe, I creep along from tree to tree, listening for the least sound. There is naught but the soft whisper of the snow sifting through the branches and once the small scream of a rabbit taken by an owl. When I have gone a good piece, I make my way along the edge of the woods, the boy guiding my every step, and we head north toward Tennessee.

27.

~POLLY ALLEN~

Marshall, North Carolina
April 1863

"The eyes! The eyes!"

Lawrence's strangled cry breaks through my sleep and I am instantly awake. Home for a few precious days of leave, he is in sore need of refreshment, of an escape from this endless war, but once more he is gripped by the same nightmare that has plagued him since the unhappy incident at Shelton Laurel. In the half-light of our moonlit room, I see that he has thrown off the covers and lies curled on his side, clutching at his pillow, shivering and drawing long shuddering breaths.

"Lawrence, my love, I'm here. *Shh, shh*. It's just a dream." Pressing myself against his back, I wrap one arm across him and speak softly into his ear, trying to bring him awake and out of the black terror of his nightmare. As I hold him, the shivering lessens and his breathing becomes more regular. At last one of his hands moves to clasp mine. He heaves out a long sigh, straightens, and rolls over to face me and nuzzle at my breast.

"I'm sorry, my poor Polly, sorry to inflict my infernal weakness on you again. This cursed dream—it comes every night unless I drink myself into a stupor." His eyes shut and I fear he may drift back into sleep and the nightmare.

"My love, it's no weakness," I tell him, sitting up and speaking briskly. "Let me light the candle and pull up the covers. Then we'll lie here all cozy while you tell me the dream, just as you remember it. Perhaps the telling will put an end to it."

Heretofore, he has refused to say more than that the dream is to do with the war. Of course, I think. The war. What else haunts us day and night? What else could inspire such terror?

We have become a house of dreams. My own slumbers are too often disturbed by dreams of the brutes who invaded our home and I suffer again the rough hands, the whisky breath, the abject fear and helplessness. I cannot tell Lawrence of *my* dreams, knowing that it would only add to his pain. And little Annie screams in the night, sobbing that the bad men are in her room and when I have hugged and caressed her into wakefulness, assuring her that the bad men are gone and will not come again, the tears break out anew and she bewails her lost brother and sister.

I fetch Lawrence a cup of water with the tot of whisky he asks for and, taking a companionable sip myself, settle back beside him, my eye on the wavering candle flame. He is propped up against the pillows and his eyes are half closed. I am tempted to let him fall back to sleep but instead I lay my hand on him.

"Tell me the dream now, my love. From beginning to end. Is it to do with what happened in the Laurels?"

He is quiet for a moment then a sound, something between a sob and a laugh breaks from his throat. "The Laurels, the goddamned Laurels. I'll never be free of them." He opens his eyes and gestures to the case bottle of whisky at the bedside. "Pour me another tot, sweetheart. 'Anodyne courage,' Cousin Keith calls it. Perhaps it will dull the ache of returning to the old nightmare again."

When I begin to protest that I have no wish to cause him pain by the recital of the dream, he reaches across me for the bottle and lifts it to his lips. I hear the liquor gurgle as he swallows. He returns the bottle to its place and lays a hand on my breast.

"Don't molly coddle me, my dear. I'm awake now and no longer a frightened child. I'll tell the damned dream through and be done with it." His voice is stronger now and tinged with his old teasing humor. "It always begins with me riding along a narrow, winding trail somewhere in the Laurels. I can hear behind me the rhythmic tramp of my troops. It is nighttime and a misty fog hangs about the trail, but there must be a full moon as the outlines of the twisted laurel bushes towering above me on either side are clear. I ride on through the fog, looking straight ahead, but from the corner of my eye, it seems I see dark shapes shifting and leaning toward me.

"My horse is not my usual mount but a smooth-gaited grey that carries me noiselessly along the trail. This goes on for some little time and suddenly I realize that I no longer hear my men marching behind me. I turn in my saddle to look, but my horse has just rounded a bend in the trail and, though I cannot see the men, I assure myself that they are close behind. The horse keeps moving steadily on and I try to check his pace so that I don't outstrip my men..."

His hand on my breast tightens and I lay my own over his. He draws a long breath and continues.

"And that is when I realize that I have no reins. The grey is moving faster and faster and I have no reins to slow him or pull him to a halt. Again I twist round in the saddle to look for my men; again I see nothing—not even the road, only a laurel thicket—a laurel hell, as some call it. And the horse keeps steadily on. I pull on his mane and try to shout out a *Whoa* but no sound emerges and the nag paces on, his head bobbing up and down, his ears pricked forward. I think of jumping off but fear to find myself surrounded by the laurels—men have been lost forever in laurel hells, you know."

I find that I am shivering. This dream frightens me and I fear to know where it leads. But I squeeze his hand and listen. It is, I think, the only thing I can do for my poor husband.

"It goes on and on—the silent, smooth ride along the winding trail, ever closing behind me as I pass, the laurels crowding nearer and nearer. And for some months—for I have had this dream for months now, Polly—this was where I would awaken. But a few weeks ago, I began to stay in the dream long enough to glimpse a clearing ahead, a moonlit clearing with a little rough-built cabin..."

I open my mouth to speak but the sight of his eyes, fixed and staring, stops me and I content myself with stroking his hand and pressing myself to his side. After a pause, he continues.

"I would see the cabin and wake, unsure if what it held was good or evil—an escape or a trap. Every night I fell asleep, dreading to find the answer. And every night, the horse brought me closer till a few nights ago it stopped at the door and I dismounted. But when I began to climb the log steps to the door, they grew from a simple half log to a tall set of wooden steps which I counted as I climbed."

"Lawrence," I begin but the telling spills on, like a runaway spool of thread unwinding across the night. He is rapt in the recitation, unheeding of my growing anxiety.

"There are thirteen steps—thirteen, like those of the scaffold. And until tonight, I awoke on the top step as I hesitated at the closed door. But tonight…" His voice catches and he motions to the case bottle. Another sip and he resumes the tale. "Tonight, when I raised my hand to knock, the door swung open. And I went in.

"The cabin is filled with fog—or smoke—and though it blinds me, I take a step forward. And then I see them. Three old women, puffing on corncob pipes, clouds of smoke billowing around their heads, filling the cabin and pouring out the open door. *Oh*, I think, *it's the smoke from their pipes causing all the fog out there. If I put out the pipes, the fog will clear and I can ride away.* So I step closer.

"They are sitting around a quilting frame such as my mother used to use. It hangs there in the middle of the room, suspended by ropes that disappear up into the smoke. The old hags—and hags they are with their nutcracker faces, shapeless black clothing, and snaky white locks—pay me no heed as I move closer to look at the quilt they're working on.

"The quilt is made of squares of blue and gray and I know at once that the fabric is from the uniform coats of North and South. And then I see the coatless corpses stacked like cordwood on the floor beneath the quilt. Silver needles flash as the crones stitch, tracing intricate patterns on the quilt, heedless of the death at their feet. And as I watch, it seems the designs and colors of the quilt itself shift and change under their fingers.

"At first the gray patches spread to surround and encompass the blue, but then a great tide of blue washes over the gray, almost blotting it out entirely. And then I see red patches blooming here and there across the expanse of fabric, and blood dripping from those patches onto the corpses below till it becomes a rising tide and still the old women quilt on, heedless of the blood soaking the hems of their skirts…"

Lawrence falls silent and I pray that we are at the end, but then I remember his cry as he awakened and know there must be more. We lie there in silence as the room grows lighter with the approach of daybreak. A rooster crows somewhere, once, twice, and a third time before Lawrence rouses himself to continue.

"We're almost at the end, sweet Poll," he says. "I thank you for your patience and pray that it *is* the end and the telling will rid me of the dream. "But I must not omit the last of it, the part that came to me tonight. I stand watching as the blood from the quilt drips and puddles and swirls down the stack of bodies to wash across the floor. I want to call out to the old women that the rising blood will soon swallow the quilt, but as before, I can make no sound.

"They stitch away, heads bowed over their work, and I see that tears of blood are dropping from their faces. Then all at once they raise their heads and turn to stare at me. The bloody tears streak down and suddenly I see—"

He draws a deep breath as if to gather strength for one last exertion of will.

"Their eyes are bloodstained mirrors and in each small mirror, I see myself."

28.

~JUDITH SHELTON~

Shelton Laurel, North Carolina
May 1863

"…being as we will be bound to suffer on account of troops eating up all our provisions and killing our men and property and destroying the country." Brother Ray is reading over the petition he has wrote out for us and some of the women who have gathered here on my porch all nod like they was at meeting and there are cries of, "Amen" and "That's right." Me and some of the others is sending to Governor Vance, asking for payment for the food and other things the Secesh troops has took. We are in desperate straits, the soldiers having took almost all our stores and livestock. I managed to hide a sack of seed corn which I have shared with my neighbors but without men and beasts to help with the plowing, we are hard put to sow enough to make much difference.

"Well, I reckon sending off a petition can't hurt none," says Rody Hall, wringing her hands the way she does. "Though the Lord knows it's like asking the fox to put the chickens back in the hen house. Do any of youns really believe the Secesh will help us?"

"Now, Sister Hall, we must put our faith in the Lord," says Brother Ray. He lays down the letter on the little table at his side and gives her a look over those silver-rimmed spectacles he puts on for reading. "Governor Vance has the name of an honorable man. Didn't he push to have that scoundrel Keith held responsible for the awful murders back in January? From what I've read in the newspapers—"

But at the mention of the murders, Mary Shelton, her who was used so bad by Keith's men, goes to wailing, and it ain't no time till most all of them is weeping and boo-hooing like one thing. Brother Ray looks like he's ready to jump up and light out of here, but he has offered to send the petition off for us and first we all have to put our names to it. Or our marks.

Brother Ray clears his throat and holds up a hand for quiet, but several is too far gone in grief to heed him. At last he stands and in his best preaching voice, he hollers out, "Now let us pray. O Lord, in your mercy please grant to these grieving mothers and wives, sisters and daughters a just and merciful answer to this petition. And, Lord, we beg for an end to this terrible war and a healing for your people. In Jesus' holy name we ask it. Amen."

And by the time he gets to the *amen*, they have all hushed. One by one they go up to the table where he has the letter laid out, and one by one they sign their names or make their marks. When it is my turn, I see that the ink I made from dried pokeberries looks like blood smears on the paper.

When Brother Ray is gone, taking the letter with him, I set a kettle and bring out some mint tea for it is clear ain't none of these women ready to go home. There is so much yet to say and grieve for, and coming together like this seems to have broke loose a power of feelings in each of us and each one wants to have her say. The Laurels is a harsh place and most all has had their losses, even before this war. Babes dying of the summer complaint, husbands crippled or killed outright by a runaway horse or an ill-tempered bull, a whole summer's crop ruint by too much or too little rain—these are but a few of the troubles that are our lot.

Sometimes I think life is hardest on the womenfolk. Bearing child after child takes a heavy toll on a woman. "A tooth for each child," the old women say, and while it ain't invariable, there is few of us who still have all our teeth. I look at poor old Miz Unus who hasn't a tooth in her head—not in all the years I've knowed her.

Losing teeth ain't the worst of it either. Bearing a babe is a risky proposition—you may bleed to death or die of the childbed fever. Or the babe may be too big and the woman can't bring it out. Miss Unus is right skillful in turning a britches baby, and she has brought many a one through what looked to be a hopeless case but sometimes…

As I look at these women here on my porch, telling one another of their particular troubles, I am remembering Sarabeth. She was my best friend growing up and she married young, no more than thirteen.

Now Sarabeth hadn't even begun to bleed then and she had no notion of getting married. Like most girls, she expected that one day she *would* marry and me and her played those silly games—making charms to bring a feller to you or cutting a long peel from an apple and letting it fall to see what letter it made, for that would be the first letter of your husband's name. I recollect that when hers fell into a *J*, she giggled and whispered to me that she hoped it meant Jamesie, a boy who lived in the next holler.

Well, as it come out, it weren't Jamesie but his father Big Jim. He was a widow man whose poor wife had given him fourteen children, nine of which was yet living. When she died of the fifteenth, he begun to look about him for another wife. It weren't so much that he needed someone to tend to the children, for his oldest, the one just before Jamesie, was a likely girl who could do all that was needful. No, Big Jim just wanted someone young and fresh in his bed and so he cast his eyes on Sarabeth.

I remember Sarabeth coming over to our place in the spring of the year to bring my mama a setting of eggs from their Dominiker hen. Sarabeth was acting awful queer, kindly fearful but puffed up too, switching around like she was somebody and putting on till I said, "Sarabeth, what is the matter with you?" and she said that she was going to be married and busted out crying.

My folks was talking about it later that night when they thought we was all of us asleep up in the loft. The others were sleeping hard, but I always was a nosy little somebody and I had pulled my pallet close to the edge to where I could hear most every word. My mama said it was a scandal and that a girl that young and small didn't have no business wedding, especially a feller like Big Jim.

"Rough as a cob, that one," said she. "I purely hate it for that little thing."

And Pap harrumphed and said anyone who fooled with cattle knowed enough not to put an over-sized bull to an under-growed heifer. "But Sarabeth's daddy owes a right smart of money to Big Jim, along of buying that piece of bottom land offen him, and what I have heard is that Big Jim says he will forgive the debt if he can have that little girl."

My thoughts and memories are broke into by a burst of bitter words. "Damn ol' Keith for a black-hearted villain and damn them all to hell," Elizabeth Shelton is saying. "I make my young uns say that every night, just before their prayers, and I make them promise that when they are growed, they will go after the men who killed my brothers and my uncle Jim and his boys too. And Davy not but thirteen years of age."

I see Marthy nodding and looking at something in her hand. When I go around again with my jug of tea, I see that it is Davy's bone ring she is holding and that her eyes are brimming. I give her a little pat on the shoulder to let her know I understand.

Now they are jabbering every one of them about revenge and what is the right and wrong of it and is it a Christian thing to take revenge. I set the jug down and lean against the porch railing and remember the last time I saw Sarabeth.

It was the fall of the same year that she married. Now that she was wed and busy with a house and family, I only seldom saw her. And when I heard she was in the family way already, I felt kindly shy of her. She was a woman now, it seemed, whilst I was yet a girl. But I missed her bad and so I cracked some black walnuts, cooked them up with sugar the way I knowed she liked them, and set out for Big Jim's place.

Sarabeth was setting on a little stool by the fire, churning. Big Jim and most of those young uns were outside working up some wood but there was two little uns rolling around on an old quilt and playing with a gourd rattle. Sarabeth's big belly filled her lap and when I said something about her being a mommy soon, her face twisted up and the tears begun to spill from her eyes.

"Why, Sarabeth," I said, reaching over to hug her, "what in the world?"

She wiped her face with her apron hem and went on churning. Up and down, up and down the dasher went while she bit her lips together to keep from busting out crying.

"I'm scared, Judy," she whispered. "I'm scared of having this baby. It hurt something terrible when Big Jim first put it in me and that weren't hardly nothing to the size of a baby."

I didn't have a thing to say to that, except that it mustn't be too bad or folks wouldn't keep having young uns. I gave her the sugared nuts and tried to talk about the coming spring and what kind of garden she would put in and how proud I'd be to help her anyway I could. But then the butter started to come and she wouldn't let me help wash it, just thanked me for the candy and told me to come back soon.

I did, too, though sooner than I meant to. Not three weeks later, Jamesie came riding up our lane on his father's plow horse. I was outside fetching water from the spring and the sight of his face sent a chill through my heart.

"Is it Sarabeth?" I asked. "Mama's over to the Nortons—"

"Miz Unus sent me after *you*, Judy. She's been there since yesterday and can't do no good. She said—she said you have small strong hands and better sense than most and you'll have a better chance of doing what needs doing."

His face was bright red when he said this and I reckon mine was too. But I clumb up behind him on the big horse and off we went—

"Why, Judy Shelton, where are you wandering? Miz Unus has asked you three times what you think is the best thing for us to do, being only women." Liney Norton is shaking my arm and I realize all the others are standing and making ready to leave.

It is like I was waking out of a dream and I speak without thinking. "It's the women who'll save the Laurels. I say the best any of us can do is to have more young uns to make up for them that's taken. More boys to work the land and more girls to bear their children. That's what the Laurels need."

"How can I have more children?" one busts out crying. "They killed my husband."

"Listen here," I say. "How many young uns do I have? And all without a husband. Honey, you don't need a husband; you just need a man."

And at this they all catch their breath and cut their eyes at one another. Then Miz Unus lets out a cackle and one by one they begin to laugh, the first happy sounds out of this gang in some time. One, whose husband was too old and lame to be conscripted, says that she will lend him out to any as wants. "He ain't much to look at but he can still big a belly," she says, patting her own and grinning like one thing.

As they go off, chattering like a bunch of young uns, I think about what I have said. And I think back to Sarabeth and that last dreadful day.

I did all that Miz Unus told me but my sweet Sarabeth had been laboring for a day before they sent for Miz Unus, and by the time I got there, she was past knowing that it was me, pushing my greased hand up inside her to try to turn the babe that was already dead. My hand was on the curve of the babe's back when Sarabeth gave one mighty shudder and went still.

It seems queer that to be remembering Sarabeth and her dying like that at the same time I am telling my friends to get themselves in the family way.

Mayhap my words will send some of these women to their deaths in childbed, soldiers in the everlasting war to hold fast to what is ours. I don't know. I spoke without pondering on it. But I reckon there's ways and ways of fighting for what matters.

And I wonder when will I see Abner again.

29.

~MARTHY WHITE~

Shelton Laurel, North Carolina
May 1863

Miz Judy's words are in my head as I leave the others and take the path to our house. Have more young uns to make up for them that's taken. I had thought to have young uns with Davy—five boys and five girls. I even had names picked out—Davy and Sam and Jim to start with and Judy for the first girl. I would have liked some real pretty names for the girls—like Esther and maybe Rosalee or Ida Mae.

But it don't matter what Miz Judy says about not needing a husband. I reckon Davy was the only feller who didn't mind the way I am. All the others round here call me Dummy and think that I ain't right in the head.

And then I think about how some talked of raising up their young uns to take revenge on the Secesh what murdered our men. Being as I ain't likely to have any young uns to train up, I reckon I will have to do it myself.

I could learn to shoot a rifle, I think, and track down that black-bearded feller who shot my Davy. Picking up a dead branch laying by the path, I hold it to my shoulder and aim at a big chestnut, pretending that Black Beard, the soldier with the silver locket, is standing there. I pull the trigger that ain't there, and in my mind, I see Black Beard's hateful shape jerk and twist, just like Davy did.

For I saw it all.

I followed when they marched our fellers off, wanting to see Davy for as long as I could, to memorize everything about him before he got took off to prison in Tennessee. I was careful, slipping through the laurels and keeping well hid. When they turned off the road, I hung back, then crept along to get as close as I dared.

And I watched as they lined them up. I watched as they shot them.

I heard Davy begging for his life and saw how they made a game of shooting him till Black Beard shot him in the heart. I would kill every one of those soldiers if I could.

The hate rises up in me so strong that I drop the branch and make fists of my hands. I bare my teeth and a growling sound pushes out of my mouth. The way I feel at this moment, I could knock a man down and tear out his throat like any panther. I can almost taste the salt of the blood.

I am so swimmie-headed with hate and sorrow and anger that I set myself down in the path till I can catch my breath. A picture rises up in my mind of Black Beard, and I wonder where he is now and how I will ever get a chance to get back at him for killing my one true love. But in my mind, I am seeing him, not when he was shooting Davy but that morning when me and Miz Judy was handing out pones of cornbread to the prisoners and the soldiers too.

Black Beard was the only one of the Secesh to say a thank you.

Still, setting here in the middle of the path, I make a plan. I will use a drawing charm, like the one the girls use to bring a feller to them. They will take something that belongs to the feller they're trying to catch or, if they ain't got that, his name wrote on a piece of paper will do. They will cross it with bindweed and say, "Safe find, Safe bind, Bring him to me, soon or late. Bring him to me for my mate." I will have to leave out the part about for my mate. And since I don't have nothing of Black Beard's nor do I know his name, I will try to get a Seeing of him, the way Papaw showed me afore he died. But first I must gather some bindweed.

I leave my bed in the early morning dark to feel my way along the foot path across the pasture and into the woods. The sky to the east is growing lighter as I wind my way between dim poplars and on to the clearing. First light finds me at the still pool in the woods—naught but a little cupped-out place just an arms' span across. Paying no attention to the dew on the bank, I lay down on the thick green moss and lean out to gaze into the clear water.

Like a looking glass it is—showing the big treetops overhead against the brightening sky, like as if they're leaning over to get a glimpse of themselves. And in the midst of them leafy clouds, I see my face, heavy braids a-dangle to either side. I let loose a sigh and my breath sets ripples to chasing one another, making my image shiver and break up into little bits of me.

Recollecting what I'm there for, I draw my head back some and commence to breathe slow and gentle through my nose, waiting for the water to go still again. In my head, I can hear Papaw speaking to me, plain as if he was at my side.

Now, Marthy, you can't force it. You just got to empty out your mind and wait for what may come. And they ain't no guarantees neither. The Sight has run in our family all the way back to the old country. And you seem the likeliest one for it to light on for unlike the general run of womenfolk, you can't chatter but you can listen. Like I say though, they ain't no guarantees—

Somewhere off I can hear a redbird calling and the harsh cry of a rain crow. But those sounds seem far away, like something in a dream, and they fade to nothing as I watch the pictures take shape and move on the surface of the water.

There is an apple tree, white with blossoms, and as I watch I see a bird bringing a twig to the nest it is building. It is so natural that I look up and behind me, thinking that I must be seeing a reflection but there are only poplar trees all around. When I look back at the pool, I see that the bird and the apple tree are beyond an open window and I am seeing inside a little room. There is a bed with clean white sheets and the black-bearded soldier is laying there asleep.

It don't make no sense. I had thought to see him, *if* I saw him, at his soldiering, not taking his ease on a soft bed. And I think of Davy, rotting in his grave, and I want to dash away this Seeing, to wake the sleeping Black Beard, to do him some great harm. I have my arm raised to splat my hand down on his image but then I recollect my purpose and reach for the coil of bindweed in my apron pocket.

There are nine long pieces of the vine. When the first piece touches the pool, the still water shivers, making the sleeping man seem to shudder, but he don't open his eyes as one by one I lay the bindweed vines across the pool, making a web to catch him in.

Safe find, Safe bind. Bring him to me, soon or late. I can't say the words aloud but I think them through three times three. Then I reach for the center where all the vines cross over the image of the sleeping body and pluck them from the water.

I hold them dripping before me and roll them into a ball which I tie tight with another piece of bindweed. I will take it home and put it under my bed tick. And every night I will say the charm, and every night it will be working to bring Black Beard back to the Laurels to pay for what he done.

30.

~JAMES A. KEITH~

Somewhere in the North Carolina mountains
August 1863

After denouncing the action in Shelton Laurel as "butchery" and "a cowardly and wicked act," the editor of *The Raleigh Standard* has worked himself up to a high pitch of righteousness and at the peak of his peroration he trumpets, "In the name of outraged humanity, we demand the punishment of the officer who is responsible for these murders."

I fold the page away and take another from my bulging dispatch case. In this edition, a month later, a self-identified "correspondent from the mountains" replies to the editor that the victims of the so-called massacre were thieves and robbers who had terrorized the community for at least a year, killing, stealing, and forcing women and children to strip off their clothes even in the dead of winter.

With a grim smile, I remind myself that truth is often what we want it to be. Certainly Governor Vance chose his path, little more than a month after the Laurel action, when he wrote to our secretary of war, urging him to take action against me for perpetrating what he called "a scene of horror disgraceful to civilization." Eager to disassociate the Confederacy from the so-called atrocity, Vance urged that I be brought to a court martial but, not satisfied at my resignation, wrote again to Secretary Seddon for a copy of the proceedings of the court martial. I think he will be disappointed.

It is Vance's opinion that the action in Shelton Laurel was murder and as such a crime against the common law of the state. Therefore, my informants tell me, the governor seeks to try me in a civil court, yet another reason to absent myself from Marshall. I did not tell Margaret where I was going, though she probably suspects the truth. It is a bitter irony to think that half a year ago we were pressing the women of Shelton Laurel to reveal the hiding places of their men, and now the roles are reversed. Margaret may be forced to endure some close questioning.

I stand by my decisions, of course. But it is a difficult legal point. According to the 1806 Articles of War, which the Confederacy and the Union both follow, guerrilla fighters like the bushwhackers of Shelton Laurel Valley can be shot even if they throw down their weapons and surrender. Unlike soldiers in uniform, these irregulars can claim no right to be treated as prisoners of war. The sticking point, the point that Vance is insisting on, is that, if captured, these irregulars may not be executed without legal proceedings before either a military or civilian court. Vance and his lackey Merrimon insist that our execution of the thirteen without a trial was murder and, just as Lawrence warned me, they claim that the military is obliged to assist the civil authorities in bringing charges against me.

There were unpleasant scenes when I returned home, seemingly a civilian once more. Little Laura and Douglas were happy, if somewhat disconcerted, to see me, but Margaret, usually so dispassionate and level-headed, revealed a side of her nature I could never have anticipated.

"Resigned from the 64th?" she stormed, her face turning red and blotched, her hands twisting at the sock she was knitting. "For doing what General Heth commanded you to do? While Cousin Allen is merely suspended half a year in consequence of the Laurels action? And though he forfeits his six month's pay, he remains with the 64th or so Polly says. Really, James, I cannot believe that you have told me the whole of the affair."

When I attempted to explain the matter, touching on the lamentable but time-honored military tradition of choosing a scapegoat in order to protect the command, and even hinting that I was fortunate to escape the noose some of the more vocal elements in the press were eager to put round my neck, she whirled to stalk from the room, flinging back over her shoulder words to the effect that she could never hold her head up in Marshall again.

"I will not *have* it. The sooner we can leave this awful place the better. For now, let us return to the farm near Mars Hill where I don't have to endure so many pointing fingers. But I think you should look out another situation—one far away from here where this scandal will not follow us. Perhaps Texas or some other western state."

Her agitation cooled a trifle when I agreed to the move to the farm and said that I would consider a farther removal. Her grim aspect softened. "At least," said she, "you will be respected as a medical man wherever we choose to settle. I shall begin making arrangements."

And true to her word, she began a campaign of cleaning and sorting and packing till the house was no longer recognizable and barely habitable. I tried to explain to her that a move out of state, especially in a time of war, would not be easily accomplished but I obliged her by assisting with the move to the farm. I also packed my books and papers and wrote to distant relatives, one in Texas, another in Arkansas, asking help in finding a suitable situation for our family.

No sooner was the Marshall house closed and Margaret and the children relocated to the farm near Mars Hill, than I began to hear disturbing rumors. Not content with, as he thought, hounding me from the service, Governor Vance was pressing Lawyer Merrimon to try me in a civil court with the avowed purpose of seeing me hang. Vance, it was said, had sworn to follow me "to the gates of hell."

Accordingly, I left Margaret and the children in the care of our faithful servants and took horse to the secluded cove where I have long kept a hunting cabin. The owner of the property and his wife are elderly, taciturn, and used to my ways. I told them no more than that I had resigned the service and was there for an indefinite stay. As in times past, it was less than an hour before my bed was made fresh and my supper brought to the door. It is simple fare but far superior to army rations or, indeed, to Margaret's frugal table. A flock of chickens and two she-goats provide eggs and milk, and old Zack is a formidable hunter and trapper. The rabbit stew that was my evening repast that first night was as succulent a dish as I remember to have had anywhere.

There was a little difficulty over payment for my keep. Zack was most unwilling to accept the Confederate currency I offered him, shaking his head and backing away. Realizing that it was imperative to secure his silence and his complete goodwill, I dug into my pockets for one of my precious gold pieces and smiled to see his eyes light up.

"That'll do fine, Doc," said he. "I reckon you'll tire of us afore I need to ask for more."

And he slouched away, leaving me to my solitude and my thoughts.

My thoughts. Before I left Marshall, I called on Polly in my professional capacity. Her health is still indifferent. She was already debilitated from nursing her sick children when the Laurelites broke into her house. I know not exactly what transpired then—Lawrence never spoke of it. But whether or not it went beyond rough handling and the terror accompanying such an invasion is something even Margaret and all her assiduous enquiries have not been able to ascertain. And of course the subsequent loss of her two children was a further blow—at one time, Margaret says, she feared poor Polly was losing her mind.

But the woman I saw when I called was perfectly rational—no touch of dementia or hysteria. My physician's eye noted a subject ill-nourished and sallow—though after several years of wartime privations, we are all ill-nourished. Even Margaret has lost much of her matronly girth.

In a case like Polly's, I would normally have recommended beefsteak and red wine, but beef is hard to come by and red wine but a memory. I mentioned a patent tonic but even as I named it, I remembered that it is probably not available, being of Yankee manufacture.

"Pray, don't be concerned, Cousin James," she said. "I do very well. It is this August heat that steals my appetite."

Her smile was still sweet and the violet shadows beneath her eyes merely enhanced her fragile beauty. I had to fight back the urge to throw myself at her feet and pour out my heart.

I demanded to feel her pulse and she held out her hand. There was nothing out of the way here but I prolonged the physical contact as long as I dared.

My thumb and forefinger can circle her wrist.

It is autumn now. The leaves are dropping from the trees and the nights grow cold. In spite of further payment, my hosts, too, grow cold. Zack only rarely makes the trip to Marshall, but on his last visit, he returned with grim news. After what I fervently hope were discreet inquiries, he learned that Vance and Merrimon are indeed building a civil case against me for the action in Laurel. They are gathering affidavits from so-called eyewitnesses in Laurel and petitioning the army to provide witnesses from the 64th. And all the while, the devil Kirk and his Union marauders go unmolested and Union recruiters have the freedom of the Laurels. It makes my blood boil.

When Zack gave me the unwelcome news of the civil case, he could hardly meet my eyes. With many a hem and haw, he finally got it out then, with even greater difficulty, added, "The wife thinks it'd be best was you to find another place now. It appears they're already searching for you and she don't want to get mixed up in all that."

The supper she brought me last night was almost inedible and she too would not meet my eyes. A bible verse learnt in my youth forms on my lips. *Foxes have holes and the birds of the air have nests, but the Son of Man has nowhere to lay His head.*

I am resigned to moving on. An old friend in the Dark Corner of South Carolina will take me in. When I can ascertain how matters stand, I will rent a house and send for Margaret and the children, though it must be done with all secrecy.

That it should come to this! From my dreams of martial glory to this thrice damnable pass. I might as well be a deserter or a runaway Negro, traveling by night, just one step ahead of the relentless, slavering hounds.

But perhaps there is yet a way to redeem all. My friends in the higher ranks have suggested that a series of *independent* actions against the Unionists of the area would be welcome, if not officially sanctioned. Though it is not generally known, my resignation from the army will not take effect except in case of necessity. Thus, I may yet serve the Confederacy in this unofficial capacity. And, mayhap, time will vindicate me.

It is something to consider.

1864

31.

~SIMEON RAMSEY~

Mac's Patch, on the border of North Carolina and Tennessee
June 1864

The summer sun is hot on my back as I work my way along the rows of corn, chopping weeds. At last the poison in my wound has gone and Mr. Suttles has stopped frowning when he undoes the bandages. The leg has begun to heal to where I can leave off the crutches and, leaning on a hoe, be of some use.

I have had enough of bed and sickness and it is a pure joy to be out under the clear summer sky. Up here might be another world, a safe and hidden place like I used to imagine before I was took by Keith. From this cleared patch atop this high peak, I can look out on all sides over rows and rows of peaceful blue mountains, stretching away in the haze to what seems like forever.

Down below, in that other world, the war is still going on and sometimes I stop with my hoe in the air, listening for the guns and the rebel yells and the cries and moans of the wounded and dying. But all that I ever hear is the rustle of the green blades of the corn, the clank of a cowbell, and the high whistling call of the red tail hawk, riding the air above my head.

Down there, other folks is trying to make crops, women without their men mostly, sometimes even without their plow beasts, all taken by the war. I have seen a puny-looking woman in the traces, dragging a bull tongue plow while two half-growed young uns stagger behind, clinging to the handles to guide it through the hard ground. I have seen fields of corn, not yet ripe, trampled to green mush out of pure meanness by soldiers and their mounts, and I have seen corn cribs raided and women crying out that their young uns will starve, cursing the men who fill their haversacks with the fat dry ears.

I have seen and heard so many dreadful things that time was I would have welcomed dying, just to be able to sleep without the boy's whispering. I have wandered in mind and body till I despaired of ever being found, of ever being whole. But here on Mr. Suttles' farm, in this high forgotten place that straddles the line betwixt North Carolina and Tennessee, I am coming back to myself and beginning to look to the future once more. And, for now at least, the boy is quiet.

I ran from the regiment back in March of last year and most of the time from then till but a few months ago is lost to me. A year out of my life, and naught to show for it but fever dreams and half-memories that might be dreams and might be real. I remember waking and thinking I must have got to heaven for I was warm and clean and laying betwixt smooth sheets and there was an angel, a tall dark woman, bending over me and spooning something sweet into my mouth. The light of a candle flickered and its glow wrapped around her like a soft garment. A white flower was caught up in the wavy black hair that hung loose to below her waist and her voice was like to the cooing of a dove.

I recollect another time, looking out the window by my bed and beyond was a gnarled apple tree, white with snow, but my head and my leg was paining me bad and I hollered out. Someone came and gave me something to drink and the next time I opened my eyes, the tree was white with apple blossoms and a bird was building its nest. It seemed as pretty a sight as ever I'd seen and made me think of a girl and a little farm with a Jersey milk cow and a flock of red chickens. But whether that was something I'd left behind, or something yet to come, or just the memory of a dream, I couldn't tell. I recollect trying to study on it and trying to call up the face of the girl and her name, but my eyelids was heavy and the next time I looked out the window, the tree was heavy with red-streaked apples.

When finally I woke to myself in the spring and wondered how I had come to this place, Mr. Suttles told me that in March of last year, a peddler had found me laying alongside a mountain trace some miles south of here with my head busted and a great ugly gash in my right leg. The peddler said I was starving and babbling with pain, but he got me onto his mule and brought me here. Mr. Suttles says this place is a refuge and a sanctuary and that I will be safe as it is too far from anywhere for either Union or Secesh to trouble themselves with it.

He told me that I had slept for days and weeks and months on end, waking only long enough to take some nourishments and be helped like a sleepwalker with crutches to the necessary house. I don't remember none of this.

What I do remember is standing guard in the cold and then slipping away from camp and stumbling through the snowy woods in the dark. I kept going till just at first light I come to a rocky outcrop with a little place at its foot, sheltered by a shelf of rock about three foot high. I was near done in and happy to slide beneath it, roll myself in my blanket, and fall asleep.

I slept through most of the day, waking with a start now and again, thinking I heard a patrol coming after me. But there had been enough snow that my footprints was long since covered and besides, I weren't of enough account for them to waste time looking for me. By late afternoon I was rested enough to move on and I left my shelter and struck out for what I judged to be the north.

It was several days that I walked, with only a few army crackers and two withered apples to keep me going. I was climbing steady, the boy whispering in my ear and telling me what I must do. There was a little trace, hardly more than a game trail, that I followed through the woods and it was bitter cold. Then the last apple was gone and, though I was light-headed with hunger, I kept on, always climbing, hoping to get to Tennessee and behind the Union lines. I had my issue blanket round my shoulders and my haversack and rifle slung across my back. The rifle weighed heavy on me and I wondered why I was still toting it, after what it had done. It seemed an evil burden and, as my feet kept carrying me up the mountain, I studied on what I had ought to do.

When I reached the top and was catching my breath while gazing at the low-hanging clouds all around me, the rifle's weight kept tugging at my shoulder. Without another thought, I pulled it off and, taking it by the barrel, sent it spinning back down the mountain into a snowy bramble patch. My ammunition went the same way and all at once I felt lighter and almost free as I set off, following the little trace that snaked its way down the other side of the mountain. I was walking fast, stumbling in my haste, then running, taking great leaps, my arms outspread like I might fly.

I don't remember nothing after that, till that first waking and the dull ache in my head and the pain in my leg and the dark angel caring for me. This is a queer place where folks comes and goes. Some stay only for a night or two, others, like me, might linger.

At the end of the row of corn, I see little Esau is waiting for me with a bucket and a dipper gourd. He came here with his mama and some others a few weeks ago, and I believe that, colored or not, he is the brightest young un I have ever knowed. His dark face is shining with happiness and he wiggles like a pup when I thank him for bringing me a drink.

"Conductor's here!" he tells me. "Tonight he's gone take me and my mama and Pearl and Zekial *north*."

He says the word *north* like it was something magic and his eyes grow wide. "Mr. Suttles says it's a long hard walk but that there's good folks all along the way who'll help us. And when we get to the north, we be *free*."

I take another long sup of water and let the gourd splash back into the bucket.

"Now, that'll be fine, won't it, young un? Just fine."

I watch him skip back to the big farmhouse, wishing that I could go with them. But it's hard enough on the conductor, trying to lead these escaped slaves to freedom, without burdening him with a deserter and a crippled one at that. I will have to bide my time till my leg strengthens, but I will see if I can get word to Cora. Could be that this conductor will make for Maryville where a many is agin slavery. Could be little Esau and his folks will spend the night in that same hidey hole Cora showed me.

Thinking of that, I go to hoeing all the harder, eager to finish for the day so I can get back to the house and beg some paper and a pen. I have a letter to write.

Mr. Suttles is hunkered by the fireplace, tending a pot of burgoo and some pones of cornbread. I look around, wondering where Esau's family is—his mama Sally has been doing the cooking these past weeks.

"Sally and her young uns are in the back room," says Mr. Suttles, giving the pot a stir and raising the spoon to his lips. He takes a taste and reaches for the gourd of salt. "I sent them to try to get some sleep before they set off."

"Can you tell me where they're headed?" I ask. "Might it be Maryville?"

He stands and motions to the table where there is an ink pot, a quill, and a half sheet of clean paper. "It might, indeed. I had a notion you'd be wanting to write to that sweetheart of yours, being as it's her father's place they'll stay at to await the next conductor."

I stare at him all amazed but before I can ask how he knows about Cora and her folks and the hidey hole, he says, "You talked a lot in your sleep when you were sick—some of it didn't make much sense but one time when Mr. Aaron was here, we were by your bed and you talked of Cora and the hidey hole, and the man with his toes cut off.

"When Mr. Aaron heard this, he flung up his hands. 'I believe I know who that is,' said he, 'for I was the one that brought those poor runaways to Maryville. They're fine strong folks, that family of Quakers, Red Strings through and through.'"

My head was all awhirl. "Not to be too quizzy, Mr. Suttles, but what are Red Strings and who is Mr. Aaron?"

There is a sound behind me and I turn to see a dark-haired man coming through the door. Something about his face seems like I must know him and I puzzle over it, studying him hard.

He smiles at me and looks me up and down. "To answer your first question, I'm Jacob Aaron, pack peddler and sometime guide for runaway slaves. You've grown quite a beard since last we met, my friend. And it seems you've found your ark to ride out the storm."

When he says this, I remember him as the peddler at the inn who warned that a war was coming, back when I was foolish enough to think I could stay out of it because it was nothing to do with me.

He nods, like he could hear my thoughts, and goes on. "As for the Red Strings of your second question, think to your Bible and the story of Rahab the harlot, who helped two Israelites escape from Jericho. She hung a red string out her window to signify that she was a friend of Israel. The Red Strings take their name from that story."

"Some call them Heroes of America," puts in Mr. Suttles who has gone back to stirring the burgoo. "The Red Strings are most of them Unionists and Quakers, but they all hate slavery. They recognize one another by the sign of the red string—a little thread hanging from a button, say, or a string caught in a window."

He pulls the pones from the ashes and lays them by to cool. "Course, out of the way as we are, there's little need for a sign here. Ain't many runaways would stumble upon this place. All those we have passing through are brought on purpose and carried off by friends like Jake. Jake was on his way here to conduct a—" Mr. Suttles looks thoughtful, then winks at me, "—a *parcel* to the North when he found you near dead along the trace."

My mind is still all a-spin, but I recollect myself enough to thank the peddler for saving my life and then I go to writing Cora. I tell her that I am safe and that if nothing don't happen, I will come to her as soon as my leg is stronger.

"Mr. Aaron, sir," I ask, "are you aiming to come back this way?"

"Like as not," says he, between sups of the burgoo. "Though I have some other stops before I return."

"I'd take it kindly," says I, scratching a few more lines, "was you to bring me a reply to this. I could pay you for your trouble."

But he won't take my money, just holds up his hand and waves it off.

ॐ

Later that night, when the peddler and Esau and Sally and the others has set off, leaving me and Mr. Suttles alone in the house, me and him walk out to the meadow atop the highest peak and stretch out on the warm dry grass under the great show of stars. The sky is like a big bowl over our heads and with no moon, the stars shine bright like little lamps across the sky.

I heave out a great sigh, wishing it was Cora up here with me.

"Reckon when my leg'll be strong enough for me to travel, Mr. Suttles?" I say. "You have treated me good but—"

Mr. Suttles don't answer at first, but then he says, "You got considerable healing to do yet, son. Just bide here with us till the peddler comes back with an answer to your letter."

I start to ask how long that's like to be, but he shushes me and points overhead where a great fireball is blazing its way across the sky. And in my head, I hear the boy speak again.

32.

~POLLY ALLEN~

Marshall, North Carolina
July 1864

My dear Emmie,

When the peonies bloomed in May, I could no longer bear to see the crimson streaks on the white flowers. They brought alive once more the horror of that day three years past when the high sheriff was shot to death on our upper gallery and his blood dropped down onto the flowers below. That day and that death, I truly believe, set in train the divisions in our county and led to the horrors visited on both sides, not least the death of my children.

I know not why the sight of the red-streaked blooms did not disturb me before—this is the third time they have bloomed since the sheriff's death—but suddenly I wanted to rip out the peonies and substitute something homely and comforting like sunflowers.

I wanted to but did not, for fear of adding the burden of my weak fancies to Lawrence's many cares. Instead I cut away all the blooms that bore red streaks and sent Juliann with them to the graveyard with instructions that she should lay some on every undecorated grave.

I think the flowers will not trouble me again for next year we will be somewhere else, if Lawrence has his way.

Lawrence resigned his commission last month after unbearable persecution over some trifling errors in bookkeeping. He reminds me that he is more fortunate than his cousin who, despite his resignation, is now being sought for a civil trial in the matter of the 64th's treatment of prisoners.

A bead of perspiration drops from my face onto the paper, washing out the numerals *64*. The heat in the parlor is dreadful but I find myself driven to my desk again, so full of unsaid words that I must write them down for fear that if they do not find expression here, they will pour forth from my mouth in some unguarded moment.

I am startled by a sound from the street, and I snatch up my much-smudged blotting paper, ready to conceal my page—though, in truth, crossed and re-crossed as it is, I doubt that any but I could decipher it. But the voices pass on and I sigh, relieved to have a few more minutes at my communion with my shadowy friend—or is it my shadowy self?

Now that Lawrence is at home, either in the house itself or, if out, all too likely to return unexpectedly, and with poor, lonely little Annie clinging to me most of the time, I must snatch moments to continue my never-to-be-sent letter. The blackberry briars are heavy this year, and Juliann has taken Annie with her to a nearby patch to fill their baskets. Lawrence, I presume, is at the courthouse again, seeking what news he can hear of the war. So I am free to add to my letter, my catalogue of woes.

I would not have either one to see me scribbling away for they would surely ask what it was I wrote and then, oh, then, what would I say? That here was my only relief from wifely and motherly duty, from the façade of a patriotic Southern woman, that here was the only outlet for my true and never-spoken feelings—the fears that haunt my days and nights, the acid anger that builds inside me, gnawing at my very soul? That, as I dare not speak the truth for fear of giving pain, I must at least write it down?

I take up my pen again and dip it into the ink that Juliann and I have contrived from blackberries, salt, and vinegar.

How goes this war for you, Emmie? Have you food enough? Writing paper and ink? Goods for a new dress? Here we eat what we or our neighbors can grow—a sparse and wearisome diet. All the things that came to us from beyond our borders are but a faint memory. I hear that those on the coast who have the means to pay live better than do we, thanks to smugglers. But very little of that sort makes its way to us.

Oh, Emmie! I confess that my enthusiasm, never very great, for our Southern Cause has worn thin indeed. At our Ladies Aid sewing circle last month, when Mrs. Morris chirped out a whole series of catch phrases—the *Glory of Sacrifice, Our Heroic Dead, Our Southern Honor*—I had to leave the room for fear that I would fly at her and do her an injury with my knitting needles.

Margaret scolded me when I told her I would no longer host the Ladies Aid Society, nor attend the meetings. When I ventured to hint at my despair, she sniffed, in that annoying fashion of hers, saying that the loss of my two children might have happened war or no and reminding me that I still have my husband, whole and unharmed, food—of a sort—and a roof over our heads. I found her arguments unanswerable and so did not, instead making excuse after excuse till she ceased to ask me.

And now she and the children have closed up their house and moved to the family farm near Mars Hill. She gives out that it is in order to keep a closer eye on the servants and the running of the farm as Dr. Keith is obliged to be away on business, but Lawrence hints that James has gone into hiding to elude the civil authorities that are said to be gathering evidence to bring him to trial. And, oh, Emmie, I am horrified to learn that, should he be found guilty, he will hang. Hang, like a common criminal!

You know, none better, what were once my feelings for the man. A girl's passing fancy, no more. But I have retained a real regard for him and the thought of him running through—

The sound of a heavy footstep outside the window and Lawrence's voice calling out to someone in the street startle me. I hastily blot my page, fold it, and hide it in my pocket, just as Lawrence opens the door.

When I re-read what I wrote yesterday, I am shocked at my own frankness and fervor. But I must admit that, despite the heat, I slept more soundly last night than I have done in some weeks and that my spirits have been far less oppressed. I can listen calmly now as Lawrence rants on about Kirk's Brigade preying on loyal Confederates as well as recruiting for the Union in the Laurel Valley.

"If I still had the 64th…" He is pacing back and forth on the upper gallery as I sit in a rocking chair, darning one of his socks and listening like a good and dutiful wife.

He stops in front of me and takes my hand. "Polly, I can bear this no longer. I have it in mind to leave Marshall—indeed, to leave North Carolina. The story of the—the incident in Shelton Laurel greets me everywhere I go, growing more and more monstrous with each re-telling. And though it is universally acknowledged that the culpability falls on Cousin James, as his superior officer, I am inescapably tainted as well. It may be that in time—"

He drones on, speaking of a new life elsewhere, of Arkansas where he has a second cousin.

I rock and darn and nod, hearing it all without caring. There is nothing here for me but the grave of my children, and in my heart, I know the claims of the dead should not outweigh those of the living. Annie, too, will be better away from this house of unhappiness.

Perhaps before we make this move, I will destroy that interminable letter which has become my secret vice. My shadowy Emmie, you have been my sole confidant and what shall I do without you?

We wake to find that Juliann has disappeared, together with her few belongings and, of all things, a little book of Bible stories from the parlor. I had thought that she loved us—surely her grief at the children's death was real. But I console myself with the thought that it is one less mouth to provide for.

I had not known she could read.

1865

33.

~JUDITH SHELTON~

Shelton Laurel, North Carolina
January 1865

"Huzzay! I hear them in the next holler! It must be midnight! Mama, can I fire the shotgun now?"

Dan'l has been waiting outside for the sound of gunfire that will tell us it is the New Year. The damned Secesh made off with my mama's Seth Thomas eight-day clock so we got no way of knowing when '64 ends and '65 begins. But now I hear guns going off all up and down the valley and the faint sound of hoo-rahing from our nearest neighbors. It is eighteen and sixty-five and I pray God that this year will see the end of this cruel war.

While Dan'l is out making our share of the commotion, the girls fling open the doors and windows and I go to sweeping with the new broom I made last week. I sweep all the corners, under the table and the beds. I sweep out the old year and all its bad luck and worse times, sweep it out the door into the night. We have come through a world of ugliness and sorrow, but we are still here.

When the sweeping is done, we shut the windows and build up the fire. The young uns is too excited to go to bed just yet, so I send Ellender after some apples and we set them to roasting.

As we wait for the apples to begin to sizzle and hiss, the young uns gather in close and I tell them again the old story of how the Sheltons come to the Laurels. I tell about old Roderick who fought in the Revolution 'gainst the king of England, and I tell about the Cherokee princess Glumdalclitch who was one of his wives.

I do this every New Year to keep the young uns in mind of the people they come from, to make them proud to be Sheltons. We ain't got much, and we have even less of it after these years of war, but we still have our name and we still have the land. I always think it's fitting to begin the New Year this way.

Frank and Little Sol are whispering and giggling and Frank says, "Reckon who'll be our first footer this year? It was that red-headed Norton man last year and he sure brought us a heap of bad luck."

"What's a first footer, Mama?" Linnie is rubbing her eyes and yawning, but she is set on staying awake to eat her apple. I take her on my lap and breathe in the sweet smell of her hair.

"The first footer is a thing our folks brought over from across the water. It goes all the way back to Scotland, I reckon. What my granny always said was that the first somebody that comes through your door on New Year's Day—the first somebody who ain't family, you understand—who that person is tells what the coming year will hold. A dark-haired man is reckoned the best and a red-headed woman the worst. 'Course, mostly anyone with red hair knows enough not to go calling on New Year morn. Heck Norton didn't come over last year till afternoon when his wife sent him to bring us some meat from the calf they'd butchered. Late as it was, he thought for sure we would already have had our first footer."

One of the apples pops, sending a stream of juice hissing into the fire, and Ellender hurries to take up the rest. She sets them into wooden bowls and hands them out. "Now have a care," she warns the least uns. "Let them cool a mite."

Linnie is a dead weight in my lap, not even rousing when I whisper to her that her apple is ready. I rise and carry her off to the trundle where Armp is already sound asleep, his backside poking the covers up. The babe is stirring in her cradle so I take her up and give her the breast as the rest of them finish their apples and, one by one, clamber up the ladder to the loft.

I set back by the hearth and study her little face in the firelight. She may be the prettiest of my babies yet with her little rosebud mouth and big solemn gray eyes. She was born on Christmas Day, the sweetest Christmas present there could be. A new life for old Laurel, like I told the others back when we was gathered to sign that petition for relief (which we ain't had none yet). But I took my own advice and the next time ol' Sol came 'round of an evening, I went with him to the barn loft. I didn't catch that first time nor the next, but it seemed a needful thing and Sol was willing.

I named the babe after Marthy—Marthy Jane, hoping to coax a smile outen that poor grieving girl. And she did smile, at first, and held the babe close and rocked it in her arms. But then her mouth shook and turned down, and she thrust the babe back at me and went out the door.

Marthy worries me and that's the truth. Davy was the only feller who ever paid her any mind and with him gone, she likely thinks her chance of happiness, of being a wife and a mother, is gone forever. I have got to put my mind to what I might do for her. She has turned hard these days, and her face that was so open that I knew her thoughts without any need for speech, that face that was growing so pretty, now it has closed up on itself, not giving anything away, nor taking in neither.

At least she ain't run mad like poor Mary Shelton who pulls off her clothes all the time. Some say she offers herself to any passing soldiers, gray or blue, but I don't believe that part for her kin, John and Matilda, have taken her in and are caring for her. They don't let her out of their sight. Poor Mary, she suffered so bad. She is like a little child now, and it seems to me she has forgotten the worst of all that. Anyway, I pray that she has. But Marthy ain't right, the way her eyes is always staring off into the distance like she is thinking hard about something. Or watching for someone.

A burning chunk falls off the log and onto the hearth, and I push it back with the poker Pap made before I was born. In the flickering light I look around, and it seems that all those that have gone before are here in this room with me. The marks of Old David's adze are on every log the house is built of. The copper kettle on the hearth come with David from Virginia. The cradle Marthy Jane sleeps in is the same one I slept in—and my brothers and sisters before me and her brothers and sisters before her. The coverlet on my bed is of Mama's weaving, and her spinning too. Pap's musket and powder horn hang over the fireplace, along with a bark berry basket that Mama set a great store by, saying that Glumdalclitch had made it and give it to her when she was a little un.

Here in the quiet, with the small sounds of sleeping young uns and the little piggy noises the babe makes as her toothless gums tug at my nipple, I am more at peace than I have been since the war began. Last year started with the Secesh up and down the Laurels, carrying on something outrageous, trying to starve us out, then trying to run us off—saying they would give a free pass to any as would go to Kentucky. After a while they gave it up and then came John Kirk's brother George W. and his Union brigade. Things got better after that and I was able to make some kind of crop, and we didn't go in fear of seeing what few men was left rounded up and marched away.

The babe has fallen asleep, a bubble of milk on her lips. I lay her in the cradle at my side and close my eyes to ponder on the way of things, hoping that the year will go on as good as it has begun. The sweet taste of the roasted apples is on my lips and the warmth of the fire is most like the summer sun. Could be, I think, that summer will bring Abner back..

I must have dropped off, for the first light of morning is coming in the window and the fire has burnt low. I stir myself to poke at it and add a few small bits of sumac that catch fire good. All the young uns is yet asleep, and I am stirring up some cornmeal mush when there is a knock at the door. I open it to see our first footer—dark-haired George Washington Kirk with a pair of dead possums dangling from his hand.

"Happy New Year, Miz Judy," says he, grinning like a boy. He puts his head to one side and holds my gaze. "I believe it's going to be better than the last."

34.

~SIMEON RAMSEY~

Greeneville, Tennessee
July 1865

Back in January a traveler come to Mr. Suttles's house with the news that Fort Fisher on the coast had fallen, leaving North Carolina open to the Union ships, and that Sherman was on the march from Charleston.

"What's more," said he, pleased at the tale he had to tell, "Stoneman and *his* Union troops is on a rampage through the Piedmont, burning bridges and tearing up railroads. Ol' Zeb Vance can't do a thing but wait for the end."

And that end came soon enough. In late May when everyone knew the war was over but for signing the papers, President Johnson, the same feller whose house in Greeneville I'd passed many a time, appointed W.W. Holden to the governor's seat. Holden had ran against Vance in '64 on the peace ticket, saying what a many had said before, that this was a rich man's war and a poor man's fight—and I say Amen to that.

So the war was over and the Rebs what had talked so big had lost. Governor Zeb Vance was arrested and put in jail in Washington D.C., and up that hidden mountain I was champing at the bit to be on my way to Cora. But we was still putting in crops and I hated to go off and leave my share of the work on Mr. Suttles, good as he'd been to me. Then the peddler come back with a letter from Cora. It had been wrote some time back and it said she aimed to go back to Miss Viney sometime in July and I should come there instead of to Maryville. So I bode my time and when I wasn't working on the fields or in the orchard, I turned to getting in wood for the winter.

There wasn't so many Negroes passing through now that the war was over and the freed slaves was able to travel in broad daylight along the roads leading north. But some few came seeking word of which way their families had gone and there were still some fellers like me— soldiers, Union and Secesh, running from the war and in sore need of healing. There was two in particular as was getting stronger fast and they would soon be able to take a part in the work of the place. They talked of staying on as long as Mr. Suttles would have them, so I begun to think again of leaving.

By the time it was late June I couldn't think of nothing but Cora. The crops was laid by and I had split and stacked a world of firewood. Mr. Suttles hisself said that I had ought to go on.

"For I fear you'll do yourself an injury with that ax, not having your mind on it like you should," he said, but he smiled and winked as he spoke.

"Your body has healed up just fine, Sim, but I reckon there's still a wound in your soul. Mayhap you'll find the cure for that where you're going."

And he asked did I need some money to travel, warning me that the Confederate money from my army pay might not get me far.

"I thank you, Mr. Suttles," said I, "but I have a few gold pieces I've toted in my boots all through my part of the war. There's more than enough to get me where I'm going, and I'd take it kindly if you'd let me leave one for the next pore somebody in need."

It was a fine clear morn when I set out and the sight of the blue mountains stretching out on all sides, calm and peaceful as they'd been since the world began, gave me the feeling that I had been hid away in a charmed place, like in the stories my step-mam used to tell of Sleeping Beauty or old Rip Van Winkle who slept for many a year. I had said farewell to everyone at breakfast but as I got on a good piece, I turned back to gaze at the place where I'd been so happy. I couldn't see the house, hidden as it was in a little hollow, but in the orchard I made out Mr. Suttles tending to his young trees. I reckon he felt me looking at him for he stood and waved his hat my way.

I was right glad the distance was enough so he couldn't see I was bawling like a baby. I waved my hat back at him and turned my face toward Tennessee. A few more steps and I swung around for one last look, but it was all swallowed up in a mist that came out of nowhere. The farm and Mr. Suttles might have been naught but a dream.

It is some days before I make it to Greeneville, and I only keep going by telling myself that each step is bringing me closer to Cora. This part of the world was like a bone with two dogs worrying at it—first the Confederates was in charge, then the Union come in, and back and forth it went till near everyone had suffered at the hands of one or the other. After so many miles, so many burned-out houses and barns, so many unplowed fields growing up in weeds, and all the scared-looking folks who duck out of sight when they see me passing by, I reckon I ain't much surprised when I reach Miss Vincy's house and see that the windows is busted and what had been her front garden is trampled. The lilac bush is still there but most of the branches is broke off. Only one lifts up a few new leaves and a single out of season bloom.

In the dying light of the evening sun, the place looks deserted but I catch sight of some black words scratched across the white paint of the door. Hoping that maybe Cora and her aunt has left a message to let me know where they have gone, I go up the steps and take a closer look.

The words appear to have been wrote with charcoal and some-one has tried to wipe them away, but I can still make out one word: *TRATOR*. I am studying on the meaning of this when I hear some-thing shuffling about inside of the house. At first I think it must be a rat or a coon or some such that has gotten in but then it comes near the door.

"Go away," a cracked little voice says. "There is nothing left for you to steal, nothing at all."

I have to catch my breath and it takes me a minute or so to recognize who it is. "Miss Viney," I say, leaning in close to the door. "It's me—Sim. I've come for Cora."

"Sim?" I hear a key turn in the lock and the door cracks open just the least bit. "You don't look like—"

"Miss Viney, it's this beard has got you fooled. It's me, Sim, all right. I got conscripted and been in the army and away all these years. Remember, when I was last here four years ago? You told me Cora was in Maryville and you give me a letter…" The door inches open and a thin little figure, her head wrapped up in some dirty gray cloth, peeks out at me.

If this is Miss Viney, I reckon we don't neither one of us look like ourselves. She is thin as a rail; her, who was like a sleek little hen when last I was here. She is wearing gloves and something about her face don't seem right.

She sees me staring and turns away. "I know I look a fright—it was the fire," she says.

It takes a time but the story comes out at last, how back when the Secesh held Greeneville, some no-goods in town got the notion that Miss Viney was part of the Red String folks and took that for an excuse to break into her house and plunder what little was left of her stock of fabric. They were rowdy drunk and as they was leaving, one of them knocked over an oil lamp and it set fire to the basket of mending on the table by it.

Miss Viney had hid in the kitchen pantry, thinking they would take what they wanted and be gone. But when the sound of their boots died away, she come out to find her front room afire.

"There was no time to go for water, and I was beating it out with my broom," she said, "when the flames flared up in my face…"

She turns to me again and I see now why she looked so queer—her eyebrows is all gone and her face is a shiny red.

"But I persevered and saved the house," she says, lifting her chin and squaring her shoulders, and I am minded of a little banty hen, wings outspread protecting her chicks from a snake.

"Miss Viney," I ask. "*Was* you a Red String? I know that Cora's folks likely are—"

"Good heavens!" she says, taking a step backward. "I wish I *had* been brave enough. But this is such a busy road, so near town and so many people passing, that it would be too dangerous. Besides, there is no good hiding place in my tiny house."

"Then why did they think—"

She gives a sad little laugh. "It was such a foolish thing. I was working on a piece of embroidery one afternoon, with some of my hoarded embroidery silks…"

Her eyes brim up with tears and she wipes them away then goes on. "I had just threaded my needle with a beautiful piece of vermilion silk when there was a knock at the door. So, as I always do, I ran the threaded needle into my collar to have it to hand when I went back to my sewing. I answered the door and it was three of the town's more disreputable citizens. I believe they were part of the Home Guard, but they were obviously drunk.

"'See here' cried the least drunk of the three, 'we have information that you are one of them home-grown Yankees, a Union sympathizer, and likely a spy.'

"'Tha's right,' said another. 'Got to root out Unionism.'

"The first leaned closer to peer at my collar. 'Boys, look at that there! She's a Red String all right. Likely got some runaway niggers in her house right now.'"

She tells how the three used this as an excuse to rampage through her house and steal as much as they could carry, and all the while her neighbors turned a blind eye.

"No one dared anger them, I suspect. As long as the Confederates were in power, those three did as they pleased. But even now, my neighbors avoid me." She wiped her eyes and went on. "I suspect I remind them of their own cowardice. It doesn't matter; I will be moving to Maryville as soon as—"

"As soon as Cora comes?" I put in. "You aim to go back with the one what brings her?"

She looks up at me, her mouth open and her eyes wide.

"But, Sim, did no one write to you? Surely her—no, I see they didn't. Oh, my poor boy—our sweet Cora passed away two months ago."

❧

It is August now and I am at the old home place near the river. I come here to dig up my bank of gold coins before I set off for— Well, I ain't yet clear on where that might be. But it ain't in my heart to stay here.

When I learned that Cora had died of a lung fever, I think I would have flung myself in the Nolichucky if it hadn't been that Miss Viney needed me to stay by her till her kin from Maryville come after her. I shaved off the big beard that frightened her so and mended the windows that was busted. Then I cleaned up the yard and fixed the picket fence till it looked nice again so she could get a fair price for her house before moving on. I was walking through a nightmare, hardly able to think beyond the latch that needed mending or the dead apple tree that needed cutting. I slept at Big Quinn's and helped out there, too, though his stock was down to four sway-backed old nags and a mule. My favorites, Heck and Brute, was long gone and Big Quinn cried when he told me the Union soldiers had taken them.

On the first of August the kin from Maryville came, and we loaded Miss Viney and her little store of household goods onto his wagon. She wept over me, calling me "her poor boy" and begging me to take heart in knowing that Cora was with the angels now. I thanked Miss Viney and wished her well but could find no comfort in her words.

And now here I set, high above the river in that same place where I watched them fellers back four years ago, crossing from North Carolina on their way to join the Union, and I think had I gone with them— But you can't undo time no more than you can make the river run the other way.

The river don't change. It didn't take notice of the war. If I was to sink myself in its depths, would it wash away my memories? My pockets is full of gold pieces for, though the trees on the knoll had growed right much, I found the piece of white quartz that marks my mama's grave and next to it, the big rock for my daddy's. I had almost expected to find the rock rooted up and my bank plundered but all the gold pieces was there, shining as bright as if four bloodstained years hadn't gone by.

I set near the bluff, my pockets filled with the gold that would have bought me and Cora a farm. Enough gold to sink me to the bottom, was I to jump into the river, I think.

And who's going to take care of my mama, the boy says, *now that all her men are dead?*

He hasn't spoke in the longest time but he is speaking now, telling me what way to go. I am like a sleepwalker as I get to my feet, shoulder my rucksack, and make my way toward the crossing into North Carolina and the Laurel Valley.

35.

~MARTHY WHITE~

Shelton Laurel, North Carolina
August 1865

The ball of bindweed in the little calico bag beneath my pillow is naught but dried leaves and twigs and still no sign of the one who killed Davy. I see that Black Beard in my dreams often enough, and over and over I take my revenge but still he ain't come. It may be that the charm and the prayers are working against each other, I think, but once again this morning, as the sun shows itself over the mountain, I hold the bag in my left hand and say the words in my head. *Safe find, Safe bind, Bring him to me, soon or late.*

I say it twice and then a great anger sweeps over me and rather than finish saying the charm a third time, I jam the bag deep into my pocket, thinking to throw it in the fire. I guess I am just a blamed fool to believe any one of them Secesh soldiers would think of coming back to the Laurels, drawing charm or not.

All summer long I have found reason to work in the fields nearest the main road, hoping that when the charm fetches Black Beard along, I will be the first to see him. I have thought out what I will do and that is to beckon him to follow me and make signs that I will give him food. If the charm is working, he will follow me home like a stray dog and while he is setting on our front steps eating the food I have give him, I will fetch the shotgun and slip up behind him and blow his head off.

Only the charm ain't working. All summer I have kept an eye on the road, hoeing, then picking beans in the patch that is near the road or taking the baskets of beans to set beneath the chestnut that corners our farm. I have set breaking and stringing beans for hours, all the while staring down the road. I have thought the charm over and over but still no sign of Black Beard.

Oh, there's been many a weary traveler creeping along the road—broken-down men, most of them neighbors, some with empty sleeves, some with bandaged heads, some limping along on crutches, making their way back to the Laurels. A few can't hardly go but even the worst off of them begins to walk a little quicker as they near the particular turning that will take them to their home.

If only one of them was Davy.

There is a wedding up in the next holler this evening. One of them fellers who made it back is marrying his sweetheart. He come back without a leg, pulled along in a little wagon by a friend who'd lost an eye. Along with the missing leg, he had a great wound on his face that made it hard to look at him till you got kindly used to it. But his sweetheart was the happiest woman you ever saw. I would have been the same, had it been me and Davy.

The place is like an anthill with folks hurrying to the infare. It has been so long since there has been a play party of any kind that folks has come from as far as Sodom and even Flag Pond. Most everyone who could brought some good thing to eat, and there were so many brought layers for a stack cake that there was enough to make two fine ones. They set, tall and shining with apple filling spilling down their sides, on either end of the long table, along with the fried chicken and kraut, beans and side meat, honey in the comb, gritted cornbread, greens, stewed apples, pickles, and all manner of good things. There is even some biscuits and light bread, for George Washington Kirk came last week and brought a sack of flour to Judy.

He is sweet on her, everyone knows that, but now that Abner Tweed is back, Judy don't seem to have time for no one but him. Sol Chandley's wife likes that pretty good, but I ain't heard what Miz Tweed's opinion is.

There is a crowd clustered all round George Kirk who is rared back like he is speechifying. Folks is laughing and elbowing one another. I figure he is telling funny stories so I edge over to where I can hear better.

"And then there was the time I was traveling through the High Country—over near the Grandfather Mountain—"

I see folks cutting their eyes at one another. George Kirk's "traveling" likely meant that he was leading raids on the Secesh.

"—a sorry little farm in the middle of nowhere, but I was right hungry and I saw smoke coming from the chimney and caught the smell of something cooking. I was alone at the time, having made plans to meet the rest of my men—"

He catches hisself and says, "My traveling companions had gone ahead and we were to meet later that day. So I hello the house and a scrawny little feller pokes his head out the door. He has hold of an old musket, likely one passed down from his grandad, and he pipes up, 'Who be ye and what do you want?'

"'Naught but a weary traveler,' I say, holding out my hands to show they are empty. 'A poor pilgrim in need of a bite to eat.'

"Well, the old feller hems and haws and pokes his head inside like he's talking to someone. Then he nods to me. 'Light and come in the house. Me and my old woman, we ain't got much but I reckon we can spare you a mess.'"

Kirk spins the tale out, telling how they set him down and feed him beans and cornbread, and how he, by way of being sociable, offers the old feller a pull at his case bottle of whisky. And how after that, the old feller gets right talky, telling of how things have been in that part of the world.

"Old Methusalum has a deal to say about the war, and I am just spooning up the last of my beans when he gets onto the subject of Union raiders."

Kirk's eyes twinkle and he has to try hard not to grin as he tells the next part.

"'Now I don't know about you,' the old feller says, reaching out for the case bottle again and taking a great sup, 'but what *I* say is that them Union raiders is naught but a gang of robbing, thieving scoundrels, every last one of them. And the worstest one of them all is that black-hearted, no-good George Washington Kirk.'"

There is a hoot of laughter at this, but Kirk holds up his hand for quiet. "I don't say nothing, just set there wiping my corn bread round my empty bowl while the old feller begins to tell all manner of terrible things that this monster Kirk has done. And then he takes another sup from my case bottle and bangs his bony old fist on the table. 'Why,' says he, 'if I had me some more guns, I'd get some other fellows and we'd *kill* that damned rascal, 'deed we would.'

"At that, I jump up from the table and lean down, nose to nose with that old varmint. 'God damn you,' I holler, '*I'm* George Washington Kirk!'

"Well, the two of them's jaws drop open and the old woman falls to her knees, 'Oh, Mr. Kirk, please don't harm my husband. He can't help it that he's an old fool.'

"The old man is still setting there, some paler than he was, but he looks me up and down and says, 'Mr. Kirk, I always knowed you warn't half so mean as they said you was.'"

"What'd you do to 'em?" someone asks after all the laughing has died down.

George Kirk scratches his chin and shrugs his shoulders. "You know, I ain't half so mean as youns think. I didn't do nothing but to thank the old lady for my dinner and ride on. It wasn't till that evening I realized that old fox still had my case bottle, and I was too far away to go back for it."

There is more laughing and several case bottles come out of the pockets of folks wanting to say they shared a drink with George Washington Kirk. The womenfolk are moving back to the tables of food, and I think to slip off for one last look down the road.

I have made a promise with myself that I will stop watching for Black Beard. Either he is dead—and it has to be reckoned a possibility—or the charm ain't working. I will burn it tomorrow morning and stop thinking of revenge. That is what is in my mind. But my feet are taking me down the lane to where I can see the main road one last time.

The sun is low in the sky and dust hangs in the still, hot air. Behind me I hear the murmur of talk and laughing and the sound of a fiddle striking up "Haste to the Wedding."

And coming up the road, I see a clean-faced stranger heading to me.

POSTBELLUM

1866 and beyond

36.

~JUDITH SHELTON~

Shelton Laurel, North Carolina
August 1866

"Could you use a helping hand, Miz Judy? They was saying you aimed to pull fodder tonight."

He stands there on the porch, old slouch hat in his hand. In the light of the setting sun, his dark hair throws off glints of copper. He has put on weight and maybe growed an inch or so in the year he has been here.

"Come in the house, Sim, and get you a bite. The young uns are finishing up their supper afore we set out for the cornfield." I motion him in and see his eyes go around the room like they always do, like he was looking for something. At the table the young uns is so busy spooning up their cornbread and buttermilk that they pay him no mind. Like everyone around, they are used to Sim showing up whenever there is a job of work to be done.

Folks wonder at it, that a young man, looking for somewhere to settle after the war, would take up in a place where he was a stranger. They wonder at it but they bless his name for the help he has given one and all, especially the widows. When first he come here, there was some not right pleased with the way Patsy Shelton took him in so quick, but I reckoned she was in sore need of a strong back to help her on the place and I said as much to those who wagged their tongues. Patsy has lost her Jim, and Little Jim and Davy as well, leaving her with two little boys and a pack of girls, none of them big enough to be much use. If she can get some help from this stranger who comes asking only a share in the family's food and a place to sleep in the barn, well then, said I, I'm glad for it.

Miz Unus calls him an angel unaware, from that verse in the Bible. When some spoke against taking in strangers, she hushed them by lifting up one crooked finger and saying in her cracked old woman's voice—"Be not forgetful to entertain strangers: for thereby some have entertained angels unawares."

The moon is rising big and red. It silvers the mountain slopes and touches the rows of corn. A little breeze sets the blades a-dancing, rippling them like water, and I stop for a moment just to enjoy the gentle touch of the air on my face and the sweet rustling of the tall corn. This is one of my most favorite jobs there is—pulling fodder by the light of the full moon. It is nice and cool after the strong heat of the day and to the young uns it seems more like a play party than work.

Me and the ones that are tall enough go down the rows with our knives and cut off the tops of the stalks a little above the ripening ears. The smaller uns trail after us, putting the tops into croker sacks and dragging them to the end of the rows. Later Sim will come back with the horse and sled and haul the tops to the barn for cow feed.

I am used to making it on my own, not leaning on a man for help, but this year I planted near twice as much corn as usual. After the hard times of the past years, I think that all of us is greedy to have more than enough. Abner lends a hand when he can, but he has a big crop to tend at his own place. And though my young uns is all good workers, Sim's help is welcome. I would offer to pay him, had I any money, but instead I made him a shirt with some homespun I had put away. At first he wouldn't hardly take it, though the old shirt he wears every day is most a rag. Finally he did, though, saying he will keep it for best.

Times is better here in the Laurels, though I can name at least seven families without a man to head them. Them women lost their husbands in the war but are trying hard to hold on to their farms and keep their families together. Some others went to live with kin when the work or the loneliness became too much. It has been like God's mercy, having a strong, good-hearted somebody like Sim who will turn his hand to getting wood or plowing or anything that needs doing.

Anything that needs doing. He has helped with the loneliness too.

Though Sim has a snug little room fixed in Patsy's Shelton's barn, I reckon he ain't always there come morning. But like I told them all some time back, we need more young uns to keep the Laurels strong. And these days, ain't no one likely to be too quizzy about how a widow woman comes to be breeding.

The moon is riding higher now and I can see near as good as if it was day. But it's a world without the greens and yellows, reds and oranges of daylight and I wonder suddenly if Death is like this, all the color of Life drained away.

Queer thoughts, Judy, I tell myself. I come to the end of my row and go to the quilt where the least uns are fast asleep. Armp has one arm flung to the side and the other around his little sister. Marthy Jane is curled up by him, her wet sugar tit tight in her little fist. The patches of the quilt show gray and black in the moonlight instead of the blues and browns of daytime.

I can look across the corn and see where the other young uns are working. Something about the night keeps them quieter than usual and they whisper rather than holler. I hear Frank say something in a low voice and Linnie giggling. Sim is moving along at a good clip and I can even hear his knife slashing the juicy stalk and the swish of the top as it falls between the rows behind him. As he moves on, I see a shiver along the row of topped stalks and I know it's Little Sol. He has taken to Sim right much and always wants to work next to him.

Young uns and dogs is both good judges of character is what I always say.

When I quizzed Sim about where he come from, all he would say was that he had gotten a head wound that had knocked out much of his memory, and he'd spent a year or more at some lonely farm where they'd taken him in and cared for him. He thought he'd been a soldier and he thought he'd deserted. He knew though that he'd had a sweetheart and that she'd died.

"And being as my folks was long dead too, I had nothing to call me back to where I come from. So I set out walking."

He said he weren't even real sure of what his name was but the folks what had nursed him back to health had called him Sim. It was some time later that Patsy Shelton said he had ought to take Shelton for a last name, "For," said she, "you've been as good to me as if you was one of my own."

Across the cornfield, Ellender is singing.

Oh, the years creep slowly by, Lorena,
The snow is on the ground again.

Her voice starts shy and quiet but as she finishes her row and sees that all the rest of us is most done, she lifts it higher, sweet and true. That song that Blue and Gray both sang seems to hold in it all the sorrows and all the longing that there is.

The sun's low down the sky, Lorena,
The frost gleams where the flow'rs have been.

And one after another of us takes up the song as we finish the last few rows of corn. Sim is in the row behind me, and he is singing too, low and soft.

Yes, these were words of thine, Lorena
They burn within my memory yet—

When I turn to thank him for his help, I see a tear, shining in the moonlight, sliding down his cheek.

I knowed him for one of Keith's men when first Marthy took me to him where he waited by the road. Back at the marrying just one year ago when Marthy came and signed me to follow her, I went, hoping that it might be another of the Laurel's men coming home. She hustled me along to where he was hunkered down by the side of the road—not one of ours but another wore-out soul in need of help.

Like I said, I knowed him right off, though without the uniform and the big black beard, he looked like a boy. But a boy with an old man's eyes that had seen too much and shoulders slumped like he was carrying a world's weight on them. I think it was the set of those shoulders that kept my mouth shut back then.

I knowed him for the one who loosed the ropes when me and Miz Unus was hanging from the tree. And I knowed he weren't like the mad dogs who used Mary Shelton so bad. But what has brought him back to this place is a mystery I can't fathom. Maybe he don't remember none of that terrible time and it is naught but happenchance brought him.

Whatever his reason for being here, I will hold my tongue. No matter how many he has helped, there is some who, did they know Sim was with the 64th, would have no mercy. Like dogs that can't be broke of sheep-killing, these fellers tasted blood during the years of war and liked the flavor. They will cry up revenge at any excuse to satisfy that need.

37.

~POLLY ALLEN~

Benton County, Arkansas
December 1866

Do you remember, dearest Emmie, when we were girls reading *Ivanhoe*? How we began to imagine for ourselves romantic futures amid surroundings of regal splendor with true perfect knights for husbands? Your husband, as I recall, was to have golden hair and sapphire blue eyes and would come riding on a magnificently caparisoned silver stallion. Mine was to be tall and dark with a forbidding visage that softened when he spoke my name. His steed, of course, was a midnight black stallion.

And oh! the castles in the air we were to inhabit—yours, tall and many-turreted, its walls clad with climbing roses, overlooking a shining sea; while mine, in keeping with my knight, was hewn from the living rock, clinging to a crag above a dark and boundless forest—

A little sound, half laugh, half sob, escapes my lips and Lawrence looks up from his eternal correspondence.

"Polly?" He frowns, seeing me sitting bemused, mouth agape. "Did you nod off?"

I close my mouth and summon a smile. "Do you know, I believe that I did. I hadn't realized how sleepy I am; perhaps I had best say good night. Do you have many more letters to write?"

He glances at the clock on the uneven rustic mantel and back at the sheet before him. "I must finish this one at least—I'm trying to stir Parker to action. If he can sell our North Carolina properties, we can find better accommodations than this sad old place." He looks around the little room, crowded with the trappings of our former home, and sighs. "Perhaps I should not have put much of our capital into purchasing farmland."

It breaks my heart to see him so worn and aged. The move meant more to both of us than simply exchanging the lovely green mountains of North Carolina for the brown hills and plains of this far corner of Arkansas. It was a farewell to life as it had been—farewell to friends and family; farewell to position in the community, to servants, and not least to Lawrence's hopes of political office.

But here in Arkansas, Annie's bad dreams have stopped and she is taken up with playing little mother to her new brother. Little John, named for my brother, has done much to lift our spirits. Pray God he is spared to us. Lawrence pins so many hopes on this infant scrap of humanity.

I rise and go to Lawrence. Laying my cheek against his, I whisper that he is not to worry, that this house suits me well, the children are thriving, that when he begins to farm in earnest, growing tobacco and strawberries for the market, the sale of the North Carolina property won't matter.

He takes my hand and kisses the fingers one by one. "My sweet Poll—if only—"

But I stop the words with a kiss. "Don't be too long, my dear," I tell him as I withdraw to our bedchamber.

Sitting on the edge of the bed—for there is no room for my dressing table or a chair, I begin to brush my hair the requisite hundred strokes and, as I brush, I resume my unwritten letter.

Shall I describe my castle for you, Emmie? It is a ramshackle unpainted frame house in the northwest corner of Arkansas—a little collection of small holdings called Round Prairie Township. It lies on the edge of Indian Territory, set amidst of gray rolling fields and sparse woodland. There is not a flower or shrub to soften the dirt around the house where chickens scratch and pigs root and I have not the desire to plant any for to do so would be to admit that this will be our home henceforth.

The steady strokes of the brush do not bring the drowsiness they once induced, and I open my trunk in search of the precious laudanum.

Not much remains but I take a careful sip and compose myself on the pillows in hope of sleep. I can hear Lawrence moving about the house. Now there is the squeak of the pump outside and the splash of water.

I burnt the never-sent letters to Emmie before we moved for fear some accident might bring them to Lawrence's notice and then all my well-intended lies would be revealed. But the need to speak frankly remains and I have formed the habit of writing shadow letters in my head, shadow letters to my shadow friend.

Do all wives lie to their husbands, Emmie? Do they lie to themselves as well?

The habit of trust, of silent agreement with my husband has been mightily strained by the anonymous letters that come to me, forwarded by my brother. We left North Carolina so suddenly, and without any clear idea of where we would settle, that I told my friends and acquaintances to send any communications to my brother as I would apprise him of our address as soon as I knew what it would be. But when at last we fetched up here, Lawrence cautioned me against letting our whereabouts be common knowledge.

Is my husband a fugitive from justice? I cannot form the words aloud but my anonymous correspondent—I am almost positive it is a woman, for only a woman could employ innuendo with such a delicate and killing touch—writes that in October, not long after we took our hasty departure, a Madison County grand jury pronounced a "true bill" against my Lawrence for the murder of a James Shelton. I know that things remained unsettled in our county, even after the war came to its inglorious end, and that some of the more savage elements who had backed the Union grew bold and outrageous. James Shelton—will we never be done with the Sheltons? At least there are none here. But murder! Can this be true?

And if this is true, what of the charges Cousin Keith now faces? Was the incident at Shelton Laurel a justified military action? Or was it beyond the pale—a matter of personal revenge? One of those executed was only thirteen years of age, says my correspondent, still a child....

There was a time I would have shown these letters to Lawrence, eager for him to dispel my doubts, to deny all these charges as frivolous hogwash. We would have laughed together and tossed the accusing anonymous missives into the fire.

In the next room I hear the creak of a chair and the scratch of Lawrence's pen as he begins another letter. The laudanum bottle is close at hand and I allow myself one more sip. I must have sleep if I am to play my part—the part of the dutiful and trusting wife.

I sink back and feel the familiar low roaring in my head as I slip toward oblivion. My mind runs back to the romance and the glory that was *Ivanhoe*. The heroic men, the dastardly villains, and the noble women were all so real, the companions of my girlhood. And I had no doubt that it would be a hero such as these that would someday claim my hand...

> But, oh, Emmie! Do you remember the names, the names we would repeat to ourselves over and over till we were drunk on the romance of the names? Rowena—I would have called Annie Rowena but Lawrence disliked the name. Lucas de Beaumanoir, Conrade de Montfichet, Maurice de Bracy—

The door creaks and Lawrence tiptoes into the room, shedding clothes as he moves toward the bed. *Who is this man I have shared a bed with all these years?* I think as he slides under the quilts and reaches for me. *Oh, Emmie, does any woman ever truly know her husband?*

But I am soaring now, over the Ozarks and the long wagon road across Tennessee, back to the grave where my darlings sleep...

38.

~MARTHY WHITE~

Shelton Laurel, NC
December 1866

Come, butter, come,
Come, butter, come,
Sim is standing at the gate,
Waiting for a butter cake.
Come, butter, come—

I sing the words in my head, in time with the clack of the dasher and the swish of the clabber. Though the churn has been setting nigh the fire, on these cold days it still takes longer for the butter to make. My mind wanders about, thinking of the baking and cooking yet to do before tomorrow and the wedding.

It was in October at the shucking at Judy's place that I first begun to pay attention to Sim. Ever since he come amongst us, he had mostly stayed at Patsy Shelton's, helping her to keep the farm going. I heard folks talking about how what a blessing it was she had him there and what a hard worker and a nice, soft-spoken somebody he was, but I didn't think of him, not one way or another. Not till the shucking at Judy's.

There was great crowd of folks in the barn, setting around the biggest pile of field corn you ever saw. It was a working but it was something like a play party, too, for there was to be prizes for the man, woman, boy, and girl that shucked the most in ten minutes and Billy Ray had brought his fiddle to speed the work.

I was setting with Mommy and some of the women when I saw Judy speaking to Sim and nodding her head my way. I knowed right off that she thought to do me a kindness by sending him to come and set by me. Most all the girls of my age and even younger has sweethearts, if they ain't married already, and seeing that makes me miss Davy awful bad. So I didn't look away when Sim took the empty spot by me but smiled and nodded. When it come time for the shucking contest, every feller there had a woman to hand him the ears and he asked would I do that for him. And when he won, I could see all the company looking at us and saw Miz Unus whispering to Mommy.

It was then the thought come to me that maybe all my chances hadn't died with Davy. It even seemed that, could he speak to me now, Davy would likely tell me not to spend my life in grieving for what him and me might have had. Davy had woke me to happiness and I had thought all that had died with him. But setting by Sim, and the way he was joking and talking to me like I was someone who could talk back—that set me to thinking.

The next week he come and spent a day at our place busting wood for he had heard Pap saying that with his back in the condition it was, he didn't know how he'd manage to get in wood before winter. Sim come to the house early and set in on the big old blocks of hickory that needed busting. When I brought him some water and a piece of blackberry pie at mid-morning, he thanked me and asked did I make the pie. When I nodded *yes*, he took a big bite and said it was the best he'd ever had.

I reckon I turned bright red for I could feel my ears burning inside my sunbonnet, but I stayed and stacked the wood while he was busting. When it was all done, he wiped his brow and said that we made a right good team. "First at the shucking and now this," he said, and he winked right at me. All I could do was look away, thankful that my sunbonnet hid my face. He is the only feller, except for Davy, to treat me like an ordinary girl.

It was a few days later that Sim come back by the house. Mommy and me and Kate was outside taking turns stirring a big kettle of apple butter which had just begun to thicken. The good smell was everywhere and I could see Sim smile as he breathed it in.

"I come," said he, "to see did anyone want to go up the mountain after some hickory nuts. Last fall I come across a shagbark hickory up there that had the sweetest nuts you ever tasted. I thought we might see have the squirrels left any. But I reckon youns is—"

"Marthy," Mommy cut in, "me and Kate can finish this up. You go get your shawl and a basket. You know how your pap loves hickory nuts."

I gave her a puzzled look for I didn't know anything of the sort, but I did like she said, and me and Sim set off up the mountain.

The trail was thick with leaves that rustled underfoot as we climbed. At first Sim was near as silent as me, only asking once if he was walking too fast, and then later saying that if he remembered right, the tree was off the trail a little to the left.

"There's the prettiest little level spot," said he, "and a clearing with the hickory in the middle."

I knew that spot for me and Davy had found that tree the summer before all the bad things started. We had even went back that fall to pick the nuts but the squirrels had got them every one. I couldn't tell this to Sim so I just followed him into the woods, glad he was walking ahead of me for my eyes was leaking tears.

I was wiping at them with the tail of my apron when he stopped so sudden I walked right into him.

"Look at that purty thing, Marthy," he said, pointing to a bush covered with red berries. "See how the outside pops open to show the berries? Hearts a-bustin' is what my daddy called 'em."

I nodded and put my face close to the bush so he couldn't see the tears that had started up again. But he reached inside my sunbonnet to put a finger on my chin and turn my face to him.

We stood staring at one another for a moment and I saw his eyes was shiny wet.

"We both have busted hearts, I reckon," he said, reaching out to pick one of the little pods. Then he took my hand and led me on into the clearing where I saw the hickory was heavy with nuts. He didn't even look at it, just pulled off his jacket and laid it on the ground.

"Let's us set a spell before we go to gathering the nuts," said he. "I want to talk to you."

At last the butter has made and big clumps are beating against the wall of the churn. I dip out the butter into a vessel of cold water and pour off the buttermilk into a crock. Mommy is mixing up some bread and calls to Kate, telling her to tote the buttermilk to the spring house and take care not to spill it like last time.

I work the butter over and over, pouring off the milky water and adding more clean till at last the water comes clear and it is time to mix in the salt. And just reaching for the salt gourd brings it all back—the hard winter and no salt, the men going to Marshall and doing what they done. And all that followed.

And Davy is dead and I am salting the butter for my wedding.

That day we went up the mountain after hickory nuts, Sim told me about his sweetheart and how he'd thought his life was over when he found she had died.

"I reckon you felt the same when your Davy—when he was taken from you. Miz Patsy told me you and him was sweethearts."

The lump in my throat was like to choke me. I put my hands to my face and nodded.

"Hearts a-busted," he said, holding up the little seed pod. "Maybe we belong together."

The butter print Sim carved for me makes a big four-leaf clover on the top of each print of the yellow butter. It is a four-leaf clover or, if you look at it another way, it is four hearts. One for each of us—me and Sim, my Davy and his Cora.

"Oh, now don't those look fine," Mommy says. She is full of smiles these days. When Sim come to ask if he could marry me, she didn't hardly credit it, thinking to have me on her hands the rest of her life. And when Sim told her he had some money put by from before the war and that Miz Patsy was going to sell him a pretty little rise of land with some fields and a fine cabin site, she was struck near dumb as me.

And all that has come to pass with the neighbors helping Sim to raise a little cabin on the foundation that Davy had begun. It is to that same little cabin we will go after Preacher says the words here tomorrow evening. It seems so queer to think it, that the dream I once had is about to come true—that dream of me setting in the doorway in a blue dress and braiding my hair, waiting for my husband to come home...

There is so much strange in this life. Last year all I wanted was to have my revenge on that old Black Beard what shot Davy. But my drawing spell didn't work and now I find I'm just as glad. As many times as I have gone over that awful day in my head, I have come to see I have been hating the wrong man. It was ol' Keith who give the order. And it was ol' Keith threatened to fire on Black Beard if he didn't shoot Davy.

I set the last of the butter prints on a plate, cover them with a clean dishtowel, and start for the springhouse. There is a skift of snow on the ground, but the sky is clear blue, boding good weather for tomorrow.

Talk is that ol' Keith is a wanted man—on the run with a bounty on his head. No one seems to know where he has gone to but I hope they catch him. Or better yet, I hope he is dead and burning in hell.

39.

~JAMES A. KEITH~

Asheville, North Carolina
February 1869

I am burning with mixed rage and humiliation as I hear the guard ushering yet another group of gawkers to peer through the grating of my cell door. Not much longer, I remind myself, shall I be forced to endure this ignominy.

"Yep, that's ol' Keith in there all right. Boys, I reckon he's the most savagerous criminal we got in this here jail—that's why come there's someone at this door night and day."

I recognize the drawling speech of Hiram Ledbetter, the guard I've been at pains to conciliate. He often entertains cronies in the hallway outside my cell door. I suspect they are charged for the privilege, but I keep my back to the door as much as possible, hoping the interest will, in time, wane.

"—forty-seven men and boys it was, ol' Keith and his troops murdered. They shot John Metcalf through the head and ran him through with their bayonets. They took and hanged another feller and then cut him down and dragged him through the laurel bushes and left him laying under the leaves. And there was one feller they shot down while he was a-plowing; do you credit that, boys? To shoot a man doing naught but trying to make a crop to feed his family?"

I turn over the page of the tattered newspaper Hiram has been induced to bring me, closely perusing the columns. Over a month old, this copy of *The Western Democrat* from Charlotte may serve to keep me from going mad as I await a further trial here in Buncombe County.

When the war ground at last to a halt, I had been living a double life—pursued by the Confederate civil authorities—damn Vance and damn Merrimon and his lies—while conducting partisan activities in support of that same Confederacy. And when the Confederacy gave way, no sooner had the surrender been signed, then the Union troops were after me. 'Ere long, as my rag-tag forces one by one laid down their arms, I was a wounded lion at bay and soon was captured.

Truly, it was almost a relief when I was taken prisoner. After two years and more, much of that time constantly on the move, sleeping sometimes in friends' homes, sometimes on the bare ground, finally in my own home but always looking over my shoulder, alert for the sound of pursuers—after these trials the spare but, on the whole, clean accommodation at Castle Pickney in Charleston Harbor was not unwelcome. With no hope of escape from the closely guarded island prison, I could only wait and make my plans.

At my door Hiram is settling into his tale for an evidently appreciative audience. "And then there was that pore widder woman—"

Oh, God! Now for the widder woman and her little dog. Daniel Ellis's wretched publication two years ago of his so-called adventures as a Union guide has given Hiram a wealth of stories to tell—no matter that the Ellis book is little more than a tissue of scurrilous lies—the lies and exaggerations of a traitor to the Southland, one who helped deserters flee to the Union states. But I make no doubt that the widespread distribution of these same lies is much of what drove the fervor leading to my persecution.

"Fourteen fine hogs that pore widder woman had, and Keith and his men shot them every one and piled them on the floor of her house. And not content with that, they shot her little dog and tossed it atop the carcasses."

There is a chorus of disapprobation. I hear one of the men hawk and spit. From the corner of my eye, I see a pool of tobacco juice spreading on the floor by my side.

I pull the newspaper closer. Another article warns of the dangers of poisoned liquor, asserting that a recent rise in murder and violence can be traced to the common practice of sophisticating liquor by adding various substances to enhance its potency. Strychnine, the author say, is used to replace hops—

"—and just like ol' pharaoh in the Bible, Keith commanded his men to kill the boys too, to prevent them growing up. Why, all over that part of the country, to this very day, mothers make their young uns mind by telling 'em ol' Keith will get them—"

If this goes on much longer, I could wish for some strychnine. But at last the visitors have looked and heard their fill—and, no doubt, the time is near for the guard to change

I should never have been captured but for a foolish desire to return to Madison County in hopes of catching a glimpse of Polly. With what stealth and cunning did I make my way through the mountains and how like a lovesick swain did I creep through the night to the house where I believed her to be.

Alas, all was boarded up, proclaiming the family's removal—to Arkansas, as I have since learned. A bitter irony that on return to my home in South Carolina I was captured.

Perhaps Lawrence was wise to quit North Carolina for the West. I can understand the feeling that there is nothing more here for a loyal Confederate. I even hear tales of groups emigrating to foreign countries—but I doubt Margaret would agree to such a move. Arkansas, though, might be an agreeable change.

And if someday my children's children ask of my part in this war to preserve our way of life, I shall simply say that after leaving the 64th I continued to serve the Confederacy honorably till it ceased to exist. I have nothing, nothing at all, to regret.

I lie in the dark on my hard bed, shivering under a thin blanket, and sleep will not come. There are some hours yet to wait before my friends can commence their operation. Again I relive my first trial in December. The Asheville courthouse is a wretched little building, erected on the site, and utilizing the bricks, of a previous courthouse, burned four years ago. There is talk of a new one—just as there is talk of the railroad coming someday to Asheville—but I have my doubts that this backward town will ever rise much above its muddy origins as a stop on the Drovers' Road.

It was in this miserable court that the first of what are meant to be my eight trials was conducted. I am charged with seven counts of murder in the Shelton Laurel incident as well as arson at Deaver's grist mill.

When I was arrested by General Canby's Federal troops, I had expected to be tried by a military court, but Canby quickly grew shy of the case and sent me from Castle Pinckney to Raleigh. And the Reconstruction government there sent me here. The prosecutors, aware of the abiding sympathy in this part of the world for the Southern Cause, have decided to try me serially—one charge at a time, hoping eventually to light on a jury that will convict.

They were disappointed in the first trial on the tenth of December when I was charged with the murder of one James Shelton, an accursed Laurelite and notorious bushwhacker. Though much was made of his youth—fifteen, it was said, as if a fifteen-year-old cannot hide behind a tree and use a rifle; the jury's verdict was quick. Not guilty.

What should have been a joyous moment was merely a return to this wretched cell as there were yet six counts of murder pending. And the second trial is delayed while my counsel pursues an appeal. It is our contention that the North Carolina Amnesty Act of '66, granting pardon for all felonies and homicides committed by troops of either side while acting under orders, applies to me and to whatever I may (or may not) have done. It seems indisputable. I was acting under General Heth's orders and can bring witnesses to attest to it.

The sticking point, as the prosecution has argued, is that the Amnesty Act was repealed in '68. Whether or no I can claim this shield will be left to the North Carolina Supreme Court—and I doubt there will be any justice for me there. Moreover, a plan is afoot to consolidate the remaining charges and move the trial back to Raleigh. There the chance of a conviction is strong.

So rather than wait for this charade to play out, I believe that I must take the option already set in motion with the help of several true friends. The muffled scrape of a ladder against the outer wall and the chink of chisels tell me that succor is at hand.

I have to suppress a grim chuckle as I imagine Hiram profiting doubly by my escape. No doubt he will charge the curious for a look at the hole in the outer wall which is even now almost large enough for me to wriggle through. My friends are quiet and diligent—another quarter of an hour and I shall be on my way to freedom.

A pocketknife is thrust through the growing hole and I reach for it greedily. As I rip my blanket into strips, I can imagine Hiram regaling his goggling audience with the thrilling story of my escape.

"Well, boys, I can let you see how ol' Keith got loose. It'll have to be quick for workmen are on the way to patch up the hole. Two bits apiece is all I ask, and for another two bits I can let you have a piece of the blankets he knotted together to climb down.

"Thankee, thankee. Step right in. Yon is the hole cut in the wall. Go ahead, poke your head out. A right smart drop from the third floor, ain't it?

"Well, a course he must have had help. But it was in the night and I was home in bed, listening to my old woman snoring. So I can't even begin to hazard a guess how they worked it.

"But, boys, I'll tell you one thing. Ol' Keith is long gone."

40.

~SIMEON RAMSEY~

Shelton Laurel, North Carolina
July 1869

More and more on these hot summer nights I find myself waking long before dawn. I know I should roll over and get my sleep out, but I can't seem to do a thing but lay here next to Marthy, my heart racing whilst I think black, hopeless thoughts. I tell myself it's just the burden of all the jobs there is to do—finishing the barn roof, clearing another field, building a corn crib—but these is just the everyday worries. My thoughts circle round and round like black carrion crows, and though I try to stay in the here and now and think on things I have some chance of mending, the thoughts fly faster and faster in a circle that narrows and narrows into the same old place. And I am back on that cold morning, standing before the shallow ditch and the line of shivering men waiting for what is to come.

I can see the snow clinging to the dead grasses and the bare trees and I can smell the stink of fear on the prisoners as they watch the firing squad form up. I see their pale faces as one by one they come to understand that this is their day to die. I see the boy jerk back as the balls hit his arms and I see the terrible knowing sweep over him as the others fall on either side of him. I taste the bitter bile rising in my throat and feel the greasy curve of the trigger on my finger. And, clear as if it was happening now, I hear Keith's horse stamping and blowing and the leather creak of the saddle as Keith turns to look at me. And I hear the boy begging for his life. I lay there all a-tremble in my warm bed, next to her that would have been that boy's wife, and it tears at my vitals, the lie I am living.

Four years dwelling amongst the kin of that boy—and in the dark I see again the terror in his blue eyes and hear him cry out, *Let me go home to my mother and sisters.* I hear him sobbing and pleading for mercy as some of our men begin to mock him—and I feel the cold hard chill of the colonel's revolver muzzle at the back of my head.

I shake off the memory that has set my heart to racing and take deep breaths till it slows to normal. Marthy is pressed up agin me, but she is sleeping hard and don't notice as I lay back the covers and slide careful out of bed. Once I start remembering the dead boy, there's naught I can do but to get up and walk till I can't hear him no more and till he stops looking at me with them sorrowful empty eye sockets.

I get my clothes from where I left them on the chest at the foot of the bed and my boots from by the fireplace and creep out as soft as I can. The leather hinges make nary a sound as I shut the door behind me.

The old quarter moon is still riding high enough to give a little light, and I pull on my clothes and set off down the eastward trail that leads into the woods. Marthy won't wonder where I am; she knows that I don't sleep good sometimes on account of bad dreams, and that walking is my best cure. If she could talk like a regular woman, she'd likely quiz me about those dreams, but as it is, when I come back after walking for hours, she'll just greet me with a smile and a kiss and set right in to making some breakfast for me.

I wonder if she thinks of that boy as oft as I do. Or as oft as I think of Cora. Sometimes I feel like we are both of us leading a shadow life and only pretending it is real. I am in the boy's place and she is in Cora's. I look around me and I see this fine farm, just what I had dreamed of when I hoped to marry Cora—waving rows of corn with bean vines twining up the stalks, the broad green leaves of pumpkins spreading beneath. We even have the Jersey cow and the flock of red chickens I used to picture to myself. But it was *Cora* in that dream I had, not Marthy. Marthy is a good helpmate and loving in every way—and I love her the best I am able—but she ain't Cora.

At the fork, I take the path that leads up to the bald where our neighbor runs his cattle, thinking to watch the sunrise. Sometimes the sight of the sun jumping up from behind the dark shape of the mountain and flinging his gold over the clouds and treetops is enough to make me believe in the kind of redemption the preacher talks of and to ease my mind for a while. Lord knows I need it bad today. I had thought to find that redemption here in the Laurels by helping the boy's family in their time of need, and then by marrying his sweetheart when she seemed to want me. And sometimes I feel near to happy in the life we have cobbled together out of the leavings of our past. But then the dreams come back and I find myself walking the trails to the high places, walking in search of something that will get the dead boy outen my head.

It is a steep climb and the half light of the dawning day creeps through the leaves, growing stronger as I near the open bald ahead. I can see the trail good now and am puzzled at the sight of hoof prints—horse or mule and fresh, so far as I can tell. I almost turn back, not wanting to meet with the rider—for there must be a rider; no one lets their horse critters run loose. But then I think of how far I've walked in hopes of seeing that healing sunrise, and I keep on till I'm at the edge of the woods with the soft mound of the bald above me. I think I can make out where the horse went off to the right but in this thick grass, it ain't easy to be sure.

There is a little gang of cattle laying quiet and peaceable in the shallow bowl just below the top but no sign anywhere of a horse and rider. I figure that whoever it was is likely long gone, and I keep climbing, up and up till I am standing at the top of the bald and looking at the ridge to the east. The sky is lighter now but over where the sun will rise it is clabbered up with heavy gray clouds. I hunker down to wait and see will I catch even the least glimpse of the sun. It seems like I have come on a fool's errand and the heaviness of my heart is most more than I can stand. A fool's errand—and as I search the thick clouds for a break in their heaviness, I wonder if my life here in Laurel has been that—just a fool's errand.

While I watch, the lower clouds draw back a mite and the sun looks out at me. But it is not the smiling golden sun I'd hoped for. This is an evil-looking thing, swollen and deep red as a boil about to bust. Dark, angry clouds hang about it and the seeing of it is like a curse. Then, in the blink of an eye, the clouds sweep back over it and veils of mist roll over the mountainside and hang about me.

What bad sign is this? I think. *No healing gold, just angry red, the red of the blood that poured from the boy's chest when I shot him.*

I stay where I am, feeling the dead boy like a weight on my shoulders. *He won't never leave me,* I think, and I bury my face in my hands.

Just then I hear a horse's whicker and look up to see a man moving through the mist, leading a pack horse and coming my way. I am so low in my spirits that I don't even stir. He could be an outlaw—there are plenty of them around, men who will kill just for the fun of the thing, men who got a taste for killing in the war. *Or,* I think, *he could be a ghost.* I feel a crazy laugh coming and think that if he is a ghost, maybe I could send the dead boy off with him. Everwho or everwhat this man is, I am in such case that I purely don't care.

I am laughing like a fool as the man comes up on me, his feet making a solid thump on the ground. Not a ghost then. I stop my laughing and throw up my hand to say howdy. He drops his lead rein, and the horse goes to cropping grass while the man pulls off the big pack he has on his back and hunkers down beside me. Something about him tugs at my memory, and I study him careful out of the corner of my eye, wondering if I know him. From the looks of the horse, he's a peddler, for the beast is heavy laden with packs and odds and ends tied on here and there. I eye the coil of new rope, hanging from one side along with some cooking pans and a thought creeps into my mind.

"I will lift up mine eyes unto the hills, from whence cometh my help," the peddler says, waving toward the Butt Mountain and, without meaning to, I give him the next verse, "My help cometh from the Lord which made heaven and earth."

"You know your Bible," says he, "do you still study it?" He turns his eyes on me and it all comes back. He was the peddler at Suttles's place—the one that saved me—and he was at that inn on the Drovers' Road, right before the war, talking about a storm coming. How could I forget those black eyes that appear to have seen everything?

"I was right about the storm, wasn't I?" he asks, like he could hear my thoughts. And I realize that just now I am in a place like when I was up at Suttleses' on Mac's Patch—a place where time and what is and what ain't don't have no purchase. It is as if maybe just a night has passed instead of all these long and terrible years. I remember back to that inn and me, fool that I was, thinking that me and Cora could stay safe and out of the war that was coming. Thinking that we could hide away in some deep cove.

I don't question how he knows me but answer back honest.

"Right you were—dead right. That blamed storm swept across the land and didn't none escape it."

The peddler is quiet for a while, staring at the mists and swirling clouds like he is seeing some story unfold. At last he turns his head and his great dark eyes are full of sorrow.

"The storm's not over, my poor friend. It's still raging and all this part of the world is fast in its grip."

I nod and we set there silent, side by side. There ain't no more need of words. The peddler has closed his eyes and is rocking back and forth just a little, while his horse grazes all around. I keep looking at the coil of rope hanging from the pack, trying to gauge its length. It looks unused but the bright hemp is tarnished along the top of the coil as if it had hung there many and many a day, through all manner of weather.

The horse moves toward the trees below, and I note a fine big oak with stout branches just high enough. The feeling grows in me and I reach in my pocket for the gold piece I always carry. *A fair price for peace of mind*, I think.

"The rope's not for sale," says the peddler, not even opening his eyes. "Not for you, my friend."

41.

~MARTHY WHITE~

Shelton Laurel, North Carolina
July 1869

The rooster's crow wakes me but rather than open my eyes, I lay there a minute, trying to make sense of the dream I was just in. It was a restless thing, like so many dreams are and, in the way of dreams, people kept shifting. As best I can recollect, I was following a man along a path through briars and brambles, uphill and down, trying my hardest to catch up to him but he just kept going and I couldn't call out. Sometimes in dreams I can talk and sing too, but in this one I couldn't make a sound. All I could see of the man was his back and he just kept going while the briars caught at my skirt and the roots growing across the path slowed me.

In the funny way of dreams, it seemed I knew the man I was chasing and sometimes it was Sim and others it was Davy, Davy all growed to manhood, and sometimes it was both of them at once. It made a kind of sense, in the dream.

I still dream of Davy now and again, and of the sweetness of that first love. I remember how I thought I'd not be able to bear living without him. But Sim has brought a different sort of sweetness into my life and I stretch out my arm to touch him and let him know how I feel. It is so good when we tumble together in love and I smile and reach for him.

My hand touches naught but emptiness and the chill bed clothes. I open my eyes, sigh, and roll out of bed. His clothes and boots is gone and I hurry to the door in my nightshift to see if I can catch sight of him but it is no use. There is nare sign of him. The sun is already breaking through the morning mists, and I hear the clank of Bessie's bell as she moves toward the milk shed. I am ashamed to have slept so late but these days it seems I am starved for sleep, nodding off before it's even black dark and still slow to rise of a morning.

As I watch the mist floating up from the hollers below, I think maybe I should have tried to get him to talk to me about what sends him off to walk the mountain trails like this. He never speaks of much beyond the farm and what needs doing, but I know there is a great trouble eating at him. This going off happens more and more these days; he sets out climbing the steep trails till he is wore out. And when at last he returns, it is like he is walking in his sleep and can't take joy in ary thing. Usually the fit wears off by the next day and he is moderate cheerful and will fun with me some but sooner or later—and the bad spells are coming closer together now—it will happen again.

I wonder could Miz Judy help, was I to find a way to tell her.

Bessie is bawling now and her calf shut away in the stall is answering her back most pitiful. I throw on my work clothes, get the milk pail and a little water from the kettle, and head for the barn.

She is ill-tempered with the wait, switching her tail and tossing her head when I try to tie her, but when I put some hay and a little grain in the manger, she settles enough that I can wash off her nasty, dirt-caked tits. I unch my milk stool up close to her flanks and clean her bag good.

When her bag is clean and I reach behind me for the milk pail, I see the hornet waiting like always atop the post that the gate hangs on. He is a big, handsome black one with a white face and he stays near at milking time so as to buzz down and pick flies off Bessie's back. It is a marvel to watch how quick he does it.

The milk sings into the pail and the rich smell fills my nose, making my stomach grip. I swallow hard, hoping the uneasy feeling will pass off. Bessie has her ways but her good Jersey milk with all that cream for butter makes her worth humoring along.

I finish up the three tits that is for us, leaving the far hind one for the calf, who is still making a fuss in his stall. After I hang up the milk pail out of the way, I let the calf out. He gives a little hop and rushes over to his mama to begin butting at her bag and slobbering each tit till he finds the one that still has milk. He is the prettiest thing—dark red with a black brindle stripe to his coat—and I stand watching as he snorts and sucks.

The hornet has taken two flies already and is waiting again on his post. I see a big fat fly promenading across Bessie's flank and, quick as can be, I reach out and slap it. Then I set it careful on the post by the hornet. He lifts up, legs a-dangle, as my hand come near then sets back down and takes the fly. He goes off with it and I have to wonder what Sim would think, could he see me feeding a hornet. Maybe it would make him smile.

The calf is most done and I untie Bessie so she can nuzzle and lick him some. I hate that we have to keep them apart, but was we to leave them together, we wouldn't get hardly any milk and the calf would get too much and likely take the milk scours. More than one young calf has been lost to that nasty flux.

A big old fly lands on Bessie's side and I slap it right quick. I look around and see that the hornet is just now coming back to his place and, without thinking, I stretch out my hand with the dead fly on my fingertips.

The hornet hovers near the post, drifting up and down like he is trying to make up his mind then, quick as anything, there is a dry whisper across my fingers and the fly and hornet are both gone. *Oh!* I think, looking at my fingers and touching them to my lips, *I have to show Sim this trick. I reckon it will make him smile for sure. This and my other news.*

42.

~SIMEON RAMSEY~

Shelton Laurel, North Carolina
July 1869

I leave the peddler there on the bald with the mists around him and I light off down the trail like something big and mean was after me, not rightly knowing what just happened. When I reach the woods, I look back but there is no sign of the peddler nor his horse. The cattle are up now and moving across the face of the bald and behind the clouds I can see that the sun has climbed high in the sky.

How long was I up there? I think. And I wonder if my mind is giving way. That happens to some soldiers what has seen too much and to others, like that poor Mary Shelton that got used so bad. They say she talks to folks what ain't there and pulls off all her clothes if her people don't watch her close.

I am most running down the path but when I come to the fork that would take me back to our cabin, I see people like shadows moving through the trees and singing hymns. The words I said up on the mountain—*said to who?* I wonder—sound in my head. *My help cometh from the Lord,* I whisper, and I take the path where the singing people are walking. I am swept along with them, and I find myself singing too.

Before long we come out of the woods to a pasture, and I recognize the Ray place where I did some work when first I come to Shelton Laurel. Just nigh a bold stream there is a new-made brush arbor all covered over with hemlock and balsam branches. I remember hearing that there was some famous preacher traveling through the Laurels and I figure that is what has brought so many folks to this place. Most of our neighbors are there and a world of other folks from all over the Laurels. I wonder have I been led here for a purpose, if maybe here I will find the answer to what it is that sends me out to the high places to talk with folks that ain't there.

Me and Marthy ain't been as regular at church as we had ought to, but when I come nigh the arbor they all make me welcome, calling me Brother Shelton or Brother Sim. I see Miz Judy and Miz Unus, and several others that I worked for back of this. It's mostly women here—that's the way of it these days in the Laurels—but toward the back a little knot of the menfolk who made it through the war are talking amongst themselves.

Miz Judy comes up and asks after Marthy and I say she ain't feeling too good this morning. "Well," says Miz Judy, smiling a little, "I reckon that's to be expected," and her and Miz Unus cut their eyes at one another.

As folks crowd onto the rough log benches under the sweet-smelling boughs, I look around, surprised at how many is there and I feel bad for Marthy that she is missing this. But it is too late now to go and fetch her for a short little feller in a dusty frock coat is stepping to the front and starting up with a prayer for healing. "—a healing, brothers and sisters, of all the bodies and souls torn and shattered by the terrible war we have endured. Not a one of you but has suffered and I say unto to you, redemption is at hand."

I would like to believe that is so. I have sought after it so long. Maybe what I need is right here in this brush arbor, amongst these neighbors. But can a man be redeemed when he is living a lie?

I look at the man on the bench beside me. Dolph Randall's right sleeve is empty and his skinny little wife has to do their plowing. But at least she has him back. Many a widow here is left to run a farm and feed a family all on her own. When first I came here, I helped many a one in the fields, and lay with some too, when they was wanting it. I reckon one or two of the young uns that come along several years back was mine, but none of the women wanted more than my seed. Till Marthy.

The preacher lights into his message, starting out soft and low, wheedling and cajoling us into thinking of our sins and how we have all earned the worst that God might mete out. He has a long list of sins—from gossiping, gambling, and back-biting to thieving and lusting and lying. All around me folks is shifting on the benches and being careful not to catch a neighbor's eye.

The preacher is hotting up now and he shucks off his frock coat and tosses it aside.

"We have *all* sinned in the Lord's eyes; we have *all* fallen short, like willful and disobedient children; we have *all* disappointed him. But his precious mercy is everlasting and he says unto each one of you—"

The preacher has to stop here and pull a rumpled white handkerchief from his pocket to wipe away the sweat that is rolling down his face. No one moves or hardly even breathes as he pushes it back into his pocket and goes on, pointing at first one and then another.

"He says to *every* sinner, he says it in Luke: 'then look up, and lift up your heads; for your redemption draweth nigh!'"

And he stretches out his arm, pointing up and every one of us looks up at the green boughs overhead, like we expected to see the Lord hisself roosting there.

Shamefaced, we look back at the preacher who is giving the altar call and begging all who have sinned to come forward, to confess and be forgiven, to make ready to be caught up into the great and loving heart of Jesus. There is a shuffling and rustling behind me and one of the Norton boys makes his way to the front and mumbles something into the preacher's ear. The preacher shakes his head and takes the boy by the shoulders, swinging him around to face us.

"Seek the forgiveness of the *church*, boy. Confess your sins to *them* and they shall forgive you. The grace of the Lord himself shall rest upon forgiver and forgiven alike. Speak up, boy, and trust in his mercy."

And all red-faced and near to bawling, the boy tells of lifting eggs and two chickens from a neighbor and taking a ham from her meat house. "It was during the war," he says, looking at his feet and talking fast, "and Mommy and the little uns hadn't seen meat for months. We was making it on mush and dried apples and the little uns was crying all the time—"

"I forgive you, Wash Norton," calls out a big woman from her bench. "I suspicioned it was you all along. I should have seen back then how it was with your mam and done better by her. I forgive you for your thieving—now you forgive me for my blindness."

And it is like a dam had let loose and folks are pushing and shoving to take their turn and confess to one another. I set there quiet, listening to their puny little sins and marveling at how their faces light up as they are forgiven and make their way back to where they were setting, only to have those around them smile and pat them on the back. All the while, through the tales of thieving and gossiping and bearing false witness, the weight of the dead boy is heavy on me and I hear him whispering that I should make things right. My breath is coming short and I feel my hands trembling but still I set there.

Miz Judy ain't gone forward, never mind all them woods colts she has birthed. No, she is setting there at her ease, her belly all a-swell with what folks reckon is Abner Tweed's child, never mind that he has a lawful wife and young uns by her. Miz Judy just sets, her face not showing nothing. I reckon a strong-minded woman like her don't feel the need of redemption. But she don't have the dead boy whispering in her ear.

The last to go up and face the church is old Miz Unus the midwife, who is generally reckoned the most Christian and honest woman there is. But she turns and looks at the folks on the benches and in a quavery little voice asks to be forgiven for smothering a babe that came afore its time.

"Hits little legs was joined together to where it looked like a fish and there weren't no hole—no way for hit to—" The tears are running free down her wrinkled old face and she is having a hard time getting the words out. "It was long ago and the mother is gone now but the memory has eat at me all this time," she says. "I did it, thinking to save both mother and babe some pain for I knowed it couldn't live—"

There is a dead silence at first and then some of the women come forward and cluster round Miz Unus. Some are crying but they are all of them hollering, "We forgive you, we forgive you," and they are wrapping her round with their arms and weeping and rocking back and forth. The preacher throws up his arms and shouts *Hallelujah* and the whole crowd stands and answers back with *Amens* and *Hallelujahs*.

When at last things settle down and Miz Unus is back on her bench drying her eyes, the preacher begins to talk about the blessings we have seen as grace comes to sinners, and he is going on to say some more when I find myself on my feet and walking toward him. The boy is whispering in my ear and I can't hear nothing else. The preacher's lips is moving but I don't hear nare word.

Like in a dream, I turn and face my neighbors and begin to tell my story—who I am and what I have done. They set there all unmoving and I tell it every bit—how I never meant no harm; how the colonel would have shot me; how the boy was going to die one way or another and I had thought to save him more suffering. I tell them that didn't no one else know this, not even Marthy, and I asked them, if they couldn't forgive me, at least not to be hard on her.

I finish and stand there with my hands stretched out to them. They are wide-eyed and open-mouthed, most of them, and I begin to hear a murmuring run round the benches. I am froze to the spot but I feel something lighter and am happy that I have told my story, whether they forgive me or not. The whispering goes on as I stand there without moving the least bit. I am afraid of what may follow, but I feel more free than I have since that dreadful day. And the dead boy is quiet.

Then Miz Judy stands and comes forward. She takes my outstretched hand and looks me in the eye. "Sim," says she, "you have lived amongst us all this while, helping those who needed help. And you are lawful wed to one of our own. I reckon there's several here has done hateful things during the war, yes, and after too. Little Davy's people ain't here to speak but *I* forgive you, Sim, I forgive you." And she reaches out with them strong arms of hers and clasps me to her bosom.

She lets go so quick that I find myself wondering if it happened at all but then, just like with Miz Unus, there is a crowd around me, putting out their hands to touch me and hollering that they forgive me. I feel so lifted up in my spirits that I might just bust through those green branches overhead and sail on up into the blue above.

The place is in an uproar but the preacher calls for silence and sends the others back to the benches. He grabs my shoulder, his strong fingers like a hawk's claw, holding me there and shouts out, "Brothers and sisters, don't you feel the Spirit at work here today? How blessed is forgiveness, brothers and sisters, to forgive and be forgiven. Now, raise your voices in that sweet old hymn—"

And he lights in to "Just as I am without one plea," and the whole place takes it up, singing so loud I wonder if Marthy don't hear it back at the cabin. I know the words, for we sung it many a time in camp back during the war, but I am too bumfuzzled to sing, still feeling the warmth of all those hands on me and still hearing the words of forgiveness ringing in my ears. I stand there like a scarecrow with a foolish smile on my face and the tears running down my cheeks, happy but fearful too. For now I must tell Marthy.

The preacher still has me in his grip when the last verse is sung but he raises his other hand and calls out, "For the Lord himself shall descend from heaven with a shout, with the voice of the archangel, yes, it's coming, beloveds, it's coming. Yes, the time is coming when we shall be caught up to meet the Lord in the air, oh, hallelujah, it's a-coming!"

And all the folks is waving their hands and amen-ing and hallelu-jah-ing as he gives me a little shove to send me back to my seat. When the folks has settled down some, the preacher holds up a blue cloth poke he has laying on a table by his Bible.

"Remember, beloveds, it is more blessed to give than to receive. And is not the laborer worthy of his hire? Your offerings will help me to travel these mountains bringing the Word to others in need. Haven't we had a great blessing here today? A great anointing of the Spirit? Oh, beloved ones, pass this offering bag amongst you and put in what the Spirit tells you."

The poke moves along right quick, cash money being scarce around here. By the time it comes to me, I can feel that there is just a handful of coins, light ones at that, and a few paper bills. I look at the little preacher who is pretending not to watch the poke as it passes from hand to hand and dig into my pocket for my lucky gold coin. I look at it for a moment, thinking that if I had thought to buy a rope that would send me to hell, the least I could do was to give it to this preacher who has brought me forgiveness and a hope of heaven.

A stray sunbeam glints off the coin just as I drop it in the poke and the little preacher sees it, too, for he turns up his eyes and mouths the words, *Thank you, Jesus.*

The meeting breaks up soon after the offering is taken and, as I mingle with the others, Miz Judy comes up to say that quick as she can run home and fetch them, she will bring over some dried herbs for Marthy to make a tea with so's she will feel better. One and another of the folks smile and nod at me as I hit the trail for home, feeling blessed and washed clean of the past. Once I have told Marthy the truth, I think, I can put all this evil behind me.

43.

~MARTHY WHITE~

Shelton Laurel, North Carolina
July 1869

On the way back from milking I was sick again, like I am almost every morning, but it passed off quick. I nibbled a little bit of yesterday's cornbread and it stayed down. Now I have put on my pretty blue dress, the one I stood up in to be married, and I look about to see what else needs doing before Sim comes home. The new milk is in the spring box and I have set a churning with the cream from the past two days. Biscuits is made and keeping warm in the ashes and sausage too. If he wants, I can fix him an egg for the hens are laying extry good just now. Even with the old speckledy one setting, we are still getting nigh a dozen a day and I am putting some by to trade with the peddler when next he comes. It is most time for him to be here in the Laurels. He always comes to Miz Judy's place first, and she has said that she will be sure to send him our way this time.

The thought of the peddler sets me to wondering might he have some domestic with him. I would like to start making baby clothes now that I've missed my monthlies twice. Mommy will show me how to cut them out. And I will need to make some hippens for its little bottom too. Oh, there is so much to do, so many happy things. And I won't wait any longer—I will tell Sim today, quick as he gets home. If that glad news don't make him smile, I don't know what will.

I get my sewing basket, where I have been saving squares of cloth for the longest time—just the prettiest, finest cloth—no work britches or rough homespun but real store boughten cloth. Miz Judy has give me a bit of pink and Miz Unus had some pale blues, and my mommy found some lavender with little flowers on it and some light brown. And I kept the scraps from this very blue dress I have on now. I take my basket to the door where the light is good and I can set and watch for Sim whilst I begin to sew the squares together. I have decided on a plain four-patch and I pick out two pinks and two browns to make a start.

It is hard to credit all this —that I am a married woman, setting in the door of my cabin, breathing in the spring-sweet smell of the apple bloom and waiting for my husband whilst I piece a quilt for the baby that is coming.

A memory jostles around in the back of my mind and I remember that this was what I used to dream of when first me and Davy was promised. And here I am, on the same land that would have been his, setting in the door in the east-facing cabin with apple trees about —just as we had planned. Some of the rocks the logs rest on are rocks that Davy hauled. Only Davy is in the cold ground atop the little hogback ridge next to Miz Judy's. He is still just thirteen years of age and he won't never enjoy a fine day like this again.

The day suddenly don't seem so fine, and I put the little patches back in my basket and set off to the path that runs through the woods. Surely Sim will be coming that way before long, I think. And if I walk to meet him, I can share the good news all the sooner.

A little ways into the woods I come to the place where the sun breaks through the trees, making bars of shadow and light on the path, and I remember the old game I used to play when I was walking to church with Mommy and Pap and all the others. I slow my pace and, just like I used to, I step from light to dark, dark to light, and back again. I used to think doing so was some kind of charm, something that would keep me and mine safe forever. And we *were* happy—and mostly safe—till come the war. But that is all behind us now and before too long it'll be me and Sim walking this path with a passel of young uns.

I stop in the last bar of light and hug myself for joy, imagining what I will do when I see Sim—how I will tell him. I make a cradle of my arms and pretend I am rocking a baby. If that don't make him understand, then I will take his hand and lay it on my belly. I will pooch my belly out and grin at him and the sadness will slide right off his face and he will wrap me in his strong arms and pick me up and spin me around, like Pap used to do to Mommy. I will hug him to me and plant kisses all over his face…

And I will try to find a way to make him understand that I have known for the longest time that he was with the ones that hung me from the tree, that whipped the others, and that marched our men off to die. I remember him good now—staying on the edge of things like he didn't want to be there. I remember him slacking off the rope when the other soldiers wasn't looking, and I remember the sick look on his face all during the whippings. And most of all, I remember that he was the one who shot Davy.

When I found the silver locket in the bottom of his old rucksack not long after we were wed, it come over me all at once that my drawing charm had worked after all, but that instead of killing Black Beard like I'd meant to, I had married him.

I could hardy get my breath for the shame and horror of it, and I tried to figure out what to do. But the more I thought on it, remembering how good he'd been to Davy's mama and many another, the more it seemed he was doing the best he could to make things right. So I put the silver locket back and in time all the hate I had felt turned to love. And I have loved him hard.

Somewhere down the path I hear him coming. And lo and behold! he is singing. It is the church song they sing at the altar call and I marvel to hear it coming from his throat.

Just as I am, and waiting not
To rid my soul of one dark blot,
To Thee whose blood can cleanse each spot,
O Lamb of God, I come, I come.

I am all amazed and my heart leaps in my bosom to hear my love, my darling one, sounding happier than ever I have heard him sound. I don't wait another minute but hitch up my skirt and run toward him.

44.

~SIMEON RAMSEY~

Shelton Laurel, North Carolina
July 1869

The trail winds through the woods, and now the sun that had seemed sulled up and red atop the bald has turned to gold, as gold as the coin I gave the preacher. It sparkles through the leaves, making little bright patches on the hard-packed earth. I am as lighthearted as a spring lamb and I cut a foolish caper when I catch sight of the fork that will take me to our cabin. In the gladness of it all I start to croak out the hymn they was singing at the meeting just now.

> *Just as I am, without one plea,*
> *But that Thy blood was shed for me,*
> *And that Thou bidst me come to Thee,*
> *O Lamb of God, I come, I come.*

The words come easy to my mind from all the times I've sung them, both when I was a boy back home with Daddy and Sairy and with the 64th when we was in camp, but today, this minute, the words mean something, more than something.

> *Just as I am, and waiting not,*

I walk on, my voice growing stronger, happy in knowing that I have almost rid my soul of the dark blot of my past, and that I have been forgiven by God and by my neighbors. And I will tell Marthy and she will forgive me too—I would pledge my life that that's so. And I sing even louder at the thought of being rid of the boy who has kept me wakeful so many nights, for if God and man have forgiven me, surely, he will too.

> *Just as I am, though tossed about*
> *With many a conflict, many a doubt,*

Fightings and fears within, without,
O Lamb of God, I come, I come.

I have never felt so happy, never, and I know that this is a day to keep in my heart forever. *All debts paid,* I think, just as a twig snaps behind me and I hear a shout, an archangel sound, it seems, remembering what the preacher said. A feeling of glad expectation overcomes me.

At last, I think, and the boy says, *Yes, at last,* and I turn—

45.

~JUDITH SHELTON~

Shelton Laurel, North Carolina
July 1869

The sound of a gunshot stops me cold, just at the fork in the path that leads to Sim and Marthy's cabin, and I drop the basket I am carrying. The little paper packets of dried mint and raspberry scatter across the path like fallen leaves, and I kneel to gather them up. My heart is pounding as I try to think what that shot could mean. No one hunts of a Sunday. *Someone saw a copperhead*, I tell myself, and I almost believe it, but for the memory of Pete McCoy's face when Sim stood up and told his story. *Just a copperhead*, I think again, not willing to give credit to my fears and paying no mind to the sudden chill running over me.

My big belly makes me clumsy and I am scrabbling in the weeds for the last of the packets when I hear a scream, the likes of which I hope never to hear again. It is as if some woman's heart was being torn from her bosom.

I struggle back to my feet, leaving the basket in the weeds, and set off, fast as I can manage, down the path to Sim and Marthy's cabin. Something is rustling in the laurels above the path, moving quick it seems, but when I look up there is nothing to see and no more rustling to hear, so I keep going.

I've gone only a little ways, my breath coming short and a stitch in my side, when I round a bend and see them there in a pool of sunlight.

Marthy is crouching beside her man, her blue dress soaked with blood. She has wadded up her skirt and pressed it to the great wound in the back of his head and her mouth is stretched wide like she was howling.

Only there ain't no sound.

❧

It is late in the evening when we have done what needed doing and the peddler and I are setting quiet on my porch in the last light of day. Marthy is in my bed and, by the Lord's mercy and with the help of some cherry brandy, asleep at last. I do not think she will lose the child, though I'm of two minds as to whether or not the loss would be a blessing.

Mr. Aaron has said hardly a word through this weary business, beyond that he had known Sim before this and thought him a good man. I look over at the peddler and see he is staring off into the trees with as sorrowful a look as ever I saw.

"I have seen many a sad and terrible thing these past years," I say to him, "but this death and that poor girl left alone, not even able to cry out—and right after all that forgiving at the meeting and him so happy. What does God mean by it, letting such happen?"

Mr. Aaron rouses himself from his thoughts, shaking his head like as to clear it. He takes a sup of the brandy he brought from his pack and pours another tot into my cup. It burns its way into my empty stomach.

"Why did the Almighty let Cain slay Abel?" he says at last, turning his dark eyes on me. "Why did he allow all that has just happened in this land? Why do people in every place and every time suffer?"

His voice is harsh and far away, like he was remembering them other times and places. I look closer at him, studying on the fine lines about his eyes, and I wonder just how old the peddler is. I remember him from when I was just a little thing, and he ain't changed hardly a lick. My folks always said as how he could be trusted and I reckon that is why I sought his help when I found Sim dead.

I was kneeling there on the path with my arms around Marthy, trying to comfort her and make her understand that there weren't nothing could be done for her man, when I saw the peddler coming along, leading his pack horse. He took one look and I saw his lips move like he was praying. Then he come closer, his mouth turned down and his eyes a-brim with tears. He looked down on the three of us, shaking his head real slow, and said the queerest thing, something about a man's feet leading him to the place where he was wanted.

"Well, you are wanted here now, Mr. Aaron," said I. "Can you make room across that critter's back to carry this poor boy back to my place?"

I had been studying on what to do. I was right sure it was Pete McCoy done this murder, but I reckoned there might be more of the same mind. I didn't want to leave Marthy alone while I went for help, and I didn't see no point in calling in the law and stirring up more ugly feelings. So I struggled to my feet, leaving Marthy holding Sim to her, her mouth still stretched in that wordless howl.

Taking the peddler a little aside, I told him my thoughts.

"I aim to take Sim back to my place now, lay him out proper, and bury him up on the hogback where we put the others back in '63. Seems fitting. And I want to do it now before any talk of it gets around. There's those who when they learn who he was and what he done wouldn't think twice about digging up the grave and making an ugly show of the corpse. Marthy will have enough to bear without that. You bring him along now while I see to Marthy. My boys will help to dig the grave, and I'll make them swear not to talk of it."

And that was what we done. I put Marthy in my bed with Ellender to watch over her while I washed poor Sim and wrapped him in a quilt. All the while Mr. Aaron and Dan'l and Frank was digging on the grave. When they was done, Mr. Aaron hoisted Sim onto his pack beast and we clumb back up the hogback ridge and put poor Sim in the ground.

Mr. Aaron said some words, good as any preacher, and my boys and me said the Lord's Prayer. Marthy had wanted to come with us but I was feared for the safety of the babe—Marthy was spotting some and the climb up the hogback would likely make things worse. At last she listened to me and quit trying to get out of the bed.

We laid Sim a little beyond where the thirteen are, deep down with the earth smoothed over and the sod put back careful. I don't believe anyone would guess there was a grave there. I will show Marthy the place when she's able to make the climb and maybe, after some time has passed, we will carry up a pretty rock to mark it for her. I reckon they will all of them lay quiet together.

At my side Mr. Aaron drains his cup and says some words I can't understand. I think maybe he's drunk then he speaks up, clear as can be.

"They tell a story of King Solomon and the Angel of Death," he says, looking off into the trees again. "One day the Angel of Death came to Solomon, looking very sad, and said that two of the king's favorite servants were to die on the following day. When the Angel had left, Solomon, in hopes of cheating Death, called for the servants and gave them swift horses, telling them to ride as fast as they could to a town far away."

I have heard of King Solomon and all his wives but I don't remember this story. I start to say as much but Mr. Aaron goes on.

"The next day the Angel of Death came back to King Solomon and the Angel was smiling and happy. 'Why do you smile?' asked the king. And the Angel answered, 'I smile because of the mystery that is Fate. You know your two servants I spoke of? They were destined to die today in a far off city, but yesterday they were here and I could not see how they could possibly be in that place today. Yet this morning, there they were, faithful to the appointment. Marvelous are the workings of Fate!' And Solomon bowed his head, saying 'A man's feet will lead him to the place where he is wanted.'"

The peddler takes another sup and stares into the darkness settling around us. I don't understand some of his big words but I take his meaning right enough. There ain't nothing to say but I mean to remember this story to tell to Marthy, later when it might bring her comfort.

Mr. Aaron finishes his brandy and stands. "Ma'am, I will say goodnight. I'll be on my way long before morning but shall hope to see you on my rounds next year."

I watch him make his slow way to the barn. He always chooses to sleep in the hay, close to his pack and his beast. He is a queer fellow but a good soul and his help this day has been right welcome.

I go the bedstead in the dark. Upstairs I hear some of the young uns whispering but am too wore out to fuss with them. Tomorrow, I think, tomorrow...

Marthy has scooched herself to the far side of the shuck tick and is curled up with her back to me. I can hear her breathing and know she ain't asleep. I slip under the covers and take her in my arms, pulling her against my big belly just as if she was one of my young uns. She is shivering and gulping air and at first I worry she is taking a fit, but then I figure out that she is crying without making a sound. I hug her tighter and wish she could shout out, could scream and scream for it might give her some ease at last.

Her body is stiff as can be, but I pet her and whisper soft words in her ears, almost like gentling a horse. "Shh, shh, honey," I say, which don't make sense as she ain't made a sound. "Judy'll take care of you while you grieve."

As I rub her back real gentle, I feel her muscles go slack. She turns to face me and lays her head on my bosom. I see her thumb go into her mouth and after a day of fighting off tears, I am undone and bust out crying.

We lay there both shaking and wet-faced, me trying to be as silent as she is for fear of unsettling the little uns even more. "Oh, Marthy," I whisper. "Oh, my honey lamb, I am so sorry."

There ain't much you can do when someone's suffered a loss like this. Sometimes crying along with them is all there is. I smooth back her hair from her face and keep on whispering. "There, there—there, there," and slowly she begins to calm.

When finally she drops off to sleep, I inch my arm from under her and settle her head on the pillow. This young un in my belly is setting hard atop my bladder and I roll out of the bed to go outside and squat.

When I am done, I stand a moment in the cool night air, listening to an owl calling up on the ridge and, somewhere else, a fox barking. A little breeze stirs in the chestnut tree behind me, bringing the smell of cows and manure all mixed in with some flowery scent. Above me the stars are scattered across the dark sky, like someone had busted open a bag of meal. They are beyond counting, and the seeing of them sets me to wondering again about God and his ways. If he could make all that, along with the land and the mountains and the water running free, the beasts and birds and all that is fine under the heavens, seems like he might have done a better job with mankind. Especially folks like Pete McCoy.

I'll not deny that Pete was of help a-plenty while the war was on.

He kept the soldiers from stealing all my crops, and he accounted for a good many of them damned Secesh. But now that the war is over and done, seems like he can't stop killing. Like a sheep-killing dog, he has got a taste for it, I reckon. He was bragging the other day about tracking down a fellow who'd been with the 64th, finding him at his home and shooting him dead as he stood on his front porch, picking his teeth.

And why I didn't think about that when I saw Pete leaving the brush arbor, I do not know. I reckon I was so caught up in all the forgiving that was going on that I didn't think there might be some of a different mind. Sim had made it clear as could be that he was forced into all that he did but that don't make no difference to folks who have made up their minds to hate.

"How long, Lord?" I ask the sky. "How long are you going to let things go on like this?"

46.

~JAMES A. KEITH~

Logan County, Arkansas
1878

How long, James, has it been since we had any news of Cousin Lawrence and Polly? It seems strange that though we all have removed to the same state, yet we never meet nor even—"

"Remember, Margaret," I say, laying down my pen with a sigh, annoyed to be interrupted yet again in my work on my memoir, "that I attempted to establish some communication with them almost ten years ago, not long after little Mattie was born. I sent the letter to Brother Obadiah and he assured me he had forwarded it on. There was never a reply nor to my second. From what little I have learned through mutual friends, they are not very well off and perhaps this makes them reluctant to continue the acquaintance."

Margaret nods and goes on with her tatting. "A sad come down for them. Did you not tell me that he'd gone to school-teaching?"

"So I heard. At some paltry salary, perhaps twenty dollars a month." I look around our well-appointed parlor, so superior to anything we enjoyed in North Carolina, and think of my growing bank account. Between my medical practice, the farm, and my logging operation, we are numbered among the most prosperous citizens of our county.

"Poor Polly," Margaret muses. "Next you'll tell me she's taking in washing to help support the family."

There is an odd little note of satisfaction in my wife's jest that reminds me of her past jealousy. She was never quite happy with my perhaps too obvious admiration of Lawrence's wife. But in truth, that is so far in the past that it might not have been. As indeed is the whole wretched time of the War Between the States and its shameful aftermath. Nine years in Arkansas have enabled me to leave behind the unjust persecutions and indignities suffered pursuant to my loyalty to the Southern Cause, and I have begun anew, earning a reputation as an excellent physician, a diligent farmer, and a successful businessman. A pillar of the community, in fact.

Indeed, as I begin to sketch out the framework of my memoir, I think I might do worse than to remark on the trials of Job—his loss of all and how it was regained sevenfold. I reach for my father's Bible that lies on my desk and turn to Job. A lengthy book but surely there will some lines worthy of quoting.

There was a man in the land of Uz, whose name was Job; and that man was perfect and upright, and one that feared God, and eschewed evil.

Perhaps not perfect but…

Behold, I cry out of wrong, but I am not heard: I cry aloud, but there is no judgment. He hath fenced up my way that I cannot pass, and he hath set darkness in my paths. He hath stripped me of my glory and taken the crown from my head.

All too familiar, indeed.

…he sat down among the ashes…

Familiar and appropriate. My time in exile and my time in the various prisons are not unlike sitting amongst the ashes. When I think of the trials I endured, culminating with my escape from jail and our hasty removal from the Carolinas—

My darling Mattie bursts into the room and throws her arms around my neck. "Papa, you promised we would go riding this afternoon. Shall I run ask Old Sam to saddle Star and Toby?"

I acquiesce, as always, and suggest that we ride into town and call at the post office as I have letters to mail. Margaret warns our darling to wear a hat against the sun. Now that Laura is married and Douglas is away at school, this last child is grown infinitely dear to us. She is a harum scarum thing, as full of spirit as any boy, and as perfectly at home in the out of doors. I tease her that even before she was born, she knew she wanted to live here, for it was her premature arrival in Arkansas as we were on route to Texas that forced us to stay our journey. And having found the country congenial, here we settled.

Our call at the post office was rewarded with the latest number of *Harper's* and a fat letter from my brother-in-law. Now, supper over and Mattie off to bed, Margaret and I settle ourselves in the parlor again. Obadiah's letter is long and full of business matters but he has included a clipping from a local newspaper.

I send this in the belief you might find it interesting, Brother Jim. It's from some years back but even so those rascals in the Laurels are still at it, murdering one another. I thought the rustic parlance of the teller, as quoted, might amuse you.

Margaret is busily tatting but she looks up. "Jim, won't you read something to me while I work? I must finish this tonight as I promised Mattie to trim her new dress with it before Sunday."

I glance over the article to ascertain its suitability. "Of course, my dear. Shall I read this clipping that Obadiah has sent? It may go a little way to explaining what manner of brute we had to deal with in the Laurel campaign. It deals with Pete McCoy—one of the most notorious of the bushwhackers. We actually had him in custody at one time, but somehow he slipped away. I am sorry to hear he still lives. The story was evidently taken down by a reporter interviewing one of the Laurelites."

She is eager to hear it and her busy fingers ply the shuttle. I begin to read, attempting a little to affect the mountain twang.

"'Wal, Pete McCoy knew that one of the men that was in the squad of soldiers that killed the thirteen lived in Buncombe County. So Pete run him some bullets at his sister's home for his Lewin Rifle that he called Old Betsy. He walked by night and slept by day, until he found where the man lived and laid in wait behind a rail fence in front of his enemy's house. He told afterwards how the man eat his breakfast then walked out on the front porch, picking his teeth with a splinter. Pete McCoy took dead aim and at the crack of the rifle, the man pitched head first into the yard and lay still. And Pete, he patted the stock of Old Betsy and said, 'Sweet revenge.'"

"Gracious!" exclaims my wife. "How wise you were to insist we move far away. Those people—"

But my eyes have struck on a shorter article titled, "Another Revenge Shooting in Shelton Laurel." I skim through it quickly.

"Now here's a curious thing. Yet another shooting ascribed to the Laurelites—not that another murder is curious for I know, none better, the savage nature of those brutes. No, the curious thing here is that it is alleged that the victim was another member of the 64th and likewise one of the firing squad in that—incident which aroused such an unjust clamor and persecution. What's more, it says that this fellow had been living unrecognized amongst the Laurelites for some years. It makes no sense." I scan the words again. "But it can't be correct. The victim's name is given as Simeon Shelton. I feel sure we had no one of that name with us at the time."

Going to my desk, I shuffle through the papers I have gathered in aid of my memoir. The journals I kept during the war, the copies of letters I wrote, the letters I received—there is a wealth of detail and anecdote, only awaiting my leisure. I find the entry in the '63 journal—my account of the incident in January of '63—and note that I was compelled to threaten one member of the firing squad to do his duty—a Sim Ramsey by name.

"No, it's as I thought. Several Sheltons but none of that name—I would have remembered the name Simeon."

"Of course, dear," Margaret says, yawning as she disentangles her row of lace from the shuttle.

An uneasy thought flutters at the back of my mind, beating against the walls of memory. Simeon—Sim—and I recall the insolent young man I conscripted. As worthless a soldier as ever there was and it was a relief to me when he ran. I'd removed his name from the rolls at some point, since his conscription had been—irregular.

"Nothing but savages, as you always say, dear." Margaret puts aside her tatting and turns down the lamp. "Nothing but savages."

I stroll outside for a last cigar before turning in. The night air is pleasant and a rising moon, near the full, illumines the pleasant lines of my surroundings—ornamental plantings, flowerbeds, a tidy kitchen garden, and the spacious fields and pastures of my farm. A garden seat beckons and I sit, light my cigar, and lean back to savor the moment. As I exhale, the smoke rises, twining and twisting in the moonlight, and for a moment its sensuous curves make me think of Polly as she was in our youth. How long has it been since she came to me in dreams?

How long since I dreamed at all?

The shimmer of smoke fades and with it my lost lady. She is gone, just as the noble Confederacy is gone, vanished into the moonlight.

Where the teasing wisps hung, the air is clear and the moon-burnished land stretches away. I breathe out a sigh of contentment, glad to be done with dreams.

47.

~POLLY ALLEN~

Benton County, Arkansas
November 1895

Partisan Campaigns of Col. Lawrence M. Allen, Commanding the 64th Regiment, NC State Troops, During the Late Civil War. Various Deeds of Heroic Patriotism—Self Sacrifice for the Southern Cause—His Rapid Promotion— Terrific Contests with the Notorious Bushwhacker Kirk—Duel in the Defense of the Honor of Southern Womanhood.

Lawrence sighs in contentment and looks from the pamphlet's title page to me. "I still find it rather fine, don't you, Poll? 'Self sacrifice for the Southern Cause—Terrific contests with the notorious Kirk.'"

He chuckles and begins to leaf through his well-worn copy of Gaston's opus, running a finger along the pages in search of his favorite parts.

"Very fine, my dear," I say, for nothing less will do. I am busy with my mending—a dress to be re-turned and a shirt to put new cuffs on. Lawrence seeks to beguile my work by reading out selections for my approval, as if he had not read them to me many times before. In the past I have tried to turn his attention away from the pamphlet, suggesting that he read to me from one of my few remaining novels, but to no avail. He only grows testy and reproaches me.

"Your own husband's finest hours, recorded for posterity, and you aren't interested? Very well then," he said, the last time I hinted that I was familiar with the words, and put the pamphlet into a desk drawer, slamming it shut. It was days before domestic harmony returned.

This is not my noble Lawrence of earlier years. The stress of war, his resignation when the situation grew intolerable, the whispers about what they now call the Massacre in Shelton Laurel, all conspired to make life in North Carolina insupportable to him and were the beginning of the change he has undergone. But we arrived in Arkansas with high hopes and Lawrence threw himself into farming. Then came bad weather, plagues of insects, and one disaster followed another. Lawrence returned to North Carolina, hoping to augment our capital by selling the properties we'd left behind, only to find that they had been unlawfully seized. In the new North Carolina government, there is no justice for us.

"Gaston treats *you* well, too, Polly. Just listen to this depiction of the raid on Marshall: 'They went first to Colonel Allen's…'"

At first I blushed to hear these inflated accounts and wondered how Gaston came to invent such a story. But it is all off a piece—delusions of grandeur—and whether my poor Lawrence was the originator of some of these exaggerations or whether the author was simply hoping to please him, I know not.

"'…demanded of Mrs. Allen her keys to the bureaus, trunks, etc., swearing they would kill her if she refused; but she stood over her sick and frightened children…'"

When first I read Gaston's pamphlet, I asked Lawrence why there were so many inaccuracies. Why, for example, was there no mention of the incident at Shelton Laurel that caused so much uproar in the press and led to Colonel Keith's arrest?

Lawrence waved my questions aside, saying the pamphlet was meant as a general summation of *his* career and, as he was not present, the Shelton Laurel incident had little relevance to his own actions. Ah, would that it were so. As commanding officer, he has been forced to bear an undue amount of blame for an action he would never have sanctioned. My poor Lawrence…

"'With bare feet he traveled two days and nights in the rugged mountains full of thorns and chestnut burrs…'"

Ah, and now we are come to one of his favorite sections, where he shoots an enemy soldier who is crowing like a rooster over the body of a Confederate sympathizer. How often have I heard the tale. And as I nod and smile and make the proper appreciative sounds, I wonder if all of history is like this—made up of truths and lies, exaggerations and misapprehensions. Once a thing is written and published, it assumes the varnish of truth.

"'His record as a partisan fighter, fully given, would rival the wildest romance of the West for all that is true, courageous, and brave.'"

The wildest romance, indeed. But my Lawrence *was* true, courageous and brave. Because of what he once was, it is all the more painful to see him now, diminished in fortune, consequence, and health.
I ache to see him clinging to this imperfect memory of those same
years I would give much to forget.

"I believe he relates the tale of the duel especially well. 'The tall old
soldier stood apparently unconcerned, but his shot told his skill. His
wound was severe but he bore it patiently. He staked his life for the
honor of Southern womanhood.'"

Will we never have done with that word *honor*? A foolish duel long
years after the war, one man dead and Lawrence with a wound that
will trouble him the rest of his life. It all seems so unjust. Cousin
Keith, whose intemperate actions were the root cause of Lawrence's
difficulties evidently flourished in *his* new life in Arkansas. Lawrence
refused any attempt at communication but a friend in North Carolina
was diligent in keeping me apprised of the Keiths's growing prosper-
ity. The same friend recently sent me word of Keith's death this past
May, along with the report that he died mourned by all as a caring
physician, civic-minded citizen, loving husband and father, and pillar
of the Baptist church.

When I attempted to tell Lawrence of this news, he waved it away,
saying that he had no interest in that fellow. Truly, I wonder at it. But
Lawrence lives so much in the past now. At least he still manages to
teach our local school, and he talks of writing his memoir, though I
believe that at heart he is content to let Gaston's words stand for him.
He seems to find it difficult to concentrate for any length of time and
his wound makes writing for a long period painful.

I was not aware, though, of the depths of his unhappiness until my
"friend" in North Carolina sent me an account of what transpired last
year when Lawrence returned thither in yet another fruitless attempt
to recover some of our lost property. He never spoke of the incident
on his return, but I remember seeing the bright pink scar of the healed
wound on his arm and asking how it came there. A clumsy fall against
an iron fence was his reply and I put it from my mind.

He is droning on, and I am nodding and smiling, playing the only
part I can. Now he is reading from the letter he gave to his second in
the duel, to be published in the event of his death.

"'...I am called to the field to vindicate the fair fame of our beloved women of my own Southland...'"

But as the graceful and familiar phrases beat against my ears, I am thinking of that other letter and the clipping from a North Carolina newspaper of last July, when Lawrence was there.

"Colonel Allen Attempts Suicide," the headline shouts and goes on to relate that my poor husband had been jailed on the charge of altering a check, of changing $22.50—the pitiful monthly stipend he draws as a teacher—to $45.50. I cannot imagine the straits that drove him to this petty thievery. But there is worse.

About six o'clock, Jailer Jamison was called to the third floor of the jail where he found that Colonel Allen had inflicted a wound on his left arm with a pen knife that cut two veins and had lost a great deal of blood.

Lawrence left yet another farewell letter, this time addressed to the sheriff, in which he said: *I commit a rash act but my day is past—I go to appear before a higher court, and the officers thereof are true to their word—I could give bond if I had a chance to see around.*

The article gives some details of his duel, possibly as a mitigating factor: *Colonel Allen received a wound that laid him up for four months. And from the effects of which he has never fully recovered.*

No, my noble Lawrence has never fully recovered. Have *any* of us fully recovered from the war and all that followed? Will we ever?

Lawrence has never offered the smallest hint of the real cause of the jagged scar on his arm. And I, of course, will never let him guess that I know. The clipping and now the daily sight of the scar are a reminder of my vows—*in sickness and in health.* My poor husband must never again feel that self-murder is his only escape from a world no longer his, a world in which his day is past.

He seats himself again, adjusting the faded cushion at his back, and chuckles as he reads this next. "The writer is reliably informed that for twenty years after the war, when their children were unruly, mothers, in order to quiet them, would tell them that 'Allen is coming with his soldiers!'"

I sit in the darkening parlor and lay aside my mending. The light is too dim for this work now, and I strive to give all my attention to my poor, damaged husband—reading and re-reading, as if he could bring back the glories he chooses to remember.

In the chill wind that rattles at the windows and in the creaking of this dark old house, I seem to hear again the clatter of my lost Rommie's boots and his childish cry as he waves his toy sword, "See me, Mama, see me!"

48.

~JUDITH SHELTON~

Shelton Laurel, North Carolina
1900

He's gone now, that young feller that claimed to be from the Asheville newspaper. He wanted me to tell how things was here back in '63. He'd talked with folks from Marshall and heard their reckoning— what was done at ol' Allen's house and the rest of it—and he wanted to know how we saw it out here in Shelton Laurel.

I tried to tell him, to the best of my memory. The hangings and the whippings, that was mostly what he wanted me to talk about, and how we found and buried the Thirteen. He wrote it all down and said farewell, leaving me with all those other memories stirred up and circling round, like the crows on that snowy day. I remember them and the hard, cold times when all the men was gone and young uns crying with hunger—my children, all Sheltons—I made sure of that. I remember Johnnie Norton, hiding under the bed—he grew up to make a preacher—married little Davy's sister, too, after her first husband died.

And I remember poor Marthy, that sweet innocent child. What little was left of her after Sim was killed was plumb destroyed when her baby died in spite of all me and Miz Unus could do. It broke my heart to see what Marthy became, little more than the idiot girl some had called her.

I was there when she passed. A weakness of the heart, the doctor said, but I know better. I hope she's found her man and her baby too. I try to remember her at her happiest. But I remember Pete McCoy too and all the angry feelings that ain't gone yet—

Folks tell stories and pass along what they heard and some is actual and some is, well, I'll not say *lies* but two people can remember the same thing in two right different ways. I think *I* remember the way of things, though after so many years I ain't sure. But sometimes I get a true memory—true as ever was and time twists around on me and I am back with Abner when he first come home from the war.

It is a hazy afternoon and he has sent word to meet him in the little hidden cove where that big shagbark hickory stands. It was our special place, long ago, and I am ready and more to lay down with him—maybe make another young un. It seems to me that is the only thing worth doing. Blue or gray, Union or Confederate, ain't neither of 'em mattered a lick. What mattered then and what still and always matters is the land and the people to work it—the broad fields and pastures, the rich soil, the creeks and rivers, the deep woods—that land that lets us make a crop, the land that gives us life.

I reach the meeting place early and stretch out on the long summer grass, all a-quiver with thinking of Abner and the sweet feel of him moving in me. My eyes grow heavy as the sun washes over me; my limbs are loose and my breath is coming fast.

I hear the sound of his horse but I keep my eyes shut. Through my eyelids I see little dots of sunlight and then a shadow falls across me.

"Judy," he says, and I feel his fingers trailing down my face and opening the buttons of my shirtwaist. "Judy," he says again, his breath in my ear and his weight on me. "Judy," he says a third time as he pulls my skirt aside.

I claw my fingers into the rich wood's dirt of this holy ground and look up to see the blue sky beyond Abner's head.

This, I think, *this*.

AFTERWORD AND ACKNOWLEDGEMENTS

The Shelton Laurel Massacre occurred in the NC county I've called home since 1975. I'd read about the Massacre and heard, in a general sort of way, that the people of Shelton Laurel still remembered whose families were involved in this long past event and which side they were on. And that it still mattered. And at least once a week I passed by the house of Col. Lawrence Allen, the commanding officer on that cold day back in 1863. Eventually I thought, vaguely, of writing a novel about it. And I did some reading which only left me totally confused as to what was the truth. Primary sources were often contradictory and often improbable. I simply couldn't get a handle on this story, couldn't find a way to tell it.

It wasn't till the run up to the election in 2012 that I found my way. As I listened to the media and the various narratives from Left and Right, all propounded by folks who were sure they had The Truth, I realized that I was dealing with unreliable narrators—that device beloved of mystery writers wherein the narrator does not give the whole truth but only the truth as he understands it *or* as he wishes it to be understood.

In fact, I began to realize that we are all, to some extent, unreliable narrators, seeing Truth through the prism of our own beliefs, prejudices, and needs. And that's when I knew how I wanted to tell this story.

As I noted in the beginning pages, four of my main characters— Polly Allen, Colonel Keith, Judith Shelton, and Marthy White—are based on real people. I spoke with two of Polly's descendants and have walked through the house in which her children died. I have had email communications with Colonel Keith's great-granddaughter. I have adhered to the facts, as far as they are known, concerning these two but have given them an inner emotional life that is all my own invention. Judith Shelton is still spoken of in Shelton Laurel as 'Aunt Judy' and I've visited the burial site of the Thirteen which lies on a wooded ridge adjacent to the chimney that is all that remains of her home. Any number of her descendants still live in the area.

Marthy White is only known, so far as I can tell, as one of the women tortured by members of the 64th and she is described as 'an idiot girl.' The only further information I could find on Marthy was that she was married and then later living with her parents. Sim is a complete invention—though there were many like him, conscripted to fight for a cause that was not their own.

PEOPLE who have my heartfelt thanks:

Patricia Shelton Wallin and her father Casey Shelton, who shared their knowledge of Shelton Laurel with me and took me to visit the graves of the Thirteen.

Kimberly Shelton, who lent me a precious copy of Shelton family history.

Drew and Louise Langsner, who took me to visit David Shelton who told some great stories that had been handed down in his family about the Massacre.

Susan Moore for giving me copies of her ancestor Vergil Lusk's letters from a Union prison. Deciphering these eloquent missives gave me a feeling for the language of the times

Dr. James Allen, descendant of Col. Lawrence and Polly who passionately upheld his family's point of view defending Col. Allen's actions in a time of war.

Jo Ellen Reimer. Colonel Keith's great granddaughter, who told me something of Keith's life in Arkansas and asked me to be fair and to note that he died a loved and respected figure in his family and community.

Dan Slagle, who is preparing what may be a definitive history of the Massacre and who cleared up some points for me.

The helpful folks at the Madison County Library Genealogy Room

The blog *Renegade South's* post on the Massacre and particularly the stream of comments that followed led me down several useful trails

Mr. Google

All my blog and Facebook friends who cheered me on.

And as always, to my family and my husband John.

BOOKS and PAMPHLETS

Victims: A True Story of the Civil War, Phillip Shaw Paludin, U Tenn. Press

Bushwhackers: The Civil War in NC, The Mountains, William Trotter. John F. Blair Publishers

The Thrilling True Adventures of Daniel Ellis 1861-1865 Daniel Ellis Union guide

"Partisan Campaigns of Col. Lawrence M. Allen, Commanding the 64th Regiment, NC State Troops, During the Late Civil War. Various Deeds of Heroic Patriotism—Self Sacrifice for the Southern Cause—His Rapid Promotion—Terrific Contests with the Notorious Bushwhacker Kirk—Duel in the Defense of the Honor of Southern Womanhood." A.P. Gaston. Raleigh. NC. 1894

A note on the cover art: The striking image is from a woodcut by Nancy Darrell, a long time resident of Shelton Laurel.